LAW

Also by G F Newman

TRADING THE FUTURE

THE TESTING GROUND

SET A THIEF

THE GUVNOR

YOU FLASH BASTARD

YOU NICE BASTARD

SIR, YOU BASTARD

THE NATION'S HEALTH

THE LIST

THE MEN WITH THE GUNS

LAW AND ORDER

G F Newman

POCKET BOOKS

New York London Toronto Sydney Tokyo Singapore

First published in Great Britain by
Simon & Schuster Ltd in 1993
A Paramount Communications Company

Simon & Schuster Ltd
West Garden Place
Kendal Street
London W2 2AQ

Simon & Schuster of Australia Pty Ltd
Sydney

A CIP catalogue record for this book is
available from the British Library
ISBN 0-671-71598-4

Typeset in Plantin 10/13 by
Hewer Text Composition Services, Edinburgh
Printed and bound in Great Britain by
Harper*Collins*, Glasgow

'The ultimate expression of law
is not order, it is prison.'

PROLOGUE

'Of course, the ramps and fit-ups,' he said over the rim of his glass, 'and the trade-offs, they are something most decent coppers deplore, but without them you'd never nick anyone at times.'

There was no irony in his voice, no smile at the corners of his mouth, as he stood at the bar talking with his colleague. The only problem he had with those sort of moves was when they resulted in complaints, and a detective had his own collar felt. But to say so would be to point out the obvious.

That was both his public and private justification for whatever detectives did. Fred Pyle had been a detective for nearly fifteen years, a detective inspector for five years, and with the Robbery Squad for a year and a half.

The man at the bar with him nodded, raised the gin and tonic, and emptied the glass. He was a detective chief inspector and had been through the same conditioning process, and had developed exactly similar patterns of thought which, Pyle assumed, helped him do the job day after day. He knew that the DCI was neither a deep thinker nor a philosopher – the job didn't bear thinking about philosophically. What it amounted to was: Do it, nick someone, keep your numbers up, keep it all ticking over, while creating the impression you were winning. He had to believe that.

At one time such belief was relatively easy. But these days there were some distinct obstacles to the faith: courts no longer automatically believing policemen; the Met's Complaints Investigation Bureau – which might have existed solely to impede policemen; a commissioner whose bias was towards the uniform branch and whose intention, it seemed, was to disband the CID or, failing that, decimate it so that it was left with no rank above detective sergeant – effectively stripping it of any operational powers. He had publically expressed his concern about the autonomy of the CID, saying they were a law unto themselves. That was especially so with the Squad. Their power was close to absolute, and the Commissioner resented it. His appointments seldom favoured them.

Action by the Complaints Investigation Bureau was causing the CID particular aggravation, as complaints were taking vast numbers of detective-manhours. There were outstanding complaints against no less than eighteen Squad officers out of a full strength of one hundred and ten. Four of them were under suspension. A number of these allegations were a legacy of a massive complaints operation which had brought a whole gang of Avon and Somerset policemen to London to investigate wrongdoing in the Met; they had returned home, ironically, to face an investigation into their own wrongdoing by the Yorkshire CID. Pyle was one of those under investigation; Tony Simmons, the DCI he was drinking with, had to bear the brunt of more senior officers' irritation at this state of affairs. Each new complaint added ammunition to the Commissioner's arsenal to use both against the CID in general and the Squad.

'The investigation'll have to run its course, Fred,' the

DCI said, 'for what it's worth. I don't doubt they'll want a word.'

'They already interviewed me once this week.'

The DCI smiled grimly. 'That was in your own right.'

The latest complaint to be investigated was against the senior detective sergeant on Pyle's squad.

'Be the same waste of time,' he said. 'You can't wonder at so many villains keeping their liberty.'

'Maybe it's too many CID earning, Fred,' the DCI said.

'I wish one or two would bung me,' he replied, sharing the joke. 'I keep getting missed out, Tony.' He smeared brown sauce on the last of his onion bhaji before pushing it into his mouth. He chewed it twice and swallowed it, then immediately downed his neat scotch. 'You want another one before I shoot off?'

'No, I got one to meet myself, Fred.' The DCI looked at his watch. He was night-duty officer for the Squad. Pyle and his squad had the current night duty.

'Make it a quick 'un then.'

'The thing is,' he said in a slightly didactic manner, 'what chance have you got with the filth.' It wasn't a question, but he glanced at the man with him at the bar, and when he didn't respond immediately Jack Lynn added, 'You got no chance, have you? The slippery bastards'll not only cop a nice earner off you, they'll go and nick you as well, 'they want you.'

'Well, maybe they don't want me very much, Jack.'

'I wouldn't fancy making a book on it,' Lynn said.

The man told him how, having been picked up by the CID with stolen bearer bonds in his possession, he had bunged the DI and pulled himself clear. It sounded reasonable when he had said it, but now he wasn't so sure. There was something wrong about this villain, but he didn't know what it was. He felt he had been pumping him from the moment he had walked in to the after-hours drinker. Lynn racked his brain trying to remember what he might have heard about the villain being picked up and then released; if it had been at all sussy. Even though he didn't see him often, he knew he had been a good 'un. But that in itself didn't mean he hadn't gone to grass, and wasn't now looking for a body or two to trade in order to keep his own liberty.

Lynn motioned to the woman behind the bar.

'I'll get that, Jack.' The man nodded to her. 'When

you're ready, Sal.' He turned back to Lynn. 'Maybe you're right. I dunno . . . You gotta take a chance. Know what I mean?'

Lynn turned away, disinterested. His gaze circled the smoky club. There was a card game in progress at a table in the corner and he wondered if he had time for a few hands before his meet.

'I mean, what can you do about it anyway?' he said without looking at the man. 'I mean, fuckall, 'they come back and nick you, can you? You can get up in court and scream about them fitting you – you gotta try – or that the filth nicked your bit of dough. But you're up the steps before a wrong sort of judge, you see what good it does you. And Old Bill make sure you go up in front of a wrong 'un, 'worry about that. Specially if their case is a bit dodgy.'

He reached round to where a new Pils had been put and sipped it. As he did, the thought came into his mind that this man had dug him out, and was looking to grass him. The skin on his face began to prickle with anger. After all, this villain was supposed to go mates with him – and here he was trying to get information on his activities.

''They let you have your bit of liberty, the cunning bastards have done it for a reason,' Lynn said, winding him up. 'And not just the earner you bunged 'em.'

'Leave off, Jack. That'd mean I'd have to go on the trot.'

'I would if I was you,' he advised.

'T'rific. My missus and kids would love that. I might as well be away doing a bit of bird.'

'Talk like a mug,' Lynn said dismissively. He had a wife and two children who he thought the world of, but he knew he'd sooner be dodging around the country, avoiding Old

Bill, or tucked away in Spain, than having his old lady visit him down at Albany with the kids.

'You know Ray Turner, don't you? Well, he was tucking up banks with a Visa card the other week. Having a right good earner. He'd done about six grand's worth, he had. He was coming out of a bank in Hammersmith, he just got into his car, when zoomp! a car pulls right up in front of him. Bang tight like that.' He demonstrated with his hands. 'He couldn't pull away. He's ready to have a fight, but the geezer who gets out of the car is a DS on the Squad. He was just driving along when he spotted him – didn't know him – just on instinct, sussed something was going off.'

'Didn't know him? Fuck his luck!'

'Oh, that's not the best of it,' Lynn said. 'After the filth flashed his ID, he nicked every penny. Well, that's all right, you expect that, I mean, it's a chance you take – he did leave him the Visa card so he could go and do a bit more for himself.'

'As you say, Jack, s'chance you take.'

'Right. But what the dirty monkey done then was give him to the Fraud Squad. They went and nicked him later that day. Only, he hadn't done enough for them to have an earner too!'

'Is that right, Jack? Snaky, no-good bastards.'

'You'd do well to go on the trot,' he advised. 'But 'sup to you though. I mean, 'you wanna take a chance.' His attention went back to the card table. One of the players got up to leave, unhooking his jacket from the chair. Lynn slid his shirt cuff off his Rolex day-date chronometer – he had given a grand for the watch and expanding bracelet, both were eighteen carat gold. He wouldn't have time for a game, he decided, knowing how he'd get involved then have to leave. That would mean leaving whatever he had contributed to the pot. All he had time for was another drink.

'Sal?' he said, motioning to the fat barmaid.

'What did I tell you? Regular as clockwork,' the balding man said from the passenger seat.

Light from the arc lamps around the perimeter of the car park spilled over the few cars that remained. One of them was the Jaguar XJ6 that belonged to Jack Lynn. He spent a lot of time looking after the car, believing there was no point having such a car if it wasn't kept tidy.

He was sitting behind the wheel watching the main entrance to the dogtrack as the last of the unlucky punters left on foot with no sort of bounce in their step. What he was watching with his passenger was a security truck as it approached the stadium. Pushing the gates open wider, the white-coated attendant waved to the driver as the truck veered off to the left and ran up the ramp towards the enclosure.

Lynn watched the two guards, armed with night sticks and wearing heavily visored helmets, climb out and lock the doors before moving on down through the stadium.

'Sometimes we're not quite ready,' his passenger said. 'It depends how much we've taken in. It all has to be collected from around the stadium, counted and sorted.'

Lynn knew the details so well that he could recite them in his sleep, and did for all he knew. Perhaps the worry of this was affecting him in that way. Perhaps not.

'What happens if you're not ready?' he wanted to know.

He had been given this information before, but it didn't matter. He needed to be absolutely sure.

'They wait. They make themselves a cup of coffee. The money can't stay there overnight.' He hesitated briefly. 'You know it was done once before.'

'What? Not recently though!' Lynn said.

'Just about a year ago. That's why they won't leave it overnight now. At one time the takings on the Tote were left in the office safe from the Thursday and Saturday meetings and banked the following Monday. Until that safe had been cut open,' Andy Harrington said. Along with every detail of his job he had told him his life history, just about. How he had gone to work for the Tote not long after the war, and had worked there ever since, suffering injustices, being passed over for promotion.

'There's no problem if the guards don't appear again within a couple of minutes?' Lynn said, bringing the conversation back to the present. 'Their mate in the van don't call Catford nick and tell them he thinks there's one going off?'

'No. They're sometimes in there for as long as twenty minutes. When we've had a big night, that is.'

'What's the biggest night you've had since you've been working there, Andy?'

'About seventy grand, it was. On the Saturday before the Spring bank holiday four years ago. It didn't stop coming in. No one seemed able to pick a winner that night. The Tote jackpot was just on seven grand, and even that didn't go. They'd like a few more like that.'

'Wouldn't be bad, would it? Seventy grand for a night's work.' There was a note of expectation in his voice.

'The average would be nearer forty-five thousand,

though.' He glanced at Lynn as though afraid that figure might cause him to lose interest. It didn't. 'Well, say between forty-five and fifty,' he added quickly.

'In nice safe used notes what you don't have to go again on,' Lynn said. 'How bad's that? No problem spending them when you want. No hungry placer grabbing the lion's share.'

Clearly his passenger didn't know anything about that, and he wasn't about to explain the pros and cons of selling stolen money to him.

'Look, I'd better be getting back,' the older man said, glancing at his watch by the light that slanted through the windscreen. 'They might start wondering if I'm too long.'

'Yeah, don't make yourself sussy, Andy, 'n' fuck it all up.'

Reaching for the passenger door handle, the older man started out of the car, but stopped. 'The thing is, when's it likely to go off? Have you got any idea?'

Lynn didn't want to commit himself yet, not to this man anyway. "S hard to say. The sooner the better.'

'I should make sure I'm off sick that week.' He smiled nervously, like he was seeking Lynn's approval.

'Be nice to get a look at that office where the money's counted, 'fore I decide definitely,' he said. It wasn't essential, but that was where he was planning to have it.

'That will be difficult, I think.' His passenger seemed embarrassed at not being able to lay this on. 'Getting a job as a cleaner or something is the only thing I can suggest.'

The look he gave him was a straight blank to the proposal. He wasn't happy about even this man seeing his face; letting everyone in the office see it would make him a million.

Like someone attempting to redeem himself, his passenger said, 'I could get an impression of the key to that door from the corridor.'

'Be handy,' Lynn said. 'Do them in a piece of cuttlebone, not soap. That don't leave traces on the surface of the key. Forensic scientists can detect soap weeks later. They'd know right off it was an inside job. 'S not bolted, that door, while they're in there, is it?'

'I've never known it.' He checked his watch again. 'Look, I must go. You'll pop down Saturday night, will you?'

'Yeah, I'll take another look.' He smiled reassuringly. 'We'll have a nice little earner here.'

'I could certainly use it. I'll see you then.'

'I'll give you a bell. Mind how you go.'

Lynn watched as he walked briskly across the car park. It amused him that this man, who had probably been law-abiding until now, should at the age of sixty-two turn to crime. He thought about the grievances that had led him to this. He wondered how many people there were like this man who had as much information about money their employers handled, people who'd never make a move for it, never get the opportunity he had given Andy Harrington, but would retire with the company's thanks and all that resentment they'd carry away. Mugs.

Such thoughts ceased as the two security guards reappeared, each carrying a cash container. He knew their routine almost by heart, not from simply watching this operation, but from the numerous times he had watched similar security-truck collections and deliveries. He was a blagger: plotting for weeks on end, scrupulously noting details, however small or apparently insignificant, was part of his trade. He had been lucky. How long his luck would last was something he didn't like to contemplate. There was little alternative; he couldn't quit the life, so he was better off not thinking about the almost inevitable nicking that would some day come his way.

Lynn watched one of the guards rap the back of the van with his nightstick and the small hatch door slide open. The two guards put their containers inside and the door closed again. Then they unlocked the cab and climbed in. The glow from a match illuminated the cab as one lit a cigarette while the other filled out his log.

He considered and dismissed the possibility of going after the money here, knowing those guards would, for the few quid they earned each week, try all sorts of moves to protect it. He could not understand that mentality. It wasn't their money, why should they give a toss? The other disadvantage of doing it here, in full view, was that it might give others ideas. All it needed was for someone to get those gates shut. The one road out could be blocked by a couple of cars. And as soon as anything started, the third guard in the truck would be on the radio for help; legging it with those cash containers would be a dead give-away, and some of them automatically destroyed their contents. Going after the money up in the Tote office was almost certainly the best place, he concluded.

The car engine fired immediately and surged with power as his foot touched the accelerator. High-performance cars had always appealed to him, and having a new one, even though the finance company had a large interest in it, pleased him. Pushing the stick to drive, he let off the brake and the Jaguar purred out of the car park after the security truck. He wasn't about to follow it, but was heading north, back across the Water.

The grey XJ6 came through the junction at the bottom of Oxford Street and into Tottenham Court Road just as the lights changed. Instinctively, he glanced about him, looking for lurking policemen. He didn't usually take chances when driving, preferring not to give the police any kind of opportunity. Making a left-hand signal, he pulled over and parked on a yellow line, but at that time of night the clampers had gone home. On climbing out, he carefully locked the door, then walked around the car and checked that the other doors were locked, even though he was within sight of the police station. He had no faith in the police to recover the car if it was stolen. Reassured that the car was locked, Lynn automatically checked in the direction of Goodge Street, then towards Oxford Street, not knowing what he was checking for.

He had just turned forty. Having got there without seeing it as a watershed, he saw no reason to change his way of life. He was earning regularly from what he did, and without thinking about it he believed that could continue for a long time to come. Earning like he did gave him a comfortable lifestyle. He dressed well and lived well. A hand-stitched suit covered his well-built frame – there wasn't much fat on him – the taste slightly conservative on account of his wife going with him when he chose his suits. He knew he was considered a fairly sharp dresser, and unless out doing a bit of work he preferred to go suited and booted. He wore large gold links in French cuffs and Hero deodorant. His dark, wavy hair was receding slightly and worn decently short. He had a haircut about every three or four weeks. There was little about his appearance that identified him for what he was. He had a flattish, bland sort of face, and someone once said his eyes were a little too close set, but there was nothing he could do about that. His was a good face, there was nothing particularly memory-jogging about it. Like so many villains, he had implicit belief in the individual, in free enterprise, and had voted for the Conservatives at the last three elections.

Satisfied that he wasn't being watched, he eased the camel-hair coat off his shoulders, as though taking some rucks out of the back, and stepped into the unlit doorway of the after-hours drinker where he had been earlier that night. He had decided definitely that he was going to make the one at Catford. Now he had to see about putting a firm together.

No light appeared behind the door, but he heard a board creak and knew someone was there. Shortly the door opened on the dark, narrow entrance hall. 'Hello, Chas,' he said in a familiar manner to the man who had opened the door. 'How's it going?'

'There's one or two Old Bill in,' he informed him. 'Thought I'd mark your card, Jack. Know what I mean?'

'They practically live in this place, don't they?' he said.

'They're just knocking out some bent scotch, s'all.'

Immediately beyond the darkened hallway was a small reception area where coats could be deposited. There was a door which led to the lavatory shared by both men and women, and a payphone fixed to the wall beneath which crates of empty beer bottles were stacked. At one time there had been a book for signing-in guests, but it had fallen into neglect and finally disappeared. The room beyond, which comprised the club, was L-shaped, with little more than the bar and a makeshift proscenium arch where occasionally a stripper or an off-key singer performed. The whole works including the seating couldn't have cost the owner more than a grand to set up.

There were usually a number of what he would call reliable people in there drinking. Most of them villains, or vaguely connected. The filth weren't shy to use the place, especially as the booze was free to them. At the bar two detectives were drinking with the owner. Lynn went to the opposite end. He didn't want to get involved with the filth. For the few card games and bit of off-track betting that went on – nothing terribly illegal – the proprietor was obliged to entertain the local Old Bill when they came looking. The alternative would have been shutting up and finding another manor.

'Pils, Sal,' he said to the barmaid and turned to check out the club. The card game in the corner was still going, but with only one of the players from earlier. He caught the eye of one of the others, and with a gesture offered him a drink. 'What's John drinking, Sal? Give him one.'

She peered through the cigarette smoke and identified John Tully, then reached for the vodka bottle. Lynn put a fiver on the bar and didn't get any change.

'Nicking a nice few quid, John?' he said, setting the drink in front of him.

'Wish I was, Jack. Haven't had a hand yet. A ten,' Tully said to the table, and showed his card, stopping another player going nap and taking the pot.

'Fuck my luck!' the blocked player said irritably. 'I could've done that the other way.'

'Cheers, Jack.' Tully put another two pounds into the pot.

'You wanna sit in, Jack?' one of the players asked. 'Might change my fucking luck.'

'Gotta get my bit of spends somehow.'

'Gonna stand you in a score, son,' the player said, doing a quick count of the pot.

'Well, let's see if I can't nick a nice few quid.' His mood was buoyant, a winning mood, he decided. He separated a twenty-pound note and threw it into the pot. Extra cards were added to the limited number used in napoleon to accommodate the additional player. Lynn took off his jacket and put it on the back of his chair.

At the table there were two prospects for the bit of work he had in mind. Of the two, John Tully was the firm favourite. Lynn didn't know the other man so well. He probably wouldn't ask him unless he got stuck. All he knew about him was that he had it off from time to time. He would wait till the game was over then put it to Tully. There were too many grasses around to mention anything here, to say nothing of the filth at the bar. Whispers about one you had plotted were picked up all too easily, but there was no way to prevent it happening; someone you put it to, thinking he was doing you a favour, would mention it to someone else to see if they were interested.

The feeling he had about his luck was accurate. He took two hundred and fifty pounds out of the first pot, a hundred and sixty out of the second. There wasn't a third.

'You always was a jammy git,' Tully said as they were driving away from the club in Lynn's car.

It was late and there was little traffic about, apart from a few empty cabs plying around with their signs down. Working for brasses or villains, he surmised.

'Thought Tony Holder was gonna block me on that last hand. He was well sick, wan' he?'

'Well, can't say I was exactly pleased, Jack. Know what I mean? Thought I was gonna nick that. 'Been handy, pay the rent.' Tully was shortish, powerfully built, with a large head; he had a large stomach that suggested he liked food. He was in his early thirties and had been a villain ever since childhood, as far as Lynn knew.

'Where you living now?' Lynn said. He had offered him a lift, assuming he still lived his way, which was Kentish Town.

'Same place, more or less – Swiss Cottage. Got a flat with this married woman – she's got a couple of kids,' Tully explained, as though called upon to justify himself.

'Yourn?' Lynn asked.

'Leave off! – nice kids, though.' He smiled. 'S'pose I am like a father to them. The ol' man pissed off.'

'Happens all the time, John.'

'Yeah. No-good slag!' Tully said.

There was silence in the car for a moment.

'This is a nice motor, Jack. How long you been running this?' It had been a while since they had seen one another.

''Sonly six months old. Trouble is, you go and make too many Old Bill sick driving about in a car like this. They can't stand it. They have to wipe their mouths though – it's clean.' He glanced at the man next to him, at the road, then at Tully again, assessing him. 'What you been doing lately? Doing any work?'

'Why, got something in mind, Jack?'

'I expect to have shortly. Could be very nice.'

'I could be interested. But the thing is, I got something

of my own going off. Depends what you got in mind, Jack, and when it's going, I s'pose.'

''S blag at Catford dogtrack,' he said.

He looked over at Tully, expecting some kind of reaction, but the villain just stared through the windscreen, like he was considering the proposition. 'I'm light about two, I reckon.'

'I always thought you had a regular firm, Jack. 'S what I heard.'

'No. Nothing definite.' He hesitated. 'Well, Stevie Murry and Terry Hutt got nicked on that one down at London Bridge a couple of months ago.'

'Yeah, I was offered some of that, wan' I?'

'You did well to give it a miss. They were well lollied. The filth ought to let them have bail, I would think. Help 'em out. They been stuck down in Brixton for two months now waiting to go up.'

'That's fuck all. Peter Collins has been waiting seven months to go up the steps. 'S fucking murder. You go and do your bit of bird 'fore you even get weighed off.'

A grin spread across Lynn's face. The remand situation wasn't funny, but a sense of proportion had to be kept. 'This one I got in mind's gonna be worth about six or seven apiece, 'a bit of luck.'

That clearly impressed Tully. 'As much as that?'

''S got to be there, no problem.' He resisted sweetening the proposition. If anyone came in with him he wanted them to do so on its merits rather than promises he couldn't fulfil.

'The thing is, Jack, I'm committed to this other one. What I mean is, it's all down to when yourn's going off, like. It's one I was putting together myself over at Abbey Wood.'

'I can't say definite yet. I gotta take another look on Saturday. But it's gotta be soon. Soon as possible. It's silly leaving it. I mean, if I know about it then someone else might.'

'Oh yeah, you're better off doing it. Look, give us a bell at the weekend. M' plans should've firmed up by then, 'a bit of luck. I'll know definite, like. But I do fancy it, Jack.'

'What's your number? – the thing is, I don't wanna leave it much later than Sunday.'

'Well, I'll know, won't I? I'll be able to tell you.' He picked up a business card from the top of the dashboard and scribbled his phone number on the back of it. 'If I ain't in, I'll almost certainly be down the hall. My Ann'll know where I am.' He put the card prominently back on the dashboard. 'Why don't you give Ginger Chapman a bell, 'you're short-handed? He was looking for something.'

'He's a fucking hippy. You can't rely on people like that, John,' he said. 'Probably be well doped-up.'

'His hair's a bit long, is all,' Tully said. 'Do the next right there, Jack.'

''S enough, John.' He wouldn't ring Chapman, he decided, as he followed Tully's directions to a block of council flats.

'I'll give you a bell on Sunday, then.'

'Yeah. Good luck, Jack.'

At this stage of plotting half of his time seemed to be spent sitting around in cars watching the prospect, or waiting to meet someone. If that someone didn't show, or he failed to see what he expected to see, then he began to wonder if the job was going to work for him or if he shouldn't find something else.

Lynn spent another Saturday evening at Catford dog-track and stayed until the end, watching as the security truck arrived, waiting for the guards to emerge with the money, meticulously timing them as though it would make some difference. Afterwards he followed them out past Catford Bridge station, watched as they made a left turn onto Catford Road. He then turned right into Ravensbourne Park Road and parked his wife's Austin Metro and switched off the lights.

He was waiting for his man from the Tote. When he had spoken to him earlier he had blanked the idea of meeting in the car park again, in case someone spotted them. His contact offering yet another excuse to leave the office might have made him sussy when the blag finally went. Something might have jolted someone's memory. The filth wouldn't take long to crack someone like that. He wondered about him now as he waited, whether his man might not be a prime suspect anyway. He didn't know a lot about him, or what his firm thought of him.

Maybe there were things the man hadn't told him that he ought to have told him before making a decision. One big plus in all this was the fact that Andy Harrington didn't know anything about him.

Watching through the driving mirror, he saw a maroon Montego crawl along the line of parked cars. Lynn put his arm out of the window and signalled to the driver. The car tucked into the space behind, and his contact climbed out and glanced carefully about before climbing into the Metro.

'All right?' he inquired.

'Yes, fine. We had a good night.'

'I'll go round the block,' Lynn said, starting the car. 'Otherwise we might get done for sus. It only needs someone in the street to do a busy and call the police. Two men sitting in a car in a Neighbourhood Watch area are a million. Unless they think they're gays!' He laughed.

'Don't go too far. I haven't locked my car.'

'That'll be safe enough,' he assured him. 'It's all spades around here – they only nick big motors.'

The older man gave him an uncertain look, then glanced back at his car. 'We had a good night,' he said. 'Took in just over forty thousand.'

Dividing that by four, even after taking a bit extra for his own Xs would give all involved a nice earner. Lynn didn't comment on that.

'D'you fetch the impression of that key?' he asked.

Removing a large wad of tissue paper from his pocket, his contact unfolded it and produced a four-inch piece of cuttlebone. Lynn reached up and put on the interior light, then inspected the impressions as he steered. They were clean and well formed, and the man had had the foresight to take two of each side of the key.

'They'll do. You did well there. I'll get my keyman to cut one from that all right. I'll send it to you to test.' He switched out the light.

'Good. I was a bit worried in case it wasn't right.' He smacked his hands together in an excited manner, as though concluding some business. 'When do you think? That you might be doing it, that is?'

'A couple of weeks or so, I'd say. 'Bit of luck.' He sensed this man's disappointment and glanced sideways at him. 'What, you desperate or something?'

'No! No, of course not,' he replied quickly. 'It just seems to be going on forever.'

'I know what you mean. Try not to think about it till it's done.'

His contact gave a nervous, excited laugh. 'A nice few quid will be handy – they owe me.'

'You'll get a taste soon enough,' he assured him, and turned the car round to head back.

There was a lot to do in putting one together, besides getting the firm. Things that he wouldn't consider telling this man about. There were tools to get, the sort that would have the right effect. There were cars to have rung; it was no good dragging any old car that put you at risk of having your collar felt before you even got to the blag. The cars had to be well rung so that they could be parked up safely. There was the getaway route to be worked out. There was never any way to tell what might happen in traffic; that would probably prove the most unpredictable part of the blag.

All of this arranging took time. But one most immediate

problem was getting his team. It was pointless making moves towards cars, guns or anything else until he had enough of a firm to do the job properly. He was beginning to wonder about that. Names were getting scratched from his shortlist, faces who, for various reasons, couldn't make it. A couple had said right off that they didn't fancy making one, without hearing what it was. He preferred a straight blank, then he knew it wasn't anything about the blag they didn't fancy. With these knockbacks he considered reducing the number he would need, but four, including himself, was the minimum. Five would be better. If the other little team he sometimes worked with hadn't been nicked or had been given bail, they'd have had a taste, if only to provide for their families while they were away! He thought about the blag they had been nicked on, and why he hadn't gone for it when it was put on offer. There had been something wrong about it, he hadn't known what, but he followed his instinct in these things. Now he was beginning to get a bad feeling about Catford.

The Plough on Clapham Common was a popular lunchtime pub, especially at the weekend when they put on a lot of food and kareoke. He didn't know if it was as popular in the evening as he rarely came south of the Water to do his drinking, and the only reason he was using the pub now was to meet a villain. All he ever came to South London for was business.

Alan Parker lived not far from the pub and it had seemed the obvious place for a meet. But Lynn felt irritated by the choice, as there was no room to sit down, much less have a quiet chat.

'Sorry, pal,' he said to a customer as he elbowed his way

out from a short section of bar as another man tried to get in. He made his way to Alan Parker, who was pressed into a corner, and gave him his pint. ''S fucking murder, this.'

'Where else have they got, Jack?' Parker said. He was in his early thirties, about three inches shorter than himself, with a deceptive build. Looking at him you might have thought he couldn't do much, but Lynn knew different. He had an old look. Around his vivid-blue eyes were blocks of flesh that sometimes developed on boxers' faces. His blond hair was long, but he was prepared to tolerate that, for it was stylishly bunched in a pony tail – hair in rat tails like some of the soapy bastards wore was what he couldn't stand.

Glancing round, making sure no one was listening, Lynn said, 'You looking for a bit of work, Alan?' There was no need to qualify the work.

Without even asking what it was, Parker said, 'I don't think so, Jack. I mean, I wouldn't do you no favours getting involved – I'm getting a lot of aggro from the filth on account of some videos I done a couple of weeks ago.'

'Fuck a duck!' Lynn said. He had been convinced Parker would have some of it. 'I thought there was s'posed to be a recession on.'

Parker scoffed. 'You wouldn't think so, would you? Try moving two hundred videos.' He sipped his drink.

Lynn considered him, then said, 'I'd take a chance, 'you fancy it?'

'No, I don't think so. I mean, I got Old Bill calling round my place every day, they worry the life out of me. It'll cause you a lot of ache, Jack. 'S all.' He drank some beer. 'You stuck?'

'Can't get no one to work with me, can I? You'd think I was a fucking grass!'

'Sorry, Jack. I'd like to have some of it.'

Lynn finished his drink decisively.

The bottom of the list hadn't been reached, but it was coming in sight. Again he considered whether the difficulties he was having were an indication for him to give the entire prospect a miss. Such thinking brought a whole new set of negative feelings about the blag. But he chose to ignore them. It was going ahead; there was a little firm to be had somewhere.

The telephone bell was barely audible at the best of times beneath the soundproof canopy near the tea bar. Punters on the nearby tables rarely answered it. John Tully had no intention of doing so as he considered his shot.

Since the arrival of snooker on the TV, Sunday lunchtime was no longer a quiet affair at the snooker hall – nor any other time, come to that. There were games in progress on all fifteen tables that transversed the badly lit room. Not much light got through the shaded windows, and the lamps over the tables were designed to light only the playing area.

'John!' the man who ran the hall called, bending to look beneath the hood. 'Telephone, son.'

John Tully didn't respond. Instead he played his shot, then straightened slowly and watched the ball run. It didn't go where he intended. 'Fuck it,' he said. He moved along the table where his opponent, Micky Fielder, was leaning on his cue.

'Your old lady chasing you for dinner, John?' Fielder said, and stood off the cue he was leaning on.

'Probably,' Tully said good-naturedly. ''S what comes of being in love, Micky.'

He glanced at Fielder who stayed watching him as he went to the phone, sensing his curiosity about who this was. Fielder was that sort of bloke, always making himself busy, asking questions that caught you off guard and which you found yourself answering. He always felt he said too much. One of these days he would find himself grassed.

Even though he knew it wasn't possible to make the one Lynn was offering him, John Tully was still almost tempted by the repeated offer. Despite what he had going off himself he wanted to say yes to it, as he knew he'd stand to earn more than he would from his own one. But that alone wasn't enough to persuade him. His blag was his blag, and being the governor was important to him. The fact that it was worth less than the other one was something he'd live with.

'Sorry, Jack. I'd like to help you out. But this one I've been plotting's going off. I mean, I do fancy yourn. Sounds like a right good earner.'

'Oh yeah, it should be,' Lynn said down the phone.

'I don't suppose there's any chance it's gonna be put back?'

'No, I wouldn't have thought so, John. It's gotta be done.'

'Pity, that,' Tully said, still half-tempted.

'Yeah, that's the way it goes. Another time, John.'

'You want me to put anyone in touch, 'I hear of anyone?'

''You hear of someone tasty. Be a bit slippery.'

'Yeah, you too. See you, Jack.' He replaced the phone and ducked out from under the canopy. He paused to assure himself that he wanted his own blag more than Lynn's.

When he got back to the table Fielder was carefully chalking his cue. Tully glanced over the green baize.

'Oh,' Fielder said, as if by way of an apology, 'I nicked the yellow, brown and green.'

'Down to me, is it?' Tully retrieved his cue and considered the three balls left on the table. 'Not a lot of chance here, have I? What's in it, Micky?'

'About six.' Fielder waited for him to line up the blue. 'D'you get your marching orders, John?'

'It was Jack Lynn,' he replied, and played his stroke, taking blue. 'He has one going off down at Catford – he's a bit light-handed.'

'He's a nice fella,' Fielder observed. 'You having some?'

'Wouldn't mind.' He moved round the table to look at pink. 'I've got enough on my plate. You wanna be put in, Micky?'

'Me? Do I fuck. Not my game, is it, blagging?' Fielder said.

Tully stooped and tried for pink, but he didn't make it. He didn't care any more about Lynn's blag, putting it from his mind.

‘So I gave her a pull,’ he said, and hitched his trousers which had slipped off his large waist. It was a frequent habit he had and most of the time he wasn’t even aware that he was doing it. Eric Lethridge was standing by one of the thirty or so desks placed in lines in the main Squad office. ‘Well, we get back to her room, this DSS hotel she’s staying – I mean, it’s a right rat’s nest – you can’t believe the place she lives in – but you know, you don’t care when you got one about sixteen on the firm. ’S all she was, I swear to you,’ he added to deal with any doubts. ‘So she says, she says, “Do you want to make love to me?” just like that. “Well,” I said, “it’s either that or you’re nicked!”’ He shook his head in anticipation of the conclusion. ‘So it winds up me giving it one. I’m giving it a right seeing to when, as casually as you like, she says, “Oh, I s’pose I ought to tell you, I’m attending the clinic for this discharge I get” . . . ah, it slaughtered me!’ As he reached this point in his story, his hip-grinding movements, resembling those of too large a dog on too small a bitch, ended and he jerked back, arching his spine as though withdrawing suddenly from the infected girl.

His audience exploded with laughter. The four detective constables, whose ages ranged from mid-twenties to late-thirties, were standing around the desk where one of them, Ray Jenkins, had stopped halfway through typing a report. They were part of the night relief, which was one of the ten separate squads, each employing ten men under a detective inspector.

The Squad office was about forty feet long by twenty wide, and crowded with furniture. The desks, belonging to no particular detective, were littered with typewriters and computer screens, plastic trays, some full of reports. On a desk near the door was chained the huge duty book, into which were entered all investigations and movements of detectives. On other tables at the side of the room were telephones; eight more hung on the wall under acoustic canopies. Jammed against the walls were metal filing cabinets, which got a lot of use with detectives continuously pulling out files for cross-reference in order to keep the paperwork moving. Most of the current searches these days were done on the computer. The whole area had a desolate, impersonal, neon-lit look, with only seven men in the office.

A telephone started ringing. Phones were usually answered quickly, as it often meant a job away from the hated paperwork. That evening no one jumped. Lethridge might have flattered himself that it was because his story was more important, but not even DC Warren Slater, who was typing at a desk close to the ringing phone, bothered, nor the seventh detective with his feet on a desk further along the room. Tonight they were waiting to go on raids and he assumed they didn't want to get involved elsewhere.

Finally, when the laughter died, he gave a satisfied smile, and moved across the office to answer the phone himself.

Glancing at DC Slater, he said, 'You lazy bastard, couldn't you answer this?'

Slater – the only one doing any work – looked up, his

fingers continuing to hit the computer console keys. He swore when he made a mistake.

'Robbery Squad,' he said into the phone. 'Sergeant Lethridge.' The voice down the line asked for his governor. 'You've got the wrong office. You want the DIs' office . . . I don't think he's in.'

'I know. The thing was,' the voice said, 'we was supposed to have a meet.'

'Hang on a minute, I'll go and check.' He laid the phone down and moved out of the office, hitching his trousers.

He was forty-four years old, and overweight, despite his active existence. He had a tiredness about him that wasn't entirely accounted for by his work. He pursued women as actively as he did villains. His sexual appetite was large, and he enjoyed the reputation it gave him: it was said about him that if it moved he would stiff it. Despite the hierarchy's edicts to the contrary he still freely associated with villains: that was the way to keep your ear to the ground. He wore a serious, almost permanently disdainful expression on his fleshy face, which only occasionally broke into a smile. He had been a policeman a long while but, having been a detective sergeant for six years, he had no expectation of making DI: to do that he would have had to go back into uniform then re-apply for CID. Returning to uniform, at whatever rank, wasn't a promotion as far as he was concerned. Few detectives ever chose to go back into the uniform branch. His dark, sleeked-down hair with its high, off-centre parting made him look a bit like a 50s ad for hair cream, and he was proud of it; his clothes had an outdated appearance, like he was waiting for fashion to come round again. Separated from his wife, he often found himself at a loose end, though during his marriage he had never diligently gone home. There had always been reasons not to, such as one to meet somewhere; still were, only now excuses weren't necessary.

Detective inspectors on the Squad worked out of a single office, smaller than the main squad room, with four desks between the ten DIs who worked there at various times during the twenty-four hours – rare indeed was the time when all the DIs were in the office together. Like all the offices on the fourth floor, it was cluttered with filing cabinets and screens, and had a familiar impersonal look.

Detective Inspector John Redvers was the only person there. Lethridge knew he should have been at home trying to sleep in readiness for the raid they were jointly making later on. Instead he was seated at his desk in his overcoat, like he was on the point of leaving, but the pile of reports he was checking said different. Scotch in a styrofoam cup stood on the desk close to his hand, the bottle would have been tucked away discreetly in the bottom drawer. None of the governors objected to the drinking that went on, but would have objected to an open bottle of Johnnie Walker advertising the fact.

'Fred around, guv?' Lethridge asked. 'Guv' was how most detectives addressed more senior officers.

'Had one to meet, didn't he? A snout, I think,' Redvers said, lifting his eyes from the report.

'He's on the phone now. I thought he might have popped back.'

'Stuck up some old tart somewhere,' Redvers surmised. He finished the scotch in the cup. 'You want one downstairs, Eric?'

'Aren't you going home?'

Redvers glanced at his watch. ''S hardly worth it.'

'Let me get a number from chummy. 'S not exactly hectic in there.' Spending an hour in the Tank, their bar on the ground floor, would help relieve the monotony.

Rising with a dismissive laugh, Redvers said, 'The time the night tour find anything more than their pricks to pull, Eric . . .' It was said without rancour. There was little animosity between the individual squads, certainly none between the one DI Redvers ran and that which he was on; they worked together too often. 'I'll see you downstairs.'

When Lethridge got back to the phone, whoever had made the call was gone. He dropped the handset back on the rest, and put the call from his mind.

Underground train meets with grasses were favoured by Fred Pyle. They were casual and anonymous and almost always safe. People rarely noticed the other passengers on the Underground, even though the scats were arranged opposite one another; there people could have epileptic fits, break a leg, get raped, and fellow passengers would mostly avert their eyes rather than risk the possibility of getting involved.

The Circle line was his preference, as the train passed through St James's Park station, which was only a short walk from the Yard. Like so many of his contemporaries, he avoided unnecessary expenditure of energy, otherwise he'd never have got through the sort of day he all too frequently put in. The only trouble with these meets was, he thought as he waited on the edge of the platform, they weren't always reliable. He checked the time, then glanced along the platform to the opening of the tunnel. The signal behind him showed green, but there was no other sign of an approaching train. His eyes moved on to the other people on the platform, his brain automatically registering their details; two Asians; a female secretary who, he decided, had worked late for her boss, then turned down his subsequent offer, and a young couple wearing leather jackets. His gaze moved on across the tracks; the prospects were no better over there. He looked up the tunnel again, growing impatient.

At forty-three he inclined towards heaviness, due to consuming large amounts of scotch and snacks at irregular hours. He didn't mind when he ate, but wouldn't miss meals altogether, believing that way he avoided an ulcer. His five-eleven helped to carry the extra weight, but his fleshy face and thickening jowls signalled it. He still had his own hair, which pleased him, especially as some of the younger CID officers had lost half of theirs. It was a grey-sand mixture and he wore it short. He wasn't concerned to follow current fashion – two of his detectives had pony tails; a small knot in his Squad tie; his shirts and suits, charcoal or dark blue, his wife usually bought for him, off the peg, from M & S. He had never dressed as well as the time, when on division, he and another detective had nicked some villains who were breaking an expensive men's outfitters. They had helped themselves to a dozen suits and twice as many shirts. He never bragged about what he earned, but strove to keep a low profile, and for the most part managed to. His face was often expressionless. Over the years he had learnt to detach himself emotionally. What followed was the ability to control his face muscles, especially those around his mouth and eyes. Eyes were the most revealing part of the face, and he avoided betraying his thoughts by developing a cold glaze. The fact that he often worked long, exhausting hours helped him to achieve this. Perhaps the most revealing thing about being a detective was, ironically, that he revealed nothing. He rarely smiled, apart from at the odd joke, and then never dropped his guard. If he showed anything resembling feelings, it was usually a ploy to gain some advantage. He had married as a young constable to a WPC, who subsequently resigned, and they stayed married despite the strains the job put on their relationship. Their two children, both in their early teens, kept them together. If asked, he would have to say he was not unhappily married. But family had always been forced into the inferior role to work. That wasn't a conscious choice, but simply the way of things.

Automatically he checked his watch as the west-bound train burst out of the tunnel. He had been waiting around twenty minutes, and if his grass wasn't on this train he'd give him a miss. He searched the carriages as the train slowed towards him.

He gave no sign of seeing his contact as he boarded the carriage and walked the length of it, checking out the other passengers. None of them showed any interest in him, not even when he took a seat next to Micky Fielder and ignored other empty seats. He glanced round at the grass, who by comparison was flamboyant. Fielder was about the same age, and had thick dark hair, with greying sideboards. He took trouble over his apearance. His hair had been well cut and he wore an expensive three-quarter black leather coat, which looked as though it had just been nicked. His lamp-tanned face was mobile and his eyes darted about the whole time.

'Did you miss one, Micky?' he asked. Their meet had been set for as close to ten o'clock as the train passed through St James's Park station.

'They cut a bastard out, didn't they? They do anything to save money, the Underground.'

'I could've been doing something better with my time. Thought you'd blanked me.'

'I wouldn't do that, guv. I tried giving you a bell . . .'

Pyle said nothing, but then Fielder needed little prompting to tell all he knew. He was a compulsive grass. Some had to be worked at with all sorts of strokes and promises before they would impart their information, and sometimes it was only achieved by a direct threat to their liberty. Most grasses responded to threats; that was how Fielder had initially fallen under his spell. He had nicked him for a breaking and had let him bargain for his liberty. He always listened to such propositions as it made no difference to him whether a villain like Fielder went down. All the while the grass offered him information he'd get whatever immunity Pyle could give him.

'Picked up a nice little whisper, didn't I? Very nice.' Fielder waited, like he was expecting him to acknowledge his efforts. Pyle didn't. 'Ever heard of Jack Lynn? Comes out of Kentish Town.'

Even though he managed to keep a whole catalogue of villains and their strokes in his mind, some going back years, that particular name meant nothing to him. 'What's he do, Micky?'

'Blags is what I hear – s'posed to be one or two nice little tucks down to him. He keeps well active. He's putting one together now. He's a bit short-handed, looking to get another couple, he is.'

'You in line?' It was a perverse compliment.

'Me, guv? Leave off, I'm not in his class. Robbery's not my game, is it?' He flexed his shoulders, adjusting his coat. 'A bit of screwing does me. You go pulling blags with other villains you wind up grassed, know what I mean?' Fielder seemed unaware of the irony in this.

'What's he putting together? Did you find out?'

''Course . . . that's why I called you. It's the Tote

down at Catford dogtrack. 'S what I heard. I'd say it was about right.'

'That's a bit ambitious, Micky. Be a nice little taste if they have that off.' He glanced round as the train slowed in the tunnel for a signal, then picked up speed again.

'He's a bit near the mark, this one, guv . . .' He paused, with an anxious look. 'I'd say so. He could get it done, this one. You any idea what that'd come to, guv? That Tote? It was done just last year, it was. It was worth about thirty grand *then*.'

Pyle remained purposely unimpressed. That way he extracted maximum information from this particular grass. 'I know it was, Micky, but they were only banking their takings once a week. Securicor collect it now after each meet.'

'Its still got to come to a nice few quid,' Fielder said.

'When's it supposed to be going off?'

That question caused Fielder to shift uncomfortably in his seat. Clearly he hadn't got the most vital piece of information he needed in order to capture the blaggers bang to rights.

'Ain't got that for you yet, guv. My party didn't give me it.'

''S not a lot of value then, son, is it?' He didn't conceal his disappointment. 'What d'you think the chances are?'

Taking up the challenge, Fielder said, 'Oh, should be a doddle. Just means punting around a bit more. Should be able to get it all right.'

'I'd appreciate that, Micky. Be a nice earner off the insurance for you if we nick them.'

The train ran into Victoria Station. Both of them watched the doors slide open, saying nothing as passengers climbed in at their end of the carriage. Some walked along the aisle away from them. When underway again with the rattle of the wheels almost drowning out their conversation, Pyle said, 'You okay for a bit of dough?'

'Oh yeah,' Fielder promptly replied, like he was eager to impress. 'I had it off the other night, didn't I?'

'Pleased to hear it, Micky,' he said as if not interested in the details, then noted casually, 'Anything worthwhile?'

'Tucked up this office in Putney.' He gave the location of the break-in. 'A bit of cash and some blank Amex – it was a doddle. They could have put a notice out, know what I mean? 'I get those travellers' cheques placed it'll have been a right good 'un.' He hesitated and glanced at the detective. 'The thing is, guv, could you do anything with them?'

Pyle considered the question. At one time he would have taken them, but nowadays American Express travellers' cheques were too much aggravation. Or maybe it was the thought of the trouble he was currently having with the Complaints Investigation Bureau. He went through the motions to encourage the grass. 'What do they come to?'

'There's just over two grand's worth.'

'What were you expecting? A monkey?' That was an optimistic figure. A twoer would be more reasonable.

'Wouldn't be bad, would it?'

'I'll have a word with someone,' Pyle said, extending hope. 'Mind how you go, if you do them yourself. I don't want to have to spring you from some local nick. Specially if you haven't dug up anything more on this Catford blag.'

Fielder grinned sheepishly, as if believing he was joking. He had a lot to learn, Pyle thought, and knew the grass would never grow old enough to know the half of it.

The fourth-floor corridor of the main block at Scotland Yard was a seemingly endless neon-lit square tube and a labyrinth of offices off it. Those along the left-hand side belonged to the Squad, and most of their doors remained open as if to invite anyone in. Occasionally the DCS's door was shut if he was having a meeting; sometimes the two superintendents' door would be closed, for the same reason. Rarely was the DCIs' door closed. The doors on the opposite side of the corridor were always shut, some even locked. These offices were used by Criminal Intelligence branch, who obsessively guarded their information. Their inquiries often went on for months, sometimes years, before they came up with enough target villains; after that amount of work it was disheartening to have the suspect given prior warning by some detective who was earning. It happened. He had done it himself.

Pyle stepped from the lift and turned wearily along the corridor. Since leaving his grass he hadn't thought about his information; instead he had been in an after-hours club, hoping to see another villain about something else. But now he was back at the Yard Jack Lynn was occupying part of his thoughts. Perhaps it was his age, or perhaps he had drunk too much scotch, but night-duty lately was leaving him more and more tired, he noticed. His kids had woken him too early that afternoon. They little appreciated that he had to stay awake through the long night.

Turning into the DCIs' office he found it deserted. He needed to talk to Tony Simmons about the blag at Catford. All the lights were burning in this office, which was about the same size as his own, but with only three single desks. There was more noticeboard space, and filled with announcements about vacancies in various constabularies; papal-like edicts from the Commissioner, angry memos from different departments about reports or forms or tests returned incorrectly; 'Wanted' posters, circulars – it was a whole week's reading.

What he had for his governor would keep. As he started away one of the telephones rang and he answered it.

'Chief Inspectors' office.'

A man down the line asked for the DCI by name. 'He's just stepped out. Can I take a message?' The caller wanted to know how long he would be. 'Can't say.' Pyle wondered if he was a grass, but doubted it. DCIs weren't that active. 'Tell him Terry called.' He replaced the phone and scribbled the message on the pad along with the time, two-twenty.

In the Squad office there were a dozen or more detectives hanging around like lads on an outing waiting for the coach to arrive. Men from John Redvers' squad were creeping back to assist the night-duty squad with Method Index raids. Only three of the detectives so far present were busy. They were taking the opportunity during this lull to catch up on some paperwork. All would have had paperwork outstanding, but Pyle knew that was something to be put off to the last moment.

'Haven't any of you got homes to go to?' he said as he passed a group of detectives.

'Chance'd be a nice thing, guv,' DC Ray Jenkins replied. It was a familiar complaint.

'Well,' he retorted, 'you'd only sleep, or give the old lady some,' – regardless of the female detective with them. He knew he could make such remarks to his men simply because whatever was their lot was his too.

He continued up the long office to find Jack Barcy, the number two DS on his squad, at a desk aggressively hammering out a report on a typewriter. He knew Barcy would rather have been hammering a statement out of a suspect. He was tall, lean and hungry-looking, with cold, emotionless eyes. There was no doubt about the position he held on the squad: he was the violence specialist, always ready to give stick. Paperwork was for him, more than any other detective, something to try to put off forever.

'Found your true vocation, Jack?' he mocked.

Barcy scowled as his fingers continued to crash the keys, like he wanted to break the typewriter. Because of his poor application to paperwork he knew Barcy was never going to rise above his present rank, and only because of his better-than-average results did he keep his place on the Squad. A lot of detectives had been transferred out for much less than Barcy got away with.

'Where's the duty chief?' Pyle asked. 'He out?' He assumed he was from what Tony Simmons had said in The Feathers earlier that evening.

'He's probably popped over the Middlesex Hospital to give that nurse one!'

Automatically Pyle glanced at the clock. 'That probably means a late start on these raids.'

'You got one to meet then, guv?' Barcy asked, leaning back in his chair.

'Me? I'm a respectable married man, Jack.'

'I've heard you say your prayers too, guv.'

'I've got to get promotion somehow, son.' He didn't smile. 'D'he say what time he'd be back?'

'Not to me, he didn't.'

'Couple of hours' sleep before court tomorrow would be handy. That's not a prospect if we don't make these raids as planned. There's an active party called Lynn. Jack Lynn, with a double "n", I think. A blagger out of Kentish Town. Have one of the lads pull up his CRO file, will you? I'm going to get my head down for an hour or so.'

Twenty detectives crammed into the DIs' office. They had drifted along there for the briefing because that was where Pyle and DI Redvers were. They were divided into four squads, as they were to raid four separate addresses, though in that confined space it was difficult to tell who was going visiting with who.

'What's this, a bit of bustlebunching, Simon?' said a DS from Redvers' squad as another detective squeezed past him. He was leading one of the raids. Pyle, Lethridge and Redvers were leading the others. The briefing, like most at this level, was informal and Pyle did it as it was his operation.

'It starts to get light around a quarter to six, for the benefit of those who aren't usually awake at that time,' he said. 'So we'll be hitting these addresses simultaneously at around five-thirty. There'll be little chance of resistance, I wouldn't have thought.'

'Well, what if one of them's got up for a leak, guv?' Warren Slater asked with a grin. The DC was young and wore his long hair in a pony tail and had more than enough to say for himself, especially to the WDC next to him.

'I suppose that might conceivably be armed resistance,' DCI Simmons put in. 'You could nick him for that.'

'But make sure he has it in his hand,' Pyle added. There were chuckles from some of the detectives who were more loyal to him than the DCI. 'John, you're liaising with the DI over at Paddington.'

'They visiting with us?' Redvers wanted to know.

'I don't think he's bothered, John. He might want to send someone along,' he said. Then, turning to the DS on Redvers' squad, 'Ian, Paddy Kennedy over at Acton'll hold your hand. Our two are both down at Peckham,' he said in the general direction of Eric Lethridge, even though he had been in on every stage of planning the raids.

'The DI out there's not a bad sort,' Simmons said. Peckham had been his own division.

'What's this, then,' Redvers asked, 'favouritism?'

'Well, your squad has gone and drawn the easy ones to nick,' Pyle countered. 'Oh, what channel are we on?'

'Channel six,' Lethridge informed them, hitching his trousers.

'Remember,' Simmons said, 'this is only a Method Index raid. There is no guarantee that any of these four were involved on the blag last week.' That said, he added, 'But of course they are all villains, so you don't be too polite.'

These were targeted from information in the Method Index files, which were searched for the most likely suspects, each preferably with some connection to the others. Pyle hadn't found the connection between these four villains but still they remained the best candidates.

As the detectives began to disperse, a DC who was the newest recruit to his squad approached. 'Guv, 's it all right if I take my own car out to Peckham? – I've got that one at Bromley Magistrates' Court in the morning. I could shoot straight off then.'

'That's okay, Roger,' Pyle said. Most detectives wouldn't have asked.

''S that something I didn't see?' Simmons wanted to know.

'From when I was on division, guv. The suspect's only just got out of hospital.'

The DCI nodded. 'Shouldn't hit them so hard.'

'Leave your car at the nick, Rog', Pyle said to the young detective. After dismissing him he turned and took a pastel-coloured foolscap file from his desk and handed it to Simmons. 'Something a snout gave me earlier. Jack Lynn. He looks like he might be a worthwhile suspect. He's supposed to have one coming off down at Catford.' He gave the details as he glanced through the CRO file. It was thick and well established.

'He's not been idle, has he?' Simmons said.

'From what I hear there ought to be a few more down there. We missed him on a couple.'

'One of your regular grasses, Fred?' The DCI was weighing up the prospects.

Pyle nodded. 'A right good 'un an' all.' He watched his governor read on briefly, then nod.

'Start a file, Fred. See if we can get something on him this time. He looks as if he might be due.'

'Overdue, I'd say, guv.'

He didn't know Jack Lynn personally, but from the limited information he had gathered since talking to his grass there was no doubt it was this villain's turn. It was almost a game the CID played with the felonry, with both parties knowing where, sooner or later, the spotlight of police attention would fall. Most villains strove to make it later. All manner of strokes were tried: other bodies would be traded, or more worthwhile crimes, or money simply put on offer. But occasionally when the detective decided it was someone's turn none of those would do. Sometimes that decision was arrived at out of anger or disgust with the crime, sometimes out of mere perversity. Whatever the reason prompting the attention, at the bottom of the line there was always a clear-up rate to nod towards. Fred Pyle had no problems keeping his numbers up. Jack Lynn would go.

As far as he knew, none of the villains they expected to find at the addresses they were going to raid would be armed, so the detectives weren't issued with guns, nor was the Armed Tactical Support Unit being called out. What he did instead was encourage his people to take along baseball bats and sawn-down snooker cues. These would give the CID the advantage which their numbers might not. DC Peter Fenton, who was not averse to putting some stick about himself, kept track of their tools. He had them wrapped in brown paper dogfood sacks. Other detectives were collecting last-minute things. Fred Pyle moved out of the office and along the corridor after them. John Redvers fell into step.

'What's the DI like out at Paddington, Fred?' Redvers asked. 'Frank Polden. You know him?'

'Yeah. Lazy bastard. You won't have any trouble with him at this time of the morning.'

'Pity. Thought perhaps we could leave it all down to him.' They stepped into a lift.

The DI at Peckham was waiting for Pyle with the night relief, but didn't protest when he told him he wouldn't need his lads. He simply said, 'Pleased to hear it. Some of them have had a long day.' He took Pyle and Lethridge through the details of the target addresses, but told them nothing about the location that they couldn't have got from the area map. A lot of the local villainy these days involved blacks.

The address which Pyle was raiding was in a street of late Victorian terraced houses that had been built for the lower middle classes, tradesmen who aspired to a grandness they couldn't afford. The houses had tiny front gardens, some with motorbikes or broken cars lodged behind bits of shrubbery. The paint-flaking facade was in marked contrast to those belonging to upwardly mobile couples who had moved into the street, to use as a staging post before the recession checked their rise.

Parked without lights, Pyle's blue Sierra was distinguished in the line of vehicles only by the four men sitting in it. He had this car at his disposal most of the time he was on duty. They had a couple of minutes in hand before the hour that the raids had been synchronized for; it was unlikely that a minute or two either way would make much difference, but he waited anyway. There was no conversation in the car. Earlier there had been animated talk between the two DCs and the driver about a case reported in the *Sunday Sport* of a dentist and his anaesthetist who'd been stiffing their patients wholesale.

Pyle glanced at his watch. It was twenty-eight minutes past five and it had yet to get light. 'Give us that, Frank,' he said to the driver, reaching for the r/t handset. Into the phone he said, 'You awake back there?'

'Just about,' Jack Barcy replied from his car parked at the back of the houses. Their exchanges on the air were casual. 'So quiet you'd think no one was at it.'

'About two minutes, I reckon, Jack.' Pyle stared down the road towards the target house. Suddenly the street lights popped out, then the first glimmer in the eastern sky was noticeable. 'Okay, we're going in now.' He handed the phone to the driver, who would stay with the car.

Pyle and the other two detectives walked abreast at an unhurried pace across the road to the house. They climbed the steps, and Pyle hammered the door-knocker and stabbed the bell-push, shattering the morning stillness. Before the noise had faded their car stopped at the gate.

Somewhere along the street a dog barked. Then another.

He rang the doorbell again. A long, insistent ring that demanded an answer. The door was eventually opened by the target, Clifford Harding, in trousers and a vest, no shoes or socks.

A baby was wailing now.

'Took your time, son, didn't you?' Pyle said, pushing straight on into the hall, followed by the detectives. 'Thought perhaps you were going to try legging it.'

'Here, what is this?' Harding said.

'You're an active villain, Clifford. We're detectives, you know there's no real point in protesting. All right,' he said to the others, 'make it thorough. Give Jack and the lads out the back a shout.'

'Look, you got a warrant, have you? Coming here upsetting my family this time of morning. You're well out of order.'

Pyle looked at him, then nodded. 'Keep it up, son, and you'll get plenty.'

Harding fell silent and stayed that way. He was clearly frightened. Early-morning house calls by detectives were meant to have that effect. Pyle knew he'd have no trouble here.

He watched his men go through Clifford Harding's house thoroughly, but not tidily. Carpets were taken up, some floorboards too; loose skirting boards removed, cupboards emptied, even dismantled; they searched anything and everything that looked like it could hide something – money most likely, part of the proceeds of the robbery that had taken place at Barclay's Bank in Lewisham last week as Securicor was collecting money. One of the guards had been beaten severely when he had refused to part with the cash sack. Forty thousand pounds in old unrecorded notes had been blagged. The local CID had got nowhere with their initial investigation, and the Squad's subsequent involvement hadn't pushed it much further ahead. The only positive development to date had been the injured guard coming off the danger list.

Standing in the living room, where he provisionally questioned Harding about his movements, Pyle watched dispassionately as the house was systematically turned upside down.

The villain, who had dressed in anticipation of being taken in, protested each time something got broken or was spilled. 'Look, for fucksake. Tell 'em to leave off, will you?'

Such protests were restrained compared with those of his wife, who followed the detectives around the house, clutching her youngest child. 'You no-good bastards!' she screamed. 'Coming here upsetting my children. You lousy sods, I could murder you bastards.' The only peace they got was when she went to comfort her other kids.

The orange and brown carpet in the hall was taken up, but nothing was found. The detectives didn't replace it.

Harding watched, shaking his head. 'Look at that

fucking mess. You haven't got a warrant, I know you haven't' – as though he believed it would gain him something.

'Don't be silly, Clifford,' Pyle said. 'You think we'd take a liberty like that? That would be right out of order.' It was a standard reply, but here it was faintly mocking. They had warrants for all four raids this morning. He paused and looked at the suspect. Harding, with his thin frame, round shoulders and bad posture, was about the same age as himself, he guessed. There the similarity ended. He didn't accept that often-touted theory of similarities between CID and villains, that only a quirk of fate put the villain on one side of the law, the CID on the other. Probably they weren't so different when they started out. As a kid, he scraped through without getting himself nicked or taken before the courts. Other kids he knew weren't so lucky. Perhaps that was how it had been with Harding, but it wasn't really of much concern to him now.

'Of course,' he said, 'you could save yourself all this aggravation . . .'

'I already told you. I weren't nowhere near Lewisham.'

''Course you weren't. Your alibi sounds terrific.'

'Guv!' There was excitement in DC Fenton's voice. The reason was the shooter he had found.

'Handle it carefully, son,' Pyle cautioned, finding a felt-tip pen and pushing it down the barrel. 'We'll want his fingerprints off it or his brief'll get up in court and say we planted it. 'S a million. Where was it?'

'The cupboard under the sink. Beneath the floorboards there.'

A ruthless smile parted his lips when he turned back to Harding. 'This is it, I'd say. Wouldn't you, son?' The villain said nothing. 'There's nothing to say, is there? The gun makes you bang to rights.'

The compound at the rear of Peckham police station was deserted. The arc lamps fixed high on the building spread a harsh light across the area. A Panda car was parked with its lights on and with static issuing from the radio as a constable, who looked like he had all too recently put on more weight than his uniform wanted to accommodate, emerged unhurriedly from the building, letting the door bang. He went across to the car, showing no interest in the blue Ford Sierra that turned into the yard with the body. He would always be uniform carrier, Pyle concluded, as he watched his uncomfortable movements, feet at ten to two and his boots going over at the side.

In the back of the car Clifford Harding looked like he was facing his moment of truth, living his biggest regret. 'If only you could turn the clock back, Clifford,' Pyle commiserated, 'wouldn't that be something. You wouldn't get caught twice with that shooter we found at your house. Without doubt it makes you a million to do a nice piece down the road. Being nicked before you had it off, and provided for the family, I s'pose that hurts.'

He guessed that once the villain was over his initial shock he would begin to think more practically, try and find some solution. Maybe there was a way out. Maybe there wasn't. One thing was for sure, something would be tried.

The interior of the 60s-built nick was as tacky as the

fast-degrading exterior suggested, the traditional colours of green and cream prevailing, and was badly in need of repainting. The furniture in the back reception area had seen a lot of service. The overall impression the place created was depressing, but Pyle had little or no time to spare to be sensitive to his surroundings. Even though paid overtime had been officially cut to a total of fifteen hours a week, he still tended to find himself dulled to the finer needs of existence.

He entered the charge room, which was narrow with a high ceiling and no windows. There was a tall charge desk in the centre of the room, like some obelisk in honour of a more distant epoch, while opposite was a long bench bolted to the floor. There was nothing here that could have been picked up and used as a weapon by any violent suspect.

The two DCs followed him in with Harding.

'Sit down,' Pyle said, indicating the bench. 'It's going to be a long night, Cliff.'

Harding didn't move. 'I want to call my brief,' he said, as though believing he had some kind of rights.

When he lifted his head to speak, Pyle noticed how gaunt his face was, how prominent his bones were, the kind which opened easily from a punch.

'You're going to need more than a solicitor, son. A miracle's what you fucking well need.'

Still the suspect remained standing, as if to challenge the detective's statement.

'Sit down,' DC Fenton said, putting his hand on the villain's shoulder. Harding didn't argue.

'Slip up and find the DI, Rog'. Tell him we're here.' Pyle moved off across to the custody officer's room. It was one of several doors beyond the charge room. Visiting him was more than mere courtesy as he was supposed to know about everything that went on there concerning prisoners. 'Have you got a minute, Skip?'

The pear-shaped sergeant climbed out of his comfortable chair. 'Morning, sir. Your other lads got here a short while ago. They're in the cells.'

Pyle acknowledged the information. He had spoken to DS Lethridge on the radio earlier about their nicking. 'Got another cell spare, have you?'

'You can take your pick,' he said with what looked like an apologetic smile. 'We've only a couple of black dealers we want to keep. The rest are drunks. We can soon throw them out. Save giving them breakfast.'

'A quiet room'll be handy.' He winked at the custody officer who knew at once what he wanted: a room where the initial interview wouldn't be recorded.

The sergeant indicated a door at the side of the large room, which opened into a windowless cubicle about eight feet square. There were two such rooms, one either side of the corridor that led down to the cells. Both were painted in dark green and had a scarred table and two straightback chairs.

'That'll do. Come on, son,' the DI said to Harding, who was encouraged to rise by DC Fenton.

The local DI came through from the back reception. He glanced at Harding as he was taken into the room. 'Busy morning,' he commented.

'I won't be sliding off to bed in a hurry.'

'He the one with the shooter?'

'Under the sink.' There was a smile on Pyle's face. 'Some of the hiding places villains use make you die.'

'They get a fucking sight sillier, I swear they do.' The local man shook his head in mock dismay.

There was a pause. They had little to say to one another. Pyle guessed he wanted to go home.

'Wasn't anything you needed us around for, was there?'

'I don't think so. Thanks for your help.'

'Well, make yourself at home – use my office if you want. It's quiet up there. Most of the relief are still here if you need any of them to chase things up. I s'pect I'll see you around sometime tomorrow.'

'I expect so,' Pyle said and went into the interview room.

'What about that brief then,' Harding said to him.

'I don't remember promising you a solicitor, Clifford.'

'I'm supposed to be allowed a phone call.'

Pyle looked at him. 'Who told you that? It's a fairy story. You were caught bang to rights. Weren't you just.' It wasn't a question. 'Sit down, son.' The felon remained standing. 'We'd better understand each other,' he warned, 'it'll save a lot of aggravation. Whatever favours you get now, you get because I want to give you them, and for no other reason. So sit down like you're told, and we'll see how you shape.' Still Harding hesitated, but finally he sat. 'Now in order for us to progress in the fastest manner possible, there's certain information I want from you. Like your whereabouts last Monday week. Who you were with on that blag, who had the dough off you, and where you got that shooter from.'

Harding's mouth fell open. 'Oh, is that all?'

Pyle clearly surprised him when he shook his head. 'That's just the start. I'm going to know a lot more about you and that blag before we're through. I'm going down the cells to see your mate now . . .'

'What mate?' Harding said.

He smiled. 'You're going to have a little chat with these lads. When I come back I'll expect some answers. Right.' Harding simply stared at him. 'You'd better know it's right, son.'

Pyle glanced at DCs Fenton and Humphries as if giving them the licence to treat the suspect however they saw fit. Although there was no certainty that Harding had been connected with the armed raid at Lewisham, the gun they had found indicated that he was heavily involved in something, so information about that would do instead. The assumption that he had taken part in the blag in question was a good starting point.

Terry Clark, the villain who Lethridge had picked up, was still in his underpants when Pyle pulled open the door. He was sitting on the edge of the shelf bunk in the bleak brick cell. There was a flushing toilet in the corner at the end of the bunk and a window made from glass bricks high in the end wall opposite the door, but nothing else. DC Jenkins was leaning against the wall behind Lethridge; another DC was sitting on the bunk near Clark.

His arrival made the cell crowded. He sniffed the stale air, which was heavy with disinfectant.

'Don't look at me, guv,' DC Jenkins said. 'I didn't shit myself.'

'Someone did. How's it going, Eric?'

'Usual old story. Don't know nothing,' Lethridge mocked. 'Do you, Terry?'

'Fucking right I don't. What about my fucking clothes? Sitting around like this in this fucking pisshole. I'll catch m' death of cold.'

'They were your choice of going-away clothes, weren't

they?' Lethridge said. 'Running down the garden like that.'

'Popping in to one of the neighbours', were you, son?' Pyle said. From the end of the bunk he lifted a folded blanket, which smelled of disinfectant, and offered it at arm's length to the prisoner. 'There you are.'

'Piss off! I ain't putting that soapy thing around me.' He flexed his shoulders as if to menace him.

Pyle didn't care for his manner. It wasn't merely defensive, like Harding's, but aggressive. He decided this suspect was likely to get a bit of stick before they got what they wanted. Perhaps he didn't have what they wanted, but still he would get the treatment.

He let the blanket drop. 'Can't say I blame you. Wouldn't be so bad if they were washed after some of those drunks had vomited over them. I think they splash disinfectant on them and hang them up to dry. So what about it, Terry?' His tone was reasonable, even though he was putting pressure on the villain. 'D'you want to put up your hands? Save a lot of trouble.'

'Some fucking chance, I should think.'

'All right, let's do it step by step. Where were you the Monday before last?' Pyle asked.

'That was a long time ago, I have a short memory.' There was a smile on Clark's face.

Pyle glanced from the young man to the large-framed detective with a bright red beard alongside him. There was an implicit threat in the gesture. ''He gives you a couple of rabbit punches he might jog your memory.'

'It'd fucking well need the four of you, an' all.'

'He's a hard man all right, guv,' Lethridge said.

'Or just thick. Can't remember what he did eight days ago.'

Clark adopted a thoughtful pose. 'Oh yes, I do remember. I was with my solicitor. Why don't you give him a bell and ask him?' He smiled, like he had said something clever.

'I'd say you'd better think about that, son. I'd say you were down at Lewisham tucking up that bank.'

'Not me, pal. Not my game, is it? Ask your mate.'

'You'll do all right,' Lethridge said. 'Your alibi's not worth a rub, and you know it.'

'I got no worries. All you done is give me a pull on my form. What d'you think, I just got off the boat?'

'It's a bit more scientific than that, Terry,' Pyle told him, hoping that they'd find something for this flash bastard. 'Not much, I grant you, but a bit.'

'I don't fancy your chances when my brief gets to work.'

Mocking laughter parted Pyle's lips. 'He must find your faith in him very touching. You fuckwit, you *sound* like you're just off the boat. You'll be weighed off almost before you even get to see your brief. Who is it he wants, Eric?'

'Gladwell, guv,' Lethridge informed him. 'He's supposed to be well bent.'

''S what I heard. Even less of a problem then, especially if we slip him on the list before the right sort of judge – someone like Morgan-Stevas would do. He's heard so many strokes. What sort of credibility do you think you'd have with that judge?'

Terry Clark sneered. 'You can't do that.'

'I can't?' Pyle said. 'Let me enlighten you, son. There's nothing easier than making sure villains like you go into the lists before a particular judge. Morgan-Stevas favours hard-working detectives; he detests villains who put a lot of stick about. All it needs is a quiet word with the clerk of the lists. Judges do it themselves all the time, Terry. They have their clerks juggle the lists.'

That left Clark looking a little less confident. Pyle smiled.

'It might sound all right when Gladwell gets up in court and slags us off, Terry,' he said, 'but when it comes right down to it, son, it only impresses villains. You add up his results, see if you find them quite so impressive.'

Clark flexed his shoulders as if to dispel his doubt. 'I'll take my chances.'

'You really could save us a lot of time and effort. You won't find us unappreciative. We've got homes to go to. You think these lads don't want to go home rather than fuck around here until you crack?'

'They don't mind, guv,' Lethridge put in. 'Looking forward to a couple of days away from home.'

'You gonna call him for me or what?'

The four detectives merely looked at Clark.

'I want to know how long I'm going to be kept here.'

'I told you, until we crack you.' He leaned closer to the man. There was menace in the gesture. 'As far as anyone out there's concerned, you no longer exist. Not until we say you do.'

'Leave off. I know my rights. You can't keep me here. Under the PACE rules you have to charge me or take me before a magistrate. He'll make sure I see my brief.' There was anxiety in Clark's voice.

'It's the Squad what nicked you, Terry, not some wooden-tops. You pulled a right stroke with that security guard, you wicked bastard. Don't whine to us about your rights, because you haven't got any. Not now you've been nicked by us. We tore up the Police and Criminal Evidence Act. What you've got, son, is information we want, and you'll stay lost, and assisting with our inquiries, for as long as it takes.'

'Yeah. We'll see about that,' Clark said, and flexed his shoulders again. 'Don't cost me nothing sitting here . . .'

'Then stand up!' Without warning his hand shot out and seized Clark's genitals, pulling him up. He was compelled to rise in order to alleviate the sudden, crushing pain. He cried out.

'What's that, painful, Terry?' Lethridge inquired.

Clark clawed at the air. Pyle expected him to lash out. But there were four of them, and no sound would escape from the cell. It was doubtful if anyone would have taken any notice if it had. Even in his suffering the villain seemed alert to how dangerous his position was.

'Leave off, for fucksake. Leave off, you bastard . . .'

'That's not nice, Terry!' Pyle said. 'I'm not a bastard, am I, Eric?'

'You've impeccable credentials, guv – a senior detective on the Squad. He should show a lot more respect.'

'About right.' All the while he was squeezing his balls.

'Le' go, will you . . . Le' go . . . fuck you . . .'

'That's not respectful, Terry. Let's have a little respect.'

There was a rap at the cell door, and a uniformed constable pulled it open. He waited.

Clark finally cracked. 'Please,' he said in a polite tone.

Pyle released him, then turned to the uniform.

'Inspector Redvers is on the phone for you, sir.'

'Good luck.' He turned back to the felon, who had sunk back to the edge of the bed and was holding his balls. 'I think you'll find you've a lot to say to us, son.'

He went out, leaving the interrogation to DS Lethridge.

Activity wasn't brisk in the front office when Pyle went to the telephone, nor was it likely to be until the day relief came on. He doubted if it would amount to much even then. This was one of the busiest nicks in Area 3, but mostly all they ever collared were blacks. Now there were only two or three policemen about. Pyle would have bet money they were drinking tea.

'John,' he said, picking up the phone. 'How did it go?'

'Nothing,' the detective inspector said. 'The bastard had skipped. He wasn't long gone. I reckon he got a bell from someone down here.' He was at Paddington Green police station.

'Could be.' Pyle was unconcerned. The suspect wasn't worth expending too much energy on. There was nothing he could do about the runner now. 'How'd the other fella go?'

'They nicked him,' Redvers said. 'I'm on my way over there to see how he shapes. What about your end? Any good?'

He told him about Harding and the gun.

'That sounds nice. Going to be a long morning?'

'With luck we'll get what we want a bit lively. I'll see you later, John. Cheers.' He replaced the phone and stood by the table for a moment and thought about Clifford Harding, who was clearly frightened for his future prospects, and not a little desperate; however, that didn't mean he'd necessarily take the easy option.

'All right, Clifford,' he said, back in the interview room. 'How about it?'

The two DCs had taken him through his story. His minding the gun for a man was all it amounted to.

'Well, what is it you want from me, then,' Harding said, 'a signed statement?'

Pyle wasn't put off by his sarcasm. 'Be handy. And to have you plead to it in court.' He paused and watched him. 'Let's start with a few names, shall we?'

'What names?' Harding tried.

'You know the names we want, son. You've got them all right. The names of the lads who were on the blag with you last week. What do you *think* I'm talking about?'

Harding remained silent, like he was lost for an answer. Perhaps he was, perhaps he didn't have the names, perhaps he wasn't involved on the robbery. Not that that small fact would make much difference to the treatment he got now. Pyle glanced purposefully at the two detectives with him, then back at Harding.

'Says he hasn't got any names,' DC Fenton said. 'He was at home with his wife and kids, guv.'

'Perhaps he was. But that's the worst place you could have been, Clifford. Terry Clark, Brian Finch, Dennis Cooper,' Pyle informed him, putting up his thumb and fingers for each of the other men who had been raided that morning. 'They'll do nicely. Oh yes, we might as well throw in Jack Lynn. He was involved as well, wasn't he?'

'For all I know. You might go and nick them for that blag,' Harding said. 'But I wasn't on it, I promise you that.'

In his way of saying things that made them sound irrefutable, Pyle said, 'Don't talk silly, Clifford, you were seen.' He watched the villain closely and saw his sense of desperation grow.

'By some slag you stuck up to lolly me. By some dirty slag you *told* it was me!'

Pyle shook his head. 'No need for strokes like that. Not this time, for fucksake.' He dragged up the second chair and sat opposite him. 'What about the shooter we found, Cliff? Or do you think we materialized it? You fancy trying to say it was ours? We planted it there?'

Harding said nothing. Anything he might say in answer to such an invitation would cost him something later.

'It's well known we carry round shooters to fit up suspects with, guv,' Fenton said.

'He doesn't believe that, do you, Cliff? Sure you don't. You know we don't do those sort of things.' He smiled. 'You know what that gun's going to get you, with your form? Ten years, without me even trying, son, especially if I put you up before Morgan-Stevas.' He was the stick to beat any active villain with. No judge currently presiding over a London Criminal Court had such an open loathing for the felonry. Villains had a dread of going in front of him.

'You realize you were grassed, son, don't you?'

Harding raised his eyes to look at him. Something he avoided doing often. 'I don't think so,' he said. 'That's just a get-up.'

Pyle didn't let the pressure off. 'Your mate down in the cells put you right in it. Well, it's the only sensible thing to do when you're nicked. Save yourself, any way you can. They all do it, Cliff. But imagine keeping a shooter in your own house. Who ever heard of anything more stupid, especially for a professional villain?'

'Who said villains have any sense, guv?' DC Humphries commented like he wasn't sure of himself.

'This oversight wasn't just folly, it was insanity. Especially if you go mates with grasses.'

Harding was becoming nervy and irritable. Having his sleep interrupted as he had would have done nothing to induce calm to start with. Chips began to fly off him as he started to crack. Pyle knew it would happen as the pressure increased, but gave no sign of satisfaction.

'All right,' Harding said, 'you done me for the gun. It was stupid, I was like some fucking wolly. But that's all you got.'

'It's enough, son. More than enough. That would be about the last thing you ought to be done for.' He paused, letting the implications of that work on Harding. He had previous convictions with a firearm which was one of the reasons he had been selected for the Method Index raid. 'Give me the others on that blag last week and I'll drop the firearm charge.' The proposition was made in a matter-of-fact way. 'Drop it right out.'

'I can't, can I? I mean, fuck I, I don't even know the guys you stuck up, do I?' He hesitated, as if realizing the detective wasn't impressed. 'Well, I do know one of them – not very well. Lynn, I know. Jack Lynn.'

Pyle remained unimpressed. 'Then you're in trouble, son. Bang in trouble.'

In the war of nerves Harding was clearly suffering heavy losses. 'I'd like to be able to help you,' he said.

'Help yourself, you mean,' Pyle reminded him. 'I don't need any help at all to get you sent down.' He waited now as Harding glanced at each of the DCs. The chances of his offering something if they were alone would be better, Pyle decided, than in front of these two. Villains planning to put up names rarely wanted witnesses to their treachery. 'Pop down and see how he's getting on with the other fella, Peter, will you?'

'Yeah.' DC Fenton knew what was going on.

'Haven't you got to shoot off, Rog'?' Pyle inquired, catching the eye of the other DC.

'If I could, guv,' Humphries said, but didn't stir.

'You'd better shoot off then, hadn't you – time to get down to Bromley, have a word with your witnesses.'

Finally DC Humphries got the message and departed.

'What did you have in mind, Clifford?' Pyle asked when they were alone.

Harding shrugged and said, ''S up to you, guv.' He waited.

The DI refused to take the initiative. He waited also.

Haltingly Harding said, 'I could put a nice earner into you. Be well safe. I mean, if that charge could be dropped out – the shooter, like . . . know what I mean?'

The fact that he didn't react seemed to make the villain more nervous. Pyle was enjoying this turn of events.

'The dough would be double-safe. There'd be no problem on that score. I mean, what's it worth to you, d'you think . . .?'

Pyle waited a moment longer as if seriously considering the offer. 'It's a bit late to do it that way, I think. I mean, my entire squad's involved, and most of another squad. That's about twenty CID. They'd all want a taste, and not just fivers and tenners.' He wasn't averse to taking an earner in the right circumstances, but these were far from right. 'You wouldn't have enough to go into us all. Even if you had the lion's share out of Lewisham.'

'I wasn't on that. That's straight, guv. I promise you.'

'About as straight as a dog's dick,' he said. 'You've no reason to lie, have you, Clifford?' – mocking once more. 'Who was it down to, then? Jack Lynn?' The suspect didn't answer. 'If you want the firearm charge dropped you've got to be practical, son. Your money's no good to me. You've got to offer me something else. Something I can use. Give me the villains who did that blag.'

'I can't. I really can't. I haven't got them.'

'Well, what have you got? You go mates with Jack Lynn. What's he having these days?'

'His old lady, I s'pose. I haven't seen him for years.' Harding waited. 'I don't go mates with Lynn. The few times I've seen him in recent years was just by chance. Lynn don't mean much to me. I'd lolly him to get a result. Yes, I could, I mean, I'd sooner he did a bit of bird than me, that's for sure. I want a deal. I'd part with every penny I could scrape together to keep my liberty.'

'He's supposed to be well active,' Pyle said, like the matter was of no importance. 'That's the word on Lynn.'

'I heard that,' Harding said. 'But I didn't get no offers.'

There was a rap at the door, and DS Barcy put his head inside the room. 'Guv, got a minute?'

He stepped back to allow Pyle out, then pulled the door to. Barcy had remained at Harding's house with another detective to complete their search.

'Nothing else there,' he said, 'apart from these.' He produced a plastic bag which contained six bullets. 'Up behind the sink, they were.'

'Good hit, Jack.' Pyle took the bullets. 'The right size, are they?' They were. Had they not been then he might have found some that were. His thoughts moved on. 'No bent gear at the house? Perhaps a telly or video?' The more pressure he could get on Harding, the better the final result.

'Nothing worth a look, guv. His old woman went berserk after you left. Screaming, she was. Set the kids off. They thought they weren't going to see their Dad again. A right upset, it was.'

That fact lodged in Pyle's brain. 'She tell them that?'

'She wound them up about their Dad.'

'Did she telephone anyone, Jack?'

'She tried calling a solicitor, but all she got was an answerphone.' Then, as if anticipating his governor's next question, he added, 'Wasn't any of the outfits likely to cause problems, guv. Just a local brief, it was.'

'Good. I'll want you to do a bit of visiting, to check some alibis. See how things shape with him first.'

He went back into the interview room. 'My DS just came from your place,' he said in a concerned manner. 'Your kids were upset.' He watched Harding, suspecting that he had found a more acute pressure point. Villains were perversely sentimental about their kids.

'What? What's wrong with them? – fucking upsetting them like that. You were out of order.'

'Missing their Dad, that's what's wrong with them, son. Still, all you villains are the same. Don't ever think of your kids when you're at it, do you?' The words were affecting Harding, but there remained only one way he was going to get off the hook. 'They'll miss you for a long while, from what I can see of it.

Probably even forget you altogether. It happens all the time, son.'

That wasn't intended to comfort Harding. He lowered his head as if to hide the emotion charging across his face, those reactions he had no control over. Pyle saw it all.

'What about the gun?' he asked. 'What d'you have in mind for it?'

'Nothing,' Harding said. 'I was just minding it for someone.'

'Someone you met in a pub! 'S always the way, son. What about these, then?' he said sharply, dropping the bullets on the table in front of Harding. His manner during interrogation changed frequently and without warning, often leaving villains confused. 'You'd better come up with some answers, Cliff, if you want a deal. Good answers, the sort I want to hear. Otherwise you'll be a long time away from your family, I promise you.' There was a pause, another change of tack. 'Right, where d'you get the shooter?'

Harding hesitated, and said, 'Can we have some sort of deal?'

'Depends on what you give me,' he replied, suggesting nothing was easier.

'The gun dropped right out, that is?'

'I'd say my governor would agree to that, if you put the right sort of stuff on offer, Clifford. 'S up to you entirely. I mean, you've got nothing at all to lose, have you?'

Still Harding resisted. 'I don't know about that Lewisham blag. I mean, those fuckers pulled a right stroke, they deserve nicking, hurting that guard like that . . .' He hesitated again. 'But Jack Lynn, if you're really interested . . . if he's at it, I could probably go and find out what he's having for you.'

'That means you'd have to be let loose before I get a result,' Pyle said. But suspecting how Harding felt about his family, he knew he wasn't likely to run away, so it wouldn't be that difficult to pick him up again if he didn't come through.

With an apparent sense of desperation now, Harding said, 'I won't have it away, I can't. I mean, I can't, can I? What about my family?'

'Family ties might impress a magistrate when granting bail.'

Harding's breathing was growing shallow with anxiety. 'How could I have it away? I mean, I couldn't take m' family on the trot, even if I wanted to. I just want to get myself out of trouble.'

'Oh, I believe you, Clifford. Then, I'm very trusting. But it isn't down to me. My governor's the one who has to be impressed.' He paused and considered Harding as he registered this new impediment to his freedom. 'As a gesture of faith you'd better give me the dealer you got the gun from, hadn't you?'

This was the final point of commitment, after which there would be no turning back. But Harding hesitated again. Pyle thought for a moment he was going to back off. Finally the villain nodded.

'Wally Marks . . .' The words almost didn't emerge.

'Who?' Pyle said, wanting him to say the name like he meant to give it to him.

'I'm not a grass.'

''Course you're not, Clifford. You think the gun dealer

wouldn't have traded you had your situation been reversed? That name again?'

'Wally Marks. He has a greengrocery business out at Charlton. He does a bit of dabbling on the side . . .'

Pyle looked at him and nodded. The information was a start; he didn't despise Harding for grassing any more than he would have admired him for holding out. As far as he was concerned all this villain represented was a means to an end, the end being the capture of a few more villains. What he had given him would possibly have some bearing on his final result, for he was an active villain, and the shooter suggested he had something plotted. He would eventually go for that. There was no more loyalty between detectives and felons than was generally found between felons. He knew that if you put enough pressure on them, then offered them an out, almost always they would come up to expectation.

By the time he got back to the office it had turned nine o'clock, three hours beyond what should have been the end of his tour, and he wanted to go home and sleep. There was little chance of that, not before his court appearance with a lad he had nicked for robbery. He felt soiled and unshaven, and at times like these regretted being a policeman. Had he been out on division running a CID office he would have had a comfortable nine-to-five routine. Despite himself he wasn't seriously looking for a transfer out of the Squad. Few ever seemed to do more than two or three years there and he would doubtless regret it when his time came to be moved. There was a possibility that he'd get the boot sooner as a result of the current complaint he had against him, and maybe even have to go back into uniform. There was substance to the complaint, but still he was banking on it not being substantiated. He had subsequently altered the contemporaneous notes that were taken during an unrecorded interview with a villain. The villain who had been badly advised – if advised at all – had made a complaint that he was stitching him up; the move wouldn't gain him anything when he came up for trial. Pyle had done nothing less than he deemed necessary to ensure the blagger went to prison. The subsequent complaint didn't cause him to regret what he had done, and wouldn't stop him doing it again. Now it was just another of the problems he had to contend with.

There was a lot of activity on the fourth floor at that time of day. Detectives and uniform policemen and civilian personnel were going about the business of getting their day started. Some of the detectives were trying to get last-minute papers and reports sorted for court. Most of the movement came from the paper-carriers, shifting the bumf from one office to another.

'Morning, Fred,' said a detective in a neatly pressed short-sleeved shirt. His face looked less than fresh, with huge, sagging ribbons beneath his eyes.

'Have it in last night?' Pyle asked as he went past.

'Not even in my hand.'

He turned back and called, 'Graham!' The detective stopped at one of the doors along the corridor and waited. DI Graham McHale was one of the few detectives from Criminal Intelligence who wasn't totally possessive about his information. 'D'you have anything on a villain called Lynn? Jack Lynn? He comes out of Kentish Town.'

'Doesn't ring any bells. What's his line?'

Pyle gave a precis of the villain's CRO file, but saw that it rang no more bells with McHale either.

'I'll have a look for you, Fred. You around later?'

'Looks like it. Good luck.'

There were four other DIs in the communal office, bending to their hated paperwork. Each glanced up and greeted him as he moved along to his own desk. Alan Welch was sitting typing a report on his side of the double desk. Pyle's arrival provided a reasonable excuse to stop.

Welch took out his tobacco bag and made a cigarette. 'You had it off last night.'

'Nothing much,' Pyle said. His arrests rate was good. He could afford to be modest. 'One looks halfway promising.'

Welch leaned back in his chair, waiting for something more. He had the lowest arrest quota on the Squad but was well thought of, mainly because he dealt efficiently with his paperwork. His presence was less of an inspiration to the other detectives than a vindication. He was proof of what most argued, that while they were burdened with paperwork they couldn't capture villains. Although Pyle coped with his own reports he foresaw the possibility that one day he might be doing nothing else.

He remained standing at his desk in his overcoat as he sorted through the work that had collected in his 'posts' trays. There were reports for his attention, memos for his information; his own carefully written reports that had been sent back because there was inadequate information, and others with the marks of approval from more senior ranks and for him now to take on to a further stage. None of it was so important it wouldn't keep until he came on duty that evening. He certainly wasn't going to come in after court to clear it, not when the trays would be full again by his next relief. He slid the papers back and reached into one of the drawers for his electric shaver. The batteries were running low and the blades seemed to turn reluctantly, giving him an indifferent shave. The wasp-like buzz of the machine added to the general noise of conversation, printers and telephone bells which filled the room.

'Some brief phoned you, Fred. Gladwell. Alex Gladwell. He wanted a word about his client you nicked. Clark.'

The information suddenly pleased Pyle. When villains'

solicitors were that quick off the mark it usually meant their clients were at it, and especially when the brief was Alex Gladwell.

'D'he say what he wanted?'

'Wants you to call him the moment you get in.'

'Some chance!'

He wouldn't be in a hurry to talk to the brief, and would keep him from his client for as long as he could.

'Perhaps he wants to go into you, Fred.'

'That would be handy. I could use it.'

He continued shaving, picking up the phone with his free hand and punching out his home number. As he waited for his wife to answer he noticed another detective enter the office. He was Maurice Head, a DI who had been under suspension for the best part of three months, having been named in allegations of fabricating evidence. The villain concerned ran a couple of clubs in the West End and some brasses at the time of his arrest had threatened to take a lot of detectives with him if he went. Whether or not his threats had been taken seriously Pyle didn't know, but he had subsequently carried them out, causing all kinds of problems. Maurice Head had been one of about twenty detectives named, and one of fourteen who had been suspended. One or two others had had the sense to resign before the investigation was concluded. The consensus was that the result wouldn't favour the CID in general and especially not those detectives under investigation. Head wasn't supposed to enter the building, no policeman under suspension was, but getting in wasn't an insuperable problem. Pyle watched him stop and speak to the DI at the desk near the door. The exchange of words was conducted as if Head was a beggar. Without wishing to admit it, Pyle felt a bit sorry for him. It was too easy to dismiss him because he had come on top. Such a problem could happen to anybody. But he did think him foolish for hanging on in like he was instead of turning in his papers, even though he understood why he didn't. Head had put a lot of villains away in his time – even if some of his moves were swift – and Pyle knew how much he liked being in the CID. It was a way of life that was not let go of easily. He himself would almost certainly try to hang on in similar circumstances.

His wife finally answered the phone. 'Edith. 'S me,' he said. 'I'm still here. Only just got in.' His wife had little to say. He didn't tell her specifics of his job. All she could ask was how he was, where he was. 'Be back later this morning. I'm not sure when. Depends what time I get finished in court. Shouldn't be long . . .' He acknowledged DI Head with a nod as he stopped at the desk to speak to Alan Welch. His wife was telling him how she might be out shopping. 'All right. I'll see you later . . . bye, love.' He replaced the phone. 'How's it going, Maurice?' he asked. He could almost see the enormous black cloud that had been over the man ever since his suspension.

'Pissed off with hanging around, I am.' His thick hands pulled on the ends of the patterned scarf he was wearing. 'Just ducked in to see if there was any word.'

Pyle knew that the real reason would have been because he was feeling lost, out of touch, even lonely; though he doubted if Head would ever admit such things.

Welch said, 'I've not heard a thing, Fred. You?'

If anyone was likely to hear it would have been DI Welch. His ear was closest to the ground around the Yard.

'Not a whisper,' Pyle said. He finished with his shaver

and blew the head clean. He removed his black briefcase from the bottom drawer of the desk. His eyes met Head's. As much as he sympathized with him, he wished he wouldn't keep showing up like this. Despite himself he said, 'Tell you what, Maurice, that investigation going on for as long as it has, there's no way you're not going to wind up nicked . . .'

'Oh, good fucking luck, Fred!' Head said.

It was the best advice he could give him. 'You know as well as anyone what your best move is. Sorry, son, but it stands to reason . . .' He paused, not wishing to debate the matter. It was ground they had been over before. 'I'll see you later.'

He went out and along the corridor to the DCIs' office. 'Is Tony still around, guv?' he said to Trevor Watson, the DCI who had the day relief. The third DCI on the Squad was currently on sick leave, and hadn't been replaced.

Trevor Watson barely made the minimum height required for service in the Met, and looked more like a bank manager than a detective in his neat three-piece suit and semi-starched collars. He wore a silver chain across his waistcoat with a silver Omega which he claimed belonged to his grandfather, but which Pyle suspected he blagged from somewhere. He had sharp, pointed features, a slightly pedantic manner that wasn't popular with the lower ranks. He often returned reports to them for redrafting or retyping if there was the slightest error in them.

'Just missed him.' Watson carefully marked the place to which he'd read in the report in front of him. 'He's gone out to Barnes on that complaints inquiry.' Despite the ever-increasing size of the Complaints Investigation Bureau, most senior detectives were from time to time called upon to investigate complaints. Most did so reluctantly. Any who did this work with anything resembling cheerful willingness were usually seconded on a permanent basis.

'Was it urgent, Fred?'

'Just a development with one of the bodies from this morning's raid's all.'

'Did you talk to that brief who phoned?'

'Not yet.'

'Didn't waste much time, did he? Is his client involved?'

''S odds on. I left Eric down there – I got one in court,' he reminded him. 'Did you see Maurice Head?'

'He looked in,' Watson said. 'I wish he wouldn't. I didn't want to be the one to categorically tell him not to. I advised him to resign. About the only advice I could give him in the circumstances. It might save him being nicked, and save his pension. The Commissioner'll accept it all right if he gets it in now.'

That was almost standard in the police force – the last thing the hierarchy wanted was the attendant bad publicity when policemen were arrested, charged and sent for trial, especially policemen as senior as Maurice Head. Far better was the alternative of quietly resigning with all his pension rights intact, and with the unspoken agreement that he wouldn't subsequently be charged.

'Maybe I ought to stick mine in,' Pyle said, alluding to the complaint investigation he had against him.

Watson grinned as he turned away to answer the phone. 'DCIs' office. Watson . . . I drafted the report yesterday,' he said in a tone which suggested he was talking to his boss. 'It's just being typed . . . doesn't look like it'll be much of a result, guv . . . Yes, soon as I get it back.' He replaced the phone.

Pyle said, 'They're wasting their time. Chummy'll get a result, and that'll be that as far as the complaint goes, you see.'

'The Rubber Heels like to make themselves busy, Fred. Incidentally, what's happening with that lad you have going up this morning? Any chance he'll plead to it?'

'I'm hoping so, guv. Save us a lot of time at court – the witnesses aren't all that. The CPS was far more confident about going to court on the evidence than I ever was.' He didn't consider the Crown Prosecution Service shrewd, and having something thrown out of court was far less of a reflection on them than on him as the detective in charge of the case. 'I suppose if it's put to him right.'

'Offer him something?' Watson said. 'Not too much.'

'It's his liberty he wants, guv.'

'Yes. Don't they all? See what he says, Fred. It will save a lot of time and effort.'

Cells below magistrates' courts were little different from those at police stations. They provided as standard a bench-bed, usually without a mattress, and rarely a toilet of any kind. The walls were scarred with graffiti, names and legends of those gone before, who expected a result or had been weighed off. Like most cells there was room for about five paces, depending how tall the prisoner was.

David Shepley wasn't particularly tall, and looked less than comfortable in his suit, which had obviously been bought in a hurry on the advice of his solicitor to try and create the right impression. He has been wearing jeans and a flying jacket when Pyle had nicked him. He paced in an agitated way. Pyle assumed he didn't like the proposal he had made.

'. . . I don't know. I just don't know, do I? The thought of having to plead guilty, it's really gutting me. It's ruining me.'

Pyle was unmoved by Shepley's visible distress. 'Well, let's be practical, David,' he said. 'You know you've got some coming. About eight years, at a guess, unless you're very lucky. I mean, you can go and gum up the works by pleading not guilty at trial. That's your right, David. But all it will do is piss everyone off. And what'll happen meanwhile? I'll see to it that you're remanded to Brixton before you ever come to trial. You'll be in Brixton for about six months, maybe longer.' He paused to let that dim prospect sink in. There were interminable delays in getting prisoners up the steps from the magistrates' courts, the lists in the Crown Courts were getting endless. 'It's your best bet, David. They'll have to send you upstairs anyway. That's going to mean a delay of months. But meanwhile you can have bail – I won't object. You could even go and do a bit more villainy, and provide for your family while you're away.' The offer was reasonable.

'You make it sound easy, don't you?' Shepley said.

'It is. You've got to have a little faith, 's all.' He added a little sugar. 'When you finally go up and plead, I'll be able to tell the court you were co-operative. I'll even leave out your previous. That alone'll save you a nice piece. But the thing is, David, I do want to know you're going to plead guilty.'

Still Shepley hesitated. 'Jesus. The thought of pleading to it, it guts me, it really does, I mean I got no chance then, have I?'

He ceased his pacing, and looked at the DI as if appealing for something better. He didn't get it.

'You think you have anyway? With a brief on Legal Aid? I s'pect he advised you to plead not guilty.' He saw from Shepley's expression that that was so, as if suddenly believing the brief was part of some conspiracy against him, which he was, if inadvertently. 'They get a bigger fee for taking it all the way. They're not interested in the final result. It doesn't make any difference to them. But you have to be realistic about this. You can't really expect the system to provide an adequate defence for those who offend against it. It's not reasonable. The system works for me, David, not you. Think about it. Ask yourself what chance you have got. I mean, what chance?' He shook his head. 'You've no chance, son.'

'My brief's up in court. He's expecting me to plead not guilty.'

'Then you need to tell him different.'

'Bail won't be a problem?' Shepley asked. 'There are one or two things that need sorting at home. Be handy.'

'It won't be if you agree to plead to it. I'll have a quiet word with the magistrate.' He wouldn't, in fact, but then he didn't anticipate any problems with bail.

'I'd better tell my brief, then.'

'You're the one employing him, David. You help the system, it helps you. See if I'm right.'

Shepley's decision would save him a lot of work. The alternative option would almost certainly have amounted to an acquittal anyway. He would give Shepley what help he could. It made no difference to him if this villain was out doing a bit more. Now he'd get home and to bed at a reasonable hour.

The exam had him completely baffled. He read and reread the questions a hundred times, but they were meaningless to him; the English they were written in might as well have been Sanskrit. He struggled a while longer before wrenching himself into wakefulness, though his mind wasn't ready to let go of sleep. He hadn't had enough rest for him to function well on his next shift. His muscles ached and his eyes hurt; there was a pain in the back of his neck which crept steadily up under his cranium now. He thought about taking some tablets to lose it. Where it might go to he didn't know, and wondered if the pain was the result of the beta-blockers he had taken before going on that raid in the early hours. A number of detectives used them in that way. He didn't know if they suffered pains in the head as an aftereffect. Probably it was nothing that a couple more hours' sleep wouldn't cure. He wanted to just roll over and go back to sleep, despite his foul-tasting mouth and his bladder, distended close to bursting. But he couldn't go back to sleep. Not now. He had already done so once. His wife was in the bedroom; her presence had woken him as she set a mug of tea on the night table.

'Fred . . . It's gone five, love,' she said in her permanently hoarse voice. She went to the window and drew back the curtains, which were floral patterned and seemed to keep out little of the daylight. The bedroom wasn't large, then nor was their semi-detached house which they had only half paid for. Their taste were for floral patterned wallpaper to go with the curtains and a matching duvet cover. Or rather that was his wife's taste, which he went along with. He didn't take much interest in the house, except when she tried to spend too much on appliances, and he had no practical interest in DIY. If anything like decorating needed doing, then either a decorator or Edith did it.

She was in her late thirties. Her hips had thickened, so too had her stomach, but in her coarse, round face, framed by her short black and grey hair, were traces of the woman who had first attracted him. She always waited until he got up. He rubbed his eyes, then massaged his face, which felt dead and bloodless.

'Golly!' he said. 'I can hardly open my eyes. 'S that the time? Only feels like I got my head down a few minutes ago.'

'You ought to sleep longer. You were late getting to bed.'

Instinctively he knew what this was about and was seeking excuses before she had even suggested anything. Maybe she knew that too. Yes, he thought, she always knew such things. She was the wife of a detective and could often read people in the same way he could. He wondered if she suspected that he saw other women when he got the chance, but didn't dwell on the thought.

'My back hurts like a bastard.' He reached round to knead his spine in the region of the adrenals, then saw the mug on the night table. 'What's this, tea?'

'I was just having a cup . . .' she said.

He looked at her. His eyes, even in their sleep-weakened state, were from habit seeking to disprove the validity of her statement. He guessed that wasn't the whole truth, that she would have had an ulterior motive for staying in the room after waking him. Her habit of uneasily smoothing her skirt, which she was doing now, told him something was on.

'The kids have gone to the cinema,' she informed him as she came back to the bed. The information could have been for no reason other than to reassure him that they wouldn't be interrupted. He wasn't reassured but irritated. 'It's a Death Metal film. I'm sure they're going deaf. They play their sounds far too loud.'

He didn't respond, but sipped the tea before reaching up to massage his neck and his tense deltoid muscles.

'I'll do it, Fred,' she offered.

At his side she began to knead his neck and shoulders. She had done a good bit of that over the years, and was quite skilful.

'Didn't they have any homework?' he asked. 'It's important they get good results at school if they're to get to university.' Maybe that was what his dream was about.

'They did it before they left school,' she said.

'When did they do their schoolwork?' he asked while she eased herself down onto the bed behind him and continued massaging his shoulders. Automatically he leaned forward to avoid her. He didn't want to make love now. He rarely enjoyed sex when he woke up. All he wanted to do then was take a pee and have a shower, brush his teeth. As if suddenly feeling desperate, Edith threw her arms around him and held him close, pressing her face against his back. But still he didn't respond. There was a pause. He grew more tense, hating this demand that was being made, the contact like this. Finally Edith leaned away, releasing him. 'I despise myself for being so weak,' she said. 'I know you work long hours, I know that. But the excuses seem to get more frequent. You chose to do what you do.'

'Be a funny sort of place without policemen,' he said.

'It's still been a long time, Fred . . . I do have some feelings.'

'I'm tired, love. I can barely manage tea when I first wake up. You know that.'

He pushed the duvet back and swung his legs over the edge of the bed. Reaching round behind him, he massaged his adrenals again, more for her benefit than his relief. He groaned as he rose. 'I've got a few days' leave soon.' The information was offered like it contained a firm promise, but Edith seemed unimpressed. Maybe she had heard too many other excuses, had seen too many of his leaves get cancelled. The call to duty ruined their sex life. He heard her sigh as he shuffled out to the bathroom.

The water, as hot as he could bear from the shower, helped him wake up fully. As he stood under the power jets he found himself inexplicably getting an erection, which took his thoughts back to his wife. It was a long while since they had had sex together. He knew that she never looked elsewhere, and wondered if that day would arrive. He was curious to know how he might react to such an event. Not as well as he liked to tell himself he would. Maybe he ought to go back in and make a show. He still enjoyed having sex with Edith, but he was tired, and he was running late – not that he had to clock-in. He decided to see how he felt after shaving, though guessed she would have gone back downstairs to get his breakfast.

To his surprise she was still sitting on the bed when he came back into the bedroom, and more surprised to find he still had a touch-on.

'Edith?' he said, coming to her side. He put his hand on her head and pushed his thick fingers through her hair.

She looked at him and smiled. 'I'll get your meal,' she said, but didn't move.

Crouching on his hams in front of her he put his hand on her knee. She wasn't wearing tights and the flesh was smooth and soft, and contact with it excited him a little, more so when he slid his hand between her thighs. The flesh there had begun to crepe, but he didn't mind that. She didn't move as he reached in further under her skirt, other than to ease her legs apart for him. By this time he had a full erection. Discovering that she wasn't wearing pants, he became seriously hard. She sighed as his fingers eased her apart and slid inside, past the short cropped hairs. She was very wet. It was worth avoiding sex for a while to find her like this, he thought.

After a few moments he rose and untied his bathrobe; she twisted herself round on the bed and wriggled her skirt up over her waist. She pulled him on top of her and helped guide him straight in as though she did not want to risk him changing his mind.

He would be late getting to work. It wasn't important.

Work was the last thing Pyle felt like, but he knew he had a long way to go through the night. Having just come on duty, he was sure he wouldn't make it to the end of his shift, especially not if something demanding broke. With luck there'd be a quiet stretch and he'd be able to get his head down. Tony Simmons, the night-duty officer, wouldn't mind. He'd probably be out visiting his nurse anyway.

Moving along the corridor towards his office, Pyle heard his name called as he passed the open door of the chief superintendent's office. Going back to the door, he found Detective Chief Superintendent Ernie Jeymer standing by his desk putting papers into his briefcase. The office was the same size as most along the left-hand side of the corridor but had only one desk, which gave the chief superintendent the amount of floorspace relative to his status.

'Evening, guv,' Pyle said.

There was no greeting from Jeymer. He was a big, brusque man with a bristly grey and brown beard and spiky eyebrows. He tended to get upset easily, especially if he wasn't kept completely in the picture. On the other hand, he soon got over his explosions and wasn't one to harbour a grudge. Pyle didn't know if the hierarchy ever upset this man. He couldn't think why they would – unique among policemen, he never seemed to complain about them. He was the sort of detective who accepted that those above him in rank were there because they knew better, and he expected the same response from those below himself.

'What's happening with those villains you nicked this morning, Fred?' he asked.

'Still assisting with our inquiries, guv,' Pyle explained. 'I've only just come on.'

'One of their solicitors has been trying to reach you most of the day – Gladwell. He's been threatening a writ of habeas corpus unless Terry Clark is either charged or released. Silly bastard'

'Some chance, the way Clark was shaping, guv.'

'Gladwell sounds like he ought to read PACE – he'd know how we can treat suspects then. But why upset him unnecessarily.' It wasn't a question. 'Keep me posted, Fred.' He turned back to putting papers in his briefcase.

Pyle stopped at the DCIs' office to talk to Tony Simmons. Trevor Watson was there on his own, and he didn't seem pleased. Whether it was because he was still there or as a result of his phone conversation wasn't clear.

'. . . Well, stay on watch there,' he was saying. 'I'll try and get someone out to take over . . . I can't say when. Just stay put.' He snapped the phone down.

'You got shares in this little firm, guv?'

'Didn't show much of a dividend last year, Fred.' Watson clicked his tongue. 'I was supposed to be taking the old lady out this evening.'

'What's it, her birthday?'

'Something like that,' Watson said.

'Is Tony in yet?'

'No. It's him who's holding me up.'

A uniformed messenger, one of the battalion that trudged around the Yard, came in to collect the 'posts' from Watson's desk. The DCI snatched a pink folder from the top, before the uniform bore it away.

'Not that one, son.' He passed it to Pyle. 'Jack Lynn's CRO file. Looks as though he might be worth spending some time on.'

'Aren't they all,' Pyle said. He believed that about any villain, apart from the one-off criminals who got caught, learned their lesson, and never offended again. Almost certainly Lynn would be having something, have had something since the last entry on his CRO computer, or would be plotting something. Pyle knew that most felons were recidivists, and no matter what lengths society went to in its attempt to reform them they'd always revert to type. But there weren't enough detective manhours to go randomly checking through the computers and then looking up villains. You simply had to wait for something to go off then dig out the likely suspects. Random checks would probably get them into a lot of trouble over the infringements of civil liberties; there was always someone ready to shout on behalf of the villains. He wasn't much concerned about their rights, believing that most of them gave those up when they went into crime; while most detectives could be trusted to keep their own sense of proportion in these matters.

Detective Chief Superintendent Jeymer came into the office and dropped a pile of pastel-coloured folders on Watson's desk. 'Get Tony to have a look at those. And don't forget that request from Beckenham. Someone needs to go out there to assist them. I'll leave it to you, Trevor.'

'Sounds like something for the Regional Crime Squad.'

'Wouldn't give them the satisfaction.' Jeymer started out. 'I'll be in the Tank for half an hour,' he said over his shoulder.

'Night, guv,' Pyle said.

Watson turned to answer the phone on DCI Simmons' desk. 'Chief inspectors' office. Watson . . .' He waited, glancing round at Pyle. 'How are you fixed for going out to Beckenham, Fred?' Watson turned back to the phone before Pyle could reply. 'Hello, hello . . . Obviously someone didn't like the sound of my voice.' He replaced the phone. 'They've a couple of robberies they're getting nowhere with.'

'I'm not exactly scratching for work myself, guv.'

'Well, see if you can't do something to help.'

The prospect didn't inspire him.

When he reached the DIs' office the place was deserted and the phone on his desk was ringing. He answered it unhurriedly. It was Alex Gladwell, Terry Clark's solicitor. 'Oh, good evening, Mr Gladwell,' Pyle said expansively. 'I was just about to ring you . . .' Nothing was further from his mind.

'What is the current position with my client?'

'At present he's at Peckham police station, helping with inquiries into the robbery at Barclay's bank at Lewisham last week.

'Has he been charged?'

'I haven't charged him.'

'In that case I presume you will be releasing him shortly or taking him before a magistrate,' the solicitor said.

There were no legal grounds for the police to detain a suspect unless charged, other than under the Prevention of Terrorism Act, but few villains knew exactly what the position was, or, if they did, were in no position to enforce their rights from a police cell. And while solicitors knew of course, it wasn't necessarily in their client's interest nor their own to force the issue. Pyle knew this solicitor wouldn't push the point.

'We're not holding him, sir,' he offered. 'He's simply assisting us with our inquiries.'

'Voluntarily?' the solicitor asked like he was doing more than going through the motions.

'I'd say so.' He opened his briefcase and lifted out papers.

'Taken at six in the morning, and held for fourteen hours? Come on, inspector. You can't seriously believe that's reasonable. Why hasn't Mr Clark been allowed access to his solicitor?'

For a moment he thought Gladwell was talking about a third party.

'He made no request to contact you.'

'I'm putting you on notice, Inspector . . .' he paused as if he couldn't remember his name, 'Pyle. Unless my client is either charged forthwith or released, I'm going to apply to the court to order him to appear first thing –'

'That'll be perfectly in order, sir,' Pyle said, calling the brief's bluff. 'The court will inform the custody officer at Peckham police station. He'll do as ordered.'

'Ah.' The solicitor's tone changed at once. 'I see. Then you are charging my client?'

'I'd say there was a good chance.'

'I'd like to see him if that's possible.'

''S not a problem . . .' Pyle paused. 'If he wishes to see you.'

'Between ourselves, inspector. What do you think?'

Pyle had the sort of relationship with some solicitors where they could ask questions like that and get the right answer, or could ask what was to be done for help. Alex Gladwell was one such, but over the phone their relationship remained correct. It had to be so for the Complaints Investigation Bureau often listened in on the conversations of detectives who had complaints against them.

'Well, thank you for your trouble, inspector. I appreciate it.' Gladwell made it sound as though he had given him all he needed.

When he replaced the phone, Pyle found DS Lethridge in by the desk, looking like he had been on the piss all day, rather than sleeping like any sensible detective on the nightshift.

'Eric,' he greeted. 'In early, aren't you?' Leaving him to conduct the interrogations that morning, he hadn't expected him in until around midnight, depending what time he got through. 'What's the situation down at Peckham?'

'Clark stuck up an alibi. Doesn't amount to much – his old lady and some villains,' he said. Pyle knew that no one would believe any of those; wives and friends of villains were inevitably liars!

'The lad with the shooter, well, it's fairly obvious that he was going after something, but it doesn't look like Lewisham was down to him.'

'I'm not worried about that,' Pyle said. He had other plans for Clifford Harding, which Lewisham blag would mess up. 'What about that lad John's squad picked up?'

Lethridge shook his large head. 'He's not shaping at all.'

'Still, not a bad sort of average for Method Index raids. Pyle nodded. 'Maybe we'll find something else for him. It seems a pity to spend time on a villain only to have to let him go. Round up some of the lads, Eric. See if we can't catch that one John missed. 'S no hurry. I want a word with the chief about Harding.'

'You think Brian Finch might be a prospect, Fred?' DCI Simmons asked, pushing aside the huge pile of statements he was reading through.

'Make it look like we were winning, wouldn't it?' Finch was the fourth villain on the Method Index raid, who had avoided DI Redvers' squad. 'The way he scarpered, someone out of Paddington must have given him the bell.'

'John told me. A fact of life, Fred. I mean, what can you do, complain to the Bureau? I daresay we've all done one a favour like that sometime.'

'Still pisses you off,' Pyle said. There had been a number of times when he had earned from villains for just such a timely phone call.

'Give the local CID a miss when you turn him over this time,' DCI Simmons advised. 'Look up that girlfriend of his as well, Fred. He might have slid in there.'

'I had planned to,' he said. 'What about Harding? What do you think about having a deal with him?'

'Fine, if you want to get your collar felt.'

That was like the official warning. But Pyle wasn't going to let it go at that. He waited.

'I don't like the idea of dropping him out altogether, Fred. Mind you, I don't mind if he's led to believe that's what'll happen.' He seemed uncertain about the matter. He was the duty officer, there was none on the Squad higher than him at present, unless he chose to call back one of the supers or the chief superintendent. But Pyle knew he wasn't likely to do so for a decision at this level. 'What do you think yourself, Fred? Is he going to come up to scratch?'

'Difficult to say. He's well placed. It wouldn't be hard for him to find us something worthwhile on Lynn.' He shrugged. 'Depends what he's offered, I suppose.'

'What about Criminal Intelligence? They have anything for you?'

'To be perfectly honest, guv, I haven't checked back with them.' It wasn't that he had been too busy to do so, he'd simply forgotten. 'I think Jack Lynn might prove the more worthwhile of the two. The other fella, Harding, he might only have been minding that gun, like he claims.' He didn't really believe that, but did believe the risk involved in having Harding at liberty to punt around was worth taking.

'With a firearm charge on the sheet, a magistrate would expect us to object to bail,' Simmons pointed out. He wasn't someone to take chances. 'I suppose he wouldn't be much use to you down in Brixton.'

'I could have a word with the beak,' Pyle offered.

Simmons looked at him. 'That's what Eric tried, didn't he? Now he's got Complaints up his daily.'

'He was unlucky, that's all, guv. Most of us do it now and then – get some help for a grass. Only there was some aggravation between that magistrate and his clerk, and the clerk complained.'

'Eric'll be lucky not to get disciplinary action taken against him. Still, it's a chance you take – do the job right.'

'We could leave Harding out altogether.'

'Be nice to have some kind of hold, Fred.'

'It's there, guv. It would only be a matter of finding him again. That wouldn't be too difficult in his circumstances.'

'Got a family?'

'Four young kids. He thinks the world of them. He wouldn't go far.'

'How did it go with the gun-dealer he put up, by the way?'

'We nicked him. He's at Peckham. From the way he's shaping he'll go all right,' Pyle said. 'And one or two more besides, I shouldn't wonder.'

'Good. All right, take a chance on Harding. But see if they have anything across the corridor on Lynn first.'

The offices used exclusively by Criminal Intelligence were much like the Squad's offices, too small for their requirements, impersonal, overstuffed with filing cabinets and an excess of computer terminals. A prominent feature was the noticeboard which took up almost entirely one wall. It resembled an elaborate set of family trees made up of photographs of villains with arrows and information connecting them to other pictures. Most of them were in conference or nightclub-type settings, inevitably in long shot; some had been circled.

DI Graham McHale pointed to a circled photograph of Jack Lynn. 'That's the most recent picture we have of him. Taken about six months ago. You see that?' He indicated the prison mugshot that was arrowed away of the centre group. 'He's changed a bit.'

'Good living, I suppose,' Pyle said.

He was grateful for the vanity which made villains unable to resist having their photo taken in clubs with hostesses, but resented the apparent good times they had.

'He was with a villain called George Bennett. This one here.' McHale pointed out a squirrel-like man in the picture. 'The Regional Crime Squad nicked him for a job out in Bromley. A bank. It was suspected that Lynn was involved, but there wasn't enough to nick him. You know what they're like,' McHale said.

Pyle nodded. The Regional Crime Squad were notoriously cautious, and painstakingly careful before making an arrest. 'They still interested?'

'They have a nibble now and again, Fred. The way they work it'll be another two years before they bite.' The DI from Criminal Intelligence yawned.

'What else you got? Anything?'

'Another rumour. A security van blag out in Wimbledon which might have been down to him. Around about that time he was seen in bad company. He was seen hanging out with a lad called Alf Kitchen, who was believed to have been involved.'

'Was he nicked?'

'No. Only one person was for that job. One or two more were pulled in. But later released.'

'D'you think he sold the Regional Crime Squad two bodies?'

'Appears that way.'

'Looks like he's had a good run.' He paused and thought about Lynn. 'Yes, he's well overdue,' he said. 'How did he stand? Was he putting those blags together?'

'That's possible, Fred. We've heard nothing.' McHalc waited. 'That's all we have. The rest is on his CRO file.'

'Makes him a bit more interesting. Good luck.'

'You got anything for us, Fred?'

He measured the DI with a look, then shook his head. 'Only a whisper that he's putting one together. 'S all. Not where or when.' He wasn't about to give over his information for them to give any CID who came looking for it. He had found Lynn, so he intended to nick him.

The block of flats where Brian Finch's girlfriend lived in West Hampstead was fairly modern, built within the last ten or fifteen years. It might easily have been council property, but probably it wasn't – there were no prams parked either in the entrance hall or on the landing, and no graffiti on the walls. There was no lift and the flat Pyle was visiting was on the top floor. That was six flights of stairs.

'Wouldn't you know it,' he said to DC Humphries.

'Keeps you fit, guv,' the DC replied.

'I'd say I was fit enough, Rog'.' By the fourth landing he wasn't showing much sign of fitness.

The caretaker had admitted them to the building. He seemed disappointed when summarily dismissed. Pyle had had both the exits covered. DS Lethridge would be sitting in his car at one, with another two detectives waiting at the back of the building.

The block was L-shaped, with open walkways. The door to the flat they were visiting was open, which made Pyle wary. Maybe someone had left in a hurry. Or maybe she liked fresh air. When he rang the bell a dog began barking. It was an Alsatian, and came bounding along the hallway and stood at the threshold, baring its teeth, like it had something to say. DC Humphries edged back, but Pyle refused to be intimidated, especially not by an Alsatian.

Having done a course with dogs in the uniform branch, he knew the breed well.

'Go on, you bastard, 'fore I break your arms!'

The young detective grinned, clearly not trusting the dog.

'Stop it! Stop it, Judge, that's a good boy. Be quiet now,' a woman said, coming along the hall. The dog quietened as she caught him by the choke chain. 'Most people run from Judge,' she said to Pyle. 'You're very brave.'

'Of course I'm brave,' he replied with an expressionless face. 'I'm a police officer.'

She appeared nonplussed for a moment. She was in her late twenties, and attractive in a tired, greasy-skinned sort of way. She had a good face, with strong bone structure, but had the slightly haunted look of the lonely. Her body was well shaped, Pyle noticed, and carried her jeans and the T-shirt she wore without a bra. He had a simple means of categorizing women: those he'd give one, and those he wouldn't. He'd give her more than one.

'Is that who you are?' she said. 'The police?'

''S Brian Finch here, love?'

She started to shake her head, but Pyle pushed into the flat as though invited. Humphries followed.

'Do you have such a thing as a warrant?' The protest was feeble. The dog remained silent.

'Of course,' he said over his shoulder. He reached into his pocket, as if to produce the appropriate paper. 'Roger . . .' He indicated a bedroom off the hall for Humphries to search. Pyle went into the other room without producing his warrant.

The small living room was over-stuffed, but nowhere would it conceal the man they were looking for. He saw that at a glance. Humphries was equally brief searching the bedroom. That left only the bathroom and small kitchen to search. Finch wasn't in either.

'Now perhaps you'll believe me.'

Pyle looked at her, feeling himself reacting to her hostility. There was something about angry women that always aroused pockets of sexual interest in him. But he had never quite worked out why. Perhaps it was because it provided a potential opportunity to do them violence. 'Slip down and check with Sergeant Lethridge,' he said to the DC. 'Chummy might have got out ahead of us.'

The DC stepped carefully around the dog and went.

Pyle watched the woman.

'Where's the warrant?' she demanded.

'What warrant's that? Didn't you invite us in to search? Oh, I thought you did,' he said. 'I thought you said, come in, have a look round, don't mind the dog.'

As she glared at him, he could feel her anger coming at him in waves, and felt himself getting more aroused. Having a hard-on twice in twelve hours was unusual for him.

'How long's he been gone, love?'

'How long has who been gone? Who are you talking about?'

'Going to make me work for the bit of info', are you? All right, what's your name?'

'What's it to you?'

He shook his head. 'Keeps the paperwork straight, 's all.'

'It's Finch. Elizabeth Finch. Brian Finch's wife.'

Pyle would have known she was lying even had he not previously visited Finch's wife over at Paddington. He had cracked some of the best liars around, and she didn't rate. 'If you really want to be difficult, we can go to the local nick. But somehow I don't think you'd like that. A right pisshole.' He waited, his eyes boring into her until finally she glanced away. 'If you are his wife we'll do him for bigamy as well. We just left Mrs Finch. Nice woman. Bit mouthy. Especially when she knows he's been at it!'

'Brian's not married,' she said, without confidence.

'Not to you, he's not.' He watched her closely, noticing the effect that was having. 'What are you wasting your time with a villain like that for? A nice girl like you. Brian knows he's got some coming. 'S why he legged it like he did.'

'He didn't tell me he was married,' she said.

'No? I don't think I'd tell you I was married if I was looking to give you one.' In fact he'd make a point of doing so as she would obviously appreciate that kind of honesty, and that level of honesty was easy enough. 'What's your name? Your proper name?' He knew, but answers to such questions were the starting point for any successful interview.

'Libby Howard,' she answered.

He nodded. 'What are you doing with him, Libby? Slags, they're about his mark.' She didn't answer. 'Oh, I suppose he has a certain attraction. Most villains do. You'd be surprised some of the women they manage to pull. You must like suffering.'

The Alsatian, which had been lying near her feet, raised its head and began growling as DC Humphries returned.

'There's a good dog.' The DC sounded nervous. 'Good doggy.'

'He's more sense than to bite you, Rog'. Any sign?'

'No, nothing, guv.'

'He wasn't here,' Libby Howard said.

Pyle inclined his head to the DC, indicating for him to leave. 'Tell Eric to get down to Peckham. I'll see him there.'

The dog growled some more as Humphries went out again.

'D'you train him to do that? Bark at detectives?'

Finally she smiled.

'What's this? A smile – thought I had struck granite here. Always comes as a bit of a surprise to find you've been sleeping with a liar.' She gave him a startled look. 'That's what you were doing, wasn't it?'

'I don't think I can help you,' she said.

'Come on, you haven't really tried.'

'I can't help you – I have a bad headache.'

'The local nick won't improve it. Make yourself some tea. Take a couple of those.' Pyle produced a flat silver-foil pack of Disprin. 'Policemen get headaches too. I'll have a cup with you.'

She hesitated and looked at him, then took the tablets.

In the kitchen he casually picked up letters that were placed between a storage jar and the wall at the end of the shelf and glanced over them while Libby Howard waited for the kettle to boil.

'They're private letters!' She reached for them, but he pulled his hand back.

'You shouldn't keep secrets from me, Libby,' he said, as he returned the letters to the shelf. She immediately retrieved them and jammed them into her jeans pocket.

'How long have you known Brian Finch?'

She shrugged. 'What do you want him for?'

'You trying to tell me you don't know?'

'I don't. Why should I?' She seemed surprised.

'Villains have a lot of bunny. They never leave off telling people what they've done. That's why we catch so many, not because we're geniuses.' He saw her take up a pale green tea packet. 'What's that, China tea?'

'Japanese. It's the only sort I have.'

'Better make mine coffee.'

'Gosh, you really are presumptuous,' she said as she took down coffee.

He nodded, it might have been an apology. 'Being a policeman as long as I have makes me like it. You don't even realize you're like it at times.' He nodded again.

Libby Howard gave him a look. Clearly she didn't suspect this change of attitude was a ploy. He knew if you gave a little of yourself, as he had done, you made the person you were dealing with beholden to you in some way, and likely to try to please you.

'Is he in serious trouble when you find him?'

'There's a bank robbery down to him.'

'Oh well, banks have loads of money,' she tried, as if trying to cover her surprise.

'More than I've got, that's for sure,' he said. 'But a guard was hurt, pretty badly. Still, that's nothing to do with you.'

'I'm sorry. I didn't realize . . .'

''Course you didn't. Why would you?'

She was silent as she offered him black coffee.

'You got some milk, love?' She got it from the fridge. Pyle watched her, no longer wondering whether or not he might get into her, but when he would. He changed tack, deciding that she hadn't quite written the villain off yet. 'He can help himself, of course. It's not all down to him.

Only that's not how the other guy we nicked is telling it,' he lied. 'He says it's all down to Brian. Everyone tries to save himself when he's up against it. A fact of life – never was any honour among thieves.' He shrugged, as if apologizing for having disillusioned her. He sipped his coffee. 'Did you take your tablets?'

She retrieved the foil tray and handed them back. 'I have some, thanks. It's not that bad now, anyway.'

He nodded, like any relief was his doing. His eyes circled the kitchenette. Earthenware pots and crockery were neatly arranged on the pine shelves. She was an orderly person but there was something disturbing about her order, like it was a denial of chaos. This made him more curious about her relationship with Finch, her involving herself as she was with the obvious chaos surrounding his life.

'What do you do for a living, Libby?'

'I'm a windowdresser,' she said.

More order. Pyle smiled. It was the first time he had done so.

'Don't you believe me?'

''Course. Why would you lie? I was thinking about a lad who kept a couple of female mannequins. The closest he got to a relationship with a woman. He was a bit of a sad case – ended up in Broadmoor. He couldn't be helped at all.'

'Will you help Brian when you get him?'

'I don't like seeing people taking stick for other people's villainy. But I honestly can't say, love. I mean, I'll help him if he lets me. First we have to find him.' He paused. 'You any idea where he might be?'

Libby Howard hesitated, and he knew just how helpful she would be.

'There are a couple of names he mentioned. Friends

of his. I don't know them, but I suppose he could be with them.'

Pyle didn't say anything. He waited for her to put up the names, knowing that was going to be just the start.

'Some of us have done a day's work here, guv,' DS Lethridge said as he came in through the back reception area at Peckham police station with DS Humphries. The corpulent DS looked at the time, then hitched up his trousers.

'It's results that count, son,' Pyle said. 'That right, Rog'?'

'Yes, guv,' the DC replied awkwardly.

'How d'you get on?' Lethridge asked.

'Oh, she came round all right. She put up a couple of names.' He produced his notebook and considered the names he had been given. 'Send the lads out visiting, Eric. A chance Finch might be there.'

'You were up there long enough,' the DS said. 'D'you give her one?'

'I wouldn't mind. Wouldn't mind one little bit. I will have to pop back for a statement,' he said. Ordinarily he would simply have sent someone else.

Lethridge grinned. 'Old slags can come to the station and make their statements! What's she like? Any good?'

'I've fucked worse. A lot worse,' he said, giving nothing. 'How are the bodies shaping?'

'Clark's still asking for his brief. He put up one or two. So did the gun-dealer.' He handed him the statement. 'Jack's out visiting now.'

'What about Harding? What's he have to say?'

'He's missing his family.'

'About right. I'll have a word with him.' He shut the folder.

'My governor wasn't interested in doing business with you,' he said to Clifford Harding in his cell. It might have been some cruel game he was playing, but there was more to it than that.

'Oh, come on,' Harding protested, visibly distressed. 'I mean, I give you the gun-dealer. You said if I give you the gun-dealer, we could have a result.' He began to pace about his cell, walking to and fro past a tray of unfinished supper sitting on the bench. The congealed fat from boiled bacon, blackening potatoes and dried carrots didn't exactly look appetizing, Pyle thought. 'Fuck I! I mean, I give you him, didn't I, I thought we had a deal . . .'

'I appreciate what you did, Clifford, don't think otherwise, son,' he assured him, as though that in itself was worth something. 'But my governor thinks that shooter makes you a more interesting proposition.' He paused, leaving him on the hook, letting him sense that sickening alternative to the help he had promised for help in kind. 'Personally, Clifford, I might be prepared to take a chance on you, regardless of what my governor said – but only if I was convinced you were going to come up with the goods on Jack Lynn.'

'But I can, I can. I'll do the business.'

'You think so?' Pyle said.

'Oh, fuck me, guv, I've got to. I mean, I've got to.'

'Unless you want another taste, a long one, that is.'

'I'll do the business for you. You gimme the chance.

I won't let you down, I won't. I promise I won't, straight.'

At first he appeared unmoved. Then he nodded slowly, letting Harding off the hook. 'If you do, son, then you'd better leg it. Get as far away from me as you can . . .'

'I can't. I mean, what about my family . . .?'

Pyle almost smiled at the man's aching earnestness – no criminal might ever have run out on his dependants. But he guessed Harding wouldn't be too difficult to capture again.

'What about the shooter, guv?'

'What, you want it back!' Pyle said. 'The charge has been left pending. I'll see how you shape, son.'

After he had released Harding, he spent some time on both Terry Clark and Wally Marks, the gun-dealer; then when DS Barcy returned with the two suspects Marks had put up, he interrogated those. The last two could easily be nicked for possessing firearms and for conspiracy to rob. But Pyle probed deeper, preferring to have charges for actual robberies that had taken placc. Results were always more impressive with some monetary figure, or recovery, attached to them. Ideally he would have liked to have tied Terry Clark up with Marks somehow, but they weren't connected. There was little doubt that he would be charged in connection with the raid down at Lewisham. Pyle knew he would find some means of cracking him. There would be something he would want, some pressure point he'd yield to.

As the night wore on the interrogations changed tack. The tape recorders were switched on and the questions became more specific. By the end of his investigation Pyle knew he'd wind up with some nice results. That was what made it worthwhile.

Some detectives, so rumour had it, worked nonstop until they cracked their cases. If there had ever existed such policemen, Pyle had never met them. When it was time to stop work for the day, or take a break, he did just that. He often left the detectives on his squad to work on after his departure, but knew to a man, and occasionally a woman, they applied the same rules.

Travelling north from Peckham in the back of the blue Ford, he shut his eyes but wouldn't go to sleep. DS Lethridge was in the back of the car with him.

'Bit swift,' Lethridge said, 'letting Harding go like that?'

'Not unless the wrong people get to hear of it. Is that how it looks?' He stretched and rubbed his eyes. 'He'll come. He has to, he's too active to be left loose. I'd say he was going to make one with that shooter, wouldn't you?'

'There's a good chance.'

'See what he comes up with on Jack Lynn first. I'd like to see that one nicked. You want dropping anywhere, Eric?'

'No. Cocoa'll do. I haven't got a meet tonight. Thought maybe I'd shoot up to Soho, give one a pull there.'

'About your mark, you fat bastard. You'll end up getting Aids.' There was a pause. Pyle changed tack, not wanting to discuss Eric Lethridge's sexual or marital problems. 'I have an interview with Complaints on Friday.'

'Oh yeah – been at it, Fred, have you?' Lethridge joked.

'Right at the fucking start of my leave. The bastards do it for the purpose. Be as well to get it straight what you want me to tell them.' He was being interviewed in connection with the complaint against Lethridge.

''S like we agreed. The villain I tried to help wasn't my grass.' Lethridge waited. 'That's best, Fred, isn't it?'

'Probably. That way you wouldn't have any reason for going into that magistrate for help for him.'

As the DS's immediate governor he was supposed to be informed of all and any informers that were used. This knowledge, the hierarchy believed, acted as a kind of safeguard and prevented subsequent charges against detectives. He in his turn was supposed to inform his governor about his grasses he met, but often didn't.

'But I didn't, Fred, did I? I mean, I wouldn't go into a magistrate to try and get favours for a criminal, would I? It's not reasonable.'

'Of course it's not, son.' Pyle grinned. He'd give this DS whatever help he could.

There were about thirty men crowded into the first-floor gym of the Grapes off Bethnal Green Road. Some were professional boxers, sparring and shaping up with would-be champions; there were old pros who hung around doing what they could for whoever they could, simply because they couldn't leave the game alone. There were managers and would-be promoters standing around the ring, some earnestly discussing fighters' prospects; there were people who had simply wandered up from the bars, people with nothing else to do, faces Jack Lynn only vaguely knew yet who were somehow as familiar as the place itself with its slightly humid atmosphere, and sour smell of damp leather and stale seeds of sweat caught in unlaundered clothes.

He had no connection with the fight game, but knew villains who had. Not even as a youth did he do a bit. He could use himself in a fight, but had had no wish to do it for a living. A lot of lads started boxing as an alternative to villainy, and for a number of those he grew up with the two pursuits seemed to be their only options. Perhaps there were other opportunities, but he hadn't been aware of them.

Stretching onto his toes to see over the crowd, he spotted the man he was looking for working out on one of the punchbags. Bobby Shaw had been low on the list of help, simply because Lynn hadn't known if he was out of prison.

He had run into Shaw's brother, who told him that Bobby was due out.

Several people greeted him as he crossed the gym but he drew a blank on some of their names. He stopped on the far side of the room and watched Shaw slam his fists into the heavy bag. Bobby Shaw glanced at him as one fist followed the other down in a series, but didn't speak.

'You look like you're staying fit, Bobby,' Lynn said.

Shaw stopped hitting the bag and looked at him. 'You gotta keep yourself at it, son. All that bodybuilding inside, you get fat as a pig, 'you leave off.' He was in good shape, Lynn noticed.

'When d'you get out?' he asked, leaning his weight against the punchbag as the boxer started pounding it again.

'Last Friday.' His breathing became heavy with exertion.

'I saw Terry, d' he tell you?' He waited but Shaw didn't reply. 'He reckoned you was getting full remission.'

'Was a good boy, Jack, wan' I? Yes, sir, no, sir, three bags full, sir!' He slammed his fists harder into the bag now. Lynn could feel the weight of the blows jarring his shoulder. 'Got the right pox of that fucking place.'

'You must be about ready to do a bit of work, I'd've thought.'

'Be handy. This don't earn me nothing.' He stopped hitting the bag. 'What you got in mind, Jack?'

'Something very pukka. You want to turn this in?'

'Yeah. I'll take a chance on getting fat.'

'What d'you want to be slim for anyway?'

'You got to, 'you wanna pull a few. Know what I mean, Jack?'

'Pulling my prick's about all I can manage nowadays, Bobby.' Without warning Lynn drove a right hook into Shaw's shoulder while his guard was down. Shaw responded too late. Lynn had moved back. 'Got you, you fat bastard.'

'Ah, you mug, you done m' shoulder right up. You ruined me.'

Lynn laughed, his mood buoyant. Those bad feelings he had been getting about the job had vanished. 'That's just to show you who's the guvnor at this boxing game.'

'Leave off, Jack,' Shaw said. 'You're the guvnor.'

Lynn knew he would bide his time and come back at him with a good 'un. It was a game, irrelevant, pointless, even banal, but enjoyable, even when you forgot, lowered your guard and took one.

When he outlined the work he had in mind, Shaw committed straight away. Social Security was the only prospect for the future other than villainy. 'I don't fancy getting a proper job, Jack, even if I could find one. And prison didn't exactly rehabilitate me. There isn't a lot of call for sighted basket makers these days! I got one or two names who might fancy going to work.'

One of them, Billy Braden, was already down on Lynn's list. He simply hadn't been able to reach him but had been leaving messages about getting in touch.

Bobby Shaw was clearly impressed with the prospect when Lynn took him down to Catford dogtrack to watch the collection operation by the security truck.

'It'll be a fucking doddle, Jack, won't it?' Shaw said.

'Yeah, won't be hard at all.'

'We'll want some shooters though, I'd say. The last bit of work I did, the one I got nicked for, we only had pickaxe handles. A few skulls were bashed in, but that didn't stop people having a go.'

'I s'pose they would be handy,' Lynn conceded, even though he had been planning to use guns. 'They're not gonna be a problem.'

'Got someone in mind to get them, have you?'

'Yeah, little firm I know should do them all right.'

''S not Wally Marks, is it? You hear the Squad nicked him?'

'No. What, the greengrocer out at Charlton?'

''S what I heard, Jack.'

'Fuck I! I didn't hear nothing.' Lynn was a bit dismayed. 'As it happens, I did have him in mind. I mean, well, it wasn't definite. He was one of them.'

'He was well bubbled. 'S what a lad who does a bit told me. Reckons it was down to Clifford Harding.'

'Leave off. Cliff's as good as gold,' Lynn protested. 'Least, he wouldn't put no one away.'

'Well, how else could you go and get your liberty after being nicked with a shooter, Jack?' Shaw wanted to know.

'By putting a nice earner into the filth. That's what I heard. Got one on the Squad straightened,' he said. He liked Harding and thought him reliable, but hadn't thought of him for this blag.

'You could be right,' Shaw said. 'He was always a good 'un when we was in the Scrubs together. I mean, I wouldn't wish no one back there. I'd probably pull some diabolical strokes myself in order to stay out. Know what I mean, Jack?'

'Cliff's all right,' Lynn announced, not wholly convinced.

There was a brief silence in the car as they watched the two security guards climb into the truck and start it up.

'Where we gonna do this? Just there?' Shaw asked.

'Inside's best. In the office. I got a key to the door.'

'We'll definitely want shooters, then, Jack. The way some of them mugs are. One or two of them have to have their kneecaps done before they realize it ain't worth having a go for someone else's bit of dough. Not when it's insured and all. Know what I mean?'

'Shooters won't be a problem. I can see about them tomorrow.'

He knew three men who dabbled in guns, including Wally Marks, who did the most and was the handiest. But he guessed Marks wouldn't be doing anything for a while, however he came to have his collar felt. The second dealer he couldn't reach. The third, Trevor Foley, was around.

He lived out at Willesden. When Lynn phoned him, Foley told him to come up and see him, but to give him a bell when he got there. That made sense, Lynn thought. He hadn't done business with the man before, but had met him a couple of times and knew he was cautious. That way he kept his liberty, and couldn't be faulted for it.

From the phone box outside the post office in Harlesden Road, Lynn rang the gun-dealer again. The phone was answered almost immediately but no number was given.

'Trevor? 'S Jack . . . all right?'

'Yes,' the voice down the line said. 'You didn't take long. Where are you?'

'Just down the road. What d'you want me to do? Come up?'

'Here? No. I'll meet you. You know Roundwood Park?'

Lynn didn't, but Foley gave him clear directions, then repeated them, just so there was no mistake.

The park was only minutes from the phone box, so he was the first to arrive. Sitting on the bench on the path as described, he felt a bit conspicuous as he waited. The day was damp and cold, not the sort on which people sat around in parks. The few people he saw were mostly walking dogs. The park looked well kept, he noticed; red and brown leaves that had fallen had been swept into piles, one of which was smouldering. The tarry smell of smoke hung in the air where the leaves were too damp to burn properly. Eddie Aldiss popped into his thoughts. He was an arsonist who could have made those leaves burn in a torrential downpour.

His attention suddenly went to Trevor Foley as he turned onto the path with a dog. Lynn would have recognized him a mile off in his hat and sky-blue shell-suit, clipped moustache and thick-lensed glasses. He stopped and let the dog off its lead, before approaching Lynn.

'Fuck knows what we're meeting like this for, Trevor,' Lynn said as Foley sat on the bench. 'We can get done just as easily for conspiracy here like this.'

'It's a nice fresh day,' Foley observed.

'We'll probably get done as flashers or something.'

'That'd be a turn-up for the book, Jack,' he said cheerfully. 'You want to take a walk?'

Lynn huddled deeper into his coat in the corner of the bench. 'Can't say as I do.'

'Trouble with you people living down in all that muck,' Foley said. 'All so unhealthy.'

'Willesden's not exactly fucking countryside, is it?'

'Oh,' Foley said, looking around the park. 'It has its good points.'

Lynn smiled. 'You're still doing a bit, Trevor.'

'You have to do something, Jack. Social Security won't pay the mortgage.' He checked around, but no one was within earshot. 'What sort of shooters are you after?'

'Something impressive,' Lynn said, 'so we won't have to use them. Not too big – there won't be a lot of room. A couple of sawn-off shotguns and a couple of .38s should do it all right.'

'You want ammunition?' Foley asked.

'Be handy,' Lynn said. 'Cut-down cartridges, an' all.' He knew that when those were fired from a sawn-off shotgun or even a full-length barrel, they didn't carry far and did little damage. The lead shot fanned immediately on leaving the barrel and peppered a whole area, but rarely killed anyone unless right in front of the gun. The blast scared people witless.

'When do you want them?'

'Well, as soon as possible. 'S that all right?'

The gun-dealer nodded. 'That should be okay. Give me a ring in a day or so. They'll come to a nice few quid, Jack. About eight and a half, I'd say.'

'Fucking hell! What are you doing, manufacturing them?'

'The problem is, Jack,' he explained, 'people are frightened to dabble nowadays, in case they get done as a terrorist.'

'Still a bit strong, Trevor.' Lynn accepted that he would have to pay the price. 'You want a taste of what we earn?'

Foley shook his head.

'I'll take them back off you, 'you get out without firing them.' He looked at him, then across the park at his dog sniffing another. 'You hear about Wally Marks?'

'I heard he was grassed,' he said, hoping Foley might offer some information. He didn't.

'Wicked. Can't trust no one any more. Did you try him?'

'Did I fuck. D'you hear who it was, Trevor?'

'Some no-good grass, for sure.' He shook his head. 'It's a sad state of affairs. I'll have those ready for you, Jack.'

'I'm relying on you,' Lynn said.

'Give me a tinkle, just to make sure.' He rose off the bench. 'Patch!' he called to his dog. 'Mind how you go, Jack.'

'Be lucky.'

Lynn watched him move away, stooping to catch and leash his dog as he went.

Dolly had always given him ache that the kitchen wasn't large enough, and he had always promised her a house with a large kitchen, but the way the housing market was they had no chance of selling this house and moving. Lately it seemed to be getting smaller, because his wife was pressurizing him about the kitchen, as if it was the only important thing in her life. He knew what the real problem was but there wasn't a thing he could do about it. He had started work. It wasn't the sort of work she wanted him to do, but he couldn't stop it. He would simply have to put up with her ache. When it was off and they had a good time again and her anxiety slipped away, then she would think it worthwhile, even if she didn't say so; then she would laugh again and enjoy almost every stroke he pulled as she had when they were first married. Who knows, he thought, after this bit of work they might even put an extension on the house to make the sort of kitchen she wanted.

But now she just wasn't coping and her irritation was affecting the children. The two girls were bickering as Dolly was helping to get them ready for school. He could hear the voices rising through the ceiling as clearly as if he was in the same room. Maybe it was just that their squabbling of late was as familiar as Dolly's responses.

'You bloody well shut your face, Carol,' he heard Sandra shout at her sister.

‘Hey, now that’s enough of that, miss, or I’ll put my hand round your bloody face,’ Dolly shouted.

He smiled in anticipation of Sandra’s retort.

‘Well, you should tell her to leave off. Saying my friends have got fleas.’ His youngest girl, at eight, always had to have the last word. He was proud of her for that.

‘I never!’ Carol was eleven, and large-boned like her mother.

‘Well, just pack it in, the pair of you,’ Dolly said, ‘and help your sister, will you, or you’re gonna be late for school.’

‘Well, she won’t finish, will she?’ the older girl argued. ‘Look, she ain’t even finished her cornflakes yet.’

‘You didn’t get me no sugar like I asked,’ Sandra said.

He heard Dolly bang the cupboard closed then slam the jar of sugar on the table. ‘There! Now, come on.’

‘I don’t like them. They’rc all soggy.’

‘Well, you get and eat them. You’ve hardly eaten anything.’

‘She dawdles and plays with her smelly friends – I’m gonna go without her,’ Carol announced.

‘Can’t Dad take us to school in the car?’ he heard Sandra ask. She obviously knew better than to expect her Mum to take them.

‘He might as well. ’S got nothing better to bloody well do. Go and get him up, Carol – get your shoes on first.’

He nodded to himself. More ache.

‘I will!’ Sandra said.

‘You finish your breakfast . . .’ Dolly began. ‘Sandra!’

‘I’m going to get Dad up,’ Sandra insisted.

‘Carol! Will you move yourself,’ Dolly snapped. ‘Put that comic away.’

'Bloody hell! I'm not doing nothing. Taking it out on me.'

'Less of your cheek or you'll feel my hand.'

Lynn made no attempt to get up. He had had another late night. Daylight pushing through the curtains made sleep difficult, not impossible, but he immediately closed his eyes and pretended to be asleep when Sandra came into the room and along the side of the bed.

'Dad? You awake, Dad?' she said, gently shaking him.

Without opening his eyes, he suddenly grabbed her and pulled her onto the bed and kissed her. 'Got you.' He squeezed her against himself. 'Ah, come in to bed for five minutes and cuddle my back.'

'Can I?' she said.

He knew getting into their bed when he was there was something special to her.

'You gotta go to school, haven't you?' he said, and saw her nose wrinkle in disappointment. 'What was your Mum shouting about just now?'

'Oh,' Sandra said vaguely, as if having forgotten. 'Carol won't get herself ready. We're gonna be late for school. Will you take us, Dad?' She pulled at the buttons on his monogrammed pyjama jacket.

'What's the matter with walking? You lazy begger.'

'We're gonna be late though. We'll get the stick if we're late.'

'They'd better bloody well not give you the stick. I'll be down that school and give them the stick.' As he looked at her he felt a quake of emotion in his chest that resembled a palpitation. That was how much he loved his kids. He couldn't look at them without feeling that. 'Haven't you got a kiss for your Dad?'

She had, and placed her lips against his and locked her arms around his neck. 'Oh, only one?' he said in mock disappointment. She giggled and kissed him again. Her lips were soft and wet and eager against his. 'All right, just one more, then I'll think about getting up and driving you to school.'

It was a game which he enjoyed as much as she did. She seemed a bit disappointed when he kissed her finally and eased her off the bed.

'Right! I'm coming down right now. Tell Carol she'd better be ready.'

Sandra went across to the door and stood with it open. She hung on the two door handles, and pressed her face against the edge of the door as he started out of his pyjamas.

'I don't wanna go to school, Dad. I got a tummy ache.'

He gave her a look. 'You sure, Sandra?'

She avoided his eyes. 'I have, Dad.'

'Come 'ere,' he said. He stooped to her when she sidled up to him and rubbed her tummy. 'How 'bout we go to school in my car and see how it is when we get there?'

She didn't say anything. But he accepted her silence as assent.

'Good girl. Down you go, love,' he said, straightening up. 'Tell Mum I won't be long.'

Both girls travelled in the front of the grey Jaguar as he drove them to school. Sandra was next to him and most of the way had her head against his arm, her thumb in her mouth. Carol enjoyed school and as soon as the car drew up at the gates she jumped out, throwing a perfunctory 'Bye, Dad' over her shoulder.

'You all right now, sweetheart, are you?' Lynn asked,

putting his hand on the younger girl's head. She nodded. 'There's a love. C'mon, give us a kiss or you'll be the biggest dimwit in the class.'

Sandra kissed him, then hesitated at the door. 'You gonna get a job today, are you, Dad?' she asked.

'Yeah, 'course I am, darling,' he said, a little surprised by her question, but guessed her Mum had been going on about it again. 'Otherwise we won't be able to pay for food at the supermarket, will we.'

'Mum won't get cross then, she won't.'

He thought about that, touched by his daughter's concern. He assumed all kids were concerned that their parents got on together. He had vague memories from a very early age of how he used to worry when the parents he hardly knew rowed, how he wanted them to make the peace, how anxious he felt when they refused to. Kids didn't change.

'What sort of job would you like me to get, Sandy? Would you like me to be a policeman?'

Sandra shook her head.

The schoolbell sounded. They both reacted to it.

'Come on, there's the bell.' He kissed her. 'Don't worry, love. I'll get a nice job. I'll see you lunchtime.'

'Will you come and meet us?'

'Don't think so. Be a good girl. Bye, darling.'

She climbed out of the car and ran into school.

Lynn sat staring after her for a moment, thinking about what she had said, and how she'd reacted to the current situation with Dolly. He knew the sort of state his wife was getting herself into, yet couldn't really understand it – it wasn't as if they hadn't been here before. However, he knew he ought to try and do something about it before it really upset the kids.

Dolly didn't react when he let himself into the kitchen. She was at the sink, washing up. Gingerly he felt the teapot on the table. It was cold, but he didn't really want tea. Almost as gingerly he moved in behind his wife and pressed his hips into her soft rump. Her ass had become bigger, he noticed, since she had got her own car. He wasn't exactly encouraged in his gesture, but as she didn't give him a straight blank, he made a grinding motion against her, feeling himself getting an erection. He reached round her and forced his large hands down the front of her skirt.

'How many loaves of bread today, Mrs Lynn?' he said, managing to get one hand into the top of her pants, where he felt the soft flesh of her stomach, the coarseness of her pubic hair.

She shrugged him off. 'Don't mess around, Jack. I'm not in the mood.'

'Oh, t'rific,' he said, his manner suddenly changing. 'Well, how about some breakfast then?'

'You know where it is.' She didn't turn from washing up.

'All right, Dolly, you got the hump. What's the problem, then? What's wrong?' Acknowledging what he knew to be wrong would have given her too much advantage.

'You make me tired, Jack. You make me so bloody tired.' The words burst out, and she turned to confront him. 'You keep on, don't you. You keep pushing your luck. You can't be like other men, you won't be satisfied, will you?'

Still he refused to acknowledge the problem. 'What *are* you on about?'

'You bloody well know,' she said, her voice going up slightly. 'You make me tired. Well, just don't expect me to be waiting for you when you get nicked again.

I'm not gonna wait around twenty years till I'm an old woman . . .'

'You having a brainstorm, Dolly? I should think you must be.' The momentum of the argument carried him, making him self-righteous. 'I should think you must be,' he repeated.

'Oh, don't take me for a complete idiot, Jack. I know you're at it.' Tears were filling her eyes.

'What makes you think so?' he demanded. 'C'mon.'

'You think I don't know you after all this time? How you behave? You're putting one together, I can tell.'

'You ought to be a detective, that's what . . .'

'I'd be a lot better off,' she retorted. 'You can't be like other men. You gotta be at it the whole time. 'S like a disease . . . Well, I won't be here, Jack. I'll take the kids and go.'

He changed tack to try and gain ground. It was no use lying to her, and when he exploded she saw through that. 'Well, who d'you think I do it for?'

'You!' she said. 'Who d'you think?'

''Talk silly. You think you'd have a nice home, two cars, and a bit of spending money? You think you'd have all that if I was working down the road in a factory – assuming I could get a job, that is? There are one or two people out of work, in case you haven't noticed!'

'Other people seem to manage, Jack. Least they know their husbands ain't gonna go away for twenty years. The thought of it's too much. I can't stand it. I get so frightened when you're out nowadays. One time, well, one time it almost didn't matter, there didn't seem too much at stake. We were younger and could cope better.' She had become quieter, but tears were at the brim of her eyes.

Pausing and looking at her, he said, 'You really want me to go and get a job?' expecting her to recognize what punishment that would be and so say no. He was disappointed.

'You could do, Jack. It wouldn't be easy, not the sort of money you'd get. But we've got everything we need, 'int we? You could go minicabbing with Tommy,' she suggested.

That idea had been raised more than once. In fact, occasionally he helped her brother out. He accepted there were worse ways of earning a living. At least doing minicabbing you were more or less your own boss.

'I s'pose that ain't too much like collar,' he said. He liked the way his wife responded.

'You mean it, Jack?' she said, coming to him. 'You'd do it?'

'I tell you,' he said evasively, 'I weren't having too much luck putting this one together. The way it was going I'd do myself a right favour giving it a miss. I'll give it a try with Tom, he can put a bit my way.' He put his arms around her and felt her relax now. 'But the thing is, Dolly,' he began, like the thought had only just occurred to him, 'I'm a villain. 'Something comes up, I'll have to have it!'

Alarm came into her eyes as he held her; it was as though he had pushed the wrong switch. She tried to wrench away from him, until he smiled.

'No, I'll give it a miss.' His words had a ring of conviction.

'Promise me, Jack. It's for the girls' sake as well. I mean, think of them.'

'If you get me breakfast,' he said.

'You promise me, Jack?'

'Yeah, I promise,' he said. 'I'll talk to Tommy.'

She kissed him. 'What would you like to eat?'

He smiled. 'How about you?' He pressed his crotch into hers.

Because of the increasing tension between them it had been a while since they had made love. He was less inhibited than Dolly and wasn't concerned that they were in the kitchen.

'I've got my gloves on,' she said.

'Leave 'em on. They might be all right,' he said as he pulled her hard against himself.

She ripped the gloves off.

Reaching down behind her, he raised her skirt and ran his hand between her thighs. She didn't attempt to push him off as he eased his hand into the side of her pants and stroked her vagina from behind her. Instead he discovered her need was as great as his.

'Not here, Jack,' she said. 'Someone might come to the door.'

Her protest was feeble and he ignored it. The idea of having sex in the kitchen appealed to him greatly. It was reminiscent in its spontaneity of sex on the back seats of cars: he had had more than enough there. He had first made love to Dolly on the back seat of his old Ford Cortina, and a lot of times subsequently. He had some good memories of those days, and felt a soft yearning for them. The past, he knew, could never disappoint him.

Unzipping her skirt he eased it over her hips. Another faint protest was stifled with his mouth against hers. His fingers quickly undid the buttons on the shirt of his that she was wearing, but he didn't remove it. Instead he reached round and unfastened her bra. She had large breasts that hung low on her chest. She didn't protest when he lowered her onto the table, but she seemed a little surprised, with a small, sudden intake of breath when the naked part of her back touched the cold surface. He removed her pink pants. He knew she was still worried in case anyone called to the kitchen door, but that only increased the excitement of this for him as he eased her legs apart where they cut over the edge of the table and knelt into her, kissing her vagina. Soft, slightly inhibited words of endearment emerged on her quickening breath. They grew louder and louder.

Finally when he stood and unzipped his trousers, his penis found its way out of the tangle of pants and shirt-tails like a jack-in-a-box. Kicking his trousers and pants off, he walked forward into the vee of her legs and pushed into her.

At moments such as this he told himself there was too much at risk to be leading the sort of life he led. He loved his wife, despite their occasional bits of domestic; he loved his daughters too much to be separated from them. The problem was that such moments were fleeting and bore little relation to the real need he had for being at risk.

There were a lot of faces in the snooker hall, mostly youngsters who got there early to get their tables booked, all fancying themselves serious players. Jack Lynn wasn't looking for a game of snooker but for someone who would help out on his bit of work. Ducking to see under the lamps that were strung low over the tables, he was surprised to see Clifford Harding. Harding didn't exactly miscue when he saw him, but he looked surprised.

'Jack!' Harding said as he straightened and moved around the table. 'How's your luck, son?'

If Harding hadn't spoken he would have turned away as though not seeing him. It wasn't him he had come looking for, and after what Bobby Shaw had told him about Harding's result he was instinctively wary. He didn't want to believe this man would turn to grassing but he was only human and couldn't avoid his doubts.

'Terrible,' Lynn replied. He moved between the tables and joined him. 'I heard you had your collar felt – didn't expect to see you around.'

'Yeah, more aggravation than enough, wan' it – Oh unlucky, son,' Harding said to his opponent as he tried but didn't make a shot. 'Watch me nick this now.' He moved along the table and took the blue.

'The Robbery Squad, weren't it?' Lynn said, while Harding chalked his cue.

'Yeah. There was a nice one I was going after,' Harding said. 'Then I went and got a pull on my form, that's all. They went and found a shooter at my place, they did. I must be getting silly as a fucking goat.' He scoffed as he lined up the pink. It went for him. 'That do you?'

'I'd say so,' his opponent said, and uncrumpled a five-pound note from his pocket.

'You wanna double it? Have a chance to get it back?'

'No. I gotta shoot anyway.'

'Five quid, it might be the end of the world,' Harding said as he rejoined Lynn.

'He thought it was going to take your five quid, Cliff,' Lynn said with a grin, beginning to feel easier about him now. 'You did well to pull clear of that other bit of trouble.'

'Didn't come to enough, did it, bunging the Squad? They all wanted a taste, the hungry bastards – well, according to the DI. They took every penny I had. That weren't all though, Jack. It fucked up this one I was going after, that's the nause. I got to find some work.'

Lynn shrugged. 'Blags are easy enough to find, Cliff. You kept your liberty, that's the important thing.'

'Sure I did. But it's like the Sword of Damocles over my head, even though I bunged that DI. You can't trust them, can you?'

'I wouldn't like to rely on it,' Lynn said. 'I'll catch you later, Cliff.' He started away.

'What?' Harding began. 'You fancy a game? – the table's paid for.'

'Just want to see if Billy Braden's been in,' Lynn said over his shoulder. Then something made him turn back. 'Set them up.'

The man he was looking for hadn't been in so far this evening.

'His mate Alan was in this afternoon,' the bald hall manager informed him, sweating from the effort as he did so. 'Nicked a nice few quid, he did. I thought there was going to be trouble. I think I heard Alan say he had gone to Spain for a holiday.'

The information surprised Lynn. Braden had half committed to the blag, and he was looking to get him firmed up. He didn't want to believe this.

'That can't be right,' he said.

''S what I heard, Jack. Down to Marbella. I wouldn't mind some of that.'

His gaze fell on sandwiches neatly stacked in the glass case on the counter. 'How old are they, Peter?' he asked. 'Drawing a pension yet, are they?'

'She only made them this afternoon. You want one?'

'Do I fuck. Tell Billy's mate to give me a bell, will you?' He went back to the table, where Harding was racking the balls.

Winning the toss, he let Harding break and watched him put white gently against the pyramid of reds. But not gently enough. He followed on, and managed to nick a red, then black.

As the game progressed, Lynn relaxed his guard, became less wary of the gaunt, stooping figure prowling around the table as if the fiver at stake made some difference to his life. Harding talked and acted no different from the way he had done the last time they had met; and when he said, 'What are you up to these days, Jack? Got anything in the pipeline?' Lynn wasn't even thinking that he might be a grass. He was still thinking how Billy Braden had let him down, and whether Harding would do instead.

'A little taste across the Water 'it comes off,' he replied. 'A bit iffy still. I'm punting around, you know.' He leaned across the table and potted the blue. 'Right now I'm getting a lot of stick from my old lady to get a job. Be perfectly honest, I'm thinking about it.'

'What's her problem? Change of life?' Harding reached the blue ball out of the pocket and respotted it.

'Wouldn't have thought so,' Lynn said.

'I might have a bit of work soon. I got a JCB lined up to rip out a cash machine at Hounslow. Could be worth about nine or ten grand to you, 'you fancy some of it.'

Lynn looked at him, feeling prickles of embarrassment on his skin that he had thought this man a grass. Instinct told him this proposition was straight. There was no reason he'd put himself on offer if he wasn't on the level.

'I'll keep it in mind, Cliff. But I want to see how this

one I got down at Catford goes. There might be something there for you.'

'When's it going?'

'Soon, I'd say.'

'Well, there's no rush on my one,' Harding said.

Lynn nodded and stooped to his shot, deciding Harding was as good as gold. He would square his coming on with Bobby Shaw. It was Shaw who had recommended Billy Braden after all!

He played a decisive stroke. The ball rattled around the table, striking a red which he didn't make. He looked up at Clifford Harding, and felt good about offering him a bit of work.

Back in the office following four days' leave since changing from the night to the day shift, Fred Pyle was drafting a legal aid report for the CPS, the purpose of which was to help twelve fuckwits to decide whether some villains could be successfully prosecuted. It irked him that the Crown Prosecution Service wanted a better than fifty-one per cent chance of conviction before they would undertake to prosecute. Everything he was involved with had waited for his return, so his desk was littered with reports to which he now had to attend. Some of the hated paperwork had become urgent, but at that moment he would have welcomed any reasonable excuse to leave it.

Other detectives around the office were less than attentive to theirs: two of the DIs were discussing a policewoman who both knew and one was stiffing; another was talking on the telephone about a robbery that might be going off. Ordinarily he wouldn't let any of this affect him, but today it did. His fingers dropped aggressively on the keyboard.

'Trying to break it?' DCI Watson said, stopping at the desk with an armful of reports.

'If that would get me out of this, guv,' he said, continuing to type. ''Bout time we had word processors in here. Let those lazy tarts along the corridor have some of the rubbish.' He was referring to the civilian typists.

'You make it look like you're winning, Fred,' the DCI said.

'I'd like to believe it.' He finished typing the paragraph.

'That was a bit of a result Eric got, wasn't it?' Watson commented. The investigation into the complaint against him had collapsed.

'I had my doubts for a time, guv,' Pyle said. 'Mind you, the Rubber Heels were well out of order in the first place.' Nothing was likely to make him change his opinion of the Bureau.

'It did sound a bit swift, Fred. The magistrates' clerk obviously thought Eric was at it with that grass.'

Pyle looked at the DCI. 'He might have thought so, guv. Doing a bit of trading, I s'pect,' he said, not wishing to say too much. 'Worth a try. Unless you're let alone to do the job you won't get anywhere.'

'Try telling that to the Commissioner. Still, Eric got his result.' He laid some reports on the desk. 'Bit more for you, Fred. Have your lads go through those again. The spelling's atrocious. I can't put them up to the governor like that.'

Pyle glanced disinterestedly over the reports. 'They must have slipped past.'

'Just have them do them again,' – like it was a few minutes' work. 'Especially that one Shields wrote. He always struck me as the literate sort.'

'I'll go through them myself, guv.' The prospect didn't inspire him.

'It's diary day tomorrow. Make sure they've all got their details corresponding – Alec!' The DCI saw one of the DIs slipping out.

Pyle pushed the keyboard away and glanced over the top report. There probably wasn't too much wrong with it, only Trevor Watson tried to have all reports perfect.

The telephone on his desk rang and he answered it quickly, hoping for something to drag him away from this.

'Oh, good morning. How are you?' he said cheerfully when the man on the line identified himself. He was an insurance loss adjuster, and Pyle was always pleased to hear from such people.

With the help of one of his grasses, he had nicked a little firm about eight months ago and recovered most of the money they had blagged. They had been convicted, had appealed, only to have their sentences upheld, which seemed unusual these days. True to form the insurance company hung on to their money as long as possible, but now it was time to weigh on. The grass would have to go to their offices in the City for his money.

'This afternoon?' Pyle said. 'It's a bit short notice. It depends whether I can get in touch with my informant . . . Four o'clock . . .' There was no real point in debating the matter until he had tried reaching Billy Little, the grass. He replaced the phone feeling cheerful. All he had to do now was find Little.

Sometimes he didn't bother with putting the actual grass up to collect the money; some wouldn't allow themselves to be put up anyway, even though it was a harmless process. For their part the insurance company simply needed someone other than the detective to sign the receipt for the reward. Pyle would try to contact this minor villain, who was due the reward. If not he would put someone else up. Billy Little answered when he rang his number. Pyle told him about the reward and arranged to meet him later. Replacing the phone he turned back to his paperwork with renewed interest.

'If you spent less time playing with your prick, Tony, and bent a little more to this,' he told DC Shields when he passed back the reports the DCI had returned, 'you might make fewer mistakes.'

'What d'you mean, guv?' the DC said. He looked over the paperwork. 'What have I done, left a comma out? – he's a pedantic sod.'

'Don't worry about Trevor Watson,' Pyle said, out of a sense of loyalty to a senior officer. 'He's still a practical copper.' Not wishing to discuss the matter, he wheeled around on Peter Fenton, who came along the busy Squad office to a free desk. 'Peter. Did you get a statement from that witness yet?'

'No. She wasn't in when I went down this morning, guv. She's coming in this evening,' the DC said.

'Well, keep on at her. It's been over a week now.' He moved on to DS Lethridge, who was at one of the sergeants' desks at the top of the room. 'Have the typists do these again, Eric,' he said, depositing the rest of the report on the desk. 'He wouldn't sign them.'

'He does go on a bit about a few fucking mistakes.'

'You know what he's like. Don't forget it's diary day tomorrow. Make sure they get all their details corresponding. I don't want him screaming about discrepancies over joint actions or statements. Go through them yourself.'

Once a week all detectives' diaries were handed in for checking by the DCI; not recording correctly all details of their actions was a disciplinary offence. It was rarely that diaries were written contemporaneously, despite that being the one oversight that constantly got detectives into trouble.

The insurance loss adjusters were at London Wall, in a labyrinthine building that covered the entire block. The building housed mostly accountants and firms of solicitors, and Pyle had several times got lost along those seemingly endless corridors, despite clear directions from the people on the security desk.

Fred Pyle glanced at his grass as he stepped through the lobby towards the lift with him. The furtive-looking Billy Little truly lived up to his name, being only five-feet-five in his heeled cowboy boots. He looked decidedly unsteady in them and would have had no chance if he had to leg it. For a man who needed to be inconspicuous, the grass had an odd choice of clothes. Someone half his age might have escaped unnoticed among the fashion-conscious youth, but Little, who was pushing fifty, tended to stand out in his Megadeath T-shirt and earrings.

'Don't look like that, Billy. You won't have any problems,' he assured him, noticing Little's eyes darting nervously about as they waited for the lift. 'He'll simply ask your name, get your signature and give you the reward money. Stick up a wrong 'un, if you like, if makes no difference.' He unhooked Little's jacket collar which was turned in. 'Terrific,' he said with mock approval as he motioned him into the lift.

The insurance loss adjuster was large, pink-faced, striped-shirted, in his late twenties. He showed them into a tiny, steel-partitioned office with only a small desk, two wooden chairs and a calendar on the wall. It was the sort of office where job applicants filled out personnel forms.

'Just the usual formalities, inspector,' the adjuster said, laying a thick folder on the desk and removing forms from it. 'Won't take but a few moments.' He had the speedy manner of the over-fed and glanced quickly at the grass as if trying not to give offence by letting his gaze linger on him. 'Is this the gentleman who supplied the information leading to the arrest and conviction of David and Laurence James?' he asked formally.

'It is, sir,' Pyle replied in a similar way.

'If I could just have a few particulars, then – for the record, nothing more,' he assured the grass. 'Your name and address is all.'

Billy Little hesitated. He looked at Pyle as if uncertain whether to proceed, then said quickly, 'It's Smith. It's Billy Smith. 600 Old Kent Road's where I live.'

The young man smiled, but committed the fiction to paper. 'That's SE15.' He wrote in a small, round hand. 'Well, Mr Smith, £28,000 was recovered as a result of your information. There were also two convictions, of course. Under the insurance reward agreement you are due ten per cent. £2,800. Along with the company's thanks.' His round, pink face smiled again. 'I'll need two signatures from you, Mr Smith, if you'd be so kind. One there and another there.' He indicated the place on two separate forms. And as Little scribbled the name, the loss adjuster drew out an envelope from the folder. 'They are all notes of mixed denomination. It's for you to count it if you wish. But I'm sure you'll find no discrepancy.'

'I'll take your word for it, squire,' he said and stuffed the envelope into his pocket.

Back on the street, Pyle said, 'That was easy enough, Billy.'

'Fuck I! All it wants is me to get seen with you, guv.'

Pyle smiled. He knew that wasn't Billy Little's reason for now wanting to part company as quickly as possible. There was a chance he might get away with all the money.

He searched around the street and caught the eye of a taxi driver. Then he glanced at the grass and shook his head. 'Billy Smith. 'S that the best you could come up with?'

'I couldn't think, I always go blank when I get put under that sort of pressure. But I mean, it did, didn't it?'

'For all the dif' it makes. Wasn't a bad day's work.'

The initial effort on Little's part hadn't involved a great deal, he recalled. Along with Lethridge and Jack Barcy, he had had an earner out of the original sum of money recovered and let it be assumed that the two villains had knocked out the shortfall.

'Nice little touch, guv,' the grass said. He hesitated, 'Eh, was you looking for something out of it, guv?'

Pyle gave him a blank stare. 'We agreed on half, Billy. I wouldn't say the figure was open to negotiation.' He held the door of the cab for the grass, and told the driver to take them to Charing Cross.

In the back of the cab he took the envelope and divided the money. Fourteen hundred and twenty pounds in safe notes decidedly improved his day. His grass wasn't at all put out, and would still want to do business in future even if he had nicked all of the reward money. Pyle wasn't so inept at handling people as to close off that possibility.

Both lifts in the block of council flats were out of order. That was a million, Tully thought as he started through the graffiti-scrawled hallway and up the stairs. Cole Coleman, the man he was visiting, lived on the second floor, but living in a block of flats himself Tully automatically tried the lifts.

Glancing over the graffiti he assumed the kids on the estate must have nicked a truckload of aerosol paint. Whoever it was had no concern about ozone depletion! There was a blaze of squiggles and writing up the stairs and along the wall on the second floor, cutting right across windows and doors. He considered for a moment what, as a kid, he had done instead of aerosol graffiti. Something equally as destructive.

He rang the bell and turned to lean on the walkway parapet to watch some pre-teenagers kicking a large cardboard box around on the bald patch of grass that was imprisoned by the flatblocks.

'The idle bugger's still in bed, John,' Mrs Coleman said when she opened the door. She was thin and middle-aged and looked like she did a lot of fetching and carrying. She was fastening her coat, her handbag over her arm. 'See if you can get him up, love. I'm fed up with trying. He was s'posed to be at the Social Security offices at ten.'

She stepped out and let Tully into the flat.

'And tell him not to eat all them eggs for his breakfast.'

In the small back bedroom Tully found the woman's favourite son curled in a foetal-like ball under two duvets. He considered ripping the covers off him but knew if he did he would probably have a fight on his hands. Cole Coleman went into blinding rages at the drop of a hat. So instead he reached under the cover and grabbed his cock. 'Caught you! Playing with yourself,' he said.

The young man in bed was startled. 'Fuck off, you dirty bastard!' he screamed.

'Come on, get up. Your mum said you gotta see the Social Security. You won their long-service award.'

Once fully awake Coleman quickly became reasonable. He stretched his arms out of the duvet and looked at the day, then grinned. 'Ah, it's a bit nippy, John,' he said and withdrew his arms. 'She getting my breakfast?'

'Yeah, it's on the table.' Tully lied. 'C'mon. It's eleven o'clock; we got a day's work to do.'

Cole Coleman wasn't pleased when he rose and discovered that not only wasn't his breakfast waiting for him but Mum wasn't there to cook it. He went without.

There had been a minor setback to Tully's plans. One of the villains who was going to work with him had dropped out because his Mum had had a massive stroke and wasn't expected to live. He wasn't too put out that Ernie Johnson wanted to be with her when she went. There was another prospect to take his place.

Sitting in the kitchen of Phil Hayes's flat with Cole Coleman, Tully outlined the blag. Like Coleman, he had been got out of bed, only his wife was around to cook his breakfast.

'What's it come to, John?' Hayes asked, pouring himself some more tea.

Coleman reached across the small table and helped himself to the food on Hayes's plate.

'About nine or ten grand, 'a bit of luck.'

'Sounds nice enough, dun it? 'Ere, leave off, Cole! That's my fucking breakfast.' Hayes watched the younger man dip one of his pieces of toast in his eggs.

'Ah, what I got, fucking germs or something?' Coleman protested.

'Fucking cook yourself some, you wan' it,' Hayes offered.

That didn't seem to appeal to Coleman. 'Can't your wife do some for me?'

'Yeah, hang on a minute,' Hayes said sarcastically. 'Let her go and sign on for you first!' He looked at the young man and shook his head like he thought he was a waster.

Somehow it was hard to resent the liberties Cole Coleman took, Tully thought. He had an easy, likeable way about him.

'Who else is gonna be involved, John?'

From habit he hesitated, even though he had already committed a lot of information to Hayes. He studied the man, who was in his late thirties, though looked older, even with his dark curly hair. His face was old, and lined, especially around his eyes. 'Only Cole here doing the driving,' he said, 'and Benny Isaacs. He's got the shooters.'

'Benny's very reliable. As it happens, John,' he said, 'I do fancy it. When's it going off?'

'Sooner rather than later. The thing is, it's there. It might as well be done. Know what I mean?'

They both knew exactly what he meant.

The plan was all more or less set in his mind. There were arrangements still to make, minor details that he could do himself; but it was important to make sure his little firm had it clear in their minds just how it was going to go. That meant visiting the proposed blag. This they did in a Ford Transit van that Isaacs borrowed from his father-in-law. Coleman drove over the getaway route, deciding where best to park the changeover car. Finally they stopped in McLeod Road, a little away from the entrance to the offices of the Gas Board. Coleman remained in the front of the van while the other three climbed into the back, from where they could easily plot this up without being seen themselves.

The small office block had three wide steps up to the main entrance and railings protecting bare concrete flower tubs. A seven-foot wall to the left of the block extended some forty feet to gates to the works and service department beyond the offices. Glass doors off the main entrance let onto a small foyer with stairs that could be seen at the end of it.

McLeod Road was a fairly long road whose dwellings comprised mainly pre-war terrace houses with bow front windows. The street was on a bus route, reasonably busy with traffic.

'Here it comes now,' Tully said.

Their attention went along the street as a security truck nosed out of the side-turning about fifty yards or so from where the van was parked. It crossed the traffic lanes and started towards them, then signalled left and turned in through the gates to the works yard.

'Where they going?' Hayes wanted to know. 'I thought

you said they collected from the office across the street there?'

'The money comes down from the first floor,' Tully explained. 'But they go in and out the back way.'

A woman who must almost have been watching for the security truck, her timing was so close, came down through the foyer of the office block and locked the glass doors.

'That's a regular touch,' Tully said. 'Those doors get locked every time they arrive. They come down the stairs and back along that corridor there.' He paused as if expecting the two security guards to appear on cue. They didn't. 'They'll be along in a minute' – as if to dispel any doubt creeping in. 'What we gotta do is go through those doors and get the money off them as they reach the foyer. Then they ain't got no chance of legging it.'

'We'll do them doors easy with a flogging hammer,' Hayes suggested.

'Might be a bit sussy climbing out of a motor and running up with a hammer,' Isaacs said. Tully had told him what his plan was. 'And it might take a few swings to do all that glass clear in those doors.'

Benny Isaacs was practical, and unlike most villains didn't push himself forward the whole time, but quietly did what was required of him. Tully liked that. He was short and slightly swarthy, with badly pockmarked skin. His was a face easily remembered. He had muscular shoulders and was as strong as any two blokes.

'Well, what we gonna do it with?' Coleman said. 'A gas stove?'

'As it happens, that's just what I had in mind,' Tully said.

Cole Coleman laughed. Hayes did too.

'I mean, what could be more plausible,' Tully went on, 'pulling up in the road and offloading a stove to the Gas Board? It's a million. No one'll look twice. Take it up those steps and zoomp! Straight through the door, it's done. Know what I mean? There!' He indicated the two guards who came through the hall.

The four men watched in silence as the guards disappeared with the money containers.

'Why not have it in the yard as they come out, John?' Philip Hayes suggested.

'There'll be too many mugs around who might want to have a go. A gas fitter comes after you with a bit of lead pipe, you gotta shoot him. Can't odds it.'

The thought left them silent.

'What about cars?' Coleman said. 'We'll want something a bit lively, John.'

'No problem. I got a man who should be able to do something for us straightaway.' He smacked his hands together in a decisive manner. 'It'll be a doddle, you see.'

The thought of going into those offices across the road with shooters and blagging the wages held no fear for him. He doubted if it did for any of them.

The ringer he had in mind for the two cars they would need had a car-breaking business at the Elephant and Castle. He had done one or two things for him before, including losing cars that he had reported stolen to claim the insurance on. Del Rogers was just one of the many contacts who enabled him to get his living.

Signalling right under the bridge on New Kent Road, Tully made a right-hand turn on to the narrow, unmade service road to the businesses being conducted beneath the railway arches. The ruts in the road were full of water from recent rain. The car-breaking operation Rogers ran occupied two arches, both of which were littered with salvaged parts, scrap metal, old tyres. In the uneven floor of the arches there were pools of black sump oil instead of rainwater.

Del Rogers, a puddingy, ginger-haired youth, whose pores on the exposed parts of his body seemed clogged with oil, was cutting up a car with an oxyacetylene torch as Tully pulled around in his newish Sierra and stepped out carefully between the puddles.

'Can you cut this one up a bit lively for me, Del?' he joked. 'Old Bill's up m' daily.'

'Just what I fucking well need.' He turned off the lamp and came across to the car. 'That's not bad, is it? Yourn, John?'

'Till the finance snatch it back,' Tully kidded. He was up to date on the HP payments so far, but he could never guarantee staying that way. He glanced across the yard to where two other men were breaking cars. 'Doing plenty, Del?'

'Getting a living. 'S not easy, is it?'

'I dunno. It ain't hard.' He got right to the reason for his visit. 'Any chance you can do a couple for me?'

Wincing as if in pain, Rogers said, 'I don't think so, John.'

'Fuck I, Del,' Tully said, 'I'm relying on you. I thought you was a stoneginger.'

'Well, the thing is, John, I got a lot of stuff to cut up.' He seemed embarrassed.

'What's it gonna take you to drag a couple off the street and stick different plates on them?'

'Won't you want them resprayed or nothing?'

Other cars Rogers rung for him had had a proper job done on them, so they weren't likely to get a routine pull from the Bill. That had meant a respray, changing the external features such as mirrors, racks, etc., and sometimes the interior trim; grinding out engine and chassis numbers as well as putting on new plates. But that took time.

'I'll take a chance if you're that pushed,' Tully said. The alternative would be to drag the cars himself, which he didn't fancy. He never had been much of a car thief. His first adult conviction had been for taking and driving away.

''S not just that, John. I been cutting up one or two dodgy ones lately. I've had the filth down from the Stolen Vehicles branch. They been sniffing around, giving me more ache than enough.'

'Oh, what do them mugs know?' Tully said. 'They don't know fuck all. Just looking for lost chassis and engine's numbers is all. It's worth a monkey to you, Del.' He watched the car man's greasy face cloud with uncertainty. 'Don't let me down, for fuck sake, Del. If you do I'm bang in trouble.'

'Well . . . I'll see what I can do,' Rogers said.

Tully took his response as a firm promise.

After the blagger had gone, Del Rogers had even more doubts about the proposition and wished he'd had the nerve to tell him outright that he couldn't help him. He was already in trouble with the Bill and all this would get him was a lot more. Gloomy thoughts pressed in on him where he sat in the tiny battered office caravan that was wheelless and propped against one of the arch walls. He stared vacantly through the grease-smeared window, knowing what he had to do, knowing how it would help him get out of his own bit of trouble, but he was still reluctant to do it. Why did Tully have to dig him out? He thought about running, going up north somewhere, anything but what he found himself doing. He felt he wasn't in control of his responses. Instinctively he glanced about himself to make sure no one was watching him as he reached for the phone and punched out the number he'd been given.

He hesitated, his manner tense and apprehensive, and when a voice answered, he almost put the phone back. 'Inspector McHale, I want,' he said. He was told to hang on. He said he would.

He wished instead he had hung up.

The pub they agreed to meet in at Waterloo was a halfway house for both. It was an old Free House that was somehow hanging on through recession and surrounding redevelopment, but its clientele, if it ever had one, showed no such tenacity. Nearly all the customers in the bar were demolition and construction workers, for whom most of the smartened-up pubs were no-go areas.

Del Rogers sat with his back against the wall and stared vacantly through the bar room, feeling depressed, his pint hardly touched, the cheese and tomato sandwich uneaten. He saw Detective Inspector McHale enter the pub and push up to the bar, but didn't acknowledge him, not even when he turned and motioned to offer him a drink. He was thinking about what he was doing, whether it was going to get him the help he needed, and if he should warn Tully off.

The detective arriving at the table almost startled him. He looked up at McHale, who was quite short and quite fat and whose hair had all but fallen out, leaving a few strands trailed across his pink scalp.

'What are you daydreaming about?' McHale asked, pulling up a chair and sitting. 'I offered you a drink.'

'Oh, I'm all right, thanks, Mr Mac.' He sipped his beer.

'Been here long?' the DI asked, checking the bar.

'No, a few minutes, is all.' Rogers' eyes followed the detective's, then searched the table top, hiding the shame he felt.

'Well, cheer up, Del. 'S not the end of the world, is it?'

The car-breaker shook his head like he was afraid it would fall off.

'How's that sandwich?' McHale asked, as if considering getting himself a round. But he didn't, he simply helped himself to one of those on Rogers' plate. Half of it disappeared in one bite. When after a couple of chews he had room to push some words out, he said, 'What's it you've got for me?'

Rogers looked directly at him for the first time, knowing now that he couldn't not give him what he'd got. 'I gotta ring a couple of cars for a little firm,' he said in a low voice. 'A fella by the name of John Tully. Comes from across the Water.'

'What is it they've got going off?'

With a shrug, Rogers said, 'Dunno. Just two cars is what he wants. Estate cars, some with a bit of poke.'

'They must have something going off pretty soon, then.'

'Dunno.' He was only interested in how his information might benefit him. He sipped some of his beer. 'What about those lads of yourn, Mr Mac?'

‘The Stolen Vehicles department are not my lads,’ McHale said.

‘You said you’d straighten them for me, ’I got you something.’ He suddenly felt betrayed. Here he was betraying a diamond like John Tully to the filth and he didn’t look like coming up with help.

‘Been down again, have they? Looking a bit too closely at those you’ve been cutting up?’ A mocking smile danced over the detective’s face. It made Rogers feel sick. ‘You shape up all right, Del, I’ll have my governor call the superintendent on Stolen Vehicles. You’ll get a clean bill of health. For a few weeks, at least until you do something naughty again. Where are you parking those cars for them to pick up?’

‘I don’t know yet,’ Rogers said. ‘I got to phone him when I done ’em.’

‘You’d better phone me immediately after, Del, hadn’t you?’

The look the DI gave him made him shiver.

Speculative work from Criminal Intelligence or anyone else wasn't something Fred Pyle wanted right now, and he could tell from the language the DI was using as he outlined it that the possibility of something going off was far from certain. He was prepared to let detectives working for Criminal Intelligence do the collar rather than have his lads sitting on a suspect for days and days on end.

'Ordinarily I wouldn't dream of involving the Squad on the little we have so far, Fred,' McHale said. 'But we're so overstretched with the potential robberies we're following through on we haven't got the men to spare to give this one the attention it needs.'

'You're a bit optimistic in assuming the Squad would be any less busy. Well, my squad isn't. I don't know about any of the others.'

'The thing is, Fred,' McHale said, 'it definitely looks like something is going off.'

'I'd say so,' Pyle agreed readily.

'Well, why don't you spare a couple of your lads to put down there on watch?'

'I'd like to help. But we've got so much going off ourselves that I'm even going to have to go out and feel a few collars myself,' Pyle said. It was his idea of a joke. 'Haven't you got anyone to spare? You must have someone.'

'Not if we're to do it properly.' McHale shook his head ponderously. 'Seems a shame to have to give it to the local CID. I think there might be a nice one going off here.'

'Yeah,' Pyle said, regretting the situation. He didn't like to hear about villains getting their living because the police were overstretched. 'Couldn't you stick a lad down there with a video camera?' he suggested. 'You must have one lad spare – I'd find one, but most of my lot can only just about work their video players!'

'Doesn't look too clever, something goes off, does it?'

'Better'n fuck all, I'd have thought, Graham.'

Reluctantly McHale agreed and left.

Normally the detective chief superintendent wasn't a man who moved fast. His ordinary methodical, plodding mentality was directly translated to his actions. But he was moving pretty fast as he swung himself around the door frame of the DIs' office. Pyle wondered if the building was on fire.

'Fred!' Ernie Jeymer said, 'there's a shout for help from the Terrorist Squad. Holborn. Get your lads over there right away. You too, John,' he added to John Redvers. 'Get instructions on the air. You'd better draw shooters.'

This might have been no more than his paperwork Pyle was running from as he went along to roust detectives out of the Squad office, leaving Redvers to get the firearms organized. Before he did he reached into the bottom drawer of his desk and took out some capsules and swallowed two as he went. They were beta-blockers and would help to keep him calm during this operation.

Five-shot Smith & Wesson .38s and ten rounds of ammunition for each detective were dispensed casually, but quickly now, by DCI Tony Simmons. The detectives being assigned weapons hurriedly scribbled their names in the book. The standard procedure was for the detective to load the gun in his governor's presence; and most did so before grabbing a holster from the cupboard by the door and hurrying out.

'Looks like we gotta pull them out of trouble again,' Pyle commented as he collected his gun. There was a slight recklessness in his tone due to the effect of the drug he had taken.

'Shoot some of the fuckers, Fred,' Simmons said.

Over the air the four cars carrying both him and Redvers' men were directed first to Holborn, then immediately redirected to Bloomsbury. There they rendezvoused with Brian Shilling, the Anti-Terrorist Squad DI, who was directing the operation. He sent them to take up positions where they were keeping tabs on a blue Fiat carrying two suspected IRA terrorists.

Pyle's car was parked in Great Russell Street, the narrow road alongside the British Museum, which at that time of the evening was full of people and traffic. All he hoped as he watched them bustle past was that nothing went off, for they wouldn't be able to manoeuvre at all. To add to their problems a traffic warden sauntered along and tapped the window to DC Fenton, who was in front next to the driver.

'You can't park here,' she said when Fenton lowered the window.

Pyle said, 'Tell her to fuck off and nick some motorists for illegal parking. Tell her to move her black arse out of it.'

She stooped to look at the men in the back as she plucked her radio off her lapel.

'We're on a job, love,' Fenton explained. 'Make yourself scarce.'

The woman looked blank, but finally the penny seemed to drop. She backed away.

When she had moved on, Pyle said, 'Fuck knows what they wanted us for with her around.'

Why they were needed anyway he didn't know. Certainly there seemed no great urgency about their shout now. He guessed the Anti-Terrorist Squad had seen their parcel on the move and had panicked.

'Give me that,' he said reaching across the front seat for the r/t. The driver passed it back to him. 'Brian . . . 's Fred. What's the word, son . . .?'

'Where are you?'

'We're still sat here,' he said, believing the detective running the operation was implying he had proceeded contrary to instruction. 'We haven't moved. 'S no sign of the parcel . . .'

'I think we've lost it,' the Anti-Terrorist Squad detective said. 'Anyone see anything?'

'Not a thing,' said a voice Pyle didn't recognize.

'Nothing this way,' Redvers said.

'Hang on . . .' a voice cut in with excitement. 'The Fiat's turned into Montague Place. 'S heading in your direction, John.'

'Not . . . wait a minute,' Redvers said. 'I've clocked it.'

There was silence on the air. Pyle waited tensely, even though he was not convinced they were going to see any action.

'What have you got, John?' DI Shilling asked. 'Anything?'

'No. A couple of old ladies, that's all.'

There was another silence, longer this time.

'There, guv!' DC Fenton suddenly said, pointing to a blue Fiat that turned into Great Russell Street from Bury Place. There were four men in it, not two, each with their hair lines and eyebrows meeting.

'This looks like it might be it.' Slowly Pyle read off the car number. 'It's turning into Montague Street.'

Suddenly the car accelerated.

'They've tumbled something. They're off!' Pyle informed the others over the air.

'Fuck it!' The words from Shilling exploded angrily over the r/t. 'All right, nick them.'

The driver accelerated Pyle's car along Great Russell Street and, as he cornered hard into Montague Stret in the direction of the blue Fiat, he almost ran down a party of school kids. The ones in the front leaped back on the toes of those behind.

'You mad fucker,' Pyle said and glanced round, making sure no one was hurt. The car didn't slow, but wove in and out of traffic.

Despite this breakneck speed they weren't the first to reach the suspects' car. Three other CID cars were there before them, two Anti-Terrorist Squad cars and one of Redvers'. Pyle wasn't upset about that. These sort of villains weren't shy about producing guns and blasting away. With their car trapped in Russell Square, two of the suspected terrorists tried to run, but Lethridge's car, coming into the Square from Bedford Way, cut them off. Once all seven CID cars had converged on the blue Fiat there followed an enormous traffic jam, which Pyle couldn't have cared less about. It meant a few people would get home a little later than usual, but at least they would get home. Some might otherwise not have done had the four terrorists achieved what they had planned with the explosives found in the boot of the car. But Pyle doubted if the inconvenienced commuter would appreciate that. All he would know was that the traffic was snarled and the police were doing nothing to unsnarl it.

Relief that he hadn't been shot or blown to pieces by people who drove around London with guns and explosives rarely found him thanking God, or saying how pleased or lucky he was to still be in one piece. But it manifested in other ways. It bubbled out in his words, his actions, even though he tried to repress his feelings, in case they revealed that human weakness which Pyle, like most detectives, tried to deny.

Having helped the Anti-Terrorist Squad capture the four Irishmen, their assistance wasn't required further, so Pyle and his men returned to the Yard noisily, like the local rugby team returning home in triumph.

First the guns and ammunition had to be taken back. Then DCI Simmons also became infected by the feelings of Pyle and his detectives as he checked-in the shooters.

Pyle had a bottle of scotch in his desk drawer and a pack of styrofoam cups. He preferred scotch, but in similar circumstances he would drink whatever happened to be available, even sherry.

'Did you see the look on that fucking driver's face when we pulled him from the car?' DS Middlewick said. They were safe now, back home.

'I saw it – fucking wicked. Good job that one didn't have a shooter handy, Ian. That ought to be a nice result for them.' Pyle splashed scotch liberally into the cups.

'Got right out of trouble again. The wankers.' Redvers raised one of the paper cups. 'Here's to it.'

'No thanks for it, of course.'

'One of those'd do me every day of the week,' DCI Simmons said, coming into the office. He brought his own glass. 'I don't give a fuck about getting the credit. Just so long as we get them all nicked and some asshole don't say we stitched them up and give them a result on appeal.'

The subject was an emotive one for each of the policemen present.

'Paddy had to be trying something,' Lethridge said. 'With those accents, saying they'd just rented the car for a holiday.'

'Firms are always hiring out cars full of explosives!' Pyle observed drily.

'A bit simple,' Simmons agreed. 'But they can shoot you just as dead.'

It was a sobering thought.

There was silence in the office as the detectives considered this. DI Frank Brickman came in. His squad had the night duty.

'What's this, a wake?'

'Yeah, something like that, Frank. Have a drink.' Pyle poured him a drink.

'Your old woman phoned, John,' Brickman informed Redvers. 'Said I didn't know what time you'd be back.'

'Better give her a bell, I suppose.'

Pyle thought about ringing his wife, but didn't.

'How's that other fella shaping, Fred?' Simmons asked. 'Do any good yet?'

'Not yet,' he said. 'I'll give him a day or two more then look him up.' A week was long enough for Harding to have got started with Lynn, had he any intention of so doing, he decided. He finished the scotch in his cup and poured himself another. The party would go on until the bottle was finished. He knew that instead of standing around drinking he ought to be shifting some more of the paperwork. Then what he ought to do, instead of what had occurred to him, was go home and eat dinner with his wife and watch television.

'You fancy going on somewhere, Fred? Having a few? Maybe pull one?' Lethridge said as he travelled down in the lift with him when the party broke up.

'Not tonight, Eric. Got one to meet.'

The fat detective seemed disappointed. 'Oh, give her one for me.'

Pyle smiled flatly. He didn't know that he was going to give her one himself yet. But that was his plan.

Light showing at the frosted glass of the bathroom, which abutted the open walkway, meant Libby Howard was home. A good start, Pyle decided as he pushed the doorbell and waited. The dog barked, but there was no other sound from within. He shifted the wrapped bottle of scotch, which he had stopped off to buy, to his other hand and pushed the bell again. The thought that Brian Finch might be there crossed his mind, but he didn't give the possibility serious consideration.

Finally Libby Howard opened the door. She was wearing a white bathrobe with a towel wound around her hair. She seemed surprised to see him. The Alsatian dog, which was at her side, recognized him and stopped barking.

'A bad moment,' Pyle said. 'I should have telephoned. I don't think I took your number, though.' He had it, in fact. He was in no way embarrassed by his intrusion.

'He's not here,' she said, matter-of-factly. 'Brian Finch.'

Pyle looked at her, considering her statement. 'Isn't he?' He stepped across the threshold as she invited him to enter with a sweeping arm gesture that almost lost her the head towel.

'Least the dog's friendly – knows a friend. Hello, Judge. Good old fella.' He caught the dog playfully behind the ears.

'Were you expecting him to be?'

'Bet you've not even seen him,' he said. 'Have you?'

'As a matter of fact, I haven't.'

'Well, as a matter of fact, love, I came to see you.' He watched her closely for her reaction.

She noticed the bottle. 'What's this? A new approach?'

'What's your problem, Libby? Some uniform nick you sometime for insulting behaviour?'

She laughed nervously, like she didn't know how to react. 'You could probably get me dropped out.'

Pyle shook his head. 'You've been listening to too many villains,' he said, 'that's your trouble. Policemen don't do those sort of things.'

Libby didn't protest.

'We going to stand here all night? You must be getting chilled like that.' He moved along the passage into the flat, patting the dog again.

There was an air of resignation about her when she followed him into the living room. He wondered briefly what he would do if she protested, told him to go; he wondered also what would happen if she didn't. That was more enjoyable.

'D'you want me to take the dog for a walk while you finish your bath?' Pyle said. 'Or shall I help you with that?'

She became more uncertain and looked about her.

'Looks like I'm being blanked, Judge,' he said to the dog, as if eliciting his opinion.

Libby said, 'Are you married?'

'The world's full of married men, haven't you heard?'

She didn't seem impressed; then it was an evasion, and he recalled she didn't like evasions. 'Of course I am. I've two lovely kids an' all.'

Libby nodded. 'You would be, wouldn't you? Why don't you go home to them?'

That irritated him, and he suddenly felt like slapping her. That notion excited him. 'You don't want me to go,' he said. 'You want me to take your pants off and fuck you as hard as I can.'

'What? What . . .?' she said.

He thought she was going to become hysterical, but was sure he hadn't misjudged her. Maybe the drug was badly affecting his judgement.

'You really are the most incredibly arrogant man . . . Oh, I forgot, being a policeman makes you like that.'

Pyle didn't say anything. He wanted to fuck her, so changed tack. He set the bottle down on the coffee table. 'You'd better visit the local station, love, for that statement . . .'

His words seemed to suddenly confuse her. 'You fucking bastard . . . you really are.'

'A fact of life, love – all policemen are. I thought everyone knew that.' This change from hostility to frivolity clearly confused her more.

'Does this visit have anything to do with Brian?' she asked, like she was trying to test the way forward.

'Him? Who's interested? We'll pick him up eventually. I told you what I want. You'd like me to fuck you, wouldn't you?' He held his breath for what seemed like a long while. He knew this could mean a disciplinary charge if she complained.

Finally she nodded. 'Yes, I would, very much. I've never been out with a policeman before.'

'You don't know what you've missed, Libby.' He was relaxing now. 'Take off the uniform, I'm just the same as anyone else.'

She smiled. 'I'm not so sure.'

'Take my word for it, love.' He took off his coat; then his jacket and unfastened his tie. She watched him.

'What are you doing?'

'I'm going to fuck you as hard as I can. Got another bathrobe, have you?'

'Oh, my God!' she said.

'What's the matter? Changed your mind?'

He waited, but she didn't respond. Assuming all the moves were his to make, he closed the space between them fast, but as he reached her she stepped in close to him, raised her hands to meet his embrace. She placed her mouth against his without any prelusive niceties. Her hands moved over his body as though they belonged there. His hands slid into her robe and felt her warm body. He could smell the perfume from her bath. His hands went where so far only his thoughts had been. They moved cautiously at first, gently, then more desperately, firmly palming her breasts. Suddenly she stepped back, surprising him, leaving him feeling at once bereft and wondering. But then her hands started tearing at his shirt, pulling it up out of his trousers, fumbling with the buttons; two came off in her haste and one of the buttonholes tore – Edith would repair it, he'd tell her he got into a scuffle, the thought popped into his mind. He didn't want it there. Libby's hands were shaking, he noticed, as she parted his shirt and began kissing him on the chest, biting his nipples, sharply, painfully. He wanted to push her away, but she moved on down to unfasten the belt of his trousers. They came down with his shorts and she was dragging them over his feet with his shoes and socks. She pulled him onto the floor between her legs. She raised her hips, pushing herself against him, and he knew he could easily slip into her but didn't want to just then, like this. Her lips parted, inviting his tongue into her mouth as she closed her arms around him and held him – did she want to be reassured by his physical touch? She squeezed him tightly, but he held back even as she bit his ear and his neck and his lips. Some of the bites were sharp and painful.

Finally she stopped and said, 'What's the matter?'

'Nothing,' he said and sat back on his hams and openly appraised her, ignoring the look of panic that came over her expression. She had firm, round tits, and a bushy cunt. He liked that. 'Go and put on your pants,' he told her.

At first he thought she wasn't going to do as he said. She hesitated as if she hadn't heard. He told her again.

'Just my pants?' she asked.

'Your bra as well, if you wear one.'

When at last she did as she was told his eyes followed her across to the dresser in the bedroom. She slid open the drawer and selected some large candy-striped pants. His cock was so hard now it was aching as he watched Libby step into the pants and tuck her pubic hair in beneath the elastic. She did it with what he decided was a certain coyness, which, after the way she had behaved with him just then, amused him. It was the same when she pulled a matching bra on over her breasts; she looked away as she reached behind under her bathrobe and fastened the strap in one easy movement. He remained motionless, not taking his eyes off her. Bra and pants for some reason made breasts and vagina more exciting for him. In fact he always found women more sexy in clothes than showing almost everything they had. He knew it was something to do with childhood conditioning and the taboo areas of the body that had always been associated with sin in his parents'

Plymouth Brethren household, but he had never explored that for greater understanding.

As she waited for his next move, Libby pulled a bathrobe close about her. He didn't mind that. He reached out to her and pulled her down to him and embraced her and kissed her mouth, her face and neck. How good a lover he was he wasn't sure, but felt he had some sense of what to do. Opening her bathrobe, he said, 'That's nice. I like that, Libby. You're terrific, you know that?' He accepted that she probably did, but she said nothing. He ran his hands over the outside of her bra, firmly palming her breasts through the soft material. If he left her curious to know why he preferred this to the feel of flesh, she didn't ask. His hands moved on down over her waist and round to her buttocks as she knelt before him. He slid his fingers into the top of her pants. His hands went deeper, fondling her buttocks. He closed his eyes, getting intense enjoyment from the sensation through this touch, feeling the smooth satiny garment stroking the hairs on the backs of his hands. His strong fingers pushed down further between the cheeks of her ass and he stroked her vagina. She made a little noise of pleasure as one finger found an opening. He found her wet there, and that added to his urgency. Her clitoris was too high for him to reach easily from this position, but he tried harder and found it.

His tongue slid into her mouth, caressing first beneath her tongue, then deep into her with darting movements. With his hands behind her he drew her forward on her knees until her pelvis was hard against his erection. He could have pulled her pants down and entered her then, but wanted this to go on and on. Ignoring his own anxiety about whether he would lose it, he slid her pants onto her thighs and pushed her back onto her calves and bent forward to her, then turning aside the pubic hair with his thumbs, he pushed his tongue against her. As he increased the pressure he caused her to moan more than just a little.

'Oh dear,' she said as if apologizing. That was all she said. It was enough.

He enjoyed the delay, but his anxiety was increasing and he knew he could quickly lose all the feeling he had. Rising up to get on to the bed, she scrabbled away before him and started to remove her pants. He stopped her with them halfway down. He wanted them left right there on her thighs. He thought not at all about wearing a condom against HIV, knowing there was no point; he had caught sight of a secret report that said as much – the naturally occurring holes in the rubber of a condom were nine microns, while the molecules of the Aids virus were four. If she wanted him to wear one he wouldn't object. But she didn't. She was obviously too far gone to consider it. He wasn't large, but didn't worry about it as he slid into her; he was hard enough, and the pants around her thighs restricted her, preventing her spreading her legs. He assumed she enjoyed this constriction as much as he did. Maybe she would enjoy being tied. The thought excited him more and he was ready to explore it.

Grasses were more trouble than they were worth!

It was a thought he often had when things didn't go to plan with his informers. The stick he had got from his old woman when he had returned home in the small hours of the morning wasn't exactly the grass's fault, but Micky Fielder phoning as he had and telling his wife he wasn't at work . . . What else would he expect of an informer? Edith guessed he had been with another woman, despite his emphatic denials and threats to take any wicked oath. If he was to go on seeing Libby, then he'd have to make sure to cover himself in future and get home at a reasonable hour. He hadn't said anything to the grass when he had finally contacted him at his office that morning to arrange this meet; there was no point.

'Sorry if I put you in it last night,' Fielder said straightaway as he joined him at the end of the carriage.

The remorse the grass might have felt over what he had done didn't help him any now. Fielder was at the front end of the Circle Line train as usual. The carriage was busier than when they used it for a meet in the evening – didn't any of these people work? Pyle wondered. The other passengers seemed mostly foreign – Arab, or from points farther east. There were a group of Japanese girls directly opposite. He looked them over but didn't consider them any sort of threat.

'Couldn't be helped, Micky,' he said, letting him off the hook. Then he added, 'You fuckwit!'

The grass smiled sheepishly. He seemed uncertain whether this was serious. 'Got one on the firm, have you?'

'Wish I had,' Pyle said, glancing at the girls across the aisle. 'What about Jack Lynn? What's the word, Micky?' He wasn't really in the mood to ride all the way round the Circle with him.

'Going off soon is what I heard – the Tote at Catford.' He paused. 'I heard something else. That Halifax cash dispenser in Bromley that was ripped out of the wall, that was supposed to be down to him. Pulled it right out the wall with a JCB.'

'What he do? Forget his PIN number?'

'There was some bearer-bonds from a car parked outside that car warehouse in Hanger Lane.'

Pyle nodded like he knew all this, but said nothing.

'I was told the fella what placed them was Gerry Davis. Well, he's not your average placer. He's got some smart offices in South Street in Mayfair. He's got a video company. Apparently he used to do a bit with longfirms, over Camden Town. S'posed to be well involved in snuff videos – I don't think he makes them, just imports them.'

That sounded interesting, but he wasn't convinced. 'How reliable is that, Micky, would you say?'

'What? Oh, pretty good. I'd say that was about right.'

'What else has this Davis done, d'you hear? Anything?'

Micky Fielder seemed sorry at having to disappoint him in circumstances such as this. Grasses often invented worthwhile business just to please the CID.

'Dunno,' Fielder said, 'apart from the longfirms. He's

supposed to be share-dealing now. Well, I mean, you got to be well bent to go and get a living there.'

'He sounds like he might be worth chasing up.'

The grass smacked his hands together. The train pulled into Victoria Station and both men fell silent. They watched the doors open and a rasta get in. His dreads were long and well kept.

'What does that look like?' Fielder said, with a note of disgust. 'You're hard put to see an Englishman on a tube nowadays.'

'We should meet in a taxi, Micky,' was all Pyle said. The spade with the dreads might have been worth a pull in other circumstances.

After the doors had shut and the train restarted, he went on, 'How d'you go with those Amex? Any good?'

'Ah, a right rubout, guv,' Fielder said, and adjusted his coat on his shoulders. 'I found a man to take them all right. But you know . . .' He made a crude gesture with his hand, in complete disregard of the girls opposite. 'Bits and pieces's how he wants to weigh on. What can you do . . .?'

It was the usual story. Pyle smiled.

'You weren't looking for a taste, guv?' the grass asked.

'I wouldn't earn much by the sound of it, Micky. Not even enough for flowers to sweeten the old lady.' He looked at him briefly, wondering why Fielder pursued the life he did. Perhaps his few moments of what must have seemed like intimacy with the CID were worth all the aggravation. 'Keep an eye on Jack Lynn, Micky. It's his turn.'

Pyle rose to get off at Sloane Square. He'd get the first train back. He still had a stack of work in the office.

* * *

'Malcolm!' DC Slater shouted across the squad office as a uniformed PC who Pyle knew was from TO13 came in.

Dept 13 of Territorial Operations dealt with obscene publications which until a few years ago was handled by the CID's Dirty Squad. Until too many of them got caught at it. The uniform branch didn't make it any straighter, and Pyle knew what Warren Slater was after. He needed some porno videos for a colleague's stag night he was organizing. The only thing that slightly irritated him was that the business was conducted so openly, like no one even pretended any more.

'They'll have to be good 'uns, though. No rubbish.'

'We nicked a lad last night with some terrific stuff, Warren. It even gave my governor a hard-on.'

'They'll do . . .'

'Warren!' Pyle said at the tail end of the conversation. He'd been invited to the party but wasn't sure if he'd make it now, the way his old woman was. 'See what you can find out on Gerry – or Gerald – Davis. There might be something in the computer.' Criminal Intelligence had heard nothing more than a whisper about him and his connection with the bearer-bonds, but nothing that could amount to a visit.

He went out of the office and along to the DCIs' office. Trevor Watson was there with a DI, who he was advising about a prospective charge – unnecessarily, Pyle thought.

'In my opinion, those plates won't be enough, Mark,' Watson was saying pedantically. 'His brief'll stick up a fanny about you planting them.' He glanced at Pyle.

'The age-old problem,' he said. ''S Tony about?'

'He's still out investigating complaints.'

'He ought to join the Complaints Bureau.'

'We'll all be in working for them before much longer.'

'At least we'll know who not to nick, guv – those doing a bit of work!'

'Daresay that would be handy.'

'You want to look at what I've got, guv?' Pyle offered.

'I'm not exactly scratching, Fred,' Watson said. 'Get the DCS to have a look.'

Ordinarily he might not have bothered, but Davis looked half-respectable, even if it was only a front. He knew he would need to proceed carefully with him.

But knowing how cautious Chief Superintendent Jeymer was, he decided to try and firm up his info' before putting it to him. He made a phone call. 'Inspector Pyle . . . It's about some bearer-bonds that went missing out of a car on your manor last year . . . 's a man called Davis I'm interested in . . . Cheers.'

He replaced the phone and watched DC Slater come into the office.

'No trace, guv. Nothing on the computer on Gerry or Gerald Davis.'

'If it was that easy, Warren, I'd've got it from the fucking computer,' Pyle said. 'Dig around a bit.'

There was something to this, he was sure. But he had a problem with putting it up DCS Jeymer, for anyone who wore a suit costing more than two hundred quid, and had an accent that wasn't heavily working-class, then Jeymer called them 'sir' and treated them deferentially. He was someone who liked villains in striped jerseys, and Pyle couldn't make out how he came to be running the Squad. He didn't seem capable of comprehending that those of middle- and upper-class backgrounds were, if slightly more genteel, usually more venal with so many more opportunities.

Leaning comfortably over a filing cabinet in the DC's office, Pyle watched his governor consider the proposition he had put to him about Davis. He could almost hear the questions being raised in his mind. Sure, it was a bit thin, but worth a visit.

Jeymer pulled his well-trimmed beard between his thumb and forefinger, then said, 'Rumours that he may or may not have placed those bearer-bonds; that he may have been running longfirms a few years ago. They don't amount to much, Fred, do they?'

'I don't know, guv. They might.'

'Davis is very respectable. He's always on the financial pages. I've got a few shares, Fred – I read the financial pages – you have to unless you want to get taken for a complete ride.'

Pyle shrugged. 'He'd have plenty of chances.'

'You know yourself, Fred, what he is as much as what we've got determines whether we go after him. And what we've got doesn't amount to much, does it? We can't just pull him down the road and give him the treatment like some villains.'

''Course not,' Pyle conceded. 'But he's worth a visit. I s'pose I've less faith in the financial Establishment, guv. I've only got a few British Telecom shares.'

Jeymer gave him a look. 'How good is your snout?'

'Pretty reliable. He gave me the stuff on Jack Lynn.'

That made him pull at his beard again. 'Give Davis a miss for now, Fred. Concentrate on Lynn.'

Pyle shifted off the filing cabinet and collected the folder from the DCS's desk. 'He's more of a prospect, I daresay.'

He wasn't particularly disappointed. He had enough to

do without looking for work. Maybe he'd find a way to connect Davis with Lynn. If he had more time he might have taken a chance and pursued Davis anyway.

'Are you going to Beckenham to give a hand?' Jeymer asked.

That visit had more or less fallen his lot. 'I don't know when, guv,' Pyle said, hoping it would get passed to someone else.

'Make it soon, Fred. They've been on again.'

'Where the fuck was I last Monday?' DC Ray Jenkins asked, leaning round from the desk in the squad office. Such inquiries were familiar from detectives who hadn't kept their diaries up to scratch. They were due to be handed in for the DCI to check them.

'I expect that was when you stuck up that old tart.'

'Some chance! Was that when we nicked chummy?'

'No. That was on the Saturday. Wasn't it? That's when I put down. The Duty Book just shows 'obo' both days.'

'You're wrong, Peter. I'll check in Jack's diary.'

This was all too familiar to Pyle as he came along the office to Eric Lethridge's desk where some of their squad's diaries were in, awaiting collection.

'You should fucking well write it as you do it, Peter,' Lethridge said. That was expected of the DS.

Pyle waited at the desk to talk to the DS about Davis. He was unconcerned about his detectives corroborating their diary details in this way.

'As long as they get them about right,' he said to Lethridge as he passed him the slim folder he'd brought. 'Davis. He's not worth too much attention after all. Too respectable – might spoil his image on the financial pages.'

He smiled. He tried to remain philosophical about the priorities they had in the CID. 'Check through his known associates anyway, Eric. Might give us something useful for when we get around to nicking Lynn. And ring Inspector Allen out at Ealing about those missing bearer-bonds. He was going to phone me back.'

'Any particular hurry, Fred? I'm up to my ears.'

'When you can,' Pyle said uninterestedly. 'I don't suppose it'll help much.' He searched around the office. 'Where's Jack Barcy? I want him to go out to Beckenham . . .'

'Will you get away with sending him?' Lethridge asked.

'He can take the seconds. Tell him I want a word.' He collected up the diaries from the desk.

'D'you see that new civilian typist along the corridor? She's got some form!' Lethridge said. 'Wouldn't mind a taste.'

'You got some chance, you fat bastard. I heard Tony Simmons was looking to get into her.'

'How does he find the time?'

'Fred!' a DI called across the Squad office. 'You're wanted on the phone.'

Paddington CID informed him they had picked up Brian Finch.

'Good luck,' Pyle said into the telephone. 'I'll come over and interview him. I'll be a couple of hours before I'm through here. Still, the wait'll do him good – the chasing around he's caused. Don't let him make any phone calls or see anyone . . . especially not his brief. Cheers.' He replaced the phone and sat at his desk with the pile of diaries.

DC Shields came in with his diary. 'Want to have a look at this one, guv?'

'Up to date, Tony, is it?'

'Just about, guv.' Shields waited while he glanced over the entries. 'I saw this snout earlier. I have him doing a bit for me – gave me a couple of nice things on division,' Shields explained. He waited as if expecting some comment. Pyle looked at him. 'He's put me onto a little ramp at the hi-fi factory out at Erith. There's a regular touch each week apparently. Two or three compact disc players going.'

'It doesn't sound like something for the Squad. What's it come to so far? Any idea?'

'Not really, guv. A few grand. I s'pose.'

'Reliable, is he?'

'He tries, guv, you know. Like I said, he's put one or two nice things my way.'

'You bunging him?' Pyle wanted to know.

'A few quid, guv.'

'Unless we have it off you'll lose that, Tony,' he told him. Money was drawable from the Informers' Fund by detectives only where it related to a job. Shields's information didn't amount to that. 'It's not worth pursuing, Tony, is it? A couple of CD players a week. Tell him to keep his ears open, though. In case someone decides to have a lorry load . . .' The Squad had to keep a sense of proportion. 'You could pass it onto division.'

'Erith wasn't my manor, guv, was it?'

Pyle nodded. 'About right, son.' He accepted the detective's need to protect his information, even when it meant a crime not being stopped. He not only condoned the practice, but encouraged it. Such a state of affairs helped create in detectives a sense of pride and independence which made them more efficient, despite what the hierarchy believed.

This was one where, from experience, he was convinced he knew better than those in offices he would never attain. The priorities of the Squad were such that they couldn't pursue every job they heard about, and the stereo equipment factory could probably afford the loss. If his handling of this became generally known, then disciplinary action might have resulted; but that was a chance he was prepared to take to preserve his own independence and efficiency.

D division was one of the busiest in the Met, and the divisional HQ at Paddington was, he knew, equipped with the most modern computer aids available to the police. But despite the technology, both building and division were still operated by police officers. They could be as helpful or unhelpful, efficient or inefficient, as circumstances dictated. Currently they were being unhelpful and perverse, and Gladwell guessed it was on the instruction of Detective Inspector Pyle, whose arrival he was awaiting – though for all he knew Pyle was already there and interviewing his client. He would get angry if that proved the case.

Many times during his short career, Alex Gladwell had run across pretty well all of the human factors governing the behaviour of policemen. Mostly that behaviour had helped him to achieve the clients' desired result. Only sometimes, like now, had it hindered him. He was waiting on the public benches at Paddington Green police station to see Brian Finch, and having invested over an hour of his time thus far he knew it would have been a complete waste if he went away without seeing his client. But with other appointments to get to he wasn't sure how much longer he would wait. What he was relying on was these local policemen getting embarrassed by his continuing presence and asking repeatedly how much longer he had to wait.

At twenty-eight Alex Gladwell was a solicitor who, in

the four years he had been practising, had made a solid reputation for himself. His clients were villains who came to him not because they were innocent, but because they were guilty. He made no moral judgements about what they did, but instead took the view that anyone, no matter what their crime, was entitled to a defence; his clients were entitled to the best result he could get them. Some of the methods he employed to keep them their freedom would not only have got him struck off but prosecuted. So far he had escaped unscathed.

He was short and round, with a plump, boyish face. His hair was beginning to recede and he had a mousy-coloured moustache, though neither detracted from his youthful appearance. The grey pinstriped double-breasted suits he always wore clearly signalled his profession.

He hadn't, in fact, wasted a moment of the time he had been kept waiting, having read a number of reports that were necessary for him to brief counsel in a fraud case. But now he had completed all his reading and subsequent note-taking. But he remained determined not to leave without seeing Finch or getting some satisfaction from the detective handling the case. He rose from the wooden seat and strode across the terrazzo floor to the public desk, which was like a large serving hatch. The uniformed constable sitting at a desk in the area beyond looked up, clearly made embarrassed by his presence and increasing impatience. He blushed, but it was hardly noticeable among the spots and boils that peppered his face.

'He's on his way, sir,' the constable said.

Gladwell stared at him for a moment, suspecting he was lying. He wasn't convinced they had even phoned Detective Inspector Pyle yet. Swivelling on the balls of his feet, he stepped back to the seat and lowered himself. He looked at his watch, then opened the briefcase, and took out a folder to check through the notes he had taken from Mrs Finch.

'Inspector Pyle,' he said to the constable who opened the back door to him after he had twice rung the bell. He didn't show his ID.

'Yes, sir,' the constable said. 'Inspector Polden said he'd like a word . . . And there's a solicitor waiting in the front reception. A Mr Gladwell, sir.'

Pyle raised his eyebrows, but said nothing. He had recently talked on the phone to Gladwell about Terry Clark.

The local DI looked more like a gentleman farmer than a policeman, in his crumpled tan wool suit and with his florid complexion. The standard bottle was brought out for Pyle's visit. The DC who had accompanied him wasn't in the office, but getting the witnesses organized.

'Any trouble picking him up?' Pyle asked.

'Came as good as gold – a neighbour gave us a call.' He gave him his drink. 'We turned his drum over – he had three grand there.'

Pyle didn't comment, but wondered if that was the amount the detectives had found or if they had dipped into it. It wasn't important.

''S down in the front office,' Polden went on. 'He stuck up some nonsense about winning it racing.' He scoffed. 'I wish some of my horses would run as well.'

'The luck some villains have on horses,' Pyle said, 'you wonder why they ever go blagging.'

'Was that one at Lewisham down to him?'

''Be handy. Who called his brief? One of your lot?'

'Probably. He showed up a while ago.'

'He's supposed to be well bent. 'S what I heard. I daresay one of your lads is earning a couple of quid.'

Polden simply said, 'I wouldn't be surprised.'

Pyle nodded. 'I've had the witnesses brought over. You got somewhere handy to put Finch up for an ID?'

'Do you want to parade him?' Polden said.

'I wasn't planning to.'

'We'll find you somewhere nice and quiet – we'll have to do it a bit slippery with his brief downstairs.'

Officially identification parades should have been conducted in a manner which was in no way likely to prejudice the witness. For that reason they were suppose to be held within the confines of both the police station and the precincts of the front office, the procedure always conducted by the uniform branch. In practice it was another matter, and convenience often dictated how it was done. No policemen, whether uniform or CID, enjoyed the inconvenience of parading suspects – it wasted a lot of time for a lot of people, not least the police.

Brian Finch was brought from the cells, put in an interview room and sat facing the door, which had a fifteen-inch square window of clear glass.

Singly the two witnesses, who had been collected from Lewisham, were ushered along the corridor by DC Fenton. Pyle reintroduced himself to them and explained what was happening.

'There's no doubt about this being one of the robbers,' he reassured the first witness, a man in his mid-fifties. Then to show that he was in no way biased, added, 'But I want you to make up your own mind. Okay?'

The witness, who worked for the building society opposite where the money was being collected, gave a precise nod and said, 'You want me to go into the room and see if it's him. I understand, sir.'

'No. Just look in through the window.'

Offering an encouraging smile, he patted his shoulder and sent him towards the interview room. The witness paused outside the door and peered in. There was no immediate recognition on his face. Nor any when he came back.

'What d'you say, Mr Higgins?' Pyle said.

'Well . . .' he began hesistantly. 'It could be him, I suppose, but I'm not saying it is, mind.'

'Perhaps if you had another look,' Pyle suggested. 'Take your time.'

'I don't think that would help, sir,' Higgins said. 'I wouldn't like to commit myself, to be perfectly honest. I'm sorry I can't be of more help, inspector – when I think of what they did to that guard. I'd like to help lock them up and throw away the key.'

'That's what we're trying to do here,' Pyle told him.

The man looked back towards the interview room, adopting a thoughtful expression, then finally shook his head. 'No, I can't say as that's him, sir.'

His face set in a grim expression, Pyle nodded, concealing his disappointment.

The next witness, a customer of the bank that had been robbed, was equally disappointing. She was put through the same motions, with more or less the same result. She couldn't say with any certainty that Finch was involved. Pyle imagined what the villain's brief would make of their testimony in court. There'd be more chance of a conviction if there were no witnesses.

Now he had to face the distinct possibility that Finch hadn't been on the Lewisham blag. But if not it was odds-on he was involved in something else. His swift departure prior to his house being raided suggested as much. Though what villain, regardless of whether or not he was currently active, would wait around for a dawn visit from the Squad? There was the three grand the local CID had found at his place. No way did he believe Finch had won it betting. Although sufficiently realistic to recognize that he might not have enough to charge him with Lewisham, he wasn't yet about to rule out the possibility completely.

Brian Finch was square-jawed, with closely cropped, sand-coloured hair; a villain in his late thirties whose eyes were a little too close set and whose mouth was too small for him to have been called good-looking. He rose hopefully as Pyle entered. Pyle indicated with his head for the uniformed constable to leave.

'What's this then,' Finch wanted to know, 'the treatment?' Pyle found him arrogant, but not demonstratively so. It was as though he believed himself innocent and knew therefore that it was only a matter of time before he was released.

'We'll see how you shape, son.'

'You're jumping the gun a bit. I'm not saying nothing until I've seen my brief.'

Pyle laughed. 'What the fuck d'you think he can do? You're bang to rights.'

'Oh yeah? Should be dead easy for you then, shouldn't it?'

'Like taking a leak, you see.' He suddenly found himself judging this man as Libby Howard's former lover, wondering how skilful he had been, whether she had enjoyed Finch more than him. 'You might as well put your hands up right now, Brian,' he said pragmatically.

'That's what you reckon, is it?'

'It's the sensible move, son. Gets you some help. You were grassed. Cliff Harding put you right in it. That's why he's out, and you're nicked.'

'Never heard of the man,' Finch said. 'Who is he?'

'Just a villain who puts his liberty above yours. Then, why shouldn't he? That's the sensible thing to do.'

'What am I supposed to do now, then? Grass a few I don't know, and go and get myself some kind of deal? 'S that what this is all about?'

The DI shook his head.

''S no value, son. We can't go on trading villain for villain indefinitely. We've got one in the book that someone's got to go for.' He stabbed his thick index finger at Finch. 'You've been elected.'

That caused Finch to step back and change his approach. 'You'll think differently when my brief has a pop at you . . .'

'A little kid with a whispy moustache?' he said, like he had never met Gladwell. 'He's here. Flapping around like a penguin with a hernia.'

'I want to see him. I've been asking to see him for the last two hours.'

'You'll see him, Brian, when I'm good and ready. What that'll depend on is what you give me. 'You put up as much as Terry Clark did, we'll get on splendidly.' He smiled. 'So sit down, make yourself comfortable, son.'

Finch looked at him, then sat. Pyle drew up a chair.

'Right, let's have a little chat about blags and blaggers.'

This interrogation took him no more further forward than the two witnesses had. The villain blocked every tack, and Pyle refrained from putting pressure on him. Rather he conveyed the impression that it didn't much matter one way or the other what Finch offered, as the result would be the same. The fact that he apparently wasn't trying served to confirm this.

'It's going to be a long wait, Mr Gladwell,' Pyle informed the solicitor, who was still waiting in the public area of the station when he came through. 'He's well stitched up.' Other possibilities were being juggled in his mind, things that would benefit him personally.

'Are you going to permit me access to my client, inspector?' the brief said formally.

'You'll almost certainly see him at Bromley Magistrates' Court tomorrow.'

This slightly surprised the young solicitor, whose attitude changed at once. 'Your case is that good, Fred, is it?'

'Both you and Finch know it – 's why you're here.' Or they knew something he didn't, he was convinced of that.

The solicitor pursed his bright red lips. Then glanced about the reception area, like he was making sure no one else was within earshot. 'Is there any possibility of some latitude here, Fred?'

A smile started in his brain, but didn't reach his face. That was what he wanted from this young man. He looked at him and waited.

'It might be to our mutual advantage,' the brief suggested.

'What d'you have in mind?' Pyle asked vaguely.

Again Gladwell checked about him. 'Can we talk somewhere less public?'

They went into another interview room, which differed little from the one Finch was in.

Despite previously having done business together, each proceeded warily, sounding the other out as though believing that what they were doing was strictly legal.

'I think my client might be interested in a lesser charge,' Gladwell suggested.

Pyle nodded. 'I'm sure. Pleading to it?'

The solicitor shook his head. 'He would be more interested in some alternative arrangement . . .' He hesitated there.

The DI waited. But saw that the brief wanted some commitment. 'That might be possible. What are you suggesting?'

'We're both practical men, Fred.'

'It still depends on what you're looking for,' Pyle said.

'I'm sure something beneficial could be worked out . . . I'd need to talk to my client.'

After a moment, Pyle nodded. 'That's not difficult, Alex.'

He knew the solicitor needed to consult with his client to ascertain what he could afford, rather than what his involvement may or may not have been. For that had little bearing if the police decided he should go. Gladwell wasn't long in coming back with an offer of fifteen hundred pounds to have his client dropped out. That struck Pyle as unreasonable. He told him Finch could plead to a lesser charge for fifteen hundred, or could walk for three grand. Without mentioning that his evidence wasn't such that he could have charged the villain for the Lewisham blag. Had it been otherwise, he would have blanked the offer on account of the beating the security guard took. He wanted to see someone go for that job. But Brian Finch probably wouldn't be the one. However, his not being nicked for that robbery was about the only thing this earner would guarantee. Finch had been at it somewhere, so what Pyle would do, once he had his money safely tucked away, was give Criminal Intelligence the word that Finch was plotting something and see what they could sniff out. That was the price of being a villain and having a bent brief.

The DCI had worried at him several times about Harding, wanting to know what was happening, if there were any developments. For his part Pyle would just as soon have let the situation run on, to see what the villain could get in his own time. But it wasn't entirely his decision how the informant was handled, and now he had to get on to Harding.

The meet looked safe enough. Harding had suggested the makeshift community playground where he went with his own kids. The area was fenced off from the street in a holey fashion – more kids went through the fence than the gate – and littered with brightly painted rubbish: empty oil drums, an old timber-and-doors climbing frame, old tyres, rope swings. The kids swarmed eagerly over the ramshackle apparatus in a noisy, reckless manner, watched with apparent casual concern by leather-clad mothers, who looked like pub bouncers, or by fathers who were presumably out of work. Clifford Harding had three of his kids there, aged four, five and six. The fourth was only six months old.

'They look like they're nice kids,' Pyle remarked, standing inside the playground with Harding, but separated from the other parents. ''S this all they have to play in?' His own childhood had been spent in the city so he had moved out as soon as he could when he had kids of his own. Green fields and a few trees to climb was what kids needed, or at least some safely constructed apparatus. Environments such as this bred villains, he was convinced of that; but all the while there were policemen to nick them and prisons to lock them in . . .

'The council keep threatening to put something permanent up,' Harding was saying. 'They don't do nothing, though.'

'They seem happy enough, Clifford.' He looked around the playground to a young mother who was sitting on a box smoking. She was attractive – his own wife came into his thoughts – still not sweetened. 'You'll miss them. They'll miss you too, I daresay – when I pick you up again.' He shrugged, suggesting that was inevitable, when Harding looked at him. 'It's got to be done. I expected word on Jack Lynn by now.'

Harding shook his head. 'I have been punting around. I mean, you don't just go up to the man and start asking questions. You have to suss things out. It takes time, dun' it?'

'I'll have fucking well retired before I hear from you. You haven't got time, son.' His anger flared and vanished as quickly. 'You've had your chance. You've got to be nicked again.'

This nearly caused Harding to panic and run. His eyes darted around the playground as if he was teetering on the edge of indecision. Pyle knew it was his children who were stopping him.

'What . . .?' The question came out of Harding like he had been punched. 'What are you talking about? I'm working for you.'

Pyle slowly shook his head, with a feeling of power, a

feeling of satisfaction. 'There'll be some new charges going up. Involving a security van blag out at Penge. A robbery went off out that way two days ago. A lad called Brian Finch put you right in it.'

'Oh yeah?' Harding said. 'Who's he then?'

''S worth a try, son,' he said. 'He's given us enough.'

'Look, you found the shooter at my place. Right, I mean, I'm bang to rights on that, but that's all there is. That's straight . . .'

'About as straight as a dog's dick. Penge was what that shooter was for. It won't be difficult finding someone to ID you.'

Anxiety gnawed at Harding. He understood how likely that was to happen when a DI on the Squad said it would. It had happened too many times before.

'Leave it out, will you?' Harding said, closing his eyes.

'My governor's making noises about you, Clifford. I can't justify keeping you clear any longer, not unless you give me something . . .'

'I will, won't I? I said I'd get it.'

'We're all becoming old men waiting, son.'

'Look, I heard he was making one,' Harding tried, like the words were choking him. 'Soon now. I mean, it was what I heard.'

'Tell me something I don't already know, why don't you?'

With near-sublime insight he knew this villain was resisting giving him what he had got so far. In spite of their agreement, to actually start grassing was something Harding probably couldn't bring himself to do finally. Pyle obviously hadn't put enough pressure on him, so he glanced purposefully over at his children.

'They could be in their twenties before you see them again properly.'

He watched Harding close his eyes again, this time in prayer maybe.

Finally he said, 'I heard it was the Tote at Catford.'

Pyle looked at him, his face expressionless.

A muscle around Harding's left eye twitched. 'It's what I heard. It's straight.'

He nodded. The information alone didn't put him ahead of what he had from Micky Fielder, but it did indicate that Harding was trying, albeit reluctantly.

'That's about right,' he said. 'What I want from you is when, and who's involved.'

The villain said he didn't know.

'Well, make it your business to find out, Clifford. Unless of course you want to do it the other way.' He glanced at the children once more, leaving him in no doubt about the alternative.

'Might be worth giving it to Criminal Intelligence, have them go on watch down at Catford,' DCI Simmons said, turning into his office, where Pyle followed him. Both were in their overcoats and carried briefcases, having just come on duty. The DCI was pleased about the development with Harding.

'S'pose they might get lucky and see something, guv. I don't think they have anyone spare.'

Simmons removed his coat and hung it up by the door, then switched off the desk lamps that were still burning in the deserted office. 'What's the alternative?'

'I didn't particularly want to have to give this one to them, that was all.' One of the reasons was that he might not be able to keep control, which might have presented problems if the need arose to nick Jack Lynn by means of a swift 'un. 'I think it's too close anyway.'

'D'you have anyone to spare to put down there?'

'That's a problem.'

His squad were completely stretched, and he didn't think there would be value in having detectives on watch at the racetrack anyway. There would be nothing to see until the blag was going off. Then, without his entire squad there and a few more besides, there'd be litle chance of nicking anyone.

'Well, borrow a couple . . .' Simmons suggested.

A detective sergeant looked in through the door. 'Guv. The super was looking for you earlier . . .' Simmons nodded. 'Did you get to look at that CRO file yet?'

'Give me a look back later on it,' Simmons said, and turned to the computer on his desk. He keyed in and got up the manpower availability menu which told him at a glance the position of each man on the ten squads. 'Is Sampson still off sick?'

'S'posed to be coming back Monday,' Pyle said. It was a sore point. 'I'd better have a replacement for him, guv. He ought to go back on division. Back in uniform would be a better idea.'

'What's the problem?'

'The usual. He's lazy, basically.' Although by no means an inexperienced detective, Sampson seemed forever in awe of the strokes that were pulled by detectives and Pyle didn't trust him, believing he was a potential whistle-blower.

Simmons nodded. 'Make the recommendation, Fred. I'll push it through.' He turned back to the screen. 'Take Troy, Kennedy and Martin from number six. The rest are in court all this week, and most of next I shouldn't wonder.'

'I wouldn't mind having someone taking seconds at Lynn's place,' Pyle said. 'Might be a bit dodgy, we could go and frighten him off. But I'd take a chance.'

'You think it's that close to going, Fred?'

He shrugged. 'According to Harding. My other snout seemed to think that was about right. I'm waiting to see if he can get anything else.' He had a lot of faith in Micky Fielder.

'I'd like Harding back inside just as soon as.'

The DCI was still worrying about Harding and so when he'd done his best he'd be nicked again. If it looked like he did his best, and his best got him the result he was after, then Pyle would do what he could to keep him free of charges resulting out of the firearm found at his place. That was as much in his own interest as a reward to the felon: once a villain started grassing that was the best possible lever to have under him. Most of them lived in terror of ever being identified as a grass. He would see how Harding shaped up finally, then maybe have another word with the DCI.

'He won't go very far, guv.'

'What about the Tote?'

'I left them out. There's a better than even chance the blaggers have someone on the inside. They have to be getting their information from somewhere.'

'They ought to be warned,' Simmons said, and turned away to answer the phone on DCI Watson's desk.

The disadvantages of warning the people working in the Tote would be obvious to the DCI, that was why he hadn't ordered him to warn them. The decision was being left to him; he wanted to nick Jack Lynn and his firm at it, rather than risk scaring them off so they could put together another one that the Squad maybe wouldn't get to hear about.

When he got to his own office the first thing he did before removing his coat was check his messages. He did this with the vague hope that something urgent would take him out immediately away from his paperwork. He read the scrawl across the pad.

'When did this come in – from Deptford CID, Alan?'

'Last night, I think.'

'Fuck! Did it? I wish someone had called me at home.' He picked up the phone and began dialling. 'Fucking grasses, they're more trouble . . .'

'One of them been nicked, Fred?'

'Wouldn't you know it . . . DS Linkup,' he said into the phone. The inherent risk with letting grasses have their own little ramps as means of payment, as he did, was them getting their collar felt. When that happened, usually something could be done. There was no question about him trying here, especially as they were still after essential information, like when the robbery was going off. 'Sergeant Linkup?' Pyle said when another voice came on the line. 'Fred Pyle. You rang me about one of mine . . . What d'you pull him for?' The DS explained how he had nicked Micky Fielder with some stolen American Express travellers' cheques.

'Can anything be done?' He was being necessarily deferential to the arresting officer. It was obvious they could work something out or Linkup wouldn't have phoned him. 'I'll come down,' Pyle told him when the DS said he'd do what he could to help. 'Won't be before lunchtime though – we've a DIs' meeting here this morning.' That suited Linkup all right.

Maybe this was for the best, he thought as he replaced the phone. Helping Micky Fielder might make him work harder.

During the lunch period the Deptford CID office was deserted. The odd DC wandered in to collect something or look for someone, but didn't disturb Pyle where he sat across from DS Linkup's desk at the top of the room. Dave Linkup was bulky and had a lot of dark bushy hair; he was about thirty-five and knew his way about. Pyle wondered what his clear-up rate was – pretty good, he guessed, or this man wouldn't be as amenable as he was.

'I nicked the fella your grass knocked out those Amex to,' Linkup explained. ''Course, it didn't take much pressure before he stuck Fielder up. What does he do for you, much?'

'He's been a good 'un,' Pyle told him. 'How d'you come to nick the placer?'

'He's well known here. Used to do a bit for me himself.' Linkup grinned. 'His usefulness is about over. He'll have to stay nicked.'

Pyle nodded, understanding the expediency of that.

'What about dropping Fielder right out? That going to be much of a problem?'

A telephone started ringing on a side-table down by the door. Both detectives let it take their attention. No one answered it, and soon it stopped ringing.

'Wouldn't be too difficult,' the DS said with a slow nod. 'He hasn't been charged. I left him out soon as he told me he was doing a bit for you. Leaves me light, though.'

'I daresay it would. I'd appreciate it, Dave –' intimating that he'd find something to help him keep his numbers up. 'Least until he finds what he's after for me. I mean, then if you need him you can have him back.'

The procedure for getting Micky Fielder set free wasn't at all involved. It entailed the DS going to the cells, getting the keys off the custody officer and unlocking the door. There were no other prisoners around to witness this, for those who had been in overnight apart from Fielder had been taken to court. There was no paperwork for the DS to fix, as the grass hadn't been charged, and all anyone knew was that the suspect was there helping the CID with inquiries.

Pyle waited outside the station and when Fielder emerged and came down the steps he shook his head in mock dismay.. Fielder was unshaven and looked crumpled in his three-quarter leather coat. His sculptured hair needed some gel.

'You fuckwit,' he said. 'I thought you had more sense than to do business with other grasses. I could have put myself in a lot of trouble pulling you out. And for what?'

The grass cringed visibly, but Pyle wasn't about to let him off lightly.

'For what? I'll tell you – so you can ponce a living, is all. But you're not helping me get my living, are you? I mean, what have you given me? Doesn't amount to a pratful, does it? A whisper about something that might or might not be going off. What else have you got?' His demand made Fielder fidget uncomfortably. 'Nothing! Why? 'Cos you been fucking about getting yourself nicked. You've been a good 'un in the past, Micky. Don't tell me I'm going to have to drop you out.' He made it sound as if that was a painful decision for him. He paused and looked at Fielder before adopting a concerned attitude. 'You having some kind of trouble indoors, son? Problems getting your indoor money?'

'No, I'm all right there, guv,' Fielder said. 'I was just unlucky – 's all. I ought to have known better.'

'How much did that DS nick off you?' Not for a moment did he imagine that DS Linkup was helping him out of the goodness of his heart.

'A twoer,' Fielder replied sheepishly.

''S cheap,' Pyle said. 'So what's the word on Jack Lynn? Did you hear anything more?'

'No, not yet, I didn't. I was supposed to see a geezer for a drink last night.'

That wasn't a piece of information Pyle was pleased to hear. 'You're a handy bloke! You'd better look him up, Micky, make yourself busy. I want to nick Jack Lynn. I'll be most upset if you don't help me do that.'

The grass was now into him for a big favour and Pyle knew he would try to redeem himself any way he could.

Post-lunch inertia had settled over the Squad office. It would need a reasonable shout to make detectives alert and active again, to get them away from the paperwork that had resulted out of their various visits to court that morning. Fred Pyle felt like tiptoeing through the place so as not to disturb anyone.

In the corridor he ran into a detective inspector from Criminal Intelligence carrying the standard folder. Anyone who ever moved about the Yard, unless coming in or going out, seemed to be transporting paperwork, despite all the computer technology.

'I was just about to look for you,' the DI said. 'Weren't you on those Method Index raids for the Lewisham blag?'

'Along with John Redvers' squad,' Pyle said. 'Is someone making complaints?'

'Probably, Fred – you've gone a long time without one now!' He grinned. 'You spun a villain called Harding. Clifford Harding. We've picked up a whisper that he's supposed to be making one. He's putting it about that he has a DI on the Squad straightened.'

'Maybe he has, Reg,' Pyle said. 'Not too bright telling everyone about it. I'd best have a word with him.'

Had he in fact been earning off Cliff Harding he might have been more concerned about the rumours. He wasn't worried, just annoyed that he had apparently backed a wrong 'un. Harding actively putting one together – presumably the one he had had the gun for – while supposedly punting around for him, only served to make him look a fool. Nothing much was changed by this DI's information, only his own determination that Harding would eventually go, regardless of what he came up with on Jack Lynn.

'Eric,' he said, summoning the DS into his office. 'Harding's putting it about that he's bunging me.'

'Well, it could look that way, guv.' The DS grinned. 'Any chance he's making that one with Lynn?'

'Be ironical, wouldn't it? Let's have another look at Harding. Turn him over again.' He sat back in his chair and watched the DS settle against a filing cabinet. 'Any word from Erith, Eric?'

'I talked to that DI. He reckons they came close to nicking Gerry Davis. He thinks he's well active with plastic. He wanted to take a chance on doing him over those stolen bonds. The DPP blanked it. Said there wasn't enough to charge him.'

'Ernie Jeymer's probably right then about giving Davis a miss,' Pyle commented.

'They're sending over all he's got. The DI reckons not being able to go after Davis stopped him nicking Jack Lynn. Might be true – it sounded like a load of ballocks to me.'

'Maybe we should keep Davis in our sights,' he said. 'But I can't see him coming easily. I could have a word with the Serious Fraud Office, let them take a crack at him. Other than that about the only chance would be to fit him. But to suddenly find Davis involved in robbery might be a bit of a stretch, Eric.' He grinned. It wasn't impossible.

* * *

There was an extra heavy workload which would keep him at the Yard hard at it until quite late, or that was what he had told his wife. She wouldn't expect him home for supper. He had started seeing Libby Howard on a regular basis, and in case anyone came looking for him urgently – grasses and such – he had left a number where he could be reached with the duty officer. He wasn't going to risk a repeat of the situation that had arisen when Micky Fielder had tried to get in touch with him.

Familiarity had soon crept into their love-making. There was none of the desperation of lovers with the need to perform or impress the other, no need to prove anything; there was little enough excitement because there was little enough pain. Libby seemed to like being tied up. She didn't struggle against her restraints. He wanted her to struggle, he wanted to see fear and uncertainty in her eyes, panic as she tried to break free and couldn't. He didn't know how far to go, how far without really hurting her and possibly getting himself into trouble. She wasn't a woman who he could pretend had resisted arrest, and there was no common consent to assault, no matter what the tone of the sexual relationship was. He saw another complaint looming as a result of what he was thinking of doing to her.

He rolled off her, feeling less than satisfied, and reached over and untied her wrists from the top of the bed. He noticed how the cord had cut into her wrists. He didn't look at her ankles, but suspected they bore the rope's impression too. She leaned forward and untied her feet and started to massage her ankles. He reached round to look at his watch on the night-table. It was time to think about leaving, but he made no move. She sat unmoving now with her trunk arched forward over her thighs. What was there to keep him? If he stayed and went again he would have to hurt her, and that might cause trouble. But her silence irritated him. He sensed she was dissatisfied, and the more he thought about it the more angry he became.

'What's the matter?' he said finally, breaking what he felt was an oppressive silence.

'Oh, nothing,' she said. 'Should there be?'

He reached out, and caught a handful of hair to pull her back down onto the bed. But she tensed her body to resist him. He pulled harder against the hair, feeling her arch her head forward, knowing she must be causing herself pain. He started to grow excited, when suddenly she yielded and fell back onto the bed.

'Fred! You're hurting me.'

Still he didn't let her go. He knew he should but the idea he had was mesmerizing him. Finally she cried out and broke his reverie.

There was a loud silence. He knew it really was time to make a move before this went any further, but still he didn't stir himself.

'Will Brian Finch go to prison?' she asked.

The question surprised him, and he remembered now that she had called him Brian in their love-making, and he felt angry.

'Are you kidding?' he said derisively. He hadn't told her that Finch had been picked up and subsequently released. 'He's going away for ever, I'd say.'

She didn't rise to this wind-up. Instead she said, 'Why do you always answer with a question, Fred? You nearly always do.'

'Do I . . .?' He knew he did, but despite the fact said,

'I don't think so, Libby.' And when she didn't give him an argument, 'It's a technique to draw out the person I'm interrogating – it wasn't a slip of the tongue.'

She raised her head off the pillow and looked at him. 'I'm not a suspect, am I?'

'I wouldn't be surprised,' he said. 'Everyone is at it some way or other. You've probably got something you could go for.' He smiled like he was only joking, and waited for an amused response from her. When he didn't get it he changed tack. He had no intention of letting her get away with her remark about Brian Finch.

'He'll go all right – Brian Finch. He's a villain. Prison's where all villains belong.' He paused, but there was no reaction from her. 'Have you seen him?'

'You said he was nicked –'

'You warned him I was looking for him.'

'I didn't. I swear.'

'You care a bit too much about that rascal still.' He grabbed her by the hair again. 'Don't you?'

'Fred, please.'

He released her reluctantly.

'Are you sure he was involved?'

'Why wouldn't I be? I nicked him.' He looked at her, reading more in her mask of apparent unconcern than he was sure she intended. His attitude hardened, and with it his gestures towards her became more intimate. He palmed her breasts, looking to hurt her rather than showing her affection. 'Even if that one wasn't down to him, others were. What difference does it make what he goes for? He's a professional thief. I'm a professional thiefcatcher. That simple. The idea is to stay out in front. Get a result. You sometimes have to do the job you're given in the only way it can be done. That sometimes means nicking villains for other people's villainy, if they won't come for their own. Even fitting them, when you know they're definitely at it.' He paused and looked at her, not ceasing in his painful caresses. He could see her eyes begin to water. 'What member of the public . . . I mean, all those who do nothing worse than fiddle their tax or cheat on their employers, what one of them wouldn't find that acceptable? After all, we do it in their name. It helps to keep a sort of balance. Can you imagine what life would be like if all those villains kept their liberty? Rubbish like Finch? Be fucking murder. No one's claiming chummy off the street – oh, it's been done, but what's the value? A possible conviction entered in the back of your diary, against a lot of aggravation when he complains or gets a result on appeal? But the Brian Finches of this world getting put away for ever, that makes a difference. That's a result.' He smiled, not liking himself for what he was doing, but not stopping because of it.

There was a long silence, during which Libby stared at the ceiling. Tears were spilling over her eyelids now. She made no sound, but he knew she was suffering.

'The wicked bastard deserves all he gets,' he said. He was squeezing her nipples hard between his finger and thumb.

At last Libby managed to say, 'Fred, stop, you're hurting me.'

'Yes,' was all he said. He would decide when to stop. Instead he reached down and placed one hand between her legs. She resisted him by keeping her legs closed, but he wasn't deterred. He climbed on top of her and forced her legs apart with his feet. She struggled harder to keep them closed, not saying a word. Suddenly he punched her. He didn't know where that came from, and it frightened him, but at the same time it excited him more than anything. He hit her again and again until at last there was no struggle left in her. Then he made love to her again. He wouldn't tie her up now. He had found something that excited him more.

Lately more and more of his time seemed to be spent in the snooker hall. It was a handy place to arrange meets, and more convenient than pubs where you only sat around and drank. Paradoxically, his missus was less concerned about his being at the hall than she was with him pubbing and clubbing. It was the knowledge of where he was that reassured her, and he felt no stab of conscience over deceiving her. He anticipated how sweet she'd be when he had it off and they were spending again. Maybe they'd go to Spain for a month or so, out of the way.

Stretching himself almost full length across the table, Jack Lynn played an awkward stroke on the green ball, barely touching it with the white. He slid back off the table and watched the ball trickle away into the bottom corner pocket.

Micky Fielder, who he was playing with, banged his cue on the floor in appreciation, even though that shot looked like costing him five pounds.

Lynn chalked his cue, and screwed the brown into a side pocket with a decisive stroke.

'Good hit, Jack.'

The man who spoke approached the table, waited while he lined up the shot.

Lynn glanced round at his brother-in-law. 'Tom. How's

it going?' he said, then turned to Fielder. 'You want to swallow it, Micky?'

'Do I fuck! You think you can make those three?'

The blue, pink and black balls were left on the table, but Lynn was about five points in front.

'Couldn't do us a favour Saturday, Jack, could you?' Tom asked. 'Do my minicabbing for me. I got a wedding to go to.'

'As it happens, I can't, Tom,' he said, chalking his cue again. 'I got something planned myself Saturday.' He immediately wondered if saying that was wise, but decided that his brother-in-law wasn't likely to mention it to Dolly. He glanced at Micky Fielder who sat against the edge of the adjacent table, kicking the base of his cue with his pointed-toed boots, not interested in the conversation. 'Micky'll help you out. He was looking for a bit of work.'

'That's too much like fucking work!' Fielder said. 'Anyway I done my brief, didn't I.'

Lynn hadn't considered him when he had said he was looking for some work. He didn't see him as a blagger.

''S not a problem. I'll get someone.' Tom waited while he lined his shot. 'S just that Dolly said you was thinking about looking for a bit of regular work.'

Lynn didn't make the blue, but snookered Fielder behind the black. 'I was thinking about it, Tom, to be perfectly honest.' He wondered about taking the cabbing for Saturday night as an alibi. 'I might be able to do it. Grimme a bell later in the week.'

'Oh good. I'll do that. Gotta shoot. One to pick up.'

'Good luck, Tom.' He watched him greet Bobby Shaw, who came through the tables with another man.

'No wonder you're such a fucking degenerate,' Shaw said. 'You're always in here, 'what I hear.'

'Gotta get my spends somehow, son.'

He glanced up and saw he had brought a second man, who was fat and soft-looking, and wore tinted glasses. Lynn didn't know him but winked as if they were sharing a joke.

'You fit, are you?' Shaw asked.

'Yeah, just let me nick a jack's here first.'

Shaw stooped to look under the hood as Fielder played his stroke, putting a snooker on the pink. 'Hello, Micky. Had it off lately?'

'Scratching's all.' Fielder walked round the table and joined Shaw. 'Not much about, is there?'

'Not a lot,' Shaw agreed. He didn't introduce his mate.

Playing his shot carefully, Lynn not only got the blue out of snooker but potted it as well. It was a difficult shot.

'Fuck me!' Fielder said.

With a triumphant smile, Lynn said, 'Just did, Micky. Didn't I just.'

Fielder pulled out his money, peeled off a fiver and threw it on the table. 'You did well there, son,' he said.

'I was lucky,' Lynn said mockingly. 'See you around, Micky.'

Fielder watched them start out, knowing instinctively that this was the team Lynn was going blagging with down at Catford dogtrack. He would've liked to have had the front to follow them, but didn't dare. He knew he had to get some more information on them, his own liberty depended on it, and nothing was more important. Punting around their familiar haunts and talking to some of the faces they knew, buying them a few drinks, would do it, he decided. The blag having advanced as far as it had, there would be more than enough rumours flying around, there always were.

The first two stops after the hall were to pubs where he saw one or two people he knew. The word was that Jack Lynn was doing a bit of work. That was the word on other lips when he ducked into the after-hours drinker in Tottenham Court Road.

He stood at the bar drinking on his own for about ten minutes when a man who had been playing cards came and joined him.

He was in his mid-fifties. He had been a villain and a good 'un, but had now more or less retired and ran a flowerstall.

'Getting a living, Micky, are you?' he asked, sliding his well-padded rump onto the bar stool.

'Nothing worth a toss,' Fielder complained. 'Got hold of a bit the other night, didn't come to fuck all. Why, you got something in mind?'

The man shook his head. 'Thought perhaps you could put me into something.'

'Some chance! Maybe me and you ought to see about making one. A little taste for your retirement, Ronnie.'

'Be handy. You got something in mind?'

Neither of them were blaggers, and Fielder knew that each was kidding the other.

'Not really. People whisper in your ear about things. You know how it is, Ronnie. But it's stuff you've got to have a little firm for.' He emptied his glass and set it back on the bar, but didn't signal the barmaid. 'I heard Jack Lynn was putting one together. D'he get all the help he needs?'

'I'd say so. I wouldn't have thought that was in

your line, Micky. I heard they were going shootered up.'

''S that right?' He was surprised. He'd heard nothing about guns. 'I wouldn't have none of that. But I gotta get me bit of Christmas money from somewhere. What's that, scotch you're drinking, Ronnie?'

'Cheers.' Ronnie finished his drink.

Fielder signalled to the barmaid. A couple of drinks with this man and he'd get every bit of information he had about Jack Lynn and his blag.

Underground train meets with the grass were more convenient but not as entertaining, he decided as he watched leggy fourteen-year-old schoolgirls prancing around at netball in the court across from where he was sitting on the park seat with Micky Fielder. The grass couldn't have known the game would be in progress, but perhaps he had, and this amounted to a gesture of goodwill for dragging him down to Deptford to spring him the other day. The girls were all in blue shorts and white blouses. One team wore green bands, the other red. All gave value for money, even the teacher who charged around with them.

Pale sunlight filtered through the trees, making sitting in the cold park possible, and without attracting attention. But casting his eyes around at some of the people on the benches positioned beyond the perimeter fence, he decided some were definitely suspect, and would probably have sat there in a gale-force snowstorm for such a spectacle.

'It's Saturday, guv. Last race, just after the finish,' Fielder said.

The information brought Pyle out of his reverie. Their preliminary banter about the merits of those schoolgirls was done with. He looked at the grass.

'That's when it's going off. That's what I heard anyway.'

'Saturday? That's definite, Micky, is it?'

'You know me, guv.' Fielder laughed. 'I give it as straight as I get it, I don't tart it up. They didn't invite me to make it with them.'

'That's 'cos you're a grass, Micky,' Pyle said. But Fielder clearly didn't like the joke. 'Who's involved apart from Lynn?'

'The only other name I got so far was Bobby Shaw.'

'Shaw?' The name was meaningless. 'What's down to him? Anything?'

'He's a violence specialist. He's done some for GBH.'

'About right.' Pyle nodded, preferring to think the worst of Lynn and his helpers, for then, putting them away would help justify whatever means it took.

'I heard they were going in with shooters . . . What I heard.'

'That's not surprising, Micky.'

Pyle looked away at the girls. One of them leaped up, putting the ball neatly and easily in the net, her blouse parting from her waistband with the jump, showing her bare midriff. The teacher blew the whistle and the two teams came back to the line. A game, well ordered, with all the players obeying the rules. Running parallel in his thoughts was the robbery planned to take place at Catford. It was likely to be anything but well ordered.

Ignoring the statement about the guns, he said, 'Look at that, will you?' as he watched the girl tuck her blouse into her skirt as she walked back to the line. 'It's enough to get you nicked.'

Fielder chuckled. 'I'd take a chance, guv.'

'All the time you've got someone to pull you out of trouble.'

There was a pause. The DI turned to the grass with a steady, measured look. 'How you fixed, Micky?'

Invariably such a question seemed to cause the informer some embarrassment. It was as if he looked on their relationship as that of equals, or two friends, and so questions of payment spoilt things.

'Ain't too clever, guv. That filth who felt m' collar nicked most of what I had – thought I'd be able to borrow some . . .'

Reaching into his coat pocket, Pyle produced five neatly folded twenty pound notes, which he gave to Fielder. ''S only a oner, Micky. If we have it off down at Catford, we get to split a nice earner from the insurance.'

'Be handy.'

'Give us a shout if you need another taste.' He could get him another hundred pounds from the Fund without much trouble. For a moment or two he continued to watch the girls leaping around, then nodded to himself. 'Think you're right, son. Probably would be worth getting nicked for.' He nodded again. 'Definitely going in with shooters, are they?'

''S what I heard. You know.'

'Still, that's the way it goes. You did well, Micky. Just mind how you go, all right?' He meant it.

'I'll give you a bell if I hear anything else,' the grass said as he rose from the bench. 'Don't get your collar felt here, will you?'

'Take care, son.'

Pyle watched as the grass slithered away along the path, nervously adjusting his leather coat on his shoulders.

No further information on the proposed blag was forthcoming from either of his grasses. No more was really necessary for the Squad to take action, but it would have been useful to know exactly how many villains were involved and exactly who they were. Extensive searches, plus some speculation about the known associates of both Bobby Shaw and Jack Lynn, had given the police little more than possible suspects.

Detectives from Pyle's squad, and some from the current night-duty squad, mustered in the DCIs' room. That was by consensus rather than design – Pyle had been in the office discussing the blag with DCI Simmons and DS Lethridge, when other detectives began drifting in. There was no point in moving the briefing elsewhere.

With the sixteen detectives present, half of whom were armed, Simmons was saying, 'They're planning the blag for after the last race. That means they have to wait for the money to be collected from around the track. That's what we reckon will happen – unless they plan to shut the Tote and not pay out on the last race and scoop up all the money – that would cause them too much attention. The bad lads will try and blag all the takings once they've collected in from all the different Tote offices around the track, and then slip away in the crowd. As we don't know the entire team this might present a few problems. Unfortunately chummy doesn't go around with blagger written on his shirt any more,' he added with a grin. 'Fred?'

'Right,' Pyle said, standing off the edge of a desk. 'Well, as most of you already know, we only marked Lynn and Bobby Shaw. Their CRO photos are well out of date, and the ones Criminal Intelligence supplied aren't much better. There could be as many as four more in the team, and probably are. My snout didn't know . . .'

'They are definitely using shooters, guv?' a DC asked.

'I wouldn't bet against it,' Pyle said.

When detectives went after villains without foreknowledge of their being armed they thought little about steaming in and making arrests. Having information that the blaggers would be armed dredged up thoughts he would prefer not to think, and knew everyone in the room felt the same.

Simmons said, 'Remember what dogtracks are like on a Saturday night. There'll be lots of people about. A lot of pushing and shoving. I don't need to warn you about how much paperwork will be involved if one of you shoots a bystander. Shoot a villain with a gun in his hand, if you have to shoot anyone.' Shooting an innocent member of the public was something most of them feared would one day happen to them, and so were often relieved when the Armed Response Unit was called in. They were uniformed branch and couldn't often be used in these circumstances.

With a glance at the DCI, Pyle resumed the briefing.

'Blagging the money from the office here or from Securicor when it's collected means these exits here are their only way out.' He pointed to the blackboard diagram that had been brought from the DIs' office. 'They open these gates here to get the punters away quickly. Securicor come in the same way. Up this ramp and parks on the brow. From there two of the guards walk down to the main office. That might be a good place for them to try and have it, as they return.'

'There are windows on the back of that building, guv,' a DC put in. 'They open onto that service road. They could stick the bags through to someone on the outside.'

'Be handy, if they do. That would probably mean them sticking their guns out too. That would give you a nice target, Eric, if we get that lucky.'

'You can never tell, guv,' Lethridge said.

'Jack. Your team will be in this enclosure here,' he told DS Barcy, indicating his diagram. 'Ted and Alan, here and here,' he informed the two DCs from the night-duty squad. 'If you spot them, don't challenge them until they've got the money, otherwise we're going to wind up with fuck all for our trouble. Let them get what they're there for. Let's nick them bang to rights.' He paused and considered the assembly. They still looked too much like detectives to him, despite being dressed in a variety of styles to enable them to blend unobtrusively with Saturday-night punters at Catford.

'They're only old mugs,' he said. 'Should be a doddle, with a bit of luck.' He glanced at Simmons, expecting him to add something. He didn't. 'Any questions?'

The silence that followed was punctuated by telephones ringing in other offices. One was persistent, but no one answered it. There was tension in the room, a sense of apprehension. Most of the detectives had the same anxiety in mind, and none wanted to raise it and so acknowledge their fears.

Finally DC Jenkins said, 'All right if I shoot off home now, guv? My mother-in-law's coming over.'

The tension was broken. People laughed at that more than it was worth.

'And I'd better not go, guv,' another said. 'I've got one to meet.'

'I suppose we could send Mr Lynn a note asking him to surrender himself here after they've had it off,' Pyle said. The atmosphere was becoming more relaxed.

'Well, that's it, then,' DCI Simmons said. 'Good luck.'

The car park at Catford dogtrack quickly filled to capacity, and the Squad had to get their cars in position early. They had six cars there in all, with two parked outside in the road which ran alongside Catford Bridge Station. It was the only vehicular exit from the greyhound racetrack. They had a long and tedious wait, one during which Pyle's thoughts twice turned to the possibility of getting shot. The tedium was relieved occasionally by him letting detectives slip into the stadium to have a bet or a drink at the bar. He shouldn't have allowed that but knew that relaxed detectives were of more use than those tensed and like a spring ready to snap. He made sure they were all back in their correct positions long before the last race.

The detectives became expectant as the final race approached, as if they had each bet their all on it. In a matter of minutes it was over, but nothing was expected to happen immediately. They were positioned close enough to both the main exit and the main Tote office to know at once when the blag went off. The stadium quickly began to empty, along with the car park, where utter confusion reigned, and no one seemed willing to give an inch. Pyle was sitting in his car watching this momentary madness, wondering what was happening in the stadium. They couldn't risk using their radios in case the blaggers were listening in, but he was impatient to know what the position was.

'Go and see what the fuck's happening in there, Rog',' he told the DC who was in the car with him. He watched him climb out and disappear in the direction of the stadium. 'I've a feeling this is going to be a rubout,' he commented to his driver without inviting any response.

Despite coming to that conclusion he felt relaxed and easy, the effect of the beta-blockers he had taken. The minutes ticked away no faster when he checked his watch. It wouldn't be the first time that a blag he had waited for had proved a non-starter, but it would be disappointing, nonetheless. What the basis was for those doubts he had about this one not going he couldn't say. The optimum moment for the blaggers to make their move hadn't arrived, but still those doubts persisted. It could be that Micky Fielder had got one or two details wrong, he reasoned. Grasses weren't infallible. He would wait until there was no doubt at all about this not going off before he abandoned it.

The car park continued to empty, the process becoming less tortuous as the number of cars thinned out. Other punters left on foot, some with a bounce in their step, others with a sense of resignation. He watched them go, puzzling at what they found here week after week. He wasn't a gambler himself, not on anything as random as a dog chasing a mechanical hare.

After a while the DC returned to the car.

'Nothing much going on up there, guv,' he said at the open window. 'No one's seen anything.'

Pyle nodded. 'The money's still up in the office. Go and find DS Lethridge, check with him, Rog'.'

Fifteen cars now remained in the car park, four of them belonging to the Squad. Possibly some of the others had been put there by blaggers, but more likely they belonged to people working in the stadium. The numbers and descriptions were noted and would get checked as a matter of routine.

When a Jaguar XJ6 came across the car park and through the main gates to the stadium, Pyle suddenly tensed. This was the first thing to look like anything.

He reached inside his coat and touched the gun that rested in its holster, as two men climbed out of the car at the brow of the service road. He had had a good result in his last gun examination – such results had no bearing at all when confronted with an armed blagger.

The two men from the Jaguar weren't part of Jack Lynn's firm but some kind of help for an old punter who they brought to the car in his wheelchair. One of them lifted him into the front seat, while the other folded the chair into the boot. The car drove away, passing the security truck as it came into the stadium.

Two guards armed with nightsticks climbed out and disappeared from sight. They were gone for seven minutes. Those minutes ticked by slowly indeed. The guards finally reappeared, dropped the money containers into the hatch at the rear of the truck, then climbed back into the cab and drove away. Nothing happened.

That only left the Squad on watch.

DS Lethridge approached and leaned down to the car window.

'Fucking waste of time,' Pyle said. 'Unless that was

chummy,' nodding in the direction of the departing truck.

'Think they tumbled us, Fred?'

He shrugged, unconcerned. 'We didn't advertise . . . Fuck it!' The words burst out of him and his anger vanished with them. 'Fucking rubout.' There was no question as far as he was concerned that a crime had been prevented, but that wasn't what his being a policeman was about. 'My snout could've got the day wrong. Maybe it'll go next week.' That thought cheered him briefly. 'What pisses me off is Jack Lynn's a villain who's been at it too long. He is well overdue. We've given this too much attention to let him keep his liberty, Eric. He ought to be behind bars; we know it, and so does he.' It was nothing personal as far as he was concerned, just a matter of principle; the villain had fallen within his field of interest and so it became his turn. 'If this doesn't go off, Eric, we might have to look elsewhere for Lynn. Maybe even find something for him.'

The DS looked at him, then glanced at his driver, who was staring through the windscreen. He didn't say anything, but Pyle knew he wouldn't object to the proposed fit-up.

'Checks and balances,' he said. 'Checks and balances, son. He is overdue.' He thought about that, then nodded to himself. 'Get the lads back, Eric, I'll buy them a drink.' On the route back to the yard he knew of an after-hours drinking club where they could drown their disappointment.

Monday morning brought slanting, icy rain that was close to snow. It helped no one's problems, apart from maybe the water companies. It didn't look as though it would stop. Few people chose to be outside on such a December day and Fred Pyle was no exception, even though the alternative was to sit at his desk bending to his paperwork. He stepped into the DCI's office with the preliminary report he had been given to write on another non-result they had had on a robbery. His report currently ran to sixty pages. By the time Simmons rewrote it, adding further negative details from other sources, all of which amounted to justifying why they hadn't arrested anyone or recovered the money, the report would probably go to two hundred pages.

'Thanks, Fred,' Simmons said without looking up. 'Think they tumbled you?'

Pyle knew he was referring to Saturday night.

'I wouldn't have thought so. How can you tell? I had a word with my snout. He reckons he might have got the day mixed up.' He shrugged. 'You know what they're like.' It was convenient for him at that moment to view all grasses as unreliable.

The DCI stopped typing. 'I'd like to see them go for something. What about Harding?'

'Didn't come through, did he?'

There was a pause. The two detectives looked at one

another. Pyle knew this man's thoughts. He was worried about Harding's being loose.

'Have another go at him. You can't tell with villains like that. Put a bit more pressure on him. If he's not interested in helping . . .' The DCI raised his eyebrows. 'It's about time we had him back anyway, a villain as active as that. Know what I mean, Fred?'

He knew exactly what his governor meant.

The rain had stopped by the time he had organized part of his squad to come and look for Clifford Harding. Oily water lay around the uneven tarmac surface of the battlefield-like community playground. Toddlers in coloured wellington boots skimmed through puddles, risking the wrath of parents who had been dragged there on that day. One threw a stone, splashing Pyle as he came through the gate.

'Don't do that, there's a good girl,' he said, and kept walking, unsure whether she was going to cry or splash him again.

Worry was evident on Harding's face when he looked up and saw him. His eyes darted about as if seeking a way out. There was none. Pyle was between him and the gate, and at the hole in the fence another detective waited. Others were positioned beyond the fence.

''S nice life, Clifford, isn't it?' he said, resting against the damp makeshift seat, where Harding sat with his second-youngest son. 'Sitting here watching over your kids, not a thing in the world to worry about, other than whether or not it's going to rain again.'

'How d'you know I was here?' Harding wanted to know.

'Your old lady grassed you, son. When I called at the house. How old's he?' he asked, indicating the boy.

'Going on four. 'In't you, Russ?' the father said. His son didn't comment but looked at Pyle, who avoided his eyes. 'Go and play with Darren, Russ, there's a good boy.'

He was reluctant to go. 'You come, Dad,' he said.

'In a little while. I gotta have a talk. Go on.' He pushed the boy away and watched him join his brother.

'Tragic. That's what it is, Clifford. Fucking tragic. I mean, he's going to be grown up, be a man, 'fore he even gets a proper chance to know you.'

'What?' Harding seemed surprised.

'Why do you think I'm here, to pass the time of day?'

'Don't talk like that, for Christsake . . .'

Pyle sighed expansively. 'A fact of life. You've got to go away, son. A tasty fifteen years, unless I'm seriously mistaken.' He thought about that. 'Yeah, about right. You didn't do that business for me.'

Harding glanced about the playground like he was thinking of running.

'You knew from the start what you were letting yourself in for, Clifford, but you were hoping that even if you didn't produce the goods – which you haven't – this moment somehow wouldn't arrive. Now it has, son. I know the score.'

'I'm supposed to be seeing a man tonight,' Harding tried.

Pyle shook his head. 'Sounds like nonsense to me, Clifford. Like you're offering me the prick. As if I'm silly enough to take that again!'

'That's straight – it is. It is. This fella's been putting himself about, getting something for me.'

'I haven't seen any advance on the information you had previously given me about Jack Lynn. What you got to support this claim with? You must think I'm a fuckwit or something. You've been too busy to get my info'. Instead you been putting yourself about and putting one of your own blags together . . .'

'Fuck off, guv. I've been clubbing and pubbing, trying to help you nick Jack Lynn . . .'

'A little blag of your own's what I heard. A supermarket out at Sydenham.' That was a rumour that Criminal Intelligence had passed on, but one that was going to cost Harding his liberty, regardless of whether or not he helped him out.

Harding's glance flashed desperately around the playground. Maybe he was hoping the other detectives had dematerialized.

Anticipating what he had in mind, Pyle shook his head, warning him not to try. 'Let's do it quietly, Cliff, and we won't alarm the kids. We'll get a policewoman to take them back to their Mum.'

Those words more than any others seemed to bring home to him the tragedy of the situation. Harding was suddenly struggling against tears as he became briefly involved with his son, who had wandered back to join him.

'Come on, Russ, mate. It's time to go home. See Mum. Go and get the others.' He looked round at Pyle who had risen in anticipation of trouble. 'I don't want to go, guv. I really don't.'

Pyle nodded. ''Course you don't, son,' he said reasonably. 'And I'd sooner have Jack Lynn.'

'He was well closed up. You think I didn't try?'

'Like I said, I think you were too busy on that one out at Sydenham.' He paused and looked at the villain. 'There is another way to help, son.' He paused again. 'Lynn put one up to you, Cliff, didn't he?' he suggested, laying a new foundation to put Jack Lynn away.

Harding waited, giving the appearance of being uncertain.

'What one was that, guv?'

With a faint smile Pyle said, 'Don't worry, I'll find something for him. Something he'll go for with a little help from you. 'S up to you, son. That's what gets you your liberty.'

Uncertainty turned to a stricken look on Harding's face. He hesitated for a long while. So long that Pyle thought he was going to turn him down. But finally he nodded, agreeing to what was suggested. Clearly his liberty was still more important to him than Jack Lynn's.

'About right,' Pyle said.

Leaving Harding to gather up his children, he walked across the playground, smiling to himself. He would take Harding in for now but wouldn't charge him yet. Instead he would keep him dangling and full of anxiety, until he found something for Lynn which Harding would appear to have put up to him.

Eric Lethridge came round the perimeter fence and waited.

'He's not a problem, Eric. He wants his liberty.'

The DS looked at him, but said nothing.

'Checks and balances, Eric,' he said, suddenly feeling a need to justify himself. 'Putting Lynn away will be one to us. Won't it just. He'll be well and truly fitted.' He thought about this and then nodded to himself. 'He'll go all right.'

'What about Harding?' Lethridge asked.

'I can't see a jury letting him walk – when we eventually get him to court,' he said without compunction.

The lock-up garages in Kidbroke weren't particularly busy at that time of the morning. Their busiest time there, he knew from recent experience, was between seven and nine, when people collected cars and vans for work. A number of small businesses were run from these lock-ups, and the loading up of gear by jobbing builders went on then. People had come and gone without noticing him parked in the road across from the service entrance. The prolonged inactivity was boring, he found, and sitting there meant a struggle against sleep, despite the cold and damp inside the van. He couldn't have the heater on as it meant running the engine and that would have attracted attention to himself.

Detective Constable Matthew Hill worked in Criminal Intelligence, and was alternating this observation detail with another DC on a twelve-hour shift. It was a long shift, as they were shorthanded in the department, and something he had to put up with. Reaching across to the seat next to him, he picked up the video camera there and checked it again, making sure it was ready to shoot. He had done that several times since he had come on at six o'clock this morning. The Sony 8mm camcorder was ready to run with a new battery; all he needed was something to shoot. But he had serious doubts about anyone showing up, having sensed a lack of interest in this job on his governor's part. Had DI McHale really believed this one a goer, he was sure he would have somehow found the men for a proper observation. He slid the camera back onto the seat and pulled his anorak closely about himself, paying scant attention to the Ford Escort XR3i that turned into the street and came towards him. The car made a right-hand signal, and he assumed it was turning onto the service road. Instead it pulled into the kerb and parked. His interest slowly uncurled like a cat from a sleep, and he wondered about the two men in the car, especially as they didn't get out. They sat in the front and looked around as they waited. It looked as though they were checking the street, so he slipped lower in his seat and reached for the camcorder, in case this was something. Even if it wasn't, it might relieve his boredom.

Satisfied at last that they hadn't been followed and weren't being watched, Cole Coleman signalled to Philip Hayes and climbed out of the XR3i. He carefully locked the doors, before starting along the service road to the lock-up garages. His nervous glances swept the street but he saw little, and nothing out of the ordinary. The only thought that occurred to him on taking in the parked van was that with its passenger window left open it would be an easy one to nick. Another time he might have investigated the possibility of there being anything inside worth nicking.

Inside two knocked-into-one garages was a Renault 21 estate car and a 2-litre Cavalier estate, each with a key and a spare hanging from the ignition, the petrol tanks full. Both had been reasonably well rung for the short journeys they'd be used for; he would have no quarrel with driving either one. When he drove out the Cavalier, and Hayes took the Renault, the garages were left starkly bare. There wasn't so much as a rag or a cigarette packet left to identify anyone by later. John Tully had told him time and again to be careful about such things. He liked working with Tully, he was always careful.

Coleman led the way, nosing the Cavalier out of the service road and turning towards Well Hall Road, glancing in his rear-view mirror to make sure Hayes was following. He noticed the van start now, but didn't think anything about it as he quickly made a turn-off, more concerned that Hayes shouldn't lose him.

There seemed to be a lot of traffic lights along his chosen route and almost every one of them was against him. If there was one more red light on this street the job would be fucked – the thought popped into his head at random and he almost went through the next red light. Only the care taken by John Tully and the fear of letting him down made him set aside his anxiety.

There was a church in Brampton Road, and Hayes negotiated the silver-grey Renault into a gap outside it like he was one of the congregation. The thought of Hayes ever going to church made Coleman smile. Being the getaway driver, he didn't know what alternative there was as there weren't any other spaces available. He was about to say something but didn't know what his objection was, so instead he watched as Hayes climbed out, locked the door, and walked to the back of the car and put one of the ignition keys in the petrol-filler housing. It was a precaution. Losing the ignition key happened at times during blags.

'All right, Cole?' Hayes said as he climbed in next to him.

'Yeah, that'll do, son.'

Coleman glanced in the rear-view mirror, then slipped

the car into gear. He took pride in how he glided it away, like he had been born at the controls.

The next stop was at a second-hand dealer's near Woolwich dockyard, where they collected an old, heavy gas stove that Tully had paid for a few days earlier. The burners were broken and it was caked with grease. The dealer probably thought he had a right result nicking twenty-five pounds for it, which was a lot more than its scrap-metal value, Coleman decided.

'You'll have a nice cooker there, you clean it up, m' ol' bruv,' the dealer commented as he watched them lift it into the back of the car.

Coleman was about to put up a story about why it was being bought, but was sure the dealer couldn't have cared less. He simply grunted, and they were off again. He was conscious of the time, as Tully had made timing his responsibility. He cursed loudly at the number of traffic jams along Plumstead Road, and at other drivers who delayed him by their indecisiveness.

Tully and Benny Isaacs were waiting for them where they had agreed at a bus stop on Plumstead High Street. Isaacs was carrying a large gripbag. Both men had on an excess of clothes, overcoats, overalls, hats, none of which looked out of place on this cold, damp morning. The clothes weren't simply to keep them warm, but to create a disguise: the bulk considerably altered their appearance. Among the hats they had with them was a ski-cap, a flying helmet, a crash helmet and visor. These were the headpieces they were going to wear along with scarves on the actual blag, as they hid their faces without being too obvious.

'All right?' Tully inquired as he climbed into the car.

''S been a doddle so far,' Coleman replied. ''In't, Phil?'

van, which, along with the car that subsequently ran into the new gas stove, achieved nothing but a traffic jam.

Surprise and confusion assaulted John Tully, stopping him thinking clearly over what to do about the presence of the CID. If there was anything he could do, these feelings were mixed with elation at having blagged the Gas Board money and got clear, but that feeling was shortlived as they sped away towards Plumstead High Street. The scream of police sirens filled the air; one, then two, police cars; then a third was heard approaching. They seemed to be coming from the same direction, and he wondered how they were on them so quickly, whether they had been grassed; yet still no thought came about how to escape their worsening predicament. The police car had far more acceleration than the Cavalier with the four of them in it, and so was closing the gap between them with ease.

He glanced round at Benny Isaacs who was in the back of the estate car. The thought that entered his head then must have flown right into Isaacs', as he knocked out the rear window and poked the short nose of the shotgun through. He knew this wasn't an idle threat on his part to try and make the police keep their distance. The Bill had to be stopped if they were to get away. Isaacs fired without warning, causing the police vehicle to swerve off course and hit a parked van and stop. As their car swept on along Bostall Hill so a second police car drew up alongside the first to check that the occupants were all right. The shot probably hadn't even reached the car.

The Cavalier skidded to a halt alongside the changeover car, startling Tully. 'What the fuck you doing,' he screamed – 'what's the point in changing cars with the police up our daily?' But Coleman was only a good driver, he couldn't think on his feet. It was as if he was programmed to head for the changeover car regardless of whatever else happened. Had they stayed in the first car they might have put extra distance between themselves and the police.

He followed the other three out of the Cavalier with their guns and cases, shedding some of their clothing as they went. He and Hayes each threw off a coat and the crash helmet and flying hat. Panic surged through him at the delay which ensued while Coleman was getting the door of the Renault open. The sense of panic was suddenly apparent in everyone as a third police car nosed out of a side turning.

'Come on, Cole! For fuck sake!' Isaacs said, and crashed a side window with the butt of his shotgun.

Suddenly the doors were open and they were in the car, the engine roaring with life. Tully pushed his shotgun through the window to warn off the police as they crept steadily toward them. The Renault accelerated away north along Brampton Road without slowing when it took a left fork into Longleigh Lane, weaving crazily in and out of traffic. The sound of police sirens was everywhere.

There were more than the three police cars they had so far seen. Just how many there were Tully couldn't work out, but he knew that more and more of them would be pouring into the area and there they were now heading back in their direction. He wondered what the fuck Cole was doing, While he himself was running on adrenalin and a self-preserving reflex. He wouldn't give up trying to save himself. He would want to press on regardlessly, relentlessly, even if driven into a corner. Still he would not give up until he was taken after a struggle, and that deep, deep instinct for survival had been wrestled with him to the ground, cuffed and beaten out of him.

The progress of another police car was heard in the adjacent street, speeding in on them. How far their car was ahead of the police it was impossible to say. Cole Coleman, though, pulled dangerously out of the junction into Bostall Hill Road. Glancing round, Tully saw there was almost a collision between police cars, as others coming up behind tried the same trick. He wanted to smile but didn't. He wanted to slap Cole Coleman on the back but couldn't.

The chase reached speeds of ninety miles an hour along this wide stretch of the A206, and Tully wasn't sure if the police cars were chasing them or each other simply to be out in front, as one overtook another and was itself overtaken.

Judging the traffic with computer precision, Coleman braked hard then desperately swung the car through the oncoming vehicles and into West Heath Road, a turning that brought them back to Brampton Road. He did it almost without losing any forward momentum.

'This is fucking murder,' Tully said. He was soaked with sweat and could see himself ending up through the windscreen or concertinaed in a head-on cannon. He wasn't wearing a seatbelt, he thought as he wrenched round to check through the rear window what progress the police were making.

'We're all gonna wind up nicked!' Hayes said.

'I'll shoot the fuckers first,' Isaacs informed him.

Tension in the car brought them to the edge of hysteria, almost anything could tip them over. Staying in control wasn't easy. He wasn't sure, but he might have shat himself.

'We gotta get rid of this car,' Coleman said. 'Every Old Bill south of the Water'll have its description.'

Suddenly the opportunity presented itself, and Tully felt elated that he was able to recognize it.

'There!' he shouted. 'We'll have that.'

A Volvo 740 up ahead was pulling out of a line of parked cars, and stopped to let them pass.

Coleman stood on the brake pedal, at the same time wrenching up the handbrake and locking the back wheels, putting the car into a neat spin on the damp surface. The Renault slewed across the road and came to a halt with its radiator buried in the side of a parked car, and partially blocked the road. The driver of the Volvo sat and stared at this like he wasn't sure what he'd seen. He remained unmoving right up to the point when Isaacs dragged him out of the driving seat and Coleman took his place.

The entire hijacking could have taken less than a minute, Tully decided, but it was long enough for a police car to have come up on them. Isaacs fired his shotgun at the car from the Volvo as they sped away. Cole Coleman seemed to go to pieces now, like his programmed getaway was completely out of sync, and was simply waiting for instructions, while merely keeping the car in forward motion at the greatest possible speed. Tully saw the glances he kept taking in his direction and knew he was expecting him to tell him what to do. Finally he did.

‘Do a left,’ he shouted above the roar of the car’s engine. There was no left turn at that section of the road and the order merely confused Coleman. ‘Right, you berk! I mean right.’

‘Fucking well say what you mean, for fuck sake,’ Coleman screamed back and he swung the car tightly into the turning, cannoning off a parked car.

‘You’re gonna kill us all, you mad fucker,’ Hayes said.

‘You fucking well drive, then!’

The hijacked Volvo squealed out of the side turning onto the dual carriageway of Harrow Manorway. The air was thick with the wail of police klaxons and exhaust.

Traffic was badly congested, but despite this Cole Coleman found it from somewhere and burned rubber, employing all his skills as a getaway driver. He wove in and out of vehicles, slicing through every gap that presented itself; even spaces that suggested only motorbike couriers might pass he forced the car into, rarely touching the brakes. But it was all for nothing, it seemed. Three police cars stayed close on their tail by simply following the swath their car cut through the traffic. Suddenly a fourth police car roared out of a junction ahead of them and tried to cut them off. But Coleman went straight through the red lights at the junction, swerving at a violent angle to avoid some crossing traffic, and mounted the pavement. Tully closed his eyes with the image of an old woman behind the lids. He felt no bump, but didn’t know how Coleman avoided her as he shot back onto the road into the nearside lane of vehicles. Traffic on the junction halted at the sound of the sirens and police cars swarmed through, closing on them again. Isaac gave them both barrels from his shotgun. Leadshot pattered harmlessly against the windscreen of the first police car, but the shock of it cause the driver to brake.

There was a heavy traffic tailback from the roundabout ahead, made immediately worse by a police sherpa van that must have approached along one of the adjacent roads and gone into the roundabout against the traffic in order to block their exit. Tully glanced at Coleman, knowing he had no special driving magic for getting them out of that traffic jam. They were boxed in on the offside lane by a crash-barrier fence. He tried. He mounted the kerb of the central island between the roadway and the fence and drove towards the roundabout where the police van loaded with the Bill was waiting for them.

'Fuck I!' Hayes said. 'We got no chance there.'

'Have it over the fence,' Tully said.

Coleman slammed the Volvo to a halt and the four of them leapt out, taking with them their guns and the two money sacks. Tully led the way over the barrier while Isaacs covered their retreat from the oncoming policemen, some of whom were out of their cars and running through the stationary traffic. Isaacs fired at them, scattering them before scrambling over the fence himself.

Traffic on the southbound carriageway was relatively free-moving and, with the help of Coleman, Tully immediately set about hijacking two vehicles. 'We'll have a better chance of getting away, 'we split,' he shouted.

The first car they dragged was a Granada Scorpio. It went without a hitch. Tully levelled the shotgun and the driver stopped immediately. Coleman dragged him out and clambered in, Hayes straight after him. The thought crossed Tully's mind that maybe he should go too and leave Isaacs. But he decided against it. Benny Isaacs was a good 'un, who deserved better.

Tully turned his attention to finding his getaway car, but the driver of the one he levelled his shotgun at refused to stop. The next he tried, a Toyota, he gave the driver no opportunity to run but opened fire as the car came towards him. The driver slammed on the brakes. Tully wrenched open the door and dragged out the driver. From the driving seat Tully leaned out of the window with his shotgun to cover Isaacs as he clambered in.

Back along the road, policemen had climbed the barrier and were flagging down a lorry which they got to slew across the road. But it wasn't big enough to block the whole carriageway. Tully anticipated what was going to happen, but was in no mood to stop for the policeman who tried to plug the gap between the end of the lorry and the central barrier. The policeman bounced off the front of the Toyota as it ploughed through the gap and accelerated away.

It raced on across the roundabout at Yarton Way as two police cars forced their way through the traffic that had frozen. Tully made a fast exit from the roundabout at the end of the dual carriageway and a wide V-turn on to Abbey Road. His driving skills under pressure were less than Coleman's. Making a right turn to go down New Road and through the park, he cannoned off stationary vehicles like someone drunk; then making a fast left before reaching the main junction wasn't much better. When he eventually reached Woolwich Road and tried to go right into Bedonwell Road he misjudged the turn completely and, mounting the kerb, tore out the side of the car on a lamp standard, then smacked into another car. Both he and Isaacs were dazed, but unharmed. The car engine had cut out and he didn't attempt to restart it. All he was aware of then was the wail of police sirens. They were everywhere and he knew he had to abandon this car. Isaacs shouted at him and ran off along the road. He watched him go, shedding clothing as he went and wrapping the shotgun in it.

Finally stirring himself as his basic survival mechanism surfaced through the fog, Tully took both his sack and the shotgun and ran. He wasn't sure which direction he was going in, but fled into the grounds of a Health Authority clinic, which was housed in a big, rambling, dirty-brick building. Prams and pushchairs were lined up outside. Glancing behind, he was aware that policemen from the first two cars to arrive were giving chase on foot. He felt an irrational sense of injustice that he should be the only one being chased – he assumed the others had got clear away. He turned back, firing his shotgun at the approaching policemen, causing them to scatter. The sack banged against his side as he ran, but he was loath to ditch it. As he turned by some bushes he pushed the money sack under damp leaves that had been swept into a pile, then ran on alongside the building and into the back garden, over a fence, into another garden and out into the adjacent street, where he flagged down a car by standing directly in its path. The woman driver had two small children on the rear seat. Tully wrenched open the passenger door and clambered in without explanation.

'Drive! Quickly.' It was an appeal rather than a threat.

The woman panicked and let the clutch in unevenly, causing the car to jerk away along the street. Keeping down in the seat Tully peered from the rear window.

There was no sign of the police, but he noticed the two children were staring at him. There was nothing he could do about it. He glanced at the woman, who glanced at him. 'Just drive,' he said. He had her make a right turn, then another, before telling her to stop. He climbed out, taking the ignition key. Then, wrapping his shotgun in his coat, he walked away, as calmly as he could.

Jack Lynn stroked his fingers firmly along his wife's crotch, knowing this had to be better than any kind of regular work. He was comfortable where he lay, his head resting on her arm, his face snug against her breast. He sensed her anxiety, but chose not to respond to it, not yet. He would have liked to make love to her again, but knew he wouldn't be able to if she kept looking at the clock. There was time enough before the girls came home from school for lunch, but he wouldn't convince her of that. Dolly didn't like the girls knowing anything of their sex life, and she got angry whenever they said they wanted to get in the shower with him, even when they were quite young. They were still young enough for that, he thought.

Having got the girls off to school that morning, she had come back to bed, bringing tea and toast. That was something he was sure she enjoyed doing as much as he did, despite her protests. His strongest argument for keeping the sort of life-style he had was the freedom to choose to do whatever he wanted to, whenever he wanted to. Since their last row about what he was doing, and his promise to go minicabbing with her brother, she had left him alone.

'Come on, lovey. We must move,' she said.

'Mm, in a minute. This has gotta be better than driving

a minicab.' He slid his finger into her. But now she was saying no.

'I've got to get up, Jack. No. Stop it. I mean, taking me back to bed this time of morning.' She pushed him away. 'No, stop it. Come on, the girls'll be home for their dinner soon.'

'You don't use it, you lose it . . .'

'Some chance of that happening to you,' she said. 'You'll wear it out. Come on!' She slapped his chest and pulled away.

'Ah.' He stretched. "S water hot? I'll take a bath.'

'I'll run it for you.' She got out of bed and dived straight into her dressing gown.

'I'll just have a couple more minutes,' he said.

'No. Come on, Jack. I'm running your bath.' She went out.

He reached over to the night-table to look at his watch. It was half past eleven. They would have had loads of time before the girls got back. He stretched again, then rose, glancing down at his erection. It wasn't doing him any good at all right then.

'They got away? You mean to say they got clean away? No one nicked? No one?' Pyle said with exaggerated surprise. He was in Criminal Intelligence general office, having just been given the news by DI McHale. 'What the fuck were all those woodentops doing? Playing with each other?'

'The plonks could have done better,' McHale said.

There was a bit of activity going on around the room from other detectives, who were mostly involved with paperwork. One detective was trying to raise a unit on their own r/t, but wasn't able to reach the car. Landphones were more secure anyway.

'There shouldn't be too much trouble picking them up,' McHale added as if in mitigation. 'They left a trail of evidence, by all accounts.'

'But twelve units in the area, and still they got clear.'

'It was down to John Tully and his little team,' McHale informed him. 'Our lads got it all on video. Should be handy.'

'Been handier 'we'd been there, Graham.'

'Yes,' McHale said curtly. He was evidently embarrassed by his lack in this case. 'We should have done something more. There're a lot like that, Fred, 'we had more men available.'

'The least said about it the better, I'd have thought.' He wasn't merely consoling a colleague. 'I bet there's a lot of screaming going on over in division 'the blaggers legging it.'

'You wouldn't think. 'S why I want to keep out of it if I can,' McHale said. 'It's only a matter of time before the shit gets thrown this way, Fred. Their commander got a right ballocking from the ACC, I hear. He's going to want to dump on someone.'

'It might not be too bad, 'we nick that team a bit lively.' Any arrests were for his squad to make now. Having supplied the information, Criminal Intelligence would bow out.

'That might embarrass the local commander a bit more, especially when the press gets going. Still, fuck him. I don't owe him any favours.' He turned as DC Hill came in with his video. 'What's it look like, Matt? ID them all, can you?'

'Well, it's not brilliant really, guv.' The DC shuffled uncomfortably. 'It's a bit blurred, what there is. I think the shutter must have jammed.'

Pyle followed the DI down the room to the video player and screen and saw they had nothing worth much. 'Not exactly Michael Winner, are you?' he said, shaking his head in dismay.

'It's not easy doing an obo on your own, guv.'

Pyle gave him a look. 'I shouldn't say too much about that.'

'It shows what's going on all right,' McHale commented. 'Be handy if it showed who they were.'

The ninety seconds of video tape was short on detail. None of the four blaggers could be positively identified, only what they were doing. An idea crept into Pyle's head. 'This'll probably do nicely, Graham,' he said. 'I mean, they could be anyone – it gives us more scope, doesn't it?' He grinned, knowing just what he had in mind.

'You going to get some raids organized, Fred?'

'It'll make a nice show, 'we can pick up Tully,' Pyle said.

There was need of concerted police action to redress the balance before any media got hold of what happened out at Abbey Wood and started demanding to know just how efficient the police were.

Criminal Intelligence had gathered a fair amount of information on John Tully and his associates, especially those he was likely to work with; how quickly the computer came up with the three most likely candidates on the blag with him.

Pyle organized the four raids to happen simultaneously, with no particular order of merit or preference over who arrested whom. He got Benny Isaacs; and sent DS Lethridge to raid Tully's flat; DS Barcy – the violence specialist – went looking for Cole Coleman; and a borrowed DS along with a squad from the arms unit went after the fourth suspect, Mark Johnson.

The local police station was descended upon regally by the Squad, and even though it was a relatively small influx of extra men, the system seemed ill-equipped, ill-prepared to extend them the help they expected. DI Pyle arrived with Benny Isaacs at the same time as the borrowed DS showed up with the audibly protesting Mark Johnson. Pyle's other two squads weren't far behind.

In the back reception area he caught hold of a constable who was passing through. 'Where's Inspector Kenley?'

'How should I know?' the spotty-faced PC replied.

'Find him. Tell him Inspector Pyle's here.'

The uniform went away at a run.

Pyle turned and looked at his prisoner and nearly smiled. 'What d'you reckon, Benny? Want to put your hands up now?' That was unlikely to happen.

Isaacs said, 'Not even to help a nice fella like you, Mr Pyle.'

'About right. What we'll do is have a little chat away from the front office. Then when you're ready with your statement we'll take you in and put the tape recorder on and we'll do what we call the ethical interview.'

The blagger didn't respond, but he clearly knew there could be no other option. The heavy bit came sooner rather than later these days, because of all such interviews being recorded. The same was happening with each of the other suspects he looked in on after they got rooms without recorders sorted out for the pre-interview interviews. Mark Johnson was at pains to be as helpful as possible. Although he had previous convictions, for this blag he had an alibi, which he insisted they check out. Pyle would see how he shaped before he wasted detective manhours checking out his story.

'Why don't you do us all a favour,' the borrowed DS suggested. 'John Tully's dropped you right in it.'

'No, John wouldn't do that even if it was true,' Johnson said with a note of faith Pyle found touching. 'Not John. You're pulling my leg.'

'You were the fourth man on that blag yesterday.'

'No. I tol' you, I was with m' Mum in hospital. The old girl passed away just about the time they was making it. Why don't you check that out, Mr Pyle?'

'Oh, we will, Mark. But you're a million, son. I mean, you go mates with John Tully, don't you?'

'You know I do. I mean, it's on m' sheet. 'S why I got a pull. But you see if my Mum didn't pop off yesterday. I was at her bedside at the hospital holding her hand, I was.' He was completely unemotional about this.

'If you were,' Pyle said accommodatingly, 'you've no problem, Mark. We'll see.' He was doubtful as he stepped out of the room.

Embarrassment over what had happened on his manor made both the resident DI and duty sergeant amenable to any suggestion by Pyle that might help them out of their predicament. He cheerfully exploited their unease.

'How come your two lads happened to be down at the Gas Board?' he asked in the DIs' office. 'D'you hear a whisper?'

'I wish to fuck I had. I'd've had more than a couple of DCs waiting down there. They were collecting a new stove for my missus. The fucking gas company didn't know when they could deliver it – is she giving me some stick about the damage that got done to it! I'll probably have to go and buy her another one.'

Pyle said collusively, 'So your lads hadn't booked on the air, no one knew they were there?'

'No, I told them to keep quiet,' Kenley explained.

Pyle nodded thoughtfully. 'What are they like? Half-wide?'

'They're all right, Fred. They do what they're told.'

'Their diaries haven't gone upstairs yet, have they?' They hadn't. 'Good. Well, maybe they ought to put down that they were out there on obo – gets you out of trouble,' he offered, like he was merely being helpful to a colleague. However, it wasn't quite that simple; nothing ever was with him. Anticipating the blank they might draw with Mark Johnson, he was already thinking about the most likely candidate to fill it. As such a move would be swift it would be useful to have the local DI owing you a favour, one that could be called in at short notice. But the chances were he wouldn't need any help with what he had planned for Jack Lynn.

Kenley wasn't convinced. He said, 'The commander is screaming like a bastard – the blaggers getting away like that caused a right upset here, and no mistake. He'd have put the duty inspector back in uniform if he wasn't already in uniform!'

'Well, it was all down to the wallies.'

'But what about the Criminal Intelligence lad with the video camera? How'd that come about?'

'They had a whisper. Nothing positive. They covered it with one man.'

'How are you explaining your two lads being at the scene?' Pyle wanted to know. 'That'll be a disciplinary matter, if it were to get out about them collecting that stove for your missus.'

Kenley thought about this and nodded. 'Maybe I'd better have then stick down they were on obo.'

'About right. The commander will forget this fuckup now we've nicked the blaggers.'

'I hope you're right.'

'You don't fancy going back in uniform, Frank?'

'Not even to take promotion,' Kenley said, as though it were a real prospect.

'How are our witnesses looking?' he asked in a peremptory manner. It was his case now, and reference to the local man was a courtesy.

'Oh, we've more than enough of those.'

'Not policemen, are they?' He had seen too many cases to court where the only witnesses were policemen and where the villains had been chucked as a result.

'Some are – but a lot of civilians, too.'

'Good. Get some ID parades organized. They'll probably get us further at this stage than interrogating this motley fucking crew.'

Identity parades were rather formal and conducted by the uniform branch; however, Pyle knew how to exploit witnesses' natural prejudices – by appealing to the basic, emotional right-wing leaning he figured the majority of the population had. This tendency had nothing to do with politics other than that their politics followed their emotions. Despite their faults, which occasionally surfaced in public, he knew the police were seen as the only means of maintaining the rule of law, as a last resort to protect the public from the marauding hordes. As a result he knew that no one was going to rock the boat so hard that it sank, whatever their politics. Because of the recent ruling concerning the validity of identification evidence, especially if unsupported by other evidence, particular care had to be taken so that ID parades were seen to be scrupulously fair. But left to their own devices, Pyle accepted that most witnesses were worse than useless. He would leave none of them to their own devices.

Having conducted a pre-interview himself in the company of the arresting officers, Pyle decided the suspects were all involved, so he objected to letting them speak to their solicitors, or anyone else for that matter. His problem was that they had to be put up in court within thirty-six hours or be released under the PACE rules. That wasn't long enough to get these men convicted. None of them was likely to put his hand up.

Tully and Coleman, being not dissimilar in appearance, were put in a parade together with ten other men. That was the minimum number required for two suspects going up. Isaacs had to go in on his own among seven other men. The fourth, Mark Johnson, wasn't put up; Pyle finally accepted his alibi. Two nurses and a doctor at the hospital had spoken to him at his mother's deathbed and the time had been precise, having been noted for the death certificate.

Witnesses came on in chronological order, more or less as they would appear in court. Some of them hadn't been available at the sort of notice the police gave them and would have to attend another parade; some wouldn't be called, for after talking to them Pyle discovered they hadn't seen anything at all, or were so confused they would be more than likely to help secure the blaggers' release. The whole process was tedious and time-consuming, and a lot of patience was required by the witnesses, the police and the members of the public in the line-up. The feelings of suspects weren't considered.

The woman who locked the front door of the Gas Board offices was the first in. She was taken along the line by a uniform.

'What I want you to do,' the inspector said, 'is see if you can pick out any of the men you saw at the robbery. Just take your time, Miss, we have all day. And please don't be afraid.' There was a bored familiarity to his words.

The parade was being held in the muster room. Pyle would have preferred the parade to be held in light similar to that at the time of the robbery, but it was too cold to be standing around outside today.

Walking straight past Coleman, who was in second place, the woman hesitated at Tully, who was next to him, then went on to the fourth man, and studied him. Pyle held his breath as he watched from the wall. But finally she came back to Tully and indicated him. At that moment she didn't seem certain; she would be by the time they got to court, Pyle decided.

The next witness was one of the security guards, the less injured of the two; his colleague was too ill after his beating to attend. Special parades would be held for him at a later date. He picked out Tully. 'That's one of the buggers,' he said, 'I'm sure of it.' But he drew blank on Coleman, and on Isaacs when he was paraded. Other witnesses from the Gas Board picked out Tully; but some of them even picked out Coleman. Pyle knew it would be a bit of a stretch using them, as he was convinced that Coleman would have been left outside to drive the car. His antecedents bore this out.

The confusion apparent in the civilian witnesses was absent from the police witnesses, which gave Fred Pyle a sense of foreboding, notwithstanding the fact that they were trained in observation. They had had the opportunity to corroborate their evidence, to see the video DC Hill had made, and to look at the photographs of the villains the police had on record. They would be challenged on all that in court, and soon it would be made to look like a swift 'un, even though he knew at that point it wasn't.

'How does it look, Fred?' DCI Simmons asked when he

got back to the Yard later that day. Simmons was at his desk checking through another large report line by line with a ruler. 'Get some good IDs?'

'From policemen is all!' he said wearily. 'Twenty-seven witnesses, and only twelve what I'd call positive. All of them from policemen.' Policemen might have had no credibility at all. But he was being practical.

'Might be a bit of a problem in court, Fred.'

'There are a few more to see yet. Some of them might shape up all right,' he said on a more optimistic note. 'They saw them all right, but like most of us they get a mental block when asked to walk down that line.'

'Can we make sure of them, Fred?'

He gave Simmons a look, and waited.

'They'll get some flash brief looking to make a name for himself – he'll go and dig something up on a policeman or two. Won't look too clever at all, will it? In fact it'll start to look a right swift 'un.'

Pyle laughed. 'Some fucking chance, I should think.'

'In the old days,' Simmons went on, 'it only needed a policeman to go into the witness box and say he did it, there was no doubt in anyone's mind. Not the case any more.'

'This little team did that blagging all right.'

'I believe it, Fred. But we'll need something more than coppers to make sure of our result. Either some forensic evidence to go with those IDs, or something more definite from the civilian witnesses.'

'Be handy,' he agreed, 'wouldn't it just.

In the corner of the DIs' office there was a TV and video with the tape that DC Hill had made. It had been run forwards and backwards through the machine a hundred times, and would be hundreds of times more. Every frame was frozen and studied that way. He pressed the switch and moved from one blurred image to the next. Then it suddenly hit him who he was looking at.

'You know who the fella in the flying helmet is, don't you?' he said deliberately. 'The one who's missing?' DS Lethridge, who was with him, sat back from the desk where he had been leaning his weight on his forearms. 'It's Jack Lynn. That's who it is.'

Without commenting, Lethridge took the remote control and flicked back and forth over the frames of that particular image. The face of the person in the picture was obscured beyond recognition by the straps of the flying helmet.

'It's a bit of a stretch, guv.'

'Look at him closely. It's his build, the way he walks.'

'Yes, I suppose that could be him.'

'*Could* be? Of course it is!' Taking the remote back, he studied some more frozen frames. 'That's definitely Lynn, Eric. No doubt about it. We'll give him a pull, turn his place over.'

Lethridge stood up from the desk. 'We going armed?'

'Might be an idea to take the firearms unit. What we want out at his place is something Forensic could use. Like a few hairs from his hairbrush, so they can match any in the flying helmet.' He rose, switching off the TV. 'He'll go this time, I'll make sure of that,' he said, and meant it.

Jack Lynn slept heavily. Ordinarily nothing woke him before time, apart from someone coming into the room. If the children cried out in the night then his wife got up to them. But the front and back doors of his house simultaneously being kicked in at six o'clock on the cold December morning was enough to awaken him – the noise was enough to waken the dead.

Both he and Dolly were awake long before detectives crashed open the bedroom door and switched on the light.

'What the fuck's going on?' he demanded, flinging the duvet back, ready to spring out of bed.

'Don't move, Jack,' Pyle ordered.

'Jack!' Dolly said in alarm.

He had started out of bed like he had neither heard the words nor seen the three guns that were being pointed at him. One of the girls in the next room had woken and was crying and calling for her Dad.

'They've woken up Sandra now . . .' Dolly went on.

He could hear how confused and upset his wife was.

'Stay where you are, Jack,' Pyle said, 'or we'll shoot you –'

'M' daughter's crying. You're out of order coming here, upsetting people like this . . .'

'Let your wife go to her.'

Dolly looked at her husband. 'What do they want, Jack?' she asked, getting out of bed.

She was wearing a flimsy nightdress and Lynn resented more than anything the policemen staring at her.

'D'you have to come here like this?'

'You're a dangerous villain, Jack. We had to make certain.'

'You rotten bastards!' Dolly's words were angry. 'I can't help but call you it. He ain't done nothing. Tell them, Jack.'

'Go and see to Sandra, Doll. Go on,' he urged. He knew his wife meant well, but her slagging off the filth wasn't helping the situation.

Dolly started out of the bedroom, but clearly couldn't avoid the row. She turned back and launched herself at the detective. 'You filthy bastard! You're filth, that's all . . .'

'Do like you're told,' Pyle said, defending himself. Other detectives aided him. Two others came up the stairs and crowded onto the landing.

'Leave it out, Dolly – c'mon, 's just a pull. I ain't been at it.'

Eventually she went to the children.

'D'you want to put some clothes on?' Pyle said. 'Or are they your going-away clothes?'

Lynn was in his vest and pants.

'Couldn't this have waited until tomorrow?' he asked, stepping into his trousers. 'I mean, coming here at this time of the night, worrying the life outta m' family . . .'

'This *is* tomorrow . . . Make a start downstairs, Eric, will you.' Pyle turned to another detective. 'Have a go up here. Properly.'

'I tell you, I ain't been at it at all,' Lynn protested. 'That's straight.'

'I didn't expect you to put your hands up to it, Jack.'

'I don't know what you're talking about.'

'Don't you? You will soon enough, 'we charge you.'

'Leave off, will you. I ain't done nothing.' He paused in dressing and looked at the DI, as if trying to fathom what was going on behind those expressionless eyes. Finally he said, 'I think I'd better call my brief, hadn't I?'

The detective shook his head. 'I don't think so.'

The other two detectives who had first entered the bedroom with him were busily searching. One had started methodically on the wardrobe, carefully going through the pockets, folds and linings of every item of clothing. The other one was being just as meticulous with the dressing table.

'Someone just stuck my name up, didn't they? That's what this is all about, isn't it? That fucking grass you got working for you . . .' He didn't for a moment believe this was a simple routine tug or one that he would easily pull clear of. It seemed too heavy for that. They had something definite in mind, and whatever it was he knew that their finding the fifteen hundred pounds he had in an envelope taped to the bottom of a dressing-table drawer would only help confirm it. He looked at the detective, who smiled mirthlessly at the find.

'A good start, Jack,' Pyle said.

''S only a bit of dough I keep by me. A cush' for rainy days. What does it prove?'

'That you had it off the other day. How much here?'

He told him. 'S mine though, innit?' It wasn't the

proceeds of a recent robbery, not the one these policemen had called about.

'You'll get a receipt for it. Along with anything else.'

Lynn ran a comb through his hair. It was a habit, and when he was nervous he always reverted to habitual behaviour.

'You look very nice, Jack. You fit?'

'Ain't you even gonna let me see my kids first?' he appealed.

''Course. But you try legging it and we'll shoot you.'

He knew the detective meant it.

'Go with him, Rog',' Pyle told the DC.

As Lynn started out he glanced back and noticed Pyle turn to the dressing table and pick up the comb he had used. He had more pressing matters on his mind than wondering what the DI wanted that for.

'What's it all about, Jack?' Dolly asked him as he stooped over the bed in Sandra's room.

'You going with those men, Dad?' asked Carol.

'In a little while, love,' he said to his eldest daughter, wishing he could somehow reassure her. 'It's just a pull, Dolly, 's all.'

'Why can't they leave you alone? Rotten sods.'

'They don't know how to, do they?'

'I don't want you to go, Dad.' Sandra was in tears.

'I'll be back in time to take you to school, you see.'

'Shall I call a brief or someone?' Dolly asked.

'Might be an idea. See how it goes.'

'Where they taking you?'

'I dunno.' He looked at the detective.

'Abbey Wood, I expect,' the DC said.

'Abbey Wood?' Both Lynn and his wife repeated

the name like it was some hitherto unexplored territory.

'Nowhere yet, Jack,' Pyle said, appearing in the doorway. 'Let's get started. We've got a lot to get through.'

Searching Lynn's house from top to bottom was the starting point for Pyle's squad. Doing the job properly took hours. Lynn was kept there and the search was made in his presence in some rooms, and in the presence of his wife in other rooms. Things weren't taken out and strewn around here as had often been the case in the past. There had been some angry memos about that flying around the Yard after complaints that the Anti-Terrorist Squad had proceeded in such a manner. It was less out of concern for suspects' property that had prompted the reaction than the fact that things strewn had to be subsequently moved again as the search progressed and sometimes evidence was lost. Here things were taken down, searched methodically, put back. There wasn't much of interest: no guns, no further caches of money. There were some interesting receipts in the mountain of paper which Lethridge and DC Fenton sifted through on the dining-room table, the most interesting items Lynn denied any knowledge of.

'You're wasting your time,' Lynn commented whenever they sought an explanation; 'there ain't nothing there.'

'We got time to waste,' Pyle replied confidently. But he was beginning to believe him.

'There's another one of those for that garage,' DS Lethridge said as he came through to the living room. 'That's five we found.'

'What about this garage, Jack?'

Lynn suddenly looked like a man who knew he was

in trouble. 'Don't know anything about it, do I?' he tried.

'No. I guess that's why you got it in a bent name. I don't suppose you have the key either?' The blagger simply offered them a hostile stare. 'Makes no difference. Get over there, Eric. Take a look. We'll be down the nick. You want to get your coat, Jack? Those cells get a bit cold.'

At the prospect of her husband being taken away, Mrs Lynn was unable to contain herself – not that she had been exactly either amenable or since they burst into her house three hours before. In the narrow entrance hall, which suddenly seemed very crowded with departing policemen, she launched her attack. 'You fucking bastards,' she screamed, startling the detectives. 'He's not going anywhere, you filthy bastards – that's all you are filth. You bastards, I hope you rot; I hope you get cancer . . .'

DS Lethridge caught hold of her as she lashed out and he pushed her towards the kitchen. 'Shut up, for fuck sake – go and look after your kids.'

Lynn became animated now. 'Don't you start!' he warned him pointing his finger.

'You fancy some?' Lethridge said, swinging round. 'I reckon I could manage you, and your old lady.'

'Worrying the life out of innocent people, 's all you sods are good for . . .'

'You'd better tell her to calm down, or she'll be done for assault . . .' Pyle advised.

'About your fucking mark,' Dolly screamed. The two girls at the end of the hall were screaming as well.

Lynn caught hold of his wife and held her close.

'Come on, Dolly, be a bit sensible, love. It's all right. 'S misunderstanding, 's all. Come on, be a bit sensible.'

Lynn kept hold of her like he didn't want to let her go. But he went when the detective laid hands on him. Pyle glanced along the hall at the two girls hanging round the kitchen door. Both were in tears. Lynn's gaze followed his fleetingly.

Glancing at the villain, Pyle said, 'Is it worth it, Jack, all the grief you cause them?' From the look on Lynn's face he knew what he was thinking.

'What a blinding result!' Lethridge said when he got back from visiting the garage that Lynn was holding receipts for. He told Pyle about the armoury of blaggers' tools that were neatly laid out. There were three sawn-off shotguns, cartridges, a handgun, hammers with handles drilled and looped for easy handling; axes, pinchbars, a bunch of about a hundred assorted car keys, liquid ammonia, teargas canisters, gloves, masks, and rope – for tying up victims.

'Nothing like being prepared,' Pyle said, 'is there?'

'Yeah, he must have been a boy scout.' Lethridge shook his head in amazement. 'I left Humphries there waiting for the photographer and fingerprints – bit of luck there might be a few prints.'

'I wouldn't have thought there was much chance that Lynn will even attempt to say we planted that lot, Eric,' Pyle said. 'Go and see the owner of the garage. See if he can identify Lynn.'

True to form Lynn denied all knowledge of the contents of the garage. He also denied any knowledge of the Gas Board blag. Pyle wasn't about to allow either denial to gain ground.

''S not what we've got, Jack. You were there all right, doing that blagging with John Tully.'

In the interview room at Abbey Wood nick with them was one of his DCs and a local uniform man working the recording equipment.

'Shut up! I told you where I was Friday morning. I was in bed rumping my old lady, that's where,' Lynn said.

''S that right?' Pyle said reasonably. 'What sort of alibi's that?'

'We could take a swab, guv,' Jenkins interjected drily, ignoring the tape recorder. 'Check how old the semen is.'

That amused Pyle but Lynn didn't share his sense of humour. However, he had more sense than to retaliate.

'That was where I was, I tell you.'

'I thought you'd come up with something better than that, Jack. I'm almost disappointed.'

'I won't deny I know John Tully. But I ain't seen him in months.'

'Well, don't worry about it. You'll be seeing a lot of him over the next few months . . .'

'Someone's getting you right at it, sticking me up . . .'

'You think that's all there is to it, son? If that was the case, a couple of DCs would have called round at a reasonable hour. You wouldn't have been picked up on an armed raid like this. Be sensible.'

'You definitely got the wrong fella,' Lynn said, pitching his words in a low, appealing tone. 'That blag wasn't down to me. I wasn't even near Abbey Wood.'

'What about the fifteen hundred pounds we found at your gaff, Jack?'

'That? Oh, that was just a bit of dough I keep by me. Rainy-day money, that's all.

'Where d'you get it, Jack?'

'How d'you mean? It's mine.'

'You had it tucked away all right,' Pyle allowed. 'So how'd you come by it?'

Looking like a man being driven into a corner, Lynn said, 'It's just bits and pieces what get tucked away. 'S all. It's m'cush'.'

'I wish I could afford to put that sort of money aside. I'd say that came out of that Gas Board. Wasn't a bright place to hide it, was it? I thought most villains had bank accounts with the TSB nowadays.'

'He probably wouldn't have had time to put it there, guv,' DC Jenkins pointed out. 'What with giving his old lady such a rumping on Friday.'

'No, I s'pose not.' Pyle paused and looked at the suspect. 'All right, Jack, stop playing games now. Put your hands up to it. Get yourself a bit of help from the court.'

'I tell you what, 'f I was involved, the first thing I'd've done was made you an offer. That's the most sensible move.'

'That might seem logical,' Pyle said, 'but it doesn't prove a thing.'

Slowly, carefully, point by point and taking care not to say anything improper on the tape, he took Lynn through everything again. But nothing changed. Finally, he said, 'Wasn't that just lucky for you that this celebrated bunk-up coincided with that blag?'

'Lucky for you, you mean,' Lynn replied angrily. 'You got one in hand, and I'm the body – I saw the papers. They made right mugs of Old Bill, that little team, didn't they?'

'Nothing to do with me. We just got word it was down to you – simple as that. The evidence all points that way, Jack. I'd say there was a good chance you're going down for this one, son. You're well overdue.'

The interview ended with Pyle giving the time and the place, his name and rank and the person being interviewed. The uniform policeman removed the tapes from the machine and got Lynn to sign for the copy he gave him.

Having decided that Jack Lynn was the fourth man on the Gas Board blag, Pyle intended to make certain nothing was left to chance when it came to getting him convicted. Too many villains got a result because too many detectives took their evidence for granted or were too arrogant about the process, assuming that because they had nicked someone the courts would authentically endorse that action with a conviction. Courts could no longer be relied on as a matter of course. Certainly he wouldn't like to rely on due process without a little help.

In the front office at Abbey Wood nick, he approached the custody officer, whose basic workload, like most other policemen's, was paperwork. Other policemen around the office were dealing with paperwork, mostly the result of traffic offences.

'Where's the blaggers' clothing that was recovered from the Gas Board blag?' Pyle wanted to know. 'Has it gone for forensic examination yet?'

'No, sir,' the sergeant said. 'It's waiting to go up now. It's all in the CID property store.'

There would have been little point in its going up sooner as the forensic labs only operated nine-to-five, five days a week, unless there was something especially urgent.

'Could I have a look, skip?'

'Yes, no problem.' He removed from one of his desk drawers a key with a chain and lead weight attached.

'I won't be walking off with that in my pocket,' Pyle said as he took the key and weight.

The large-property store was a small, windowless room on the ground floor. Goods, from lead off church roofs to confiscated girlie magazines, were stacked around the place; a bicycle, a lawnmower, some tins of paint, all stuff which had to be held onto by the police until the case in which it was involved had been dealt with by the court and it could finally be returned to the rightful owner.

Pyle stepped inside and locked the door after him. He found the pile of clothing tied in a neat bundle, each item tagged with an exhibit label. The leather flying helmet was the only item he was interested in at this stage. Breaking the seal and easing the hat from the bundle, he first examined inside, then removing an envelope containing Lynn's comb he freed some hairs from it and placed them inside the helmet, crumpling the hat to work them into the fleecy lining. He then stuffed the hat back into the bundle, reset a new seal and went out, switching off the light.

'Morning, Frank,' Pyle said to the local DI as he stepped into his office on the first floor.

'I hear you nicked the fourth blagger,' the DI said. 'How does it look?'

'He don't look bad. Could you get your people to organize another parade?' He could have asked the reserve inspector himself, but he had more of a relationship with the local DI.

'When were you thinking?'

'This afternoon'll do it – Lynn's not going anywhere. I have a couple of other things to do before then.'

One was to get the banknotes found at Lynn's place checked by the cashier at the Gas Board. There was just a chance the money could be identified. Also he had to see Clifford Harding, who he would now employ to help him convict Lynn.

There probably wasn't anyone anywhere working for banks, security firms or money-in-transit offices who wouldn't co-operate with the police on this type of investigation. The reason was that they knew that without the police they couldn't function as free from worry over potential assault as they did.

The cashier at the Gas Board was no exception. Fat-jowled and dandruff-flecked, he strove with obsequious delight to ingratiate himself when Pyle was shown into his office. Pyle knew he was a million to get a result here, regardless of whether the notes he had taken from Lynn were part of the Gas Board money. The cashier said how he'd co-operate in any way he could; he even went on to say what a fine job he thought the police were doing, how splendid it was that they had caught the robbers so quickly. Pyle let him say his piece, knowing that time spent here was an investment. At one point he wondered if this man wasn't at it himself.

'It's a simple matter, what you ask, inspector,' the cashier said, examining the banknotes he had been handed. 'I'm sure I'll be able to identify these.'

He seemed to accept that the money was part of the Gas Board take simply because Pyle had told him it was. 'Yes. I can identify some of these notes as part of the money made up for our cash collection. We each have our own individual way of marking notes,' he explained. 'The same as tellers in banks do. Yes. Quite definitely I would say these were from that cash collection, sir. Several of the notes seem to have my mark on them.'

'Can you be more than quite definite?' Pyle asked.

'Oh I am – I'm certain of it.'

Pyle nodded. He would take a short statement, have the cashier sign an exhibits label, then move on to tie up his next witness.

Pyle didn't visit Clifford Harding on his own, but took two detectives with him. He wanted the villain in the right anxious frame of mind to co-operate. This visit would better achieve that if it seemed Harding was going to be arrested.

Pyle waited in the blue Ford Sierra outside Harding's house while the two DCs brought him out. One of the detectives opened the door for him and climbed in the back after him. The other went in the front next to the driver. Harding's protests ceased imediately on seeing Pyle. But started again once he was over the surprise.

'What the fuck's going on, guv? I mean, what the fuck's it all about? I mean, I'm getting more pulls than enough.' Harding was visibly distressed.

'Your name keeps coming up, Clifford. Whenever we seem to look at anything, there's your name . . .'

'Leave it out. I mean, what chance would I have, keep being pulled like I am. I thought we was s'posed to have a deal. I give you a bit of help, you give me a bit.'

Pyle nodded slowly. 'That's right, son. What I want now is more help. Frank,' he said to the driver.

The car started away.

The suspect was taken to the local nick, and put into an

interview room. Pyle followed him in, shutting the door. Having got Harding to his present agitated state the other two detectives weren't needed.

'Right,' Pyle said decisively. 'What I want from you is a nice statement saying how your pal Jack Lynn put that blag at Abbey Wood Gas Board up to you. Okay?'

'Fuck I!' Harding exclaimed, clearly unprepared for that.

'You want to pull yourself free of that bit of trouble of your own, don't you? This is what does it.' He had kept this villain on the hook for a number of weeks over the firearms charge against him.

Harding hesitated. Pyle had no doubt he found the prospect sickening, but had no sympathy for him. Instead he watched him swim around the room like he was under water and couldn't to get air into his lungs. Finally he said, 'What have I got to say?'

'Just tell it like it happened,' Pyle explained. 'How Jack phoned you, and you had a meet and he put this blag to you.' Pyle watched him closely. 'Sit down, son. Make yourself comfortable.' He laid a sheaf of statement papers on the small table and uncapped his pen.

Harding remained standing. 'What about that bit of trouble of mine, guv? I mean, is it gonna be dropped out finally? You know, dropped right out?'

'It will be, Cliff. Like you'd never even seen that gun. Like you weren't even thinking of making one with it.' Pyle sounded convincing, but still he pressed his point. 'I tell you, you give the right sort of statement, help me nick the other fella, it'll be like you never even had any form, son.'

Little by little Harding was reassured. He sat at the table

and picked up the pen. 'But the thing is,' he said suddenly, 'what's going to happen if it comes on top? I won't be able to do nothing, will I?'

'How do you mean?' Pyle asked.

'Well, I mean, I won't have to go up in court and stick that up? I mean, I can't do that, can I? That'd not only make me a grass – I'm fitting one for you.'

'No, you're not, Clifford – he phoned you, like I said. You won't have to go into the box to give evidence,' Pyle lied smoothly. 'We're entitled to protect our sources of information – that's standard. Stand by what I tell you.'

Harding looked at him, then finally nodded. 'You'd better tell me what to write.'

'First we want your full name, address and a declaration that you're making that statement of your own free will without threat or favour.' There wasn't any trace of irony in his words as he watched Harding write.

There had been a lot of confusion at the scene of the robbery, and as a result there were a lot of contradictions from the witnesses who came in to the first identity parades. Pyle was determined there wouldn't be the same confusion when Lynn was put up. From the earlier statements he knew who would prove the most valuable witness; the uncertainty of some he had seen for himself in the muster room. The security man who had been well enough to attend the earlier parades had had no more than a vague impression of the blaggers; his colleague, James Lawrence, who had been too badly beaten to attend earlier, was no clearer. Pyle on the other hand had no doubts so would make certain of both security men this time around.

After exchanging a few brief and pleasant words with the reluctant solicitor who arrived at the nick to look after

Lynn's interests – he learned Mrs Lynn had simply picked him from the phone book – Pyle caught each of the two security guards separately and had a quiet word with them in one of the interview rooms.

'You won't have any trouble identifying the fourth man, Mr Mason,' Pyle said to the guard. 'He was the one in the flying helmet; dark, wavy hair, slightly receding.' – Lynn would be seen without a hat on.

'It's surprising how difficult it is, inspector,' Mason said. 'Until you walk down that line you think you have a very clear picture in your mind.'

'I know how difficult it is. But you won't make the same mistake with this one. Remember his slightly crooked nose? He was a bit of a fighter – I think he got a whack from a security guard's stick on the last blag before this one.'

A feeling of apprehension rose in Pyle as the guard looked at him for a moment. He thought he was going to raise some objection. But he didn't.

'I remember him all right.'

Pyle nodded. He knew he could rely on this man.

After priming the other witnesses in a similar way, he decided not to take a chance on any more. The three would be enough to help get Lynn put away, especially with the forensic evidence he would have. He didn't wait around through the whole of the ID parade, but stayed long enough for his three witnesses to pick Lynn out. He was satisfied.

DCI Simmons was satisfied too when he got the reports the following day.

'Those witnesses ID'ing him just about wraps it up,' Pyle said in the DCIs' office. 'I'd say he was a stoneginger.'

'I would say so. Especially with what was found in his lock-up. Was the forensic report in yet?'

'Not yet. I'll chase them up. What about the charges for all that stuff in the garage? We putting them all to him?'

'Why not? It'll look good when it goes up. Conspiracy to rob; possessing prohibited weapons; no firearms certificate. Let's have everything in, Fred. What about those blags at Bromley and Wimbledon that were supposed to have been down to him?'

'I still reckon they were. But there's no evidence,' Pyle said.

'Pity. Nor any for Catford?'

'Only what we found in his lock-up. Unless you want to stick it up on the word of my grass?'

'No. There's not that much point. But it wouldn't be a bad idea to check the possibility of tying him into any of our unsolved major blags, as we've got him. Get a warrant and check his bank accounts, see if there are any heavy deposits about the right time.'

Pyle gave a doubtful look.

'Silly as can be, some of these villains, Fred. 'S worth a try. We'll put up all we can, let the CPS throw it out if they want to.' He turned his attention to two fairly thick pink folders on the desk immediately in front of him. 'There are one or two discrepancies creeping into these statements, aren't there?'

'There won't be any concerning Lynn,' Pyle reassured him.

'No, but these others. Especially those given by the local police. What kind of idiots are they over there? Don't they corroborate their evidence before committing it to paper?'

Pyle shrugged dismissively. 'Uniform branch,' he said,

as if that explained everything. ‘Think they’ll make any difference, guv?’

‘I wouldn’t have thought so, Fred.’

Pyle simply nodded.

They were fitting him and there was not a thing he could do about it. Nothing he said or did seemed to make any difference. The situation made him feel oppressed, and depressed. He was becoming increasingly frustrated too, and was getting ready to explode. If that happened someone was going to get hurt. Quite how he had checked his anger so far he wasn't sure.

As he stood in the dock at Bexley Magistrates' Court listening to the disconnected, mumbled motions for getting him remanded, he felt sick – it was a despairing kind of nausea that rose from the pit of his stomach. There were few people in the court, apart from himself and the magistrate, his clerk, officers of the court, police, the detectives involved in the case; also his brief, who, as far as he was concerned, was about as good as nothing. How had Dolly come to find that wanker? There were no reporters around, not even from the local press, or he would have let them have it about the filth fitting him. The press, he supposed, had better things to do than waste their time on a remand. There was only one way it could go, that was for sure.

'Do you have any legal representation, Mr Lynn?' the magistrate asked, peering over his glasses.

Lynn's solicitor popped up. 'Yes, sir. I represent Mr Lynn.'

Popping up at the right time, doing the right thing, upsetting no one, that was all his brief was good for.

'How long a remand is being sought?'

'One week, your worship', the Crown Prosecution services' barrister said. 'Because of the complicated nature of the investigation, there are a lot of statements to be prepared.'

'I take it there are objections to bail?'

'Yes, sir.'

Lynn listened as the CPS man went through his objections. They were standard: serious nature of charges, fear that he would go on the trot, concern that he might interfere with witnesses. Having gone through all that, the beak asked his brief if he was making an application for bail, like there would be serious consideration given to it if he was. His brief didn't even try.

Finally the magistrate said, 'Remanded for one week, in custody.'

'To the twelfth of December,' the clerk of the court informed them.

Lynn felt like giving them some verbal as he was led out, but knew there would be a better opportunity later, when there was a jury to impress.

The remand was to Brixton prison. At first he thought it was going to be Abbey Wood nick, while the filth continued to question him about what must have been every unsolved blag that had gone off in London over the past two years. But he guessed Brixton was more convenient to them than Abbey Wood. About the only thing that could be said in Brixton's favour was that it was relatively warm in the winter, a fact which had far less to do with the heating system than the body temperatures of the densely packed inmates.

Although while on remand he kept all his options barring his liberty, he was considered a potential category 'A' prisoner, so he was watched more closely than regular remands. In theory he could have as many visits during the day as he wanted, but as none of these could be open visits they had to be restricted, as with other potential category 'A' prisoners, to availability of officers to supervise them. So in reality it amounted to one short visit a day.

Dolly came down to see him every day, bringing him a change of clothes, as he was permitted to wear his own clothes; she also brought food, as he could have all his own meals sent in, and tobacco to trade or give to others inside – money wasn't permitted.

His brief, Ronald Watson, came down to Brixton to see him. The visit didn't endear Lynn to this man one bit more; he refused even to be grateful for having someone to visit him. The visit served to confirm his opinion of the solicitor, and made him feel more depressed.

Since his last stay in Brixton, little had changed. The cells were more crowded. Most were three-up, some even four to a cell. There were newly built extensions around the place, more for greater security than comfort. But something that had changed were the visiting rooms for solicitors and police. These were now housed in a new building in the courtyard. The room he drew was some ten feet by eight feet and on the first floor of the building, with separate rooms for the screws. The prisoners were brought in through a double-locking security hatch at one end of the building, while visiting briefs and CID came in through a similar hatch via the metal stairway to the courtyard at the opposite end.

Ronald Watson sat at the table in the visiting room

holding open his briefcase before him. He was a neat, obsessive man in his late forties, whose main preoccupation currently seemed to be placing his pen in precise symmetry to his large, unwritten-upon briefpad, Lynn noticed as he paced around the room.

He knew instinctively where this man was coming from, even before the solicitor said, 'In view of the vast amount of evidence the police seem to have against you, Mr Lynn, I think your best course might be to plead guilty . . .'

Lynn wheeled on him. 'You got to be fucking joking, pal. What the fuck d'you think all that is I been telling you? They are fitting me.'

'We could seek to get the charges reduced for a guilty plea.'

'They are fitting me,' he repeated like he was talking to an imbecile.

'I don't think that attitude is going to help much,' the solicitor said.

'That attitude, for fuck sake! It's getting near Christmas and I'm stuck in this pisshole. How do you expect me to react? I want to be out, where I'm entitled to be. I want you to go back to court, get me bail. So I can spend Christmas with m' family. Blank the magistrate, go into a judge,'

'That's absolute nonsense,' the brief protested.

'About all you've done so far is fill out the Legal Aid form, and I could have done that. What about what I told you?' he demanded, staring down the table at the solicitor. 'Are you going to stick up in court that I was fitted?'

Watson seemed decidedly uncertain about that, and avoided his look. He realigned his pen.

'I'll discuss all that you've told me with counsel when

I brief him. But I can't say that it's a sound basis for a defence.'

'Oh, that's fucking t'rific,' Lynn said in dismay. 'So what d'you reckon? I gotta take my fitting? Not only that, I gotta go and fucking well plead to it?'

'If you have some evidence against the arresting officer, then we can make an official complaint against him.'

Lynn looked at the brief in amazement. 'Never in a hundred years would I have the sort of evidence likely to satisfy you, pal. You're worse than the fucking police, you are. You're doing their fucking job for them.'

'That's not fair, Mr Lynn.'

'Fair? You're about as good as fuck all. You'd better fuck off, you prick. Go on, fuck off! 'Fore I break your arms – I'll find someone else.'

Anger was boiling over in him and he only just stopped short of hitting the solicitor, and probably would have done so had the screw not made a timely appearance – so much for the rooms being soundproof.

Other visits for potential category 'A' prisoners weren't so convenient as those for briefs and the police. There was no room for relatively private conversation, no opportunity for physical contact. Jack Lynn ached with need of that when he saw Dolly behind the screen in one of the cubicles of the visiting area. She was already seated when he was brought in. The screw escorting him was a reasonable sort of guy, one of those who would do anything for a couple of quid, but as much as he seemed to want the earner Lynn offered him he said there was nothing he could do to get him together with his old lady. Visits were controlled by the gate officers who phoned through and told him where to take the prisoner.

Lynn sat on his side of the partition and put his hands on the shelf in front of him. His knuckles showed tense and white. He felt tense. He didn't attempt to speak for a few moments. He wondered what was going through Dolly's mind. She looked tired. He guessed she probably was, but he wouldn't speak about it, he was almost afraid to speak about it in case she came to the conclusion she had had enough. Perhaps she could no longer face the prospect of his going away for another five or ten years, and he knew that she knew there was a good chance he could draw such a sentence.

'How are you, Jack?' she asked, reaching out and putting her hand on the glass that separated them. There were microphones in the side panels which made it possible for them to talk to each other without shouting.

'I'm okay. How are the girls?' he wanted to know.

'Asking when you're coming home. That Sandra doesn't stop asking. Runs home from school, she does, expecting to find you home . . .' Her words trailed off.

He looked away, feeling completely gutted.

There was a long silence between them before she said, 'There's some clean clothes and a bit of food in the parcel. How long's it look like being, Jack?'

'Too fucking long,' he said, his anger rising again. There was no point in getting angry with Dolly. It would only get her upset, but he couldn't stop the words coming out as they did.

'What did that brief say about bail?'

'That prick! He's been sacked. I have no fucking chance with him. I should think the filth must have straightened him. He reckoned I ought to plead guilty.'

'The rotten bastards,' she said vehemently. 'I mean, you

know you didn't do it. Makes my blood boil to think about those wicked sods. I'd like to see them all dead. They ought to die painfully, that's what they deserve. They deserve to die as slowly as possible.'

'Oh, I ought to know better than to waste my time with a brief on Legal Aid. I mean, look who's paying him. It's the state. So why wouldn't he tell me just to plead to it?'

'What are you going to do, Jack?'

Anxiety was making her look old. He knew she felt responsible for having landed him with such a useless solicitor. He didn't want to blame her but couldn't help himself.

'Find another one. One who's gonna do a bit for me.'

'Why are they doing it, Jack? The police. Why you? I've been asking myself that ever since they arrested you.'

'It's my turn. That's what the filth said when I tried to have a deal with him. I was well overdue's what he said. What chance has someone like me got?'

'Jack?' Dolly said in a calmer tone. 'You didn't do nothing, did you? You weren't at it?'

He had told her he wasn't and assumed she had believed him, but now doubts were creeping in. The thought of her turning against him terrified him.

''Course I wasn't. You know where I was, don't you,' he said angrily.'What's the matter with you?'

'They won't put you away. They can't.'

'There'll be a lot of aggro 'they do, I tell you. I'll wind up topping someone . . .'

'They won't, Jack,' she insisted. 'What'll I tell the girls?'

'I dunno. Tell 'em . . . tell 'em I send my love. I'll see 'em soon.' He rubbed his forehead in an agitated fashion, as if going through the process of thinking. 'I'm gonna have to get myself another brief, if I'm gonna have any chance of chucking this. I gotta get one working for me. How much you got tucked away in the post office, Dolly?'

'I don't know. About four thousand, I think.'

'A fella in here told me about a brief, a right good 'un. Gladwell. Go and see him. Alex Gladwell. Got a firm over King's Cross way. Go and see him, see if he'll do a bit for me – he's s'posed to be a bit near the mark.'

'What if he can't take your case . . .?'

'Well, I don't fucking know,' he snapped, not having considered the possibility. He studied his wife for a moment, realizing she was getting upset, guessing how hard a time she was having. Someone had said it was always the wives who did the time, the husbands were merely locked up. 'I'm sorry, love,' he said more calmly. 'What a way to top up just before Christmas, I don't know. Go and see Gladwell. See if he'll have some of it. I don't know if what you've got tucked away is enough. But Tommy's holding a few quid for me, so there shouldn't be no problem. Tell him he can have something on top of Legal Aid. It should be all right, Dolly. You see.'

There was an awkward pause. He could see she wasn't entirely reassured.

'I could use a little taste, Doll,' he said with a smile, and was amused by her embarrassed reaction.

'Jack,' she said. It was almost censuring.

'Yeah, they'd probably rush in and fit me while I was at it.' He brushed his index finger against the glass like he was brushing her cheek. 'I was told this guy Gladwell is well bent. He might even be able to go and arrange bail for me so I'm out for Christmas. Tell the girls – it'll be all right, you see.'

Suddenly he was becoming more cheerful, almost like he believed his liberty for Christmas was possible.

However, he wasn't going to rely entirely on his brief to secure his release. He was also having another go at Tully and his mates, to see if he couldn't persuade them to give him an out.

'How come they fitted you like they did, Jack?' Tully asked.

Lynn had gone visiting within the prison and was in the cell which Tully shared with another potential category 'A' prisoner. The cell held all the home comforts that he could afford, all of which helped cushion the impact of what could be the start of a long prison sentence. However, none of those comforts could make you forget where you were, what your prospects were. Noises echoed through the labyrinthine remand block at Brixton with a curious sense of unreality for most of the inmates, mainly because they were all in a virtual state of limbo over their future. Cell doors and gates banged; prisoners called to one another; the prison officers' protests were feeble – far too many of them were taking too many earners off prisoners for them to conduct themselves as effectively and uncompromisingly as warders in other prisons tended to. That was where his life would be hard, Lynn knew from experience.

He considered Tully where he lay on his bunk and wondered if by his questions he was having a go at him.

'They've gone and booked me for the fourth man on that little team.' As a matter of prudence he wouldn't say whose team it was. Even though Tully wasn't leaping to help him, he wouldn't actively seek to put him in further trouble. 'Maybe someone just stuck me up.'

''S not just that, though, is it?' Tully said, like he was trying to mitigate his own part. 'Look at all the other stuff they done you for.'

'They want me put away, 's what it's all about. The thing is, they ain't got fuck all without that one at Abbey Wood.' He truly believed that was an accurate assessment of the situation.

'A right get-up,' Tully conceded.

'I mean, I know who that was down to, John. And you definitely know it wasn't down to me, right?'

'Oh, no doubt about that at all.'

'Well, the thing is, if they nick the fourth man on that little team, they ain't got no case against me, have they?'

'I wouldn't have thought so,' Tully said obligingly. 'But I don't suppose they're even trying now.'

'No, 'course they ain't. But what's the chance, d'you think, John, of getting me a bit of help?'

'I dunno. I mean, I wish I could help you out, but I can't, can I? I mean, there's no way I can help you out without putting myself in it. I mean, I'm not pleading to it. Nor are the other two. And I don't suppose the other fella's gonna put himself on offer. I'm sorry, Jack. I'd like to help you out, but I can't, can I? Sorry,' he concluded.

Lynn remained standing by the closed cell door for a long while. He could have willingly killed John Tully just then. Finally he nodded. He was sorry too.

The sense of purpose and positivity that Alex Gladwell tried to create when he went to visit villains in prison always paid dividends. Visible for all to see was the confidence it restored to Jack Lynn. It clearly made him think he was going to get a result, and not only that but one that would exact a high toll on those fitting him.

Gladwell wore an expensive chalk-stripe suit and shirts from Jermyn Street. They made him look every inch a member of the legal profession. He was only in his twenties and wasn't concerned that his complexion and baby-blue eyes made some people think he was still in his teens. His apparent youth clearly surprised Lynn, but he liked surprising people, especially with the results he sometimes got. Not only did he cultivate an appearance of being efficient, he *was* efficient, not missing a single point in Lynn's story. He looked quickly over the notes he had taken, while Lynn waited. He could feel anxiety coming off the villain and knew the reason for his unease was the possibility that he might not believe him. He would show him how to say things with confidence and believability.

Looking up suddenly, Gladwell said, 'It's all interesting stuff what you've told me, Jack, and, as far as I'm concerned, all within the realms of possibility. But do you honestly expect to go up with that story, and not only have the court believe it, but actively support you by acquitting you? Is that what you expect?'

'But it's the truth what I told you,' Lynn said urgently. 'I am being fitted by the filth.'

'But do you expect to go to the Old Bailey and have the judge support you in that contention? That's what I'm asking.'

'I don't understand what you're driving at,' Lynn said. 'I don't suppose I do. I mean, that's part of the fucking system, innit? It's always favoured the Bill, the fucking liars! They don't wanna believe for a moment that Old Bill's at it or fitting people. Or if they know it they never fucking well admit to it, do they?'

'Sometimes they do, Jack. What we have to do is make them accept that fact this time. Make them acknowledge that the police are as corrupt as you and I know them to be. That they do fit people up, that they are fitting you. Easier said than done, especially as we don't have much going for us. Your record, for one; and the other three defendants. None of them is prepared to help put you in the clear.'

'They won't do that,' Lynn confirmed. 'Means sticking up the other man, dun' it?'

'Then we need someone to put your case in court. Someone who knows what he's about, and is prepared to accept that the police get up to the sort of things we know they get up to. Someone who isn't simply going to support the status quo.' He hesitated and looked at the prisoner. 'The only thing is, Jack, the man I have in mind won't come cheap. In fact he won't take the brief just for a Legal Aid fee alone. But if we got him he would be worth every penny he gets, I promise you.'

'Well, the thing is, my liberty's at stake.'

'Your wife said she had about four thousand pounds. She told me you had access to some other money.'

'M' brother-in-law's holding a few quid for me.'

'We'll need it. What I'll do is offer counsel five thousand pounds the other way to take the brief. I'm sure we can find an area for talking around that price.'

The solicitor explained how QCs wouldn't normally take cases like his on Legal Aid, cases unlikely to prove spectacular or newsworthy. Cash inducements were a regular practice among the learned professions.

'Is it stolen money?' Gladwell asked.

Lynn didn't reply but looked away.

'If you expect me to act for you to your best advantage, then you have to be straight with me. I don't care one way or the other. I get a living by not passing moral judgement on my clients.'

'Well, the thing is, Mr Gladwell, I been getting a living from villainy for a long time.'

'That's fine. But what we mustn't do is allow the court to get that impression. What about the fifteen hundred the police found at your place?'

'It didn't come from where they said it came from.'

'You're certain of that, are you?'

'I told you, didn't I! I wasn't on that blag.'

'If you're sure, that's fine. But the police are certain to claim that's where it came from. They might even come up with some evidence to support that claim.'

'There's nothing I can do about that, is there?'

'No way you can show legitimate source of income?' He watched Lynn think about the question, then shake his head. 'Pity.'

'I s'pose I could stick down minicabbing.'

'Do you actually do any?' Gladwell wanted to know.

'Now and again, for m' brother-in-law, Tommy Jones.'

'Would he go into the witness box and say that, do you think? Perjure himself if necessary?'

'Tommy? Yeah, he's as good as gold.'

Gladwell made a note of the name. 'Has your wife any criminal record?'

'Dolly? Leave off! 'Course she ain't.'

'It's important to establish that fact, especially as she's your only alibi for the time of the robbery. Did she know how you got your living?'

Lynn shrugged. 'She was always rucking me to quit.'

'She knew, then.' He made a note. 'What about those other charges, Jack?' He referred to the sheaf of white copies of the written charges. 'Conspiracy to rob Catford Tote? Any foundation at all?'

Again Lynn hesitated.

'What's the problem? Don't you trust me?'

Lynn seemed embarrassed about answering. 'I mean, I ain't had no dealings with you before, have I?'

'Equally, I don't know you. That's the purpose of this meeting. If you don't trust me I can't do my best for you. Not if I'm only half-informed, and almost certain I'm going to make a fool of myself when briefing counsel. It's equally certain counsel will make a fool of himself.' He waited, shrewdly assessing the prisoner. 'It's your money you'll be wasting.'

With a reluctant nod, Lynn told him about Catford and how he believed he had been grassed. Gladwell leaped on that, seeing as a useful lever the likely prospect of the police trying to protect their informer. He wanted to know also about the raids at Bromley and Wimbledon that Lynn had been charged with. The same reluctance seemed to surface when Lynn told him they were in fact down to him.

'So unless the police have suddenly come up with some dramatic evidence, which I doubt, it looks like they've simply thrown these things in for good measure. The idea probably being to overwhelm the court with your apparent criminality. That's good,' he said with a smile and laid his two index fingers together thoughtfully across his cupid lips. 'If we could get those charges dropped, or at least have the police soft-pedal them . . . I'll arrange for a meeting with the detective in charge of the case and see if we can't do some business for you.'

'Do business with them?' Lynn was somewhat outraged. 'The slags are fitting me!'

'A fact of life, Jack,' he informed him. 'They might give you a cheap rate as a result. But possibly they want you away more.'

'That's what they fucking well said – I was well overdue.'

Gladwell nodded. 'I know Inspector Pyle. He's not only accessible, he's greedy as well. Although from what you tell me I doubt if he'll do you too many favours. Are you prepared to spend, what, say another two thousand pounds? Have you got it?'

'The thought of going into the filth has never concerned me, but like this, that really guts me. Is that what bunging him comes to?'

'It could well come to more than that.'

'What if he ain't having any of it?' Lynn asked.

'Then we'll have to look for another tactical advantage. We'll make a formal complaint against him for conspiring to pervert the course of justice. In fact, I think we'll make a complaint anyway. We'll see if we can't dig up something on his colleagues as well. They find that shoe pinches rather painfully on their feet.'

The vein of excitement that was running through Lynn by the close of their meeting wasn't exactly the confidence he had hoped to engender but it was something to build on, he decided.

'While you're going into the filth,' Lynn said, as Gladwell collected up his notes, 'what's the chance of getting me bail over Christmas? I mean, I could bung him a few quid. What d'you think, Mr Gladwell?'

'Not good, I'd say. I'll certainly put it to him. What's it worth to you? A grand?'

'I ain't made of money . . . Yeah, that'd be all right.'

'I'll ask him. But don't count on it, Jack. He's almost certain to want to keep hold of you now he has you.'

Lynn nodded. 'It would be nice to have Christmas with m' family. Know what I mean.'

Gladwell smiled confidently. 'I'll see what he says.'

He bought two large scotches and took them along to the table where Pyle was sitting, in the bar of The Feathers, tucked away in a recess. At that time of night there was no one around who either felt they needed to avoid. Gladwell sat and watched the older man as he raised his glass.

'Good health, Alex.'

Pyle was friendly enough. Then there was no reason for him not to be, knowing there was no way he could lose. The detective had readily agreed to this meeting when Gladwell had telephoned him. He got right to the point. 'What are the chances of our getting together on this, Fred?'

'Pretty slim, I'd say, Alex. I'd like to help you out . . .'

The detective hesitated, as though he was in a position to help and needed the right inducement.

Gladwell said, 'He wasn't expecting all the charges dropped. Just some of them. So he goes up with no lesser advantage than his three co-defendants.'

''S not up to me any more, Alex, is it?' He sipped his scotch. 'You representing the other three, are you?'

'You know I'm not. Come on, you're not expecting a conviction on the conspiracy and bank robbery charges.'

''S not a problem. The evidence is all there.'

'Is it?' Gladwell said with interest.

Pyle smiled. 'You're a cunning bastard. Aren't you just.'

He was neither expecting nor trying to trick Pyle like that. He would see the police evidence soon enough. 'If you could help, it's worth a thousand pounds to you.'

'And the rest, I'd say.'

Gladwell waited to see what the rest was.

'I'd like to, I really would. A bit of extra dough would come in handy. I promised to take the wife and kids skiing after Christmas.'

'An answer to your prayers, Fred. It would be perfectly safe. I'd make sure of that.'

'I wouldn't be worried on that score. It just can't be done the way you want it. It's down to the CPS now.' He drank some of his scotch and thought about the problem. 'Why don't you go into them? The fuckwits, 'spect they could use a few quid same as anyone else – mind you, they don't deserve it. There's a lad there called Rawlings who's handling it. Well bent, he is.' He set his glass on the table and slowly twisted it round by the base. 'Alternatively,

I tell you what I might be able to do. I could have a word about getting those other charges dropped out if he'll plead to the Abbey Wood blag. It won't cost him a penny.'

Gladwell shook his head. 'He's claiming you're fitting him. He's not taking it kindly.'

'It happens, Alex,' Pyle said matter-of-factly. 'But not this time. There was no need. I've too much evidence to fuck around like that. About a dozen eyewitnesses, for a start.'

'Police . . .?'

'Some,' Pyle said. 'Nice bit of forensic, too. He'll go all right, even with you as his brief. Tell him to do himself a favour, plead to it, get himself a reasonable sentence.'

'Oh come on Fred, that would make it too easy for you.' Gladwell smiled confidently, even though the meeting wasn't going as he hoped it would. 'I briefed Horace Macmillan as counsel today.'

Pyle was impressed. 'Nice to know Lynn's got that sort of dough.'

'There's no problem in that area, if that's worrying you,' Gladwell said, still hoping to do business.

Pyle shook his head. 'The wife and kids'll probably have to make do with Butlin's.'

They talked generally about the case over another drink; then explored the possibility of getting Lynn out on bail for Christmas, but this the DI thought a nonstarter. Finally Gladwell told him about the complaint they were planning to make against him.

Pyle looked at him. 'Thanks for the warning, Alex. Such moves are standard nowadays. I won't lose no sleep over it. Good luck, anyway.' He finished his drink in one swallow.

That left Gladwell feeling less than confident about Lynn's chances.

Because it was his investigation, the local DI was privy to all the information and all that had gone on in the case; therefore, Pyle assumed, he knew enough to know that the evidence that had just been brought up to him would cause a few problems, if not some serious doubts as to the involvement of one of the Gas Board blaggers. That was the purpose of his phone call.

What the man had had handed to him was the second bag that had gone missing with half the Gas Board's money in it following the chase. One of the uniform branch on patrol in the area had wandered around the health clinic buildings in Bedonwell Road when he had come across the bag in a pile of leaves.

'I suspect the uniformed officer had gone in for a leak or a smoke, rather than any sort of follow-up to the investigation. That'll mean another ballocking from the brass if we're not careful,' the DI said. 'That whole fucking area was supposed to have been thoroughly searched. But that's nothing to the sort of problem this find is presenting you with, Fred. Weren't you supposed to have recovered part of the missing half of the money from another source? From one of the suspects?'

'That's right, we did,' Pyle said smoothly. 'Is it all there, Frank?'

'Every penny of it. All the bundles were intact.' He

hesitated. 'Puts you up shit creek with that other bit you found at his place, doesn't it?'

'I'd say that money we found at his place was part of it all right.'

'How could it be . . .?' the DI began, but stopped abruptly.

'The cashier at the Gas Board ID'd it. No problem.'

'Well, what d'you think about this? I mean, what d'you want doing about it?'

Pyle didn't need to think about that. 'Stick it down in the rear of the Charge Book and lock it away for now. I'll have a word with my governor, see what he thinks.'

Without even bothering to see the DCI, Pyle could guarantee what his reaction would be. It was as he thought. He was even less interested in the find. It wasn't significant, he said, not now that the money found in Lynn's possession had been ID'd as part of the payroll. DCI Simmons's only concern about this find was how it added up with some of the other things they now had in hand that didn't look quite right.

'There are various pieces of contradictory evidence still coming to light, Fred,' Simmons said, leaning back from his desk. 'The forensic report on the blood samples wasn't helpful.'

'The report didn't exactly rule out the possibility of the four suspects being involved.'

'No, but the sample found in two of the stolen cars, from cuts presumably received when jumping in and out of vehicles during the chase, matched the blood of only two of the villains. And both were in the most common group.' Simmons paused. 'But neither of them had cuts on them.'

Pyle shrugged. ''S not that important. Just leave it out at their trial. There's plenty of other stuff. Some of the witnesses' testimony's a bit confused and contradictory, but if you have enough not-sures the jury tends to come to the conclusion that it was a yes. What about this money being found? Will we put it up to the CPS?'

'I s'pose we'd better, just to cover ourselves. But I don't think they'll be too interested, Fred. They're keen down there to go ahead and get convictions for all four. Especially now they're all committed for trial. You start having second thoughts about one, begins to make the others look iffy. Whatever way you book it, that money you found at Lynn's place has to be bent. We'll get a result all right, Fred. Don't worry about it.'

Pyle was anything but worried.

However, that wasn't the case with DS Lethridge.

''S all right for Tony Simmons to say that, Fred,' his DS said, standing supporting a large scotch in the corner of the Tank. 'He's not putting himself on offer, or the one with a fucking complaint against him, is he?' Lethridge had also been named in the complaint that arose out of Lynn's arrest.

'I should worry about that,' Pyle said. 'You'll have a lot more of those before you draw your pension, Eric.' He finished his drink.

''This fucking rate I can't see me drawing it. It's beginning to look swift.'

'I wouldn't have thought so. The CPS wouldn't fancy it so much, 'it did. There won't be any problems, 'we get it on in front of the right judge. Someone like Quigley'll be handy. He won't tolerate any suggestions of a fit-up, no matter how swift it looks. He knows the police don't do those sort of things.' Pyle smiled confidently. 'The chief's having a word with Rawlings in the CPS, see if he can't have a word with the Clerk of the Lists, make sure the case gets in front of Quigley. 'S as easy as that, Eric.'

It was.

Since finally parting with five and a half grand to bung Horace Macmillan for taking his case, Lynn had seen the silk only twice during the seven months he had been on remand. He had seen the QC's junior a few times and the solicitor any number of times. But he couldn't say the sum total of their meetings was a great surge of confidence. He even wondered if the advice they had given him over the committal proceedings hadn't been wrong. Whenever he had gone for trial before it was always after full committal proceedings, when everything Old Bill had was put up and challenged, and a chuck was looked for at the end. Now, having been committed by agreement between his defence and the CPS, nothing was challenged. Both his barrister and the prosecutor had been like old school chums meeting up, all smiles and small talk. The truncated committal proceedings didn't even get him up the steps any quicker as he hoped it would.

Lynn was in one of the cells below the Old Bailey court on his own. Normally you waited in a cell with all the other defendants you were going up with, but Mr Gladwell had arranged for him to be on his own as the silk wanted a word with him before he went into court. Dressed in a dark, conservative suit, a tie, and a smart blue shirt that was now a bit loose at the collar, he sat waiting on the single bench bed in the cell, thinking about the past seven months, the holidays and birthdays he had missed with his family. The girls knew where he was, having been to see him in Brixton, but he wasn't sure if they understood. His reflective mood was broken by the sound of the lock turning.

The door of the small green-painted cell, with its graffiti-scarred walls, opened and Horace Macmillan stooped through the low doorway, followed by Gladwell. The silk was tall, strutting, arrogant, the sort of person who took over all the space around him. He had a polished pink face and a loud voice that rang with confidence. His manner was so expansive he seemed to dwarf the instructing solicitor.

'Morning,' he said, adjusting his gown. 'How are you feeling? Did you get a good breakfast?'

'Right fucking slop,' Lynn said.

The barrister didn't really seem interested in his opinion of the culinary delights of the prison service, or even in having his questions answered for that matter.

'We've some good news and some bad news, I'm afraid, Mr Lynn. The good news is that we've managed to get some dirt on the police involved in the case, quite a bit of it in fact. Or, rather, Mr Gladwell has. The sort of stuff that if we get away with bringing it up will tend to damn the police in the jury's eyes. Certainly it will go a long way to diminishing their credibility. That's a risk, of course. If we attack the police then they can legitimately bring up your previous convictions. But I'd say it was worth the risk.' He paused briefly. 'However, the bad news is that the case is set before Mr Justice Quigley.'

'Fucking hell!' Lynn exclaimed. 'That wicked bastard.'

The prospect of going before Quigley filled him with genuine fear. Too many villains had been sent down for too many years by that judge for him to be anything but dismayed.

'Precisely,' the silk said, as though they were his feelings too. 'However, all is not lost. I'll endeavour, even at this late stage, to get it put out of the list and on before another judge.'

'Can you do that?' Lynn asked. 'That bastard'll weigh us off with about ten years for fuck all.'

'We can try. We'll certainly do that.'

Macmillan's smile didn't reassure Lynn one bit.

Along with John Tully, Benny Isaacs and Cole Coleman, Lynn went into the dock at the Old Bailey's number four court, jointly charged with attempted murder, robbery, robbing cars, and conspiracy to rob. Alex Gladwell, true to his word, had done a deal with the CPS, which meant Lynn went up with no additional charges. It had cost him fifteen hundred pounds.

Before the business of the trial got underway, Horace Macmillan rose to his feet to make his pitch.

'If I could crave the court's indulgence, My Lord,' Macmillan said, 'and ask for the case in respect of Jack Lynn to be put out of the list. My instructing solicitor is anticipating some new evidence which has been delayed. Evidence which could prove vital to my client's defence.'

The star of this court, and indeed any he appeared in, was Robert Quigley, who automatically seemed to see all defence counsel trying to pull a fast one over him. Mr Justice Quigley had a reputation for being the epitome of the law – biased in favour of anyone who went to the right school, had the right accent, had real money. He was classically austere-looking, in his early sixties, with close-shorn white hair, and spiky white eyebrows above his dark, thick-rimmed glasses. His nose was slightly beaked over his thin, pale lips; the ample flesh on his face was weakening and beginning to sag. If he had been known to smile, then by the face he presented in court today he might have been trying to deny it. He took a long time considering Horace Macmillan, as if trying to remember who he was rather than to consider his motion.

'I am sure you will find this court indulgent to a fault, as this trial progresses, Mr Macmillan,' Justice Quigley said. 'But don't start out by trying its patience. Unnecessary delays in criminal trials are costing the taxpayer a good deal of money. Something each of you might bear in mind with your usual and unnecessarily lengthy submissions as to the doubtless virtues of your respective clients,' he went on, embracing the other three defence barristers in the warning.

Sitting in the dock listening to him, Lynn could feel his anger rising. Justice Quigley was heavily prejudiced against the defendant, but he was clever and rarely said a word out of place, none that could be interpreted as taking other than the fair, middle ground on subsequently being read back in transcript on appeal.

But he knew what the bastard was saying by his emphasis and inflexion. He would slaughter them.

'Perhaps in the event of this vital evidence not being forthcoming when the time is relevant,' the judge said, 'you might make a further submission to this court. But it is now seven months since committal – I would have thought that ample time to prepare a defence.'

'With respect, My Lord,' Macmillan said, holding his

hands on his hips, dominating the court, 'perhaps you'd care to listen to my argument.'

'No, I wouldn't,' Justice Quigley said. 'I'd much prefer to proceed with the swearing of the jury.'

It was a clear indication to Lynn of the way the trial was likely to proceed.

There was no right of objection to any of the jury. Two were excused by the judge on account of poor health and work commitment. From the look of the twelve jurors they finished up with, Lynn tried to shrewdly assess what sort of background these people came from. The two who had been excused were clearly retired middle-class professional people who probably believed they had the most to lose from the breakdown of law and order, and who saw anyone in the dock, charged with what he was charged with, as a threat to well-ordered society. As his defence consisted mainly of undermining that order by attacking the police, they might not have been too useful on the jury anyway. A lot of middle-class people were having serious doubts about the police now; a lot of black people were too. He supposed the two black men who were on might hopefully have had some brush with the law and would as a result prove sympathetic. But they weren't young, and blacks of that age were often reactionary. Of the rest only three took fleeting glances towards the dock. One of those he was sure would elect himself foreman. The swearing of the jury was soon over.

The opening address by the prosecution was long and detailed, despite his remarks about it being a relatively straightforward case.

As the prosecutor, Gordon Harpenden-Smith, stated what he was supposed to have done, in company with the other three defendants, Lynn could feel his anger rising again and he wanted immediately to shout out his denial. Several times the words were on the tip of his tongue. He knew he wasn't going to be able to stay quiet for the full course of the trial. Harpenden-Smith was stout, middle-aged, and had three chins; he also had a habit of removing his eyeglasses when talking and waggling them up and down in his hand, rather as if he was suffering from Parkinson's disease. After about an hour of it, Lynn was thoroughly irritated by the habit, and felt like telling him to keep his fucking hands still. Had the man not been slagging him like he was he doubted if he would even have noticed the gesture.

Witnesses for the prosecution appeared in chronological order, following statements being read from the police plan drawer and official photographer. Street plans and photographs had gone in as exhibits at committal and weren't challenged. Each witness seemed to take about half a day in the witness box giving evidence. Perhaps it was his imagination being overactive, but the prosecution seemed to question them with great skill, greater skill than that which any of the four defence barristers displayed in cross-examination. The cumulative effect of the various defence counterattacks was a strong impression of vagueness among the witnesses, who variously shifted ground from: 'Quite definitely, it was one or other of the defendants', to: 'It might have been him', or, 'Not sure'; or 'It was someone like him!' Tully, Coleman and Isaacs sat quietly through the evidence, no matter what witnesses said they had done. But Lynn couldn't, and frequently sprang to his feet to protest, scream his denial, call witnesses liars; they were never simply mistaken, but were an active part of the police conspiracy to fit him. He knew that, knew how the filth operated. Despite the judge warning him about his outbursts, and telling him he would be removed to the cells if they persisted, and his counsel suggesting he calm down, he couldn't keep a check on his emotions. It was easy for that little team on the defence bench to stay calm, they weren't in the dock listening to the lies, which finally would make no difference to them personally. Some days, Lynn felt worse about what was said than others. On bad days he saw his prospects as abysmal.

It wasn't merely coincidental or ironical that by the sixth day, with the departure of the last civilian witness for the crown, more of them had positively identified him than had ID'd any of the other defendants. He knew how and why that was, and had a sick-making feeling churn his stomach. Travelling back to Brixton that evening in the prison transporter, which was an enclosed truck divided into sixteen cubicles off a central aisle, he felt depressed and defeated. His certain belief was that he was going to end up with a heavy prison sentence and was feeling murderous about the prospect. Also he was worrying about the evidence that his silk had countered with, why the man hadn't brought out such and such a point. He was hardly aware of the animated chatter that was coming from various cubicles – the van was taking prisoners from other courts at the Old Bailey back to Brixton – until John Tully spoke to him. They had hardly spoken in the past six days. It was as if each of the other three blaggers was afraid of him in case he set about them. He could have easily done that.

'They're well fitting you, Jack,' Tully said from the cubicle immediately in front of him. 'And that fucking judge, he's bending over backwards to help them.'

'What a no-good wicked bastard, him,' Isaacs added from across the aisle.

'And you slags are helping him do it,' Lynn said angrily. That was all he said, but it silenced the entire truckload of men. He was grateful that he was locked in, confined within two square feet, his knees tucked under the seat of the back of the forward cubicle, or he might have done some damage.

Lynn let his gaze find the tiny horizontal window. Wistfully considering his lost liberty and the fact that it was likely to remain lost for a long while didn't improve his mood.

The first of the police witnesses was lucid, and sounded well rehearsed. Lynn grew more depressed listening to him tell how he and Coleman had collected rung cars from the lock-ups and parked the changeover car; then from a secondhand dealer had collected the stove to crash the door with; picked up the other two blaggers and made the blag. So positive did he seem that for a moment even Lynn believed he might have done this one, and wondered how the jury could do other than believe it. This was the detective who had made the video that was there in court. The blurred, out-of-focus few minutes of tape would, Lynn was sure, prove conclusively that he wasn't there.

'It's exhibit 17, My Lord,' Gordon Harpenden-Smith QC put in helpfully. 'It has been certified by the forensic laboratory as being a true recording without editing or interference. Perhaps it would be useful for the jury to see the video at this stage?'

'I'm sure it would, Mr Harpenden-Smith,' the judge said. 'Indeed, I would like to see it also.'

There was a short recess while that happened. Lynn had seen the tape along with his barrister and knew no sane person could identify him from it. But then none of this was sane.

Harpenden-Smith need not have done anything further to score when they reconvened, the judge did it all for him. He said, 'This is quite the most remarkable video I have seen.'

Justice Quigley's comment together with the glance he gave across the court to the four men in the dock left no doubt that he believed that these men and those captured on video were the same. He said to the witness, 'You are to be congratulated on both your steady hand and a steady nerve. Especially in view of a beating you had to watch a colleage endure.' He glanced across once more at the defendants and nodded. 'Quite remarkable.'

The confidence the detective displayed while giving evidence wasn't quite so apparent under cross-examination by Horace Macmillan. The force of the defence counsel attack was savage. He proceeded as if his case was already made and won, and Lynn's spirits lifted slightly.

'Wasn't this procedure rather unusual, constable?' Macmillan asked, requiring him to explain how he came to be tailing the robbers.

'No, sir. I don't think so.'

'Presumably you've had lots of cases where you have been conveniently armed with a video camera, instead of what might have been more appropriate, a loaded pistol?' The implication was that the detective had been conducting himself in a less than proper manner.

'It was the first such situation I've been in, sir.'

'I am sure it was. Did it not strike you as odd, your being

asked to pursue a gang of robbers single-handed, armed only with a video camera?'

'It was an observation detail . . .'

'One that was, by the merest coincidence, set up only a day before the robbery? Doesn't that suggest prior knowledge of the robbery?' Horace Macmillan said.

'I don't think we're interested in that kind of conjecture, Mr Macmillan,' Justice Quigley put in, as if anticipating the QC and blocking his tack. 'The witness has stated how he came to be where he was at the time.'

'With respect, My Lord, it's my contention that the video tape offered in evidence, remarkable as it might be in content,' – sarcasm was dripping off his words – 'in no way identifies the defendant Jack Lynn.'

'Then what is the point you are seeking to make?'

'That the police had, in fact, long prior knowledge of the robbery, but chose not to prevent it or send a squad of armed detectives to apprehend the robbers as that would have left them little scope for their subsequent conspiracy to indict Jack Lynn. This quite remarkable video offered in evidence does that extremely well, if only in its inability to identify anyone.'

'In order for that to be acceptable, Mr Macmillan, you would need to establish a prima-facie case against the police. This I feel you won't achieve by conjecture,' the judge said. 'But you're welcome to try.'

The points his silk was scoring against the police were all lost again in that one gesture of the judge's, Lynn felt. The old bastard got the upper hand at every turn.

He wondered if the cross-examination was making any real impression on the jury, even though his brief underscored a number of points about the fit-up conspiracy:

leading the detective to admit he was a keen amateur video maker, then demanding to know why this video was so out of focus; wanting to know how many other people he had videotaped showing an interest in going to the lock-up garages – there were none; how he managed to tail these two cars as he did on his own, when normally about six police cars would be employed to successfully effect such a detail; how remarkably lucky he was to get so close to the robbers at the Gas Board, and undetected. The obvious conclusion was that he wasn't this good or lucky but had, with prior knowledge, been able to position himself outside the Gas Board to wait for the robbery to go off so he could videotape it and aid the police conspiracy. The silk knew his stuff all right, Lynn didn't doubt that for a moment, and up before any other judge he would have been well ahead with the jury.

The next detective in the witness box was effective if only for the sympathy he got due to the fact that he had tried to prevent the robbery and had taken a beating. Even the most liberal-minded juror could not help but respond, a response that would inevitably have some bearing on him and the other men in the dock. Someone had been commissioning an armed robbery, and this detective, single-handed and unarmed, had tried to prevent it. Real heroics!

He was examining one of the sawn-off shotguns that Lynn recognized as having been taken from his garage. He saw the trap closing over him.

'Are you able to say whether that was one of the guns used in the raid on the Gas Board?' Harpenden-Smith asked.

'It is exactly similar, sir,' the detective said. 'I recognize the same plaster binding round the stock. Also the same sort of leather loop through the handle.'

'Exhibit 27, My Lord,' the prosecution said.

As he watched the usher take the exhibit from the witness Lynn felt like calling him a prick, saying that every sawn-off shotgun ever used to make one had plaster around the sawn stock to avoid leaving fingerprints and a loop for holding it.

'It looks singularly offensive,' the judge said.

Next Lynn got a mildly pleasant surprise as Harpenden-Smith proceeded with his witness. The detective went on to ID Benny Isaacs as the man who knocked him to the ground. Lynn had expected he would identify him. However, the witness did then state how he had been there, and that he had subsequently ID'd him when paraded. With great effort Lynn stopped himself from calling out.

William Eaton was a willowy barrister in his fifties, with skin tightly drawn across his face as though having undergone plastic surgery. It seemed difficult for him to smile, for he never did, not even when he made a particularly favourable point in Tully's defence.

'How long were the robbers in the office building?'

In the witness box was DC Peter Footring. He was less sure of himself than his colleague. He didn't seem so well rehearsed.

'About a minute,' he replied.

The previous witness had said about two minutes. Possibly not an important point, other than to add to the general confusion about the robbery.

'Long enough for you and your colleague to get the gas stove loaded onto your van and run those sixty yards or so to the scene?'

'Yes. That's as it happened.'

'Why didn't you go to assist DC Brett? Surely with two of you you'd have had a better chance?'

'He told me to go back and radio for assistance.'

'Even though the detective from Scotland Yard with the video camera was doing just that?'

'We didn't know he was present, sir.'

That was a point Horace Macmillan pursued.

'How did you happen to be where you were at the time of the robbery?' the QC asked.

The detective constable didn't seem to expect the question. 'We were watching for the robbers.'

'If that was the case, you seemed curiously unprepared. No video camera?'

People in court laughed.

'We weren't sure when the robbery was going to happen. If it was, even.'

'So there were two of you there just in case it did, ready to call others to your aid, just as the detective *with* the video camera was supposedly doing?'

DC Footring agreed. Then Macmillan reiterated the point, before saying, 'Was it not true, in fact, that you weren't there because you had heard a rumour of a robbery? But, contrary to police regulations, you were collecting a stove for a senior officer to deliver to his home?'

'No, sir,' Footring said emphatically, like the emphasis would carry the argument. 'We were using the stove as cover to watch for the robbers.'

'I suggest that that isn't true at all. That you were there by the merest chance. Do you wish for an opportunity to change your mind about that? To avoid perjuring yourself?' The brief pointedly opened a folder as if about to pull out a deposition of some kind to contradict the constable's evidence. It was a ploy Lynn recognized as used by the CID during interrogation. 'In fact I have here a copy of the docket your colleague signed on collecting the stove.'

Footring hesitated, and the judge intervened.

'Mr Macmillan, I fail to see the purpose of this, or what possible difference it could make how the police came to be there. The important point is surely the fact that they were present, and witnessed all that occurred.'

'I am returning to the matter of police conspiracy, My Lord,' Macmillan informed him matter-of-factly. 'I am suggesting that the police conspired not only before the crime was committed, but afterwards also, to make certain that their evidence was corroborative, and in so doing masked their own malpractices.'

'If that was the case then I'll alert the Director of Public Prosecutions to take the appropriate steps,' Justice Quigley said in a dismissive tone. 'Meanwhile, perhaps we could take a more direct path through the facts of the case and so assist this court.'

'But almost the entire defence of my client, My Lord, rests in the sincere belief that the police conspired against him.'

'Very well, Mr Macmillan,' the judge conceded with apparent graciousness. 'We will hear your argument.'

This statement by the judge, the tone in which he made it, would seriously undermine any argument that was subsequently put, Lynn decided.

He had promised his silk that he would stay calm, stay silent; had promised the court, and most of all he had promised Dolly. But he didn't know how much longer he could sit there taking this shit.

A dozen policemen passed through the witness box, all of them involved in the chase that took place after the Gas Board robbery, all of them liars, as far as Lynn was concerned. Once the prosecution had extracted the evidence it required from them, the four defence barristers then sought to take their story apart. Each of the barristers was relying on diminishing the credibility of the police to some degree although none relied on that as much as Lynn's own barrister, Horace Macmillan. There were any number of contradictions in the police statements, and while he could see these generally worked in favour of Tully, Isaacs and Coleman they tended to work against his defence in as much as an active police conspiracy might have tidied up such loose ends.

The PC who had organized a roadblock during the chase seemed to get a lot of sympathy as he told of the injuries he had received when run down by the fleeing robbers. Harpenden-Smith made much of this before leading him to positively identify Isaacs and Tully. But counsel for Isaacs then managed to reduce the credibility of that identification somewhat when he produced the test acceleration capability of the model of the car that was hijacked and, on going through the evidence point by point, found that the policeman got to see the two suspects for only one or two seconds through the reflecting windscreen of a car travelling at seventy miles an hour.

DI Pyle, being the officer in charge of the case, was the last policeman to give evidence. He was taken through it from his first knowledge of Lynn's involvement, to his interrogation and identification. He was frighteningly professional, Lynn found, and suspected he had probably been in the witness box more times, and under more pressure. Harpenden-Smith couldn't want for a better witness. Pyle related the details of the case as if they were irrefutable facts. The prosecution didn't need to prompt him.

'How far in advance did you know about the robbery, inspector?' Harpenden-Smith asked.

'It was first brought up about a fortnight before by a colleague in Criminal Intelligence. We weren't able to do anything about it at the time through insufficient information.'

'From your subsequent inquiries you found out who was going to be involved?'

'Two of them, was all.'

'Putting a detective on watch with a video camera, is that a usual procedure, inspector?'

'It's one we're having to employ more and more, in order to cover an increasing number of investigations.'

'You try and stretch your very limited resources over as wide a field in order to give the public the best service possible?' Harpenden-Smith said.

'That is correct,' Pyle said.

'I would like to go back for a moment, if I may, to consider your earlier evidence about the contents of the lock-up garage. To refresh the jurors' memory, this contained a veritable arsenal, marked exhibits 37 to 82, photographs of which are in Bundle 2. Perhaps you would just remind the court what explanation the defendant Jack Lynn gave about the contents of this garage.'

Pyle flipped back through the notes he had with him in the witness box. 'When I questioned him about the contents of the garage, he replied, "Don't know nothing about them. I let the garage to a fella I met in a pub, a man called Richard Cook." Lynn had in his possession receipts made out to Richard Cook.'

'For money paid to him?'

'No, for rental to the owner of the garages, one James Fowlie,' Pyle replied.

'We heard earlier in this trial from James Fowlie, who identified Jack Lynn as being Richard Cook, the man who rented his garage. But prior to that, had you made any inquiries or tried to establish the existence of Richard Cook as a third party renting the garage not from Fowlie but Lynn?'

'We did. We made extensive inquiries, but the result was negative. Our conclusion was that Lynn and Cook were one and the same.'

'That the sublessee didn't exist, that the garage and its nefarious contents were the responsibility of Jack Lynn entirely?' Harpenden-Smith concluded.

'Yes, sir.'

When Macmillan rose to cross-examine the DI his tack was full of ploys to deflect the jury from the witness's evidence, but Lynn wasn't sure how successful he was.

'How long have you been a policeman, inspector?' the QC asked, glancing over his notes as though ready to contradict him.

'Twenty years, just on,' Pyle replied.

'And during that period how many complaints have been made against you?'

This was an aproach that Lynn was getting more nervous about in case it backfired as it had done a couple of times earlier when Macmillan had attacked the credibility, the truthfulness, the honesty of other policemen in the witness box. The judge always seemed to find some way of diminishing the attack, rendering it less effective, the cunning old bastard.

'Is this pertinent, Mr Macmillan?' Justice Quigley asked right on cue. 'Or are you merely pursuing the theme of police corruption with which you have doggedly persisted?'

'It is pertinent, My Lord. If you will bear with me for a while.' The implication was that he wasn't being given a chance.

'Then I would like you to come swiftly to the point.'

Macmillan bowed his head to the judge with excessive courtesy. 'How many complaints, Inspector Pyle?'

'About eleven, I think – all were unsubstantiated.'

'Having been investigated by your colleagues,' Macmillan paused, making it appear like a conclusion, 'you were cleared of the charges eleven members of the public saw fit to bring against you? Is it true that you have a complaint currently outstanding against you? For conspiring to pervert the course of justice?'

'I have,' Pyle said. 'But only from one of the prisoners in the dock. Lynn.'

'Is that to infer he no longer has any rights, inspector?' the QC asked sharply.

'No, sir.' Pyle seemed slightly defensive now.

'So his complaint per se is no less valid than anyone else's?'

'He has the same right as anyone to complain, sir.'

'Would you tell us the specific nature of his complaint?'

'Lynn is claiming that I manufactured evidence against him to get him convicted.'

'Isn't that precisely what you're doing, inspector?' Macmillan made this sound like an everyday occurrence.

'No, sir. As far as I've been able to ascertain, Lynn was very much involved.'

Justice Quigley pulled off his spectacles. It was a signal that he wasn't able to allow this attack upon the police to continue. 'Do you believe this to be a malicious complaint against you, inspector?'

'Yes, My Lord, I do,' Pyle said.

'A device all too familiar to criminals nowadays,' the judge commented, cutting the ground from under the defence. 'Proceed.'

'When arresting Jack Lynn, did you not say: "It's your turn, son. You're well overdue"? Meaning he should have been put away a long time ago?'

'No, I didn't.'

'You're quite sure?'

'Quite sure.'

Macmillan glanced over his notes, as if they contained the unremitting truth. 'When did you decide Lynn was involved in the Gas Board robbery?'

'Approximately two days after the robbery took place.'

'After you had, in fact, arrested and subsequently released a fourth man?'

'Happens all the time.'

'The police arresting the wrong people?'

'Eliminating suspects,' Pyle countered.

'So having eliminated this *wrong* man, you had a vacancy. Lynn seemed the most likely candidate, did he not? How did you discover he was involved, as you claim, in this crime?'

'Through an informer, sir.'

Lynn became alert with anticipation now.

'A source you believed to be reliable?'

'Hundred per cent reliable, sir.'

'A member of the criminal fraternity?'

'He was,' Pyle said.

'Yet still you consider him one hundred per cent reliable and truthful,' Macmillan said dismissively. 'Why did he give you this information?'

'I'm not sure, sir.'

That almost made Lynn laugh out loud, it was so outrageous.

'Could it be duress? Did you have some sort of lever on him?'

'No, sir.'

'Then revenge? That's a common motive among informers. Could that be the reason this convicted criminal chose to come to you with his information? – he is a convicted criminal?'

'Yes, sir. But I can't think that was his motive.'

'And you believe the word of a convicted criminal was enough to arrest Jack Lynn?'

'It proved so, sir. Having arrested him we found other evidence,' Pyle said.

'Let us examine some of this evidence. We have less than satisfactory eyewitnesses' testimony, apart from twelve police witnesses – all of whom, incidentally, are quite certain they didn't discuss the case or corroborate what each saw. A more disinterested bunch of policemen one could not wish to meet. We have a flying helmet which the police say Lynn wore for the robbery, only it's two sizes too small; the hair sample found inside, on which there is a forensic report, not only matches Lynn's hair, but approximately thirty-two per cent of the population of this country. Then we have the find at the garage, a garage which Jack Lynn sublet. But no extensive search was made to find the sublessee because the police were convinced they had the right man. And you came to your swift conclusion about that on the word of a convicted criminal . . .'

Lynn glanced apprehensively at the judge who was reaching for his glasses again. He held his breath for the counterblast, even though the silk made some worthwhile points for the jury.

'Mr Macmillan,' the judge said, 'perhaps you would conclude this rambling surmise, and restrict yourself to cross-examination.'

'My Lord,' Macmillan said, acknowledging him. Then to Pyle, 'Was this reliable informer named Michael Fielder?'

Pyle seemed genuinely surprised that the QC had his name.

Recognizing the detective's dilemma, the judge said, 'If you feel a need to protect the identity of your informer, inspector, then you may refrain from answering.'

'Revealing the man might endanger him, My Lord.'

The judge accepted this and indicated for Macmillan to proceed.

'This *unnamed* informer, is he an active criminal?'

'I wouldn't think so. Merely an associate of criminals.'

'Is it not true that you have a quid pro quo arrangement with criminal informers, allowing them to commit minor crimes, provided they supply you with information on other bigger crimes?'

'No, sir,' Pyle said emphatically.

Pyle remained in the witness box for three days being cross-examined, and each of the defence barristers tried to open further the credibility gap in the police evidence that Macmillan had made. Lynn felt confused and demoralized by the time the DI stepped down. He thought his cause was no further forward while, ironically, he also thought the three men in the dock with him might now get a result. They had every reason at this rate to take it all as calmly as they were; he had only barely managed to remain in court, having twice lost his temper and called Pyle a fucking liar. The judge had given him his final warning; it might well have been his sentence, too.

Although not unhappy about the way things seemed to be going in court, Pyle wasn't entirely convinced they were going to get a result. Nowadays you couldn't rely on any court to give the result you wanted. He knew he could allow himself to sit comfortably throughout the trial with the firm belief that the jury were eating up every word the prosecution was feeding them, then suddenly it could go right the other way with the jurors giving a chuck. If that was how this came out it might leave him with a lot of explaining to do, especially with the complaint Lynn had made about him supposedly perverting the course of justice. A result for Lynn would tend to support that, and it was odds-on that the blagger would proceed with the complaint, or might even sue him as more and more people were doing now instead of complaining. However, he tried not to allow that prospect to worry him, for the prosecution had a surprise in store which was certain to knock the defence sideways. Now that all the evidence from police witnesses was concluded, they were offering an additional-evidence witness: Clifford Harding. He was waiting in the cells below court, and was far from happy about the position he was being forced into; possibly the move might endanger him, and would probably cost him most of his friends, but the alternative for not doing what he was asked would cost him a lot more. Pyle had spelt out just what the alternative meant: his pressing ahead with the possession-of-firearms charge which Harding still had hanging over him. This would mean the loss of his liberty for certain. The possibility that once brought into the witness box Harding would renege on their deal and become a hostile witness was something he had considered – it had happened before with witnesses – but he didn't think it likely here. Anyway, he had the tape of Harding's confession, and he had made plain to him the consequences of going back on their deal: not only would he lose his liberty, but he would do so in addition to being identified as a grass.

Heading along the corridor for the police room, wearing his light Aquascutum mac, which was damp from the summer shower he got caught in, Pyle encountered Harpenden-Smith with one of his juniors. They exchanged a few pleasantries. The prosecutor wanted to know about the witness. Pyle told him how he was awaiting his big moment.

'Is he going to co-operate, inspector?' he asked.

'Well, he's not exactly happy about it,' Pyle informed him.

'It is important we have his evidence. Juries can get recklessly confused with such a concerted attack on the probity of the police. Harding's appearance will help set their minds at rest. Excellent. See you in court.'

Surprise hit Jack Lynn with the force of a blow in the face when the prosecution rose and begged leave at this late stage to introduce some additional evidence, and, having had it granted, called Clifford Harding. He saw him slither through the court and into the witness box like the snake he was. All the while the thought running through Lynn's head wasn't about what Harding knew, but why he would do this. Clearly he was part of the fit-up, and Pyle would have primed him, and doubtless put him on a promise. And the dirty no-good slag obviously listened to him. Anger was racing through him now as he tried to think up ways of hurting Harding. He had offered him work, and never would have suspected him capable of doing this. Fielder, not Harding, was the grass, that was the whisper he had got. But then Harding had been bang in trouble, while surviving, and keeping his liberty, must have been all that mattered to him. Keeping his liberty was all Harding might do.

'Jack told me he had this one going off at the Gas Board at Abbey Wood, worth about ten grand,' Harding was saying from the witness box. 'He said he was a bit short-handed, like, and asked me if I wanted to make it with him . . .'

Anger finally exploded out of Lynn. 'You liar!' he screamed. 'You dirty, no-good fucking liar. I'll top you! You lying fucker, I'll fucking slaughter you . . .' He started to climb out of the dock to get at the witness, all reasoning gone now. He was dragged back by two prison officers who were in the dock also.

Confusion and a babble of excited interest followed the scuffle in the dock. Silence was called for, but there was no immediate response.

'Remove the prisoner,' the judge said firmly. 'He will be held in the cells for the duration of this trial.'

Lynn didn't want to go, and put up a struggle, like his life depended on getting to Harding and doing him some damage. Other uniforms in the shape of policemen and officers of the court came to assist and, with kicks and punches, they dragged him down the steps from the dock. In the area below, where there was more room to manoeuvre, Lynn had less chance to protest physically with seven against him, but still he didn't give up. It took a while for them to subdue him sufficiently to get him into a cell and lock the door.

It took him much, much longer to even start to calm down. But still his thoughts churned angrily, and he would only have needed to glimpse Harding to fly into a rage again. Finding an opportunity to do him some real damage was all he could think of. He had nothing to lose now, he was convinced of that. Harding's appearance in the witness box had removed any chance he had of getting a result. That thought depressed him more than anything as he sat on the bench bed. His jacket pocket was torn and the sleeve was coming out of the shoulder. Buttons had gone from his shirt, and there was blood on him from a nosebleed he had given one of the police officers. A couple of his ribs ached, and his left cheek was puffy and painful, but other than that his pain was all mental.

As he waited in silence and isolation he was as close as he had been in a long while to crying. After what he guessed was about an hour a screw looked in on him, but didn't speak. Then again before lunch. This time he asked him if he wanted any food. Lynn didn't feel like eating, but he accepted the offer.

Soon after that, Tully, Coleman and Isaacs were returned to the cell for their food. They were as cheerful as a gang of scaffolders going to the cafe.

'That was a right fucking upset up in court, Jack,' Tully said. 'Should think that fucking judge'll give us all about an extra five for that.'

Lynn didn't say anything. There were a lot of questions he wanted to ask, but if he started here these three men would bear the brunt of his angry feelings. They deserved nothing less for their part in this, but he knew here he'd have a real fight on his hands.

'That silk of yourn, Jack,' Tully went on. 'He's ruining that no-good slag, he is.'

'Won't be worth a toss, his evidence,' Isaacs added like he was trying to appease him. 'He's some brief, Jack.'

'Did all right, did he?' Lynn was unable to avoid the pleasure he felt at this.

'Fucking slaughtered him. Reckoned how Harding and Pyle had a deal, Pyle had put him on a promise. He did terrific.' Tully suddenly turned to the door. 'Oi! Charlie! Where's our grub?'

Just before the court resumed Horace Macmillan came down to see Lynn. They were left alone in the cell.

'The prosecution has concluded its case,' he told Lynn. His arrogant manner as he stood, legs braced, hands clasped behind his back, pushing out his gown, made Lynn feel awkward and inadequate. He didn't enjoy the feeling. 'Superficially, the evidence is damaging. But the jury are sufficiently confused and plagued with doubts by this time for us not to worry too much.'

'Can I go back to court now?' Lynn asked. Somehow he felt he would have some control over things if he was present. Macmillan shook his head.

'Quigley is nothing if not consistent. I'm afraid you're going to have to sit it out. I'm not going to call you.'

That surprised Lynn. 'Why not? Someone's gotta say what lying slags they all are.'

'You'll have to trust me. You go into the witness box,

the first question the prosecution is going to ask is how you get your living. Can you tell them? The second question, how did you pay for your car? Valued at, what, twenty thousand?'

'But I got it on HP. For five grand deposit, was all,' Lynn protested as if making a valid point.

'Most of the jury are probably struggling to run a Nissan Micra. And probably not a new one at that. I'll say all you'd wish to say, and without allowing the prosecution any advantage. Just be patient.'

Lynn gave the barrister a peculiar look, as he suddenly felt a surge of hatred for this man, who he believed could have no real understanding of him or the many people like him who he must have dealt with over the years. All he had done was learn a peculiar set of rules by which to play a particular game, and the loser was never this man, and neither winning nor losing made any difference to him at all. At that moment he hated him and all his kind no less than he did Harding and all his kind.

'Is there anything you want now?' Macmillan asked.

'My bit of liberty,' Lynn replied automatically.

'That I will endeavour to secure for you.'

Lynn continued to look at him, seeing as much doubt in his face as there must have been on his own. The doubt stayed with him long after the barrister had departed with a jolly quip. He was alone then, and had never felt more lonely. His future was being argued over some twenty feet above his head, though he suspected it had been decided long before. At that moment he couldn't grasp the reality of the situation. It was as if he had started to float and had subsequently lost all contact with life around him. Occasionally people passed along the corridor outside his cell, nameless, faceless people, shuffling through his suddenly futureless world. The thought of hanging himself with his belt came into his mind. That's why they had left him his belt, he concluded.

Alone, waiting, he shivered as if the ghost of someone who had gone before had done that. Perhaps someone who had scratched some of the graffiti into the walls. One legend read: 'Fifteen for armed robbery – I'll do it on my prick. A. Duncan.' It was dated two weeks ago. He didn't know who A. Duncan was but the thought of him starting fifteen was more depressing for the mirror the prospect offered him. What had that villain done? he wondered, and then if some slag like Pyle had fitted him. That only made him feel worse.

The cases for the defence were concluded a good deal quicker than that for the prosecution. Then they had no defence as far as Pyle was concerned. The shortest was for Lynn's. His principal witness was his wife. She confirmed his alibi and couldn't be shaken from it. But who would believe a villain's wife?

The prosecution took a whole day delivering the closing address. Harpenden-Smith was eloquent if lacking passion. While the danger man, Horace Macmillan, was both eloquent and passionate in closing speech. His client was innocent, the victim of a malicious and vindictive police conspiracy, he insisted, and he gave the jury but one alternative: to find Jack Lynn not guilty. The speech might have been more effective had not the other three defence barristers taken a similar line.

The jury listened with studious attention when the judge summed up. They adopted thoughtful poses to show how carefully they were listening as they hung on his every word, probably in order to fill the gaps left by their flagging attention, lack of concentration, and failing memory over the past three weeks. What the judge said truly mattered.

'The vast array of evidence presented here over the sixteen days of this trial would appear overwhelming in its indication of the guilt of the four defendants. Witness after witness has testified as to their presence at the scene of the crime, and the subsequent crimes in aiding their escape from the prompt response by the police.' The judge removed his thick glasses, his tone becoming dismissive as he spelt out the alternative. 'But you must consider the elements of conflict and confusion apparent in this testimony, and ask yourselves whether this amounts to reasonable doubt. Were the witnesses simply confused in this emotion-charged situation, as people sometimes are? Or was the confusion purposely instigated by robbers who, with criminal foresight, were wearing excess clothing to first disguise themselves, to then subsequently discard when effecting their escape? You must consider those points carefully, but remember these particular robbers in their criminal confidence chose to leave their faces uncovered, and were unconcerned that they were seen. If you find the eyewitness testimony too confusing to be reliable, as is sometimes the case nowadays, especially when unsupported, then you must give some weight to the remaining evidence. First there is the garage which contained the most base instruments of mayhem one could encounter. A man found with a sawn-off shotgun in his possession can only be judged for what he surely is: a robber prepared to do violence as a means to his own wicked end.

What is the alternative? Can there be one? There is no possible legal occupation for which such a weapon could be employed. Secondly, there was a great deal of money, money for which Mr Lynn was neither able nor willing to account. But of course having such an amount of money isn't a crime in itself; however, the wholly honest man can adequately give account of such sums, and Lynn steadfastly refused to give account of this to the police. You may ask, how could he honestly have come by it? For he seems to have pursued no legitimate occupation other than casual taxi driving. Then you must give proper weight to the testimony of the gas company employee who identified some of those banknotes as being part of the money he had counted for collection by the security company. But as counsel for the defence pointed out, cashiers, along with bank tellers, mark thousands of notes during the course of a year, some of which coincidentally might have arrived among those notes found in Lynn's possession.' His tone gave the coincidence no validity and Pyle found himself nodding in agreement on every point. 'Also there is that remarkable video tape of the robbery actually taking place. If, however, you choose to set aside both the eyewitnesses' testimony and evidence presented in court, then, and only then,' he paused and looked long and hard at the jury, 'you must accept the supposition, which seems to constitute the entire basis for the defence, that there was a widespread police conspiracy afoot here. A conspiracy involving not just one or two police officers, but all sixteen who were actively involved in the case. But wait. Such a conspiracy would not have stopped there. Others would have to be implicated, senior police officers who signed and authenticated police notes would have been involved, plus both the prosecution and people in the offices of the Crown Prosecutions Service. If that is what you believe, that such people, people with hitherto blameless characters, did actively conspire against these men, then you will doubtless find the defendants not guilty, and a new form of police institution will be urgently required. However, should you choose to dismiss the defence hypothesis that there was such a police conspiracy in operation, then you should find the defendants guilty.' Mr Justice Quigley paused and replaced his glasses. 'The defence throughout this trial made much of the fact that eyewitness identification testimony was totally invalid. Not merely in this particular case, but in general. When you retire to consider your verdict, I want you further to consider the implication of this also, for it reaches far beyond this single case. If such testimony is in future to be held up as being less than valid, then it leaves the armoury of the police in their fight against crime sadly depleted. It leaves them without the invaluable support of honest members of the public, of people who are prepared to step forward and assist when their assistance is so desperately needed.' He removed his glasses again and tapped them against one neatly manicured thumb and smiled at the jury. 'I want you to go away now and carefully consider your verdict.'

A smile crept across Pyle's face as he turned to DS Lethridge, who was sitting in court with him. Both knew what the result would be. There could be little doubt after that summing-up. Not that he had much faith in juries. 'Come on, I'll buy you a pint, Eric.'

The faces of the four defendants turned expectantly towards the jury as they filed back in and took their places. Some were self-consciously avoiding looking at the prisoners in the dock, Pyle noticed. That was always a good sign, but still his mouth went dry. The jury weren't looking at him either. So it could still go badly wrong for him. What those four in the dock were feeling right then he couldn't guess, and he didn't much care. They were villains, and being fitted was an occupational hazard! Their faces were set with a slightly haunted look, each showing traces of fear. Some were coping better than others, but none of them openly cracked. He wondered if the gaoler had slipped any of them a stiff brandy. Some of those old uniform-carriers had more feeling than sense!

When the jury was seated the clerk rose.

'Who is the foreman of the jury?' he asked.

'I am,' a woman said.

'Have you reached a verdict in respect of each of the prisoners?'

'Yes, we have – with the exception of Mr Coleman.'

The exception meant further delay. Pyle glanced at Mr Justice Quigley, who clearly wasn't pleased. 'Then I may tell you at this point,' he said like he was warning them, 'that you may return to the jury room and arrive at a majority verdict, of ten to two.' The judge sent them away with a terse hand gesture.

The jury were out for another four and a half hours and Fred Pyle found the strain of waiting was having more effect on him than it should. There was no relief when the jury returned, for they were no further forward.

'Is there any likelihood of your reaching a ten-to-two majority if you were given further time?' the judge wanted to know.

'No, sir,' the woman said.

The judge's humour wasn't improved by this. 'Very well. Let us hear the remaining verdicts.'

'May I make an application for bail at this stage, My Lord?' said defence counsel for Coleman, bobbing up. He didn't improve the judge's humour.

'You may not!' he snapped.

The barrister resumed his seat. This was a distraction, but Pyle's thoughts came anxiously back to the possible verdicts of the others.

'Count one charges John Francis Tully with attempted murder,' the clerk said. 'How do you find him? Guilty or not guilty?' Pyle held his breath.

'Not guilty . . .'

That wasn't possible! He couldn't believe it. He turned to Lethridge as if for some explanation as he heard the nervous excitement bubble out of Tully at the result.

'Oh, t'rific. That's bloody t'rific . . .'

If that was the only surprise he was going to get, Pyle decided, he might have swallowed it. But it didn't prove so as the clerk went through the various counts with the foreman of the jury.

'Count three charges Benjamin Michael Isaacs with

conspiracy to commit robbery,' the clerk continued in the formal, ritualized manner. 'How do you find him? Guilty or not guilty?'

'Not guilty!'

Pyle shook his head in dismay as Isaacs giggled out loud now. He could well afford to giggle, having had a result on the two previous counts.

'Silence in court!' the clerk called as the excited murmer grew. Like Tully, Benny Isaacs got a result right the way through the card.

'This is like some bad fucking joke,' Pyle whispered to his DS. 'It makes no fucking sense at all.' He shook his head again, feeling like someone had punched him in the stomach.

'Count one charges John Albert Lynn with attempted murder,' the clerk went on with familiar monotony. 'How do you find him? Guilty or not guilty?'

'Guilty.'

The reply suddenly lifted his spirit, and Lynn's response cheered him even more.

'What . . .? Leave off!' Lynn said and gripped the rail of the dock like he was about to leap out. The prison officer nearest him put a hand on his shoulder.

The verdict of guilty on every count against Lynn caused a lot of comment from those in court. Through it Pyle watched Lynn, who was standing stock-still and disbelieving in the dock, like he was stunned. The reality of what had occurred would sooner or later penetrate his thick skull. The result was truly ironical, he found, that the one person who wasn't actually on the blag should be convicted for it, while those who almost certainly were got to walk.

Pyle was sure it struck Lynn the same way. He was equally sure that he would learn more from the lesson it provided than Lynn would. What it taught him was not to be so confident in presuming a conviction would follow guilt. Real evidence, he decided, had to have been worked on as closely as that which was manufactured. Still, it was done now, and there was no second chance this time round. But he would pass Tully and Isaacs back to Criminal Intelligence to keep tabs on.

'I can't offer you this court's thanks,' the judge finally told the jury. 'You have by your verdicts shown how fallible juries are.'

The barristers representing Tully and Isaacs were on their feet one after the other asking for their discharge. The judge gave them it grudgingly.

'Coleman will be taken back to prison to await further trial. I will hear your application for bail afterwards, Mr Robbins,' he told his barrister.

The freed blaggers dived out of the dock like they were afraid the jury might change its mind.

'Tell them!' Lynn appealed, as he swung round to watch them go. Then more desperately as they disappeared, 'Tell 'em, you slags! Tell them I wasn't fucking well involved!'

The clerk ordered silence.

Separating a file from several he had in front of him, the prosecutor rose and adjusted his gown like he was making himself comfortable for a long speech. Mr Justice Quigley glanced at him. Pyle was sure he awaited the poison in anticipation.

'The prisoner has seven previous convictions, My Lord,' Harpenden-Smith reminded the judge. If Pyle had had some sort of deal with Lynn all the poison would have been left out, which in turn would have saved him a few years on his sentence. Usually the consideration was either for a guilty plea or an earner. They had no such arrangement.

'I will hear the last three,' the judge said.

The prosecutor went through the details. Respectively they amounted to eight years for robbery, which had been his last conviction; three for conspiracy and two for stealing a motor vehicle. Lynn's brief would have a struggle to say anything worthwhile in mitigation. Even the details of his personal life sounded somehow like an offence when the prosecutor put them before the court.

'Thank you, Mr Harpenden-Smith,' the judge said when the QC finally resumed his seat. 'The Criminal Justice Act requires me to seek probation reports before I pass sentence. Are there any special circumstances surrounding the prisoner which the court should be made aware of before I follow that course?

'No, My Lord,' he said, half-rising.

'What about the fitting, you filthy bastard?' Dolly Lynn screamed from the public gallery, where she stood gripping the rail. She was in tears. 'You bastard! You rotten, filthy bastards!'

The clerk called for silence through the disturbance which followed Dolly's removal.

'Leave her alone, you fucking slags! Leave her,' Lynn shouted.

Soon after that the judge ordered him removed. He would be taken back to Brixton prison, where he would be assessed for sentencing. No one could seriously think there might be any alternative to prison for this man, Pyle decided. But, like everyone else, he would have to wait three or four weeks to find out when Lynn would be brought back to court for sentencing.

The arrogance that Horace Macmillan had displayed throughout the trial was gone when he returned to court to make his obligatory plea in mitigation on behalf of a much subdued Jack Lynn. Even the physical stature of the defence barrister seemed to have disappeared, Pyle noticed. He wondered if the brief had had any real belief in his client's innocence in the first place. Now that the trial was long over and Lynn was back at the Old Bailey for sentencing, the brief had to abide by the rules of the game and live by that verdict, and proceed as if his guilt were now an indisputable fact.

'I'm sure, My Lord, you will agree with me that the prisoner before you is a most unfortunate man. One who was given less than adequate means to equip himself for life, one who blundered forward for the most part, caught in a downward spiral of deprivation and criminality. No one has lost more as a result of his behaviour than Lynn himself. This said, My Lord, he is not a man devoid of all hope. There is a bright spark of humanity within him, one that needs the right sort of fanning to encourage it, rather than oppressive regimes to douse it completely. As you will see from the reports before you, Lynn lost not one but two parents at the tender age of four, when his mother committed suicide following his father's death. The young Jack was, with his three siblings, institutionalized. Barely knowing the warmth of a family, and despite having only critics rather than examples in the harsh system within which he was raised, he did manage to marry a warm and loving woman and produce two considerate daughters, both of whom are devoted to their father, as he is to them and to their well-being. I'm sure, My Lord, this will carry some weight with you when you come to pass sentence on this man. Just as I know you will not be prejudiced by the fact that he sought to defend himself against these charges rather than admit his guilt . . .'

Despite the appearance Lynn gave in the dock the spark of anger was still with him as he shouted, 'I was fucking-well fitted – I was, I tell you –'

At that point Horace Macmillan rested his plea. Pyle glanced over at Lynn, wondering how this villain even managed to stand here, he had shot himself in the foot that often . . .

'In the probation reports, My Lord,' Macmillan went on, 'you will I'm sure have seen one on the prisoner from Dr Ryder. Might I direct you to take particular note of what this psychologist said about him, My Lord, and about the possible effects of long-term incarceration on this man.'

'I have carefully read and digested that report, Mr Macmillan,' the judge told him. 'The circumstances of this case are quite straightforward. I have no need to give special attention to that report to help me make up my mind as to his sentence, but you are right to bring it to my notice, Mr Macmillan. Perhaps Mr Lynn's problem is that he takes longer than the average person to learn his lesson, so perhaps his previous sentences haven't been long enough.'

Pyle couldn't resist looking over at Lynn at that. He looked as if he was about to cry. If that was all he did when he was weighed off then they'd have no problems.

'John Lynn,' the judge began, glancing at the prisoner, then away. 'You have been found guilty of attempted murder; robbery; conspiracy to rob. All crimes of a professional criminal out to further his own wicked ends. For these crimes, of which I believe you were the instigator, you must bear the full consequences, as by your silence two of your confederates have gone scot-free. You are a man who has lived his life by crime, and one who, if free, might reasonably be expected to do so for the rest of his active life; therefore I must – for the sake of the public at large – seek to curtail that activity. For the attempted murder of two police officers, you will go to prison for fifteen years. As you have been found guilty of armed robbery I am required to send you to prison for a minimum of fifteen years, and do so without hesitation. Those two sentences will, however, run concurrently. On the other charge you will go to prison for five years. This sentence is to run consecutively with the previous sentence so you will go to prison for a total of twenty years. Take the prisoner below.' The judge paused while Lynn was taken away by the two warders, two of whose colleagues had joined them in the dock as if in anticipation of trouble. Pyle felt relieved when he went down quietly.

'Throughout this unnecessarily protracted trial,' the judge said, 'there have been a number of allegations against the police. Allegations which, I am pleased to say, the jury appears to consider unsubstantiated. By this one verdict the actions of the police officers have been completely vindicated. Indeed, throughout this trial, under constant attack as they have been, I have found the conduct of the police exemplary. It would be a sad day for the police institution if such cavalier accusations were proven. For if the police are dishonest, then there would be no security for the citizens of this country. I commend Inspector Pyle and his colleagues for their courage and for the diligence and the scrupulous manner in which they have conducted themselves.'

Pyle accepted the commendation without so much as a blush.

It was done, they had got a result; not quite the result he had expected, but as the judge had said, the verdict vindicated their actions. The end always justified the means, he believed. Getting villains locked away was an important achievement, however it was done.

'We got a bit of a result there, Fred,' Lethridge said, as they emerged from the main entrance of the court into the warm evening sunshine.

'Didn't we just.' Pyle was feeling pleased with himself. 'Be a long time before he does any more villainy.' There was no sense of guilt or remorse over the way he had sent him down. 'Still, it does make you wonder, Eric. Those others getting a result.'

''S not enough any more, is it? Being bang to rights.'

'In future we'd better look extra hard, no matter how good the evidence seems to be.'

They went across the road towards the wine bar.

'They can't do it, Jack,' Dolly said through her tears. 'The rotten bastards. You weren't there. You was with me . . .'

'They must have wanted me so bad . . . We'll see what happens on appeal,' Lynn told her. 'That's the next step. We'll get it started. We're not going to take this fitting lightly. There'll be murders inside if I don't get a result.' Yet paradoxically he was almost resigned to his future.

'I won't stop screaming it's a fit-up, Jack . . . I won't . . .'

Dolly was in the corridor outside his cell, speaking to him through the grille. The warder wasn't obliged to allow the meeting, but he had done so while Lynn was waiting to be collected and taken off to prison. He'd been told he would go to the Scrubs initially, and then on down to the Island, probably.

'It's time to go, love,' the warder said, appearing behind her.

'Jack?' Alarm came into her voice. 'Look, I have a million things I need to say to him. I can't just leave him, I can't. I love him; I need him. Jack!' Their fingers touched at the grille. Suddenly he felt the breath being sucked from his lungs.

'Give the girls my love . . .' was all he could think of. He wanted to tell Dolly how much he loved her, but didn't, and later regretted not doing so.

'Jack . . .' She started away with the uniform gaoler.

Lynn pressed his face to the grille, desperate for one last glimpse of his wife.

'You lousy bastards!' Dolly screamed along the corridor. 'The lying sods. He didn't do nothing! The police lied!'

Her voice was finally lost with the slamming of a heavy door, when she was shut on the far side.

Lynn was aware at that moment of the steel against his face. He felt desolate, trapped.

The dark-green Ford Transit headed along the motorway at a steady fifty-five miles an hour. The midday road was congested, but the driver seemed in no particular hurry. Lynn was in even less of a hurry to get to his destination. He saw the police motorcyclist ahead and soon the van driver made a left-hand signal for the slip road. Lynn glanced round and watched the police do the same.

'We've reached the county border,' one of the prison officers escorting him explained.

A new police escort of two motorcyclists was waiting to take over. He was a category 'A' prisoner and little expense seemed to be spared in getting him safely to prison. Right at that moment he couldn't think of a single person in the world who might be interested in helping him to make a break.

The minibus with its horizontal barred windows tended to invite stares from the free people, who then quickly averted their gaze, especially if he happened to catch their eye. He wondered if they did that out of guilt, or a there-but-for-the-grace-of-God sense of relief that made them look away so quickly. He was the only one of the four occupants of the van who was looking out of the window, sitting on his own, staring unseeingly at the passing scenery and the moving vehicles. His thoughts churned angrily as he considered the freedom of choice people beyond the bus still had. That freedom was now denied him. There was no relief from trying to tell himself that most of the people out there were no less prisoners, or that the four screws who were escorting him were prisoners themselves. They did at least have some chance of getting a result for themselves! Four seemingly endless days ago he had been weighed off with twenty years. Twenty years. The result of a fitting from the filth. Still this wouldn't sink in, and the three nights he had spent in Wandsworth prison did little to make it a perceptible reality. Sitting or pacing the whole time, as he had done, thinking about his sentence, left him feeling numb with disbelief. The initial shock had worn off, leaving a tiredness, which he was grateful for in some ways. The thoughts that rolled through his head, as if on a loop, made him want to murder someone. Over and over in his mind he killed Detective Inspector Pyle; then, his thoughts slaughtered those three slags who knew he hadn't been involved with them, but hadn't offered him an out; he next blundered bloodily on to get the vindictive judge for weighing off with twenty. Only the burden of injustice that he felt he was carrying for the entire wronged criminal fraternity stopped him hurting someone in a vain attempt to ameliorate his own hurt. His wife's protest as she had been led away after seeing him in the cells below the court was the point at which thinking became unbearable.

A family travelling along the motorway, their car overloaded with holiday luggage, stared at the prison truck as it overtook them. The kids pointed to the van as if recognizing what it was. The picture made Lynn prickle with shame and brought to mind his own children. He had seen little of Carol and Sandra during the eight months of his remand and trial, and still hadn't got used to being without them. Those two thought the world of him and he would willingly top the Bill who had separated him from them. Both would be grown women by the time he got out, unless he got a result on appeal. He was hopeful, but even so this unjust separation was a wedge being driven between them and he would make someone pay for it finally.

'You sure you don't want a few hands, Jack?' said one of the screws, as he paused from dealing the cards.

'Deal the card!' one of the others rasped at him.

'Oh, what, you losing a few bob, Ernie?'

'C'mon. You got more fucking rabbit than my old woman.'

Distracted for a moment, Lynn looked across at them but didn't comment. He had no wish to join their game. He was too close to the screws as it was. He watched the cards slide clumsily out of the dealer's hands, and thought about the stupid waste of money in sending him on his own like this with four screws and a police escort. In Wandsworth there were two other cons who were both category 'A', and like him, were due to go to the same prison. He turned away to gaze out of the window again, his agitated, angry thoughts quickly absorbing him.

At forty-one years of age, he had all his working life got his living from villainy, apart from a few brief periods when inside. Not surprisingly he had lost weight recently – his clothes were now fairly loose on him. They had a crumpled, slept-in appearance, even though he had changed them frequently during his remand period. He had retained his own clothes, not having gone through reception at Wandsworth, nor having been assessed because of a prison officers' dispute.

There was little in his appearance that instantly identified him as a villain he would have argued; however, as a criminal, and one who had never denied his criminality, he had always accepted the odds in favour of being arrested at some point and even of going to prison. He knew you had a run, and, depending on how lucky rather than how clever you were, you earned a nice few quid; then when trouble came you tried to have a deal with the filth, get a result; if you couldn't then you did your time. If you couldn't do your time, as a CID has once said to him, then you shouldn't do the crime. He accepted that. There had been no real problem over his previous arrests. But the longer the good run of luck he'd had, the nicer the blags he'd been involved in, the harder it had been to face the prospect of going down. That would never have come about, but for the diabolical conspiracy on the part of the police, the prosecution, that judge. Had he been nicked for robbing the Tote at Catford dogtrack he might more readily have accepted his good run coming to an end. Here his thoughts were drawn to the angry, hostile conclusion that everyone in authority had been part of that conspiracy, and eventually he would find the will and determine the means to do something about that. He would resist his sentence for all he was worth.

There were two meal stops en route to the prison, and for neither of them was he allowed to get out of the van, other than to go to the lavatory in handcuffs, accompanied by two screws. Food from the Little Chef was brought out to him and eaten in the van.

The crenellated gatehouse of the prison was an anachronism; the square battlements rose like some Victorian folly that someone had built on a whim, and it bore little relation to the rest of the building. Even more incongruous, perched high on the battlements were the two security cameras which swung in alternate arcs across the road in front of the huge, studded gates, picking up any movement and showing it, Lynn assumed, on the screens in the security room. The prison van must have been identified for what it was long before it reached the gates, but even so one of the screws was obliged to get out and ring the bell. The wicket gate opened and his transit papers were passed in. He watched the wicket gate close, then shortly afterwards the double gates juddered slightly and rolled open on well-oiled runners. The truck moved into the security area, and he shivered involuntarily.

Then as the huge gates closed slowly in the wake of the vehicle, and as though aware for the first time that their intention was to incarcerate him for a period longer than he could grasp in his imagination, a growing sense of panic caused him to shake. This was it, he thought. Now he was actually inside the prison, it was as though any last vestige of hope was stripped away. All the while he was on the outside anything might have happened, the minibus might even have crashed, giving him an opportunity to run. Whilst outside those gates, although under heavy escort, he hadn't entirely lost all sense of freedom.

'One on!' a gate warder shouted, informing the rest of the gate staff, like they couldn't see him in the van.

The screw who had taken the driver's papers reappeared and handed back only two of the dockets. The main gate having been closed, the warder unlocked the heavy iron inner gates at the opposite end of the security area. He swung them open one at a time, then waved the truck on.

The Ford Transit rolled slowly out of the gate security and across the yard towards reception. The steel gates were slammed in its wake. Lynn looked back as the noise echoed about him. He shivered again. Gates and doors being banged at every opportunity was what he remembered most vividly from his previous stays in prison.

Followed by two of the screws from the minibus, he shuffled through the double security gates and into the reception wing. In the main hall where newly arrived prisoners were processed a screw waited behind a metal table – it was bolted to the floor. A trusty was close at hand, to assist but his general demeanour was no more welcoming than that of the reception screw he was assisting.

The room was twenty feet by thirty, with a line of six holding cells along one side, windowless cubicles which were smaller than ordinary cells. Lynn knew that's where he was destined for the night after completing reception. Ranged behind the table was a block of Dexicon shelving that reached to the ceiling. On the shelves were hundreds of dusty, numbered cardboard boxes containing prisoners' effects. On one end of the table were flat, empty boxes, one for each prisoner, along with a box of mothballs used for storing their clothes. Into the prisoners' personal property book the reception screw entered every kept item. Usually the reception screw removed as his perks any cigarettes, tobacco or sweets. At the end of the room was a corridor which led to the bathroom, also the room where the medical officer examined reception prisoners. Next to this was the room where prisoners were fingerprinted and photographed. Every surface was shiny with cream and green stippled paint, apart from the white lines on the floors where prisoners were required to stand at a prescribed distance from the officer receiving them, as though they were contagious.

'Stand on the line,' the escort said, stooping and pointing to a line on the floor three feet in front of the table. Lynn toed it.

'One on,' the second warder informed the reception warder, and handed him the second and third copies of his transit papers.

Putting the papers on the table, the reception screw pulled his clipboard towards him. 'Full name.' Warders never said please or thank you, not to cons, fellow officers, or to the deputy governor, only to the chief officer and the governor. The brutalizing aspects of prison affected the screws equally, Lynn was convinced of that. None had any vestige of sensitivity. If they had entered the service with any, then it was quickly lost, along with any of their good intentions.

'John Albert Lynn.'

All they ever wanted was the surname, why – when they had all details on record before them? But he knew that was the way it would be from now on.

The reception warder looked up at him. 'You've forgotten something.'

Lynn simply looked back, ignoring his demand.

'In case you don't know, you'd better learn fast here, from the go. When you address a member of staff, no matter what their rank, call them sir. Understood?'

It was a try-on. Some prisoners might be intimidated, but Lynn had no intention of even starting out that way.

'You got some chance, pal,' he replied.

There was a tense pause as each looked at the other, the reception screw clearly undecided about his next move.

In a tone heavy with menace, he finally said, 'Looks to me like you're going to make a lot of trouble for yourself,

John Albert Lynn.' He shook his head. 'In future you're a number. You're now prisoner A4697. That's what you'll be for the next twenty years. Don't forget it. When required to do so you'll identify yourself by that number, then, if further required, and only then, by your name. Understood?'

Lynn hesitated. Despite himself he knew he had to go through this process. Trying to prevent it happening was pointless.

They checked through his particulars. He stated his occupation was cab driving, then he was asked about his insurance card and P45. He hadn't got either.

With what he saw as a deprecating nod, the screw said, ''Course you haven't. I daresay we'll all be obliged to keep your wife and kids for the next twenty years, even though you've contributed fuck all.'

Lynn tensed, tightening the hold he had on his inclination to spring at the screw and kneedrop him in the groin. This was only the start of the abuse, and half the time these bastards probably didn't realize they were abusing people. 'Old Bill fitted me,' he said, his hands at his side flexing into tight fists. 'The state'd fucking well better support my family.'

'Don't answer back,' the escort warder said.

The reception warder seemed unimpressed as he rose from behind the table. 'I'll give you some advice,' he said, stabbing the air with a thick middle finger, 'and you'd better fucking well take it 'cos we got the means in here of dealing with hard cases. Stay in line or you'll be on report faster than you know.' He glanced at the other two warders present, who were tense and alert.

Having screws put pressure on you in reception, trying to establish beyond doubt their authority, was standard.

But he wouldn't take too much of it, he told himself. The way he felt was enough to precipitate some kind of straightener before much longer, without this added pressure. It was waiting to happen.

Bathing was an essential part of a prisoner's reception, though in the past prison regimes, because of lack of staff and adequate facilities, bathing he remembered wasn't a too frequent part of the routine. He wondered if it was now an any more frequent occurrence than a once weekly – if you were lucky! Perhaps, with the threat of Aids spreading in prison. The idea of a bath on reception was to check the possibility of bringing contagious diseases or infections into the closed community, though the six inches or so of water he was allowed was barely more than a nod towards cleanliness.

The bathroom in the reception wing had six antiquated cast-iron baths set in the stone floor, each with huge, worn taps and scoured-off enamel. As he came in naked past the white-coated warder a trusty, who moved a mop listlessly between the baths, watched him with uncommon interest.

'Get a towel and soap.' The warder indicated some small oblongs of folded towelling on a metal table, then turned away and went out of the bathroom.

'The water's nice and hot,' the trusty said.

Lynn said nothing, but instantly he felt hostility towards this man. The prison authority tolerating homosexuality as it did was, he was sure, part of the mockery of prison celibacy. Meeting this reception queen in his present mood was the final insult. Having him there, had to mean someone in the system was trying to provoke trouble.

After washing himself for a few moments he noticed the trusty drag his mop across the floor in the direction of his bath; there, having checked that the warder was out of sight, the man stopped mopping and gave him a big smile. He had reddened lips and darkened eyes – dyes from the hardcovers of library books were used.

'I'm getting a blue veiner here, Ginge,' Lynn said, masking his anger as he glanced down at his crotch.

The trusty looked out of the door again, then stepped over to the bath, his mop still in his hands. He leaned forward as though he was going to oblige him. Without warning Lynn grabbed him by his thinning hair and yanked his head down hard. The trusty let out a hysterical shriek as he went under the water. Lynn was up and out of the bath by the time the screw reappeared at a run.

'What's going on?' he wanted to know.

'That soapy bastard needs a bath,' Lynn said.

'What happened?' the screw said to the trusty, who was on his knees, spluttering, at the side of the bath.

'I slipped, Mr Gregory. I slipped, sir,' he managed.

'Get yourself dried,' he said to Lynn, 'and get over and get your clothes sorted out.'

The screw's reaction was about what he expected. Lynn let it go and went out, drawing the sparse towel round himself.

From what he'd heard on the outside, prisons were relaxing the rules over the wearing of clothes. At one time every prisoner was compelled to dress in an exactly similar way, including wearing the ties that were issued. Nowadays, although the full clothing kit was issued, the decision to wear it or not was for the prisoner to make. In the past prison authorities had rarely seemed to learn from experience, but perhaps they were slowly coming to understand that there was no advantage in forcing a man to wear a tie or shoes, especially if he had little or nothing to lose if he chose not to.

The clothing store was part of reception and run by a trusty, supervised by a screw. Lynn watched the trusty size him up with a glance where he stood in front of the table. 'What are you? 'Bout forty-four chest?' he asked.

'Forty-two,' Lynn replied. 'Thirty-four waist. Something that fits a bit near the mark would be handy.'

The trusty nodded slowly. 'Get any snout in?' he asked.

That would determine how new or well-fitting his clothes would be. Lynn knew the score – probably the warder copped half of what the trusty got – but he wasn't going to play. It was bad enough having screws pull those sort of strokes without having one of your own kind doing it. 'Yeah, I got about three ounces jammed up m' daily.'

'Ah, you flash bastard,' the trusty said. He quickly collected up an assortment of clothes and set them on the table.

Lynn picked up a vest that was several sizes too big. He would have put up with that had it been clean, but there were stains down the front. He threw it back at the trusty, and, although the man was big, Lynn wasn't put off at all. 'Change it.'

'You gotta take it as it comes, pal.'

Pointing with his index finger to emphasize his warning, he said, 'I won't tell you again.'

The trusty clearly recognized he had trouble on his hands. He reached down another vest, while Lynn stepped into the pants. They hung down his legs like a curtain. He decided to let them go, but he wasn't about to with the trousers he stepped into. He removed them patiently.

'I told you waist thirty-four,' he said, throwing them at the trusty, whose attention was momentarily distracted by the warder who had stepped through the door.

'What the fuck do you think this is,' the screw demanded, 'Savile Row? Pick those clothes up and get them on, 'fore I fetch the principal officer.'

'Tell this ponce to get me down something that fits.'

That wasn't the answer the screw was expecting. 'Right!' he said, panicking slightly. 'Stay where you are, don't move.' He backed away cautiously, then suddenly wheeled out.

'You picked a wrong 'un, upsetting that screw, pal,' the trusty said, as if trying to mitigate his own position.

The screw came hurrying back with the principal officer in charge of the reception wing. He was Gordon Walters, who was older, heavier and shorter than his colleague. He had the look of someone who had been in the service a long while, and probably knew most of the dodges and fiddles. He was more sure of himself.

'This officer has reported you for using threatening behaviour,' Walters said.

'I just asked for some decent clothes . . .' Lynn said.

PO Walters said, 'We're not a fucking West End tailor.'

'It's not even clean.' Lynn was digging in.

'*We* make the rules,' the PO said. 'Rule 20 states: A convicted prisoner shall be provided with clothing adequate for warmth and health in accordance with a scale approved by the Secretary of State. It doesn't say anything about it having to fit you or be clean. It's adequate for your needs.

If you wanted to wear fancy clothes you should have thought of that before getting yourself convicted . . .'

'I was fitted by the fucking filth,' he protested.

'We've heard it before,' the PO told him. 'You're doing time and you'll do it our way.'

'Fuck it! Either I get clean clothes, or bang me up like this.' Having made his stand, he wasn't going to back down.

'You're going to come to a lot of grief here, 'you persist in this attitude,' the PO said. 'A lot of grief.' Then for no reason Lynn could understand, he wiped his mouth and turned on the trusty instead. 'Why haven't these clothes been laundered? They're disgusting. Get them down to the laundry, and give the prisoner some decent clothes.'

With that he departed, leaving the warder as disappointed as the trusty.

'You pulled a right stroke there,' one of the warders said as he took Lynn along to the MO's office.

Lynn didn't reply. His navy-blue battledress-type uniform fitted him well enough; so did his striped shirt. His shoes were new. It was a minor victory.

A medical examination was considered an essential part of reception, but it was so perfunctory that it could easily have been dispensed with. The MO's office was sparsely furnished; a table, a chair, a cupboard and an examination couch were the only items of furniture. The stooped Dr Eynshaw, the MO, had nicotine-stained fingers and dandruff across his shoulders. He was about thirty-five, a worried-looking thirty-five. He sat reading a newspaper and ignored Lynn, who dropped his trousers and pants where he stood at the line before the desk. Instead he marked some horses in the racing page. Finally he put the paper to one side and found a reception medical form.

'Number, name and initial,' he said, without looking up.

'Lynn, Jack Lynn.'

The MO stopped writing and looked up at him for the first time. 'Don't you understand plain English?'

'A4697,' Lynn said grudgingly.

'Take your top off. Raise your arms.' He shone his torch on his armpits, without getting out of his chair. Then on his pubic hair. The examination was briefly interrupted by a coughing fit. A blob of phlegm shot from his mouth and landed on the form. The doctor casually wiped it away with the side of his hand. 'Turn round and bend over.' When he did so the doctor shone the torch up his ass. 'Any VD, crabs or lice?' he asked uninterestedly. Then he went on: 'Are you HIV? Have you ever visited a doctor or hospital to be examined for Aids?' He seemed satisfied to accept Lynn's negative answers. 'Ever had homosexual relations?'

'Leave off.'

The doctor went on writing. 'You're fit to work.' That was the end of the examination.

Nothing much had changed since his last medical in prison. The doctor had got younger, that was all. Lynn remained unmoving with his trousers and pants around his ankles. He felt angry and frustrated. This was part of the humiliation that all cons were subjected to. Those who perpetuated the system treated the men in their charge like dogshit. That was because they were no better than shit themselves, he decided. They allowed prisoners no dignity or respect, and therefore deserved none in return. So, as if to fulfil some role expected of him, he raised his dick and pissed on the table.

'What are you doing?' the doctor demanded, leaping back out of his chair. 'Why are you doing that? Why, you maniac!'

'This is a pisshole, innit?' Lynn said. 'You look like someone who cleans pissholes, pal.'

'You're on report!' the warder bellowed at him.

That caused Lynn no concern at all as he went on urinating until he was finished.

He didn't complete reception, which would have meant being interviewed by the chaplain, the chief officer and a welfare worker. Instead he was escorted to the punishment block and placed in a cell. The following morning he was taken before the governor to answer the charge.

Immediately prior to going before the governor Lynn was put in a cell adjacent to the adjudication room, which was on the block. A copy of the report had been pushed under his door. On the back of the form he could answer any or all of the charges in writing if he wished to. He didn't, for he knew it would make no difference one way or the other. He tried to remain detached from the whole procedure. Next he was searched, then told to remove his shoes. When he did he was given a pair of carpet slippers several sizes too big for him. The soft footwear was, he assumed, to prevent him kicking the governor.

Two warders marched him into the adjudication room. There the prison governor, a picture of self-righteousness, but a lot younger than he expected, sat behind the small desk, which was bare, apart from the records of prisoners on report that morning. Also present was the chief officer, Robert Carne, who was tall and overweight. Someone had told him that Carne was moderate and liberal in his views. Lynn would wait and judge for himself. No such word proceeded the officer in charge of the punishment block:

PO Alec McClean was a thin, gaunt-faced Ulsterman who looked like he enjoyed his position. The warders from the MO's office were there too, while Lynn had no one to speak for him. The room was drab, painted in familiar institutional colours, and free of furniture or adornment. The line painted on the floor was six feet from the desk.

'On the line,' the chief officer barked. 'Toes touching it.'

Lynn toed the line. The escort warders positioned themselves either side of him, just in front of his shoulders, both facing inwards – even that proximity wouldn't have prevented him springing the governor had he chosen to.

The governor, Archie Maudling, was the best fed man in the prison, and looked the most indulged. He was heavy with flesh and had the large jowls of a much older man; his face was disproportionately large even for that large body, and pea-shaped. He wore glasses which he had a habit of pushing up onto the bridge of his nose.

'Not a favourable start,' he said. 'It doesn't bode well that you couldn't even get through reception.' He didn't seem interested in the response Lynn attempted to make. He pushed up his glasses and glanced towards the chief officer, then at the warder from the MO's office. 'Mr Maitland?'

'A4697, sir. Charged under the rule 47, sections 13, 14 and 20, in that he treated with disrespect the medical officer who was examining him during reception; that he did use abusive and improper language to the medical officer; that he did offend against good order and discipline in that he urinated on the desk and floor of the MO's office.'

'How did this come about? Through incontinence?'

'No, sir,' the warder said. 'He raised his member, sir,

and directed it.' Lynn glanced at the uniformed man, who seemed embarrassed. 'When the MO asked what he thought he was doing, he replied: This-is-a-fucking-pisshole. You-are-a-fucking-pisshole-attendant.'

'You'd better think again . . .!' Lynn said

'You'll get your turn, Lynn.'

Lynn snorted down his nostrils. He knew that, however much of a turn he'd get, the entire adjudication was a ramp and it was pointless offering any kind of defence. Prison governors always accepted the word of screws, while the governor's word was final unless you somehow got judicial review. If you didn't then it didn't matter much for relatively minor offences, but the procedure was no different for the graver offences heard by the Visiting Committee.

When he protested again he was ordered to be quiet, and the screw was allowed to continue with his lies. After the screw had finished the governor asked, 'What have you to say in your defence?'

'I was fitted by the filth,' Lynn stated categorically. 'I've no intention of doing my bird . . .'

'I'm not interested in that.' The governor was plainly irritated, possibly anticipating that he would prove a troublesome inmate. Lynn knew it wouldn't matter to this man by what injustice he had arrived here, only that now he was here he should abide by the rules. 'If you're issuing warnings or statement of intent, let me advise you, for your own good, we cannot accept disruptive behaviour.'

Lynn looked hard at the governor, not knowing which of them despised the other the most.

'Why did you urinate in Dr Eynshaw's office?'

'It looked like a pisshole to me . . .' Lynn began.

'Outside!' the governor ordered.

Before the governor had completed his order the escort about-turned him and marched him out. In the shiny green and cream corridor the older of the two warders shook his head in dismay. 'Jesus wept,' he said. 'You're not asking for trouble, son, are you? He won't put up with it, not this governor. He'll refer you to the Visiting Committee. If you still act up he'll have you transferred to somewhere like Broadmoor. That's the sort of bloke he is. I'm just marking your card.'

Lynn wondered about that as he looked at him, why he would do that for him.

The governor – advised by the chief officer and Principal Officer McClean – quickly arrived at his adjudication.

When Lynn was summoned back in, he said, 'You have been found guilty as charged. Although this case is sufficiently grave to warrant its being referred to the Visiting Committee, I have decided to deal with it. You will be held in solitary confinement for three days, and lose fourteen days' remission.' He pushed his glasses up his nose three times in succession. 'You must understand that I can't allow you to become a disruptive influence. Further offences of this nature will be dealt with most severely by the committee . . .'

'I don't intend serving my sentence,' Lynn restated.

'Address the prison governor respectfully!' the chief snapped.

Maudling's lips tightened. 'You'll only succeed in making life very uncomfortable for yourself.'

'That's ballocks. The filth fitted me up,' Lynn said, ignoring the warnings.

'Sir. I think the prisoner should be further charged

under Rule 47,' PO McClean said. 'Treating an officer with disrespect. Namely yourself, sir.'

Maudling smiled at that. 'Very well, Mr McClean. You are so charged, Lynn,' he said. Then announced without further deliberation, 'I find the prisoner guilty as charged. An additional fourteen days' loss of remission. Take him away.' He might have been a feudal king.

'It's ballocks. This is a fucking kangaroo court,' Lynn protested as he was taken out.

That was his whole procedure of adjudication from start to finish. He was found guilty even before he got to say his piece, and a prison officer saying he did it made it indisputable in this system. Rarely did a prisoner on report get a result. Lynn accepted that all screws were liars and were compelled to lie when going before the governor, as to tell the truth would almost always show them up for the petty bastards they were.

The cell in the punishment block where he was escorted to was larger than a normal cell, being about eight feet by fourteen. When the door was banged after him he leaned back against the cold, damp-feeling wall to take stock of his situation. He told himself he could take solitary confinement. It wasn't something he'd seek as a preference, but he had felt so isolated in prison over the past months that he was no worse off for being on chokey. Imprisonment itself was something he couldn't reconcile, not the varying degrees within the regime.

In the end wall of the cell was a barred window that was too high to see out of, but no furniture to stand on and get a view. The cell held only a low cot bed with a thin mattress, duck-cotton sheets and three blankets. A plastic pot stood in the corner by the door. The green and cream walls were without adornment apart from graffiti, and they were stipple-painted so that any attempts to remove the mortar from between bricks would be immediately apparent.

Being left alone now to consider his prospects, he felt a sense of dismay overwhelm him. The only way he could prevent it was by not thinking about his future. He was distracted by muffled sounds beyond the cell. He stood off the wall and listened concentratedly but was unable to identify what they were. The noise worried him, but proved a distraction from his own problems.

Boredom was the rock on which so many prisoners perished, while in solitary all that was boring was accentuated. He had no formula for coping with boredom, and when he lay down on the bed he knew that if he allowed himself to sleep now, he wouldn't sleep at night. By turns his thoughts closed in on him, threatening to send him mad, or he became aware of a screw watching him through the Judas hole in the door. Physical exercise was something most prisoners on solitary resorted to, and he was no exception, until he discovered how unfit he was. He managed to do only sixteen press-ups before his arms began to shake and he crashed on to the stone floor.

The punishment block was a single-storey building with a central thoroughfare, intersected from the entrance by inner barred gates. There were cells along either side of the corridor, and an office for the PO, and another that the warders used. A cupboard with the word LIBRARY stencilled on the door held about a dozen books. Lynn wondered if his privileges extended to a visit there.

A cheerful trusty brought a supper tray to Lynn's door. He introduced himself as Brian Lang – after the fat warder unlocked the door, then waddled back along the corridor to the next cell.

'How's it going, Jack?' Lang whispered across the threshold. 'Heard you'd arrived.'

'Not for fucking long, Bri'!' Lynn replied, but recognized immediately what a stupid statement that was.

'Mind how you go.' Lang spoke quickly and from the side of his mouth, his eyes darting back along the corridor the whole while. 'They got a special punishment routine here, 's murder.' He checked along the corridor again. 'Fucking slaughtering that poor bastard, they are.'

'Who's that?'

'Bobby Mark – the fella in the next cell but one . . . Watch out for that blond screw – Cyril Jordan.' As the warder turned in their direction he ended the conversation abruptly.

'C'mon, what you after, a fucking tip?' Jordan said.

'Just taking Mr Lynn's wine order, Mr Jordan,' Lang said cringingly, as if mocking him for the warder's benefit.

After the door was slammed locked, Lynn considered the tray, which had on it a pint mug of tea, four slices of white bread, a small pat of marge; a dollop of what looked and smelt like lumpy cat food, and vegetables that were potatoes and carrots in name only. The cutlery was plastic. He raised the plate and smelled the main dish and wrinkled his nostrils in disgust, but he knew he'd eat it. He had a similar reaction with the first mouthful of tea he tried. He spat into the pisspot. Extra bromide was put in the tea which came down to the block, he was sure of it.

Shouts from Bobby Mark and the muffled crash of the tray interrupted Lynn's meal. 'I'm not fucking well eating it, I'm not,' he heard. He pressed his ear to the door, trying to make out what was going on. 'Keep it up, you silly bastard, you'll get some more,' he heard Jordan say. But maybe, just maybe, he said 'silly boy'. There was more shouting from Mark asking to be let out. Then silence. Lynn listened throughout his meal. Silence continued, but Lynn was was more disturbed by that than by the shouting.

The only reading material in the cell was a mutilated Gideon Bible. He didn't want something to read that badly, but would use the book in the same way most prisoners did, for toilet paper – there was never enough supplied in prison. His pot had to serve him throughout the night; the screw told him there was no way he was going to be let out to use the lavatory.

A cry suddenly awakened Lynn from a shallow sleep in his lighted cell. Hearing prisoners cry out at night wasn't unusual. Some did out of fear, others from conscience; more did so when they got an unexpected visit from the screws searching for contraband. It took Lynn a few moments to identify where the noise came from. It sounded like the lad along the corridor again. He was making a disconcerting wail. Lynn got out of bed and sprang up to the window and hung there as that was the best place for listening – illegal conversations were often held that way. Finally his arms gave out and he dropped down and went and stabbed at the bell push. He couldn't avoid getting involved, even though he didn't know Bobby Mark. Someone had to try and do something; maybe someone would do the same for him.

There was no answer to his pressing the bell, nor any immediate indication that a bell somewhere was summoning a warder. He didn't attempt to go back to bed, but sat listening. After a while Bobby Mark fell silent; then after a while longer, Lynn's door was unlocked. Jordan stooped in the doorway.

'You ring your bell?' he said.

'Half an hour ago.'

'What d'you want, a sleeping pill?' Jordan was six feet, with yellowing blond hair that looked like it was bleached, and a rigidly straight back and neck, which probably helped him to see from under the acute angle of the slashed peak of his cap. He had a youngish, fleshy face and thick lips. He was a Geordie; the prison service seemed full of them.

'What's wrong with that lad? Screaming like that?'

'Like what?' Jordan listened. 'I don't hear no screaming. You had a bad dream. Get back to bed and don't ring that bell no more.' He waited like he was challenging him to make a comeback. Lynn didn't. The uniform stepped out, slamming the door.

With perseverance the press-ups came easier for Lynn. He exercised in that way in his cell both before and after breakfast. The time would come, he guessed, when he would be able to do fifty, probably one hundred. But for now twenty left him breathless and sweating.

He was that way on the floor, recovering, when a screw called Reg Allison unlocked the cell and bent through the low doorway. He was a tall man with a pronounced stoop, possibly from bending through too many low doorways. He was a long-serving officer who hadn't much time to do before retirement.

'Time for a bit of outdoor exercise, son,' Allison said as Lynn rolled over and looked at him.

'They letting me out?' Lynn asked, reaching for his towel.

'You'll do all right, son, you keep a sense of humour.'

'That might be the easiest thing in the world, banged up in here like this.'

The older man smiled at that. He had the sort of face that suggested he had seen everything and had learned to live longer with a smile. He winked, then checked outside in the corridor. Turning back, he said, 'I'll give you a piece of advice, for what it's worth. Watch your step. They're looking for an excuse with you now. Any old excuse'll do.' He winked again. 'Come on!' he said, changing his tone. 'Outside.' He stepped back through the doorway.

Lynn watched him, suspecting the advice was a trick to get him to toe the line. It would only make him dig his heels in more.

The exercise yard was oblong and enclosed by a sixteen-foot chainlink fence which was topped by rolls of barbed wire set in 'Y' brackets; this was itself enclosed within a razor-wire-topped walled compound, which was finally enclosed by a perimeter wall, and on top of that were spikes. Being a maximum-security prison, there were more video cameras than at a cup-final match. A warder with a dog was on duty outside the wire compound, while another, without a dog, was inside the exercise yard. Four prisoners were led directly into the yard by a door from the wing it abutted – that was the only way in or out. With them was Reg Allison, who locked the door after them. Walking six paces in front of Lynn, shuffling and stumbling, sobbing to himself as the four of them moved around the yard in single file, was a young man who he assumed was Bobby Mark. He worried Lynn.

'What's the problem, pal?' he asked quietly as they moved farther away from the warders. There was no response. He glanced around, checking where the warders were, then lengthened his stride and closed the gap between them. 'Is it bad news from home?' That was the single biggest cause of upset to prisoners, always made worse by the fact that they could do nothing to help.

Still there was no response from Mark. He was a big man in his late twenties, thickset, but his height was disguised by the fact that he was hunched over and hiding his face as he shuffled along. He was in a world of his own.

Lynn dropped back to the con immediately behind him as they went round. 'What's wrong with him in front?' he asked. He lengthened his stride as they came past the nearest point to the warders.

'You Jack Lynn?' the con asked when they closed the gap again.

'Who are you?' Lynn asked.

'Frank Timper. Heard you was down. How long d'you get?'

'Three days, 's all. What about him?'

'Poor bastard,' Timper said. ''S bit simple.'

''S that all?'

'Naw. He's not that simple. They give him some stick.'

'Oi! No talking, or you'll be on report,' the warder accompanying Allison said. 'Space yourselves out. Come on.'

As they continued round, Bobby Mark tripped and fell to the ground without trying to prevent himself. He lay there sobbing. Lynn started to help him and saw, close to, just how badly marked his face was. He had had enough fights to know that those scabs and bruises were caused by fists.

'All right, leave him,' the warder said.

Lynn withdrew, feeling helpless. He knew he ought to do something but didn't know what.

Lying on his bed after Lights Out he listened for any sound from Bobby Mark, and reacted to the first scream that came through the wall, followed by muffled shouting to be left alone. He sprang off the bed in his vest and pants and rang the bell. There was no reply. He searched round the cell for something to bang the wall with. There was only his shoe.

'Bobby! Bobby Mark? You all right?'

He waited. Still there was no response. Bobby Mark had stopped crying. As he listened there was total silence along the block. The cries that suddenly started from Bobby Mark again startled him. Angrily Lynn stabbed at the bell push, and held his finger against it.

'Take your finger off that fucking bell!' a screw ordered.

He ignored the order until the shutter in the door flew open, revealing Jordan's sweating face.

'What's your fucking problem?' he demanded.

'What's wrong with that lad along there?'

'What's it gotta do with you?'

'I broke the fucker's glasses . . .' Another warder, a fatter, shorter man called Oliver Dorman, said as though it was an achievement.

The shutter slammed, shutting Lynn off from this conversation.

When Bobby Mark failed to appear for exercise the following day, Lynn decided something had to be done, speculating that he was getting more stick than he deserved.

He tried several times to get some information but without success.

'Cook's run off with the gardener again, Jack,' Lang, the block trusty, said as he brought round the familiar tea, bread and marge, meat stew and pudding.

'Fuck it, I'm thinking of finding another hotel, Bri'.'

Catching Lynn's eye, the trusty winked. 'Don't stuff yourself.'

Lynn thought little of the gesture, still being preoccupied with Bobby Mark. As the warder went to close the door, he stepped forward. 'Mr Allison?' he said. The warder waited. 'What happened to Bobby Mark last night?'

Allison hesitated. 'I don't know. I wasn't on duty.'

'They beat him. How fucking badly?' Lynn said.

'Watch it, son. That'll get you in trouble.'

'All right,' he retorted, 'put me on report. See if silly ballocks wants to know about what's happening.'

The warder shook his head, then stepped into the cell. Lynn sized him up, deciding he'd have no trouble with this old screw if he tried to put one on him.

'What good will that do you?' Allison said. 'They'll charge you with groundless complaints. You'll wind up doing fourteen days down here.'

'What about Bobby Mark?' He was committed now.

'He had a fit. 'S what I heard. He has 'em all the time. He shouldn't be here really. Look, leave it with me, I'll find out how he is, let you know . . .'

Reluctant to give ground, Lynn finally said, 'He didn't look like he got that from a fit.'

'He had to be restrained,' PO McClean announced from the doorway. Neither had heard his approach. 'He was doing gross personal violence to an officer.'

Lynn looked at this man with the contempt he felt he deserved for that statement. 'I heard it.'

'Did you now?' the PO said. 'Then you'd better take it up with the deputy governor. I'll put you down on application to see him tomorrow.' He glanced at his subordinate. 'Mr Allison.'

When they had gone Lynn realized the significance of what he had done. But getting involved in Bobby Mark's fight helped him to stop thinking too much about his own problems. He turned his attention to his supper and lifted a piece of bread. As he did so he saw something beneath it that shouldn't have been there, and remembered Brian Lang's wink. Replacing the bread he checked round, making sure he wasn't being watched. Then, sitting masking the tray, he cautiously lifted the bread and found half a bar of chocolate. He smiled, cheered by this. He would remember this gesture from Lang and repay him in some way.

Applications to see the governor for any reason were taken in the adjudication room during the morning, along with the charges. But often it was the deputy governor or one of the assistant governors who heard the complaints. This morning it was Maudling's deputy.

'A4697, on application, sir, to make a complaint against an officer,' Chief Officer Carne announced.

'Is the officer who the complaint's against present?' the deputy governor wanted to know. He had a pale wispy moustache that was trying to hide a slight harelip. Prison officers were given every possible opportunity to defend themselves.

'I took the application, sir,' PO McClean informed him. 'He refused to name the officer.'

'Well?' the deputy governor said, his gaze falling upon the wall over Lynn's left shoulder.

Lynn hesitated. He had had all night to think about what he was being drawn into, and he remembered Mr Allison's advice. His being nicked again wouldn't do much for Bobby Mark. And in the unlikely event of his getting a result they would then have it in for him as well as Mark.

'What is the complaint?'

Still Lynn remained silent.

'Answer, man, or you'll be charged with insolence,' the deputy governor said, his harelip rising like a beak.

'I made a mistake, sir,' Lynn said. 'I apologize for wasting your time, sir.'

The deputy governor and the chief officer exchanged looks.

'Very well. I accept your apology. I think you'll find this change of attitude will make your stay here far easier for you.' He nodded, concurring with himself.

That easy.

On the wings there was the constant clashing and slamming of gates and doors. That was how Jack Lynn remembered stir. No one ever closed a door quietly, and for reasons of security, he assumed, gates were always slammed. After a few weeks there, you stopped noticing the banging. He wondered if the screws slammed doors in their own homes the same way.

Once through the locked outside door, entrance to the wing proper was barred by a heavy steel gate that formed a security reception area. Allison and another warder who escorted him from the punishment block waited while a wing warder came forward and unlocked the inner door.

Standing on the threshold and looking over his new environment, a feeling of panic rose in Lynn and he started to sweat as he fought it. The old wing was tall and narrow, and had spurs that were built like afterthoughts. The centre of the three-storey building was clear through to the skylights, interrupted only by anti-suicide chainlink netting that stretched horizontally at each floor. Apart from stopping anyone jumping to his death, the chainlink served to oppress you more. On each of the stone landings around the main well the cell doors were set back in the brickwork, the entrances low and restricted. The doors all opened outwards and had a two-inch Judas hole, which was designed to give a view of every part of the cell. To the right of each door, fixed to the shiny-painted green and cream wall, was a cardholder with the cell card of each prisoner. It gave his number, name and sentence, with the colour of the card denoting his religion. Most prisoners put down something, some adopted those denominations that afforded the most privileges. Catholics got fish on Friday; Buddhists got vegetarian diets, and vegans got vegan food if they made a fuss, but if you neglected to state some religion then you were banged up during chapel times. The wing where Lynn was put held both special and category 'A' prisoners. As they were considered the most dangerous in the entire maximum-security prison, they had special exercise and recreation facilities. These for the most part were training weights and table tennis, both on the ground floor. On each of the landings there was an association room where prisoners could eat their evening meal and watch TV. The main office used by the warders was on the ground floor, as was the PO's office. There was a green baize notice board fixed to the wall. Beneath the notice board stood the empty food trolley, ready on the deserted wing to collect the next meal. Lights burned on the ground floor where daylight failed to penetrate. Fixed to the wall at the end of the wing was a worn iron staircase that groped its way through the chainlink safety nets.

'On one!' Allison called to the warder who unlocked the section gate. 'A4697, Lynn.' He passed over Lynn's movement book. This went with him everywhere in the prison and was signed by the officer into whose charge he was given. After locking the gate the young wing warder glanced at the photo in the book then at Lynn before going away for the PO, who would sign the book.

Allison raised his eyes, as though cheesed off with the

procedure, and trying to draw Lynn into his disapproval. Instead he turned away, his eyes meeting those of a trusty, who had stopped polishing the floor and was leaning on his mop. The trusty's eyes darted away so not to give offence and he resumed his work.

'I expect you'll be behind your door for a couple of weeks,' Allison commented. 'While they assess you.'

The young wing warder returned with the principal officer, who carefully compared Lynn against the photo before signing the book.

Allison looked at him and for a moment Lynn thought he was about to say something, but finally he didn't and returned to the gate. The PO took the movements book to his office and the warder ordered Lynn to move off.

'Hello, Jack!' The cheerful greeting met him as he came round the first-floor landing. 'Heard you was down here.'

Lynn felt pleased to encounter a friendly face.

Alan Parker, who was descending the stairs, had lost all his front teeth since the last time Lynn had seen him in a pub on Clapham Common when he had offered him some work; and the front part of his hair was missing. Parker had aged ten years in the last twelve months. Lynn wondered if he had too. Dolly hadn't said, but then she wouldn't.

'I thought you drew the 'Moor.'

'I was for a couple of months. Fucking murder down there. I didn't stop telling them. 'S how I done them,' he said, pointing to his missing teeth. 'I'd sooner be in this pisshole. You have to have a ruck, Jack. 'S all that keeps you sane.'

The young warder looked at the con, then at Lynn. 'Move on.'

'Don't take no nonsense from Enoch there,' Parker

advised, and started on down. He called back, 'If you need anything while you're banged up, just send me the word.'

On the top landing, the warder checked off cells until they reached one with an empty cardholder. He popped Lynn's card into it. 'Your new home,' he said.

Lynn checked the inclination to tell him it wouldn't be for long.

As the screw pulled open the door, a prisoner inside jumped off the bed in alarm. 'What the fuck are you doing in here?' the warder demanded.

'I was just lying down, Mr Powell. I wasn't feeling well, sir.'

The prisoner seemed unduly nervous. He sidled along the wall of the narrow cell as the warder stepped inside. He was tall, slim and had the fine-boned face of an actor. But fear was etched deeply into his face.

'Out!' Powell snapped. 'Back where you're supposed to be 'fore you get my toe up your ass.'

That seemed about right to Lynn, the screw bullying someone like that. He wouldn't have tried it on him or Parker.

The prisoner shrank away from Lynn on emerging from the cell. He hurried towards the stairs, his head flicking from side to side. Lynn watched him clatter down the stairs like a nervous kitten.

'Simon Menzies,' Powell said. 'You probably heard about him. Molested and killed a little girl, that one.'

'What!' Lynn was suddenly incensed. 'And he's been sleeping on my fucking bed?' The offence might have been contagious.

'There's been worse than him in here at times.'

'I'd better have another cell. It's a fucking liberty, Mr Powell.'

He watched as Powell considered him, uncertain whether or not to go along with it. Finally he stepped out of the cell and, taking the cell card out, he changed it with the card outside the next cell.

'Here you are. This is Bobby Mark's cell. But he won't care where he's put when he gets out of hospital.'

Lynn was uncertain about that, thinking how the lad from solitary had enough problems without his adding to them. But when he saw the room was almost as bare as the one he had been offered, he felt it didn't matter. The space was six by twelve, with a tiled floor and shiny cream walls – they must have run out of green paint. All the furniture amounted to was a washstand in the corner, a small table and chair and a narrow, low cot bed with three blankets and ducksheets piled at the top end. There was a heavily barred window high in the end wall. The cell contained nothing else, apart from Mark's meagre personal effects stacked on the table. Seeing those, even without knowing how long Mark had done, made him feel more sorry for the man.

'This is it. There's nowhere else.'

'What about those?' he said, pointing to Mark's possessions.

The warder collected them up. 'You'll have the chaplain and the social worker round to see you soon.'

'Oh, terrific,' Lynn said.

During the two weeks behind his door he got more than one visit from the chaplain and the welfare officer. On each of their visits he repeated the statement he'd made to the governor, telling them how he'd been fitted and that he didn't intend doing his time. Probably that formed part of his assessment and went on his record. He knew that anything said to prison staff went onto your record, and then on to the Home Office computer, despite any promise of a conversation being in confidence.

Work was offered to him; a pile of mailbags to sew. He chose to sit on them instead. He didn't smoke so had no real need of spends, and the £1.90 a week he got wouldn't help Dolly and the girls. There were enough books to read, which he found preferable to sewing mailbags. Even so, he was glad when at last they opened the door.

On this wing he was ranked among the hard men, an elite who had done worthwhile villainy and had wound up with long sentences. There were about fifteen of them. Others on the wing with longer sentences had got those for mindless villainy, usually involving unnecessary damage to property. His acceptance by the hard men was shown in the respect people readily gave him. The other thirty or so prisoners there were murderers, rapists, and nonces – the child molesters who were kept behind their doors under Rule 43, and let out with an escort only.

At dinner time, which started around four when those who worked came back from the workshops, food was served from the trolley on the ground floor by a trusty. Prisoners collected their own food. There was a pecking order: a hanger-on wouldn't get his food before a villain, but definitely before the nonces.

'Get your supper,' a warder told Lynn on his first unlock.

He sauntered out onto the landing with a strange sense

of freedom. The warder pointed down the stairs to where the food was.

On the stairs Lynn ran into Alan Parker, who was about to turn along the second landing with his food.

'Jack. All right, son?' he inquired. 'Get your grub and come up here in the TV room. All right?'

''S that where you eat?' Lynn wanted to eat in the right place.

'There, or behind your door. Go on, 'fore those fucking nonces try to get their'n and someone pisses in it.'

On the ground floor there were a lot of prisoners milling around the trolley waiting their turn, as two warders oversaw things.

'Hello, son,' Stephen Collins, a major villain, said to Lynn as he was moving out with his own supper. Heads turned. Collins giving him such obvious respect made Lynn feel special. 'Al told me you was here. A fucking turn-up.'

'In't it just,' Lynn responded.

'Get stuck in 'ere,' he said. Then, turning back to the trolley, 'Who's that for?'

'It's Lentin's,' replied the trusty.

'I should fucking think so. What, before Jack gets his?' He simply took the tray and gave it to Lynn.

'Jack.' He offered him the tray. 'You'd better put a bit more on that as well. He needs fattening up.'

'Only so much food comes over from the kitchens, Stephen,' one of the screws said as the trusty heaped more food on Lynn's tray.

'Only because the catering officers are at it,' Collins said. 'The nonces will have to go short.'

As he reached the second level, Lynn said, 'I'm gonna have my bit of grub in the TV room here.'

'Not there with them mugs,' Collins chided. 'Come up to the threes,' – there Collins held sway.

'I just told Al I'd see him.'

Collins seemed slighted at that. Clearly he liked having his own way. But he grinned, finally, as though seeing Lynn as some kind of celebrity he didn't want to let go of, and said, 'All right. I'll come there for a change.'

The TV room was the size of a double cell. It had a central table where Lynn and Collins joined Parker and two other prisoners who were eating. Three more were sitting watching *Blue Peter* on a large TV tucked away in the corner.

'They're no-good fucking ponces,' Alan Parker said angrily as Lynn's case was discussed. 'Them three what got done with you, Jack.' It might have been himself involved and wronged.

How each of the men at the table had either been fitted up or unjustly weighed off; what their chances were on appeal; who was the governor among them, or who was fucking whom, was more or less the staple topic of conversation, Lynn was soon to learn.

'What the fuck can you do?' he said. 'The filth decided they wanted me long before Tully's little firm showed up.' He grew dangerously philosophical about this. Had he been weighed off with an easy five he might more readily have accepted that it was his turn.

'John Tully. He always was a no-good slag,' Collins said. He was a volatile mixture of love and hate, the sort of bloke who, in other circumstances, was as likely as not to say what a nice fella Tully was.

'They should definitely have given you an out,' Parker said.

'You stuck in your appeal, Jack?' one of the other cons at the table asked. He was Micky Dunkerton, who was in his late thirties. He was immaculately dressed compared with other prisoners, some of whom not only didn't bother with ties or coats but wandered around in their vests. Dunkerton wore a collar and tie, and his jacket and trousers were neatly pressed.

'My brief done it right off.'

'I don't want to depress you, son,' Collins said. 'But you know yourself the way that is. Either you've done half your bird before you ever get to appeal, or those slags always stick together and favour the judge what puts you down.'

He didn't enjoy being reminded of the immediate prospects for his appeal, but said, 'Don't you watch the news, Steve? The Court of Appeal is turfing them out all over the place.'

'Only if you got one of the criminal groupies working for you and can get it on telly,' Collins said.

He was a bit older than Lynn, a bit fatter, with a babyish complexion. He had an argumentative nature, and didn't like to see anyone get something he hadn't, whether it was an extra letter or a result on appeal. Clearly he liked to be Jack the Lad and dominate people. That was something he had effectively done on the outside, but Lynn suspected he was basically a coward. He had heard stories about Collins and had half-forgotten details of the firm he had once run. His reputation was formidable, he was doing thirty for various assaults, robberies and murders.

'The thing is,' Parker said, eating the last of his pudding, 'you got to get someone to look at the discrepancies in the police evidence. That's the only sure way to get a result.

The dopey sods write things down then forget to destroy their own notes.'

'Got some new evidence against the filth, Jack?' Collins inquired. 'That's what you need.'

'My brief's working on it.' Lynn believed the young solicitor he had was doing nothing else. 'He's a bit near the mark.'

'You ought to talk to Tony Scuffham down on the ones,' Dunkerton said. 'He's doing twenty-five with a recommendation. He handled his own appeal.'

'How'd he go?' Lynn asked with interest.

'Oh, it went against him, Jack. He couldn't get into what Old Bill were up to.'

''S fucking handy,' Lynn retorted. He looked at the faces of the men around the table, assessing them. They each had to be all right or Alan Parker wouldn't be sitting with them. 'It does go the other way, I tell you, I'll have to plot one up, 's all.'

'Out of here? You got to be joking,' Collins said. 'What d'you reckon I been thinking about for the past seven? Get one going, Jack, me and Bri'll make it with you. Won't we, Bri'?'

The fifth man at the table, who had said little throughout the meal, glanced over at Lynn with interest now. He was Brian Smith, who was in his late twenties and seemed to be the odd man out at the table. It wasn't simply that he had a different accent. He didn't get his living from villainy, but had been adopted by Steve Collins, perhaps because of being so different.

'I'd've thought you'd have had something going by now,' Lynn said. He would never settle down to his twenty years.

'Ain't even been attempted. Too many fucking grasses. You can't even have a shit round here without you're grassed.'

'Something's got to be tried.'

'You wait and see,' Collins said. 'There's one or two grasses I'll mark your card about later, Jack. Though you'll smell most of them a mile away.' He winked.

Straightaway he recognized what Collins was doing. He was trying to bring him into line, to give the impression that he was part of his little team. It wasn't on, Lynn decided. He glanced around the table, looking for any spare food. Dunkerton hadn't finished his pudding. 'Don't you want that, Micky?'

'No. You wan' it?' He pushed the tray his way.

'It ain't that good, is it?' Collins said.

'I'm a growing lad.' Lynn was surprised how quickly he had accepted the low quality of food.

'You look like you could do with putting on a bit,' Collins said and pushed his chair back. 'You need any snout, son?'

'No, I don't use it,' Lynn said.

'Most in here let you brown 'em for a bit. Gonna watch telly.' He rose and moved across to the TV, where, with a peremptory air, he changed channels. 'Watching that rubbish,' he chided. 'This is better.'

The protests from the men in front of the TV were muted as Collins settled in one of the chairs.

'You gonna do a bit of work, Jack?' Parker said, taking out his tobacco. 'You don't have to of course if you're appealing. Mostly making soft toys. It helps to alleviate the boredom, especially if you're in a decent shop working in a group. 'S better than staying behind your door.'

'To be honest, Al, I've been sitting on a pile of mailbags behind my door. I didn't sew one of them.'

'You don't want to do that. They just give you ache, 'you do. A talent like yourn, you could get a job in the library or the administration where there's some fiddle. Brian's in the machine shop. 'S all right, you can get on that.'

'I'd just as soon stay behind m' door as work for them mugs.' He pushed his empty plate away and leaned back in his chair.

'What do you want to do that for?' Parker said. 'You can earn bundles. Three pound eighty-four pence I went and earnt last week. They'll have to cut my missus' Social Security money.'

'But rehabilitation is a wonderful thing, Alan,' Brian Smith remarked. His accent, despite his attempt to disguise it, was so markedly different from his own or Parker's that Lynn wondered how he got here.

'Be very handy, I get out in about twelve,' Parker said cheerfully. 'Be no end of openings for basket weaving and stitching mailbags. Sure you don't want none, Jack?' putting his tobacco on offer.

'What happened to that big fella in chokey?' Lynn inquired. 'Bobby Mark. D'you hear?'

Parker glanced towards the door, then said, 'The fuckers put him in the hospital, they did.'

'I heard the whacking they give him.'

'He's as simple as soap,' Collins said from across the room.

'He's a nice lad, 'you talk to him sensibly,' Dunkerton said. 'Quiet as anything. A nice bloke.'

'He was involved in a motorbike crash,' Parker explained.

'His mate on the back was killed, it tipped him over. He ought to be up the road, Broadmoor or somewhere. He gets violent now and again.'

'Is that why they whack him?' Lynn asked. Mark interested him, and he began to feel a curious sense of responsibility towards him. Possibly he should have protested more when he heard him being beaten, pressed on with his complaint in front of the deputy governor.

'Those fucking screws pick on him. They know he can't do fuck all. You run across Jordan on the block? Tall, blond-haired screw? Definitely a reincarnated Nazi, that one.'

'What about the PO down there, McClean?'

'Cor, what a no-good slag. He's on holiday from Ulster. Couple on this wing are all right. What it is, they're scared, they know we ain't got fuck all to lose. They don't get too flash. Discipline and security is all most of them care about. You'd be better off trying to get a move to Broadmoor or somewhere. But don't use violence to get there. Know what I mean?' Parker winked.

This sort of talk did little to encourage Lynn. He knew a lad who had gone to Broadmoor, a right good villain who hadn't had anything wrong with him until sent there for attacking a couple of screws. The slight sense of euphoria he had felt at being out of his cell and with people he liked was leaving him now and a feeling of depression was seeping back in. Although his seven months on remand had cushioned the impact, a lot of adjustment was still needed. All that being on remand had done was acclimatize him to his loss of liberty, while ahead of him had remained the hope that he would get a result in court. Here there was hope of getting a result on appeal, but it was less substantial to cling to. What life would be like if he didn't get his appeal he didn't dare to contemplate.

Free association like this was something he was more grateful for than the prison authority would know. The opportunity to exercise freedom of choice about who you associated with was all a prisoner had left. He enjoyed talking to other prisoners, and listening to their stories, but finally choosing to leave their company to be on his own was a luxury Lynn had too long been without.

He was lying on his bed when Brian Smith appeared in the doorway. He had brought two mugs of cocoa and buns.

'May I come in?' he asked. Another con would've wandered in and waited to be told that he wasn't wanted. He proffered a mug. 'Cocoa. It's not very good, I'm afraid.'

Lynn didn't say anything, but leaned on his elbow and watched the younger man. He could see how uneasy he was.

'It's just about drinkable,' Smith went on, 'when you get used to it. It's taken me a couple of years.' He laughed nervously as he set down the mugs. 'I wanted to talk to you about what you said at dinner.' He looked at Lynn, then checked the landing before pulling the door to. 'Were you serious about making one out if your appeal's turned down?'

The question surprised Lynn. He hadn't expected this sort of approach so soon, and least of all from him.

'I think I'll get a result all right,' he said non-committally.

'What if you don't? Could you tolerate this for twenty

years? Even for the seven years you'd need for parole eligibility?'

'What d'you have in mind, Brian?'

'I have a plan I've been working on for about a year.'

Lynn was suspicious. 'Aren't you and Steve together?'

He laughed and shook his head. 'You heard how he reacted. Most are like that. They all get used to the prison regime. It tells them when to get up, what to eat, when to sleep. By going to prison we forfeit the right to make choices. That's why we're sent here, I suppose. But once here, if they're here any length of time, they forget how to make any choices for themselves. Or they get so that they're afraid to. Finally about the only decision you can make yourself is whether you use your pot or piss your pants. That's exactly what the system wants, Jack.' He spoke eloquently and in a way that suggested that he knew what he was talking about. 'It isn't interested in rehabilitating you – it can't, it hasn't the facilities. And what would it rehabilitate you for? Unemployment? This is where they work on you.' He jabbed his forefinger against his head. 'They want to mash that, then try to turn you into a well-responding, well-behaved vegetable. They don't need to lobotomize prisoners to quieten them down. They're achieving the same result, only in a more socially acceptable way. Look at some of the people in here, they're no more responsible for their actions than Bobby Mark is. Unfortunately they no longer even break the rules as he does.'

'I don't know,' Lynn said, instinctively resisting what this man was saying, as if to acknowledge it openly would put more pressure on him, challenge him to do something about it. 'Steve said he would make one.'

Brian Smith shook his head emphatically. 'He doesn't even believe that. He just likes to be in on everything that's going on. He wants to control everything.'

Lynn sat on the edge of the bed and sipped his cocoa. ''S not all that, is it?' he said. 'The thing is, I got m' appeal.'

'Let's hope it goes well for you,' Smith said. But what he left unsaid impressed Lynn more.

He considered the man. 'What d'you get nicked for, Brian?'

'Destroying property,' he responded defiantly, but didn't elaborate or lionize his deeds. Lynn liked that.

'How come you sought me out?'

'I heard about your reception. You sounded like you'd be the most likely to take a chance. At least I was confident you weren't a grass,' he said.

'There are enough of those about,' Lynn reflected bitterly. He would want to be part of any plan anyone half-reliable had for making one out of there in the event of his appeal not going right for him. But what he didn't want to do at this stage was think about that disastrous possibility. 'Keep me in mind, Brian, will you?'

Smith agreed readily. 'Of course. Who else is there?'

A new day in prison always began just like the day before, and the day before that. Prisoners did rely on the regime, Lynn noticed, more and more. From the time they were unlocked, to lock-up in the evening, the routine they went through and the reactions of both prisoners and screws alike followed a regular pattern. He soon realized why new inmates were given such attention. Even the thickest of them was like a lifeline coming in with new ideas and experiences.

The wake-up bell rang throughout the wing at 7.15 a.m., a strident, discordant noise that seemed to have no effect on prisoners other than to inform them that their daily routine had started. It was part of the general noise pattern, as were the groans and coughs that followed, along with the familiar shouts of protest. 'What was your old woman doing while you was on last night?' was a favourite one for winding the screws up – there were few effective ways of getting back at the people who kept you locked up twenty-four hours a day, seven days a week.

Lynn rose easily, his bladder bursting from the two pints of water he drank at night. He relieved himself in his pot, which was half-full. He shaved in cold water in the small bowl on the washstand in the corner. There was no opportunity to shower first thing, and he was by now getting used to not being able to.

Around 8 a.m. warders moved along the landings, unlocking the cells for prisoners to slop out. With familiar regularity prisoners filed out with their pisspots, some of which were lapping to the brim, while others had been used for dumping in during the night. Strictly, pots weren't for prisoners to evacuate in, and Lynn had never used his like that, even though the chance of getting out to the recess after being banged up was nonexistent. A queue began to form at the recess where the urinal, WC and water tap were, on the end of each landing.

'About time!' prisoners exclaimed on cue as they were unlocked. The tone they used depended on which warder was at the door.

Other prisoners wanting to be unlocked rang their bells, which only brought shouts for them to stop from the warders.

'M' pot's overflowing, Mr Westbury,' a con said from behind his door.

'Then fucking well tread it down,' came the reply from the overweight warder with a large head made larger by muttonchop sideburns.

There was a sour smell of urine and excrement rising up through the wing, one that never really disappeared and was only ever masked with disinfectant. After about three or four prisoners had used the recesses the smell was vile, but like everything else it was something you had to get used to. It was only their own smell, they were told, if ever they complained. Smells in prison were something that were ever present. The predominant smells, it seemed to Lynn, were urine and the peculiar smell of damp metal; at meal times it was boiled cabbage, regardless of what the meal was.

'Quiet!' the principal officer shouted as he came on to the landing. 'This is not association.'

'Ballocks,' was the reply from an unidentified prisoner.

There was laughter from the recess queue.

'Who said that?' the PO screamed. His name was Allen, and he liked discipline. 'Come on, who said that?' There was a stony silence from the queue now, interrupted only by the flushing sluice. 'Another fucking word 'I'll have you behind doors.'

Breakfast, collected from the trolley on the ground floor, was eaten in the cells. It consisted of tea, porridge made from Grade A Canadian pigmeal, one dried, shrivelled rasher of streaky bacon, unless you were vegetarian, and four slices of bread. Despite it being singularly unappetizing, Lynn ate heartily.

At nine o'clock, with breakfast finished, prisoners were slopped out again, then set to work. Lynn was lying on his bed reading when the landing warder, Westbury, opened the cell door.

'Work detail,' Westbury announced. 'Mailbag shop, you.' He moved on as if expecting Lynn to rise and go to it. But then turned back immediately, mildly surprised when he didn't. 'Oi! Get yourself onto the mailbag-shop detail.'

'No fucking chance,' Lynn said. He didn't care for any of the jobs on offer, especially not for those poor rates of pay. He fancied mailbags least of all.

'What did you say?' the warder asked.

'I ain't working.'

'We'll see about that!' he announced, then wheeled out, slamming the cell door.

When he returned with the principal officer and unlocked

the cell door, Lynn was standing pissing in his pot. He ignored them until he had finished.

'All that tea for breakfast,' he said finally.

'Mailbag-sewing detail,' PO Allen said in a tone that suggested he wouldn't stand for any argument. 'Get to it.'

'Not while I'm appealing against sentence,' Lynn said, and sat back on his bed in defiance.

'Off that bed, before I drag you off it.'

Lynn gave him a measured look. 'You'd regret it, 'you tried,' he said evenly.

'You're on report,' the principal officer said. Then he turned on his heels and went out.

'On report,' was the screws' favourite expression. Lynn understood perfectly what it meant, and what the inevitable outcome would be. He'd have the usual brief hearing in front of the governor, who would back the charging officer then summarily dismiss him with the appropriate amount of chokey. He didn't regret what he had done. He would have preferred not to have been banged up behind the door, in the same way that he would have preferred not to have been in prison; however, he felt an instinctive need to protest in case he slipped unnoticed into the prison routine described by Brian Smith and become like all the other cons who tried to do their time and keep their noses clean. He was determined not to go like that: having been fitted he wasn't going to do his bird, but would protest any way he could. Brian Smith was right, Lynn thought, about cons growing to rely on their bird. It was frightening.

The MO was the next to visit him. He was still on his bed reading when a screw unlocked and the scruffy-looking doctor stepped inside. Lynn gave the young man only a cursory glance, then went back to his book.

'How are you feeling?' the doctor asked. He seemed confused by the silence and looked at the screw. Finally he said, 'You're fit for work.' That meant he was fit for punishment also. The doctor turned and stepped out.

The medical determination that he was fit enough to be punished made the subsequent adjudication by the deputy governor a foregone conclusion. Lynn wondered why they even bothered with the charade as he listened to their ballocks.

'Responding to Landing Officer Westbury's request,' PO Allen said, giving evidence in the adjudication room, 'I went to the prisoner's cell and asked if he'd like to join the work detail for the mailbag shop. Again he refused to work, without giving any reason. His tone was disrespectful. I told him to address me as 'sir' and ordered him to get off his bed. To which he replied, "You'd fucking well regret trying to make me." I saw there was no point arguing as the prisoner was becoming increasingly hostile. I informed him that I was putting him on report, sir.'

Frustration was causing Lynn to ball his fists as he stood listening to this. He wanted to scream at them.

'Well?' the deputy governor said, turning to Lynn. 'What have you to say?' His tone was disapproving.

'No point saying anything to that rubbish.'

'Address the deputy governor respectfully,' the chief officer ordered.

'I was fitted up by the police – I'm waiting for my appeal to be heard . . .' He doubted if his words were heard.

'You will conform with the rules and regulations governing the good order of my prison. This includes working when ordered to do so. If you are determined to make a habit of wilful resistance, it's a habit we will

'Why do you get angry like that?' she wanted to know. 'Don't you think it's right that a criminal should be punished?'

'I wasn't angry,' he said calmly. 'Of course it's right, otherwise we'd have fucking nonces on the loose.'

'But it's not right for you to be punished?'

'Well, one thing's for fucking sure, 's no good relying on anyone on your side of the system to be anything like fair. All you're doing is trying to ease their consciences for putting me here. Well, you can go and fuck yourselves,' Lynn said. He laughed, feeling in control now. 'You probably all do, for all I know.'

The psychiatrist snapped her notepad shut, concluding the interview. Psychopathically overbearing, arrogant, angry at authority – Lynn could guess what would go in her report on him.

Before the seven days behind his door were up, Lynn received a visit from his solicitor, Alex Gladwell. Suddenly he was filled with excitement and anticipation. He was afraid that they would deny him the visit on account of his circumstances, but then the deputy governor had said nothing about him losing his privileges. Lynn didn't know if his brief fell under that heading anyway.

'You're supposed to sew those sacks, not sit on them,' Powell said when he unlocked the cell door.

'Oh, I will, son,' Lynn said. 'Just as soon as the needles come back from being sharpened.' Similar comments were made by the screws whenever they opened the cell door. He thought about giving one of them a surprise by actually sewing some of the bags.

The screws reacted to his protests less and less, like they

knew there was no point. Lynn saw it as a trial, and the little victories pleased him.

Alex Gladwell looked like he was still getting a good living. Most of his business was from criminals, and most of them probably got their living from serious crime, Lynn decided, and therefore probably paid a cash fee over the Legal Aid brief. Whatever Gladwell's ability at law, Lynn knew his greatest asset was in the relationship he had with the CID, and the deals he was able to make on behalf of his clients. Most of those deals involved passing money from the villain to the detective on the case, in order to help get a result. Lynn had no problem with that, and doubted there was a single turn-down from any detective who Gladwell ever approached, assuming the circumstances were right. The fact that he had tried to do some business on his behalf but had been unsuccessful didn't signal any failure on the solicitor's part, but had indicated to Lynn how much the CID wanted him put away.

'Just because DI Pyle can't do any business doesn't mean that the police can be of no assistance,' Gladwell told him. 'Putting the right price into the right policeman can still get us a lot of valuable information that will help with your appeal. What we're looking for is information about the police involvement in the case, details of which didn't come out in court. But that all costs money.'

'Do you know anything that don't cost money when you're tucked up here?' Lynn said.

Even though censorship wasn't what it was in prison they still couldn't write to each other about such things.

Gladwell smiled and glanced towards the closed door of the legal visiting room.

'How are you?' he said, like he was suddenly uncertain about whether they were being listened to.

'Oh, I'm t'rific,' Lynn said, his eyes following the solicitor's. 'You think them fuckers are listening at the door?'

'Wouldn't surprise me, Jack.' He looked at Lynn and said, 'You look fucking awful. Can't you get a bath and a shave in here?'

''S not exactly Butlin's, is it? I heard it's as hard to get out of there.'

'Sit down, Jack,' Gladwell told him, taking a seat at the table and opening his briefcase. 'I don't suppose they're listening.'

'You can't even fart in private around here.'

'We'll write each other notes, then we can eat them.' He grinned. 'You're behind the door, I hear.'

'I'll stay there if necessary, till I get my appeal,' he said defiantly. 'How's it going, Alex?'

Gladwell arched his eyebrows. 'To be perfectly honest, our first priority is money. The second priority, though just as important, is new evidence. We can't go far without either.'

There was a pause. The small round eyes of the solicitor watched him frankly. Lynn felt more dismayed than disappointed, but decided he had to be practical. He said, 'Well, I ain't got either, have I? I mean, how the fuck could I, stuck down here?' I'm not earning. Can't you get if off Legal Aid?'

'Not for the sort of digging we're doing,' he said. 'It's a nice idea, Jack, getting a Legal Aid certificate in order to go into bent police for information on other bent policemen.' He smiled. But Lynn didn't see what was funny about the situation.

'If we had some new evidence to put before the court,' Gladwell said, 'the appeal would be a simple open-and-shut case. It could amount to a miscarriage of justice as a result of the new evidence that hadn't been available at the time.'

'Well, I fucking ain't got any, have I!' Lynn said angrily. 'I dunno who the fourth blagger on that one was.'

'Don't worry about it, Jack. Your appeal's been put in. What we have got gives us a better than good chance. A bit of dosh would make things a lot easier.'

Lynn considered the problem, knowing there was only one way to go on this. At first he tried to avoid it, but knew how much he needed Alex Gladwell, and that he wasn't going to go on working for nothing. 'I'll have to sell m' house,' he said, feeling sick at the thought. It was Dolly's and the girls' only bit of security. 'I'll talk to Dolly. That'll solve the money problem. Where'll she go with the kids, though – her mother's, I suppose.' He looked at the solicitor, as if expecting some understanding of his domestic problems, but he gave no sign of doing so. 'Should be worth about forty-five grand, by the time she pays off a couple of debts and the mortgage.'

'You think it'll sell all right, in this market?'

'Yeah, it should be okay, I'd say.'

'Sorry it has to be this way, Jack,' the solicitor said. 'But going into different people costs money.'

Lynn nodded, reluctantly accepting the situation. 'Dolly will understand, and do what I ask about the house. It's a shame though, she liked that place, even though the kitchen was never big enough. We was gonna get an extension put on. The girls were settled there too. Still, they like it at their gran's. That's the way things go,' he concluded philosophically. 'You never get too far ahead before you get a knockback.'

'Our best option lies in the charges against the detectives

involved in the case,' Gladwell said. 'But we can't expect too much from the straight inquiries by the Complaints Investigation Bureau. They'll do no more than is required of them. They won't really want to nick one of their own, especially if they can give him an out. But they might have to this time, Jack. DI Pyle is being looked at under that widespread investigation into the squad fabricating evidence. If we get something substantial on him, that way we can show a miscarriage of justice. I'm going into as many policemen as I can. The more dirt we can get on that little firm the better. It'll all help.'

'What do you think, Alex? Seriously?'

'I'm a realist, Jack. I told you before that I'm not concerned how you got your living. But I do believe that in this case you were fitted. No matter how many other robberies you may have had lined up, I accept that you didn't rob the Gas Board at Abbey Wood. It's not up to the police to decide it's your turn. Whether the appeal court judges are convinced that's what they did will depend on what we come up with. If the fourth man on that blag were to be arrested . . .' He shrugged. 'But life is rarely that easy. As things stand as of now your chances are pretty good. By the time I finish they're going to be ninety-nine per cent good. I'm not going to gain a thing from telling you that if I don't believe it. Somehow we'll get you a result all right.' The solicitor looked at him, then said, 'I won't stop working on your behalf, Jack, I promise you. I'll do everything I can to get your release.' He nodded, as if confirming this. Then dropped his voice to a whisper. 'If all else fails I'll send my managing clerk into you with some hacksaw blades.' He winked.

That wasn't such a ridiculous proposition. Lynn had

heard that Gladwell's managing clerk had been used before to liaise with cons on the inside over escape details.

Gladwell spread his pudgy hands over the papers he had removed from his briefcase. 'We've a lot to get through here. Have you got time?'

'Oh, I'd say so,' Lynn replied, feeling a lot more cheerful now.

The cheerful face of Brian Smith waiting on the landing outside his cell with his supper tray as the warder unlocked the door was a welcome sight, Lynn found. It was his seventh day behind his door. He ignored the warder, not even hearing what he said, but stepped out through the doorway and breathed the air like he was breathing in freedom.

'Haven't you sewn those mailbags yet?' Smith said, openly admiring him. He smiled again. 'If I had a trumpet, Jack, I'd blow it.'

'Why's that, Bri'?' Lynn said. He had quickly sussed this lad. From previous prison experience he knew how certain types of prisoners latched onto you, wanting you to fight their battles, especially younger prisoners. Sometimes it was all right, he found; other times it was embarrassing. Instinctively he knew the attraction was partly sexual, but he wasn't able to articulate this. He didn't object to Brian Smith coming on like he did, especially as he had an escape plotted up and was prepared to wait for him on it. In some ways Lynn rather enjoyed the attention.

'I collected your dinner.' Smith extended the tray.

'To be honest, I was looking forward to getting it myself. It's the little highlights what make your day, 'you been behind your door.' He saw Brian Smith's disappointment, and suddenly winked. 'Good luck, Bri'.' He took the tray from the younger man, and they went towards the TV room together.

Bobby Mark came up the stairs with his evening meal. Lynn noticed him when the landing warder called Westbury shouted to him. He was probably going to push him around, but Lynn couldn't fight that fight now or his food would get cold.

There were six prisoners in the threes' TV room. The only difference between this and the room on the lower floor were the faces. Most of those turned from the TV and greeted Lynn when he came in but didn't stop chomping food. Collins was at the table with a black prisoner who was doing life for stabbing a policeman. Collins paused from his food and watched Lynn as he and Brian Smith sat at the table.

'Steve,' Lynn said. 'How's it going?'

Collins slowly shook his head in disapproval. 'We try to observe a bit of decorum here, son. Like shaving.'

'Oh yes,' Lynn said without giving anything. 'The trouble is you lose touch with the niceties, banged up. I tell you, Steve, there was even nights when I wasn't bothering to dress for dinner!'

'Down the slippery slope you go,' Collins commiserated. ''Fore you know it you've forgotten which knife to eat your peas with. So what's the outcome of this little ruck? You gonna join us and do a bit of work after all?'

'Hadn't thought to,' Lynn said. 'I mean, what's the point?'

''S up to you. Providing silly ballocks don't get the hump with everyone else. Know what I mean?'

'Why should he?'

The fourth con at the table was clearly someone who

was currently giving Collins his favour. He said, 'Well, you know what he's fucking well like, 'he's upset.'

Brian Smith glanced at Lynn and said, 'Fuck it! Maybe we should all refuse to work.'

Collins gave him a look. 'I'll tell you what, son. I'll take your job in the machine shop, 'you refuse to sew mailbags. How's that?'

'I made m' point, Steve,' Lynn said, attempting to defuse the situation. 'I might do a bit now. Pass the time while I'm waiting for my appeal result.'

They ate in silence for a while.

Bobby Mark stooped through the low doorway. He paused and looked across to the men at the table as if having difficulty identifying who they were. He saw the TV and was distracted momentarily. Collins smiled but didn't say anything as the big man came across to them. Lynn sensed something was wrong as he measured the man approaching the table, judging his chances if it came to a fight.

'You got my cell,' Mark said. 'You got my cell.'

'That's all right,' Lynn replied reasonably. 'You can have it back if you want.'

The offer immediately seemed to confuse Mark. He hesitated, then said, 'Oh no, it's all right. I don't mind. Mr Allison tol' me you was the one asking after me in hospital.'

Lynn felt slightly relieved that he didn't have a fight on his hands. He didn't doubt he could have put Mark away, but guessed he had enough problems.

'How are you?'

'I'm all right now. They give me some stuff in the hospital. Calms me down, like. Valium, it was.'

'Why don't you sit down and have your dinner, 'fore it gets cold?'

Bobby Mark hesitated, and glanced at the television that was clearly in the forefront of his thoughts. 'I'm gonna watch telly,' he said.

'That's all right. We'll have a chat later.' He watched Bobby Mark go over to the TV and sit down.

Collins grinned. 'Thought you was in trouble there.'

Lynn nodded. 'Given us a hand, Steve, would you?'

'He's a strong lad. I've seen him put four screws away. You gotta be simple to try that. No way do they let you pull strokes like that.'

'He seems all right to me,' Lynn said.

There were strong crosscurrents at the table, and the feeling of pleasure he had had when getting out of his cell had vanished. He sensed Brian Smith didn't like the attention he gave Bobby Mark, and saw he was having difficulty keeping the emotion off his face. Steve Collins noticed the same thing, but didn't comment.

'What'd your brief have to say, Jack?' Collins asked.

'Oh, he reckons there's a blinding chance of me getting a result.' Lynn didn't want anyone to know his business; that way no one would derive satisfaction from any misfortune of his.

'Pleased to hear it,' Collins said, and glanced at Brian Smith again. 'All you gotta do is get it on, then.'

'That's all,' Lynn replied. It might have been the easiest thing in the world.

Why Jack spent so much time trying to help Bobby Mark sort himself out, Brian Smith wasn't sure. Obviously he was a decent man who felt sorry for him, seeing the shitty deal the big loon got from everyone. Most of the other cons dismissed him, while most of the warders picked on him, knowing they were certain to get a reaction from him. There was no one on the wing easier to wind up than Bobby Mark. More than anything he supposed the man epitomized injustice for Jack, but his concern would all come to nothing and he wanted to tell Jack that as he watched the two of them in front of him now. He could hear most of their conversation as they shuffled around the exercise yard together. Jack was doing most of the work, as if he was trying to draw Mark out. 'How long you down for, Bob?' he said. But Mark didn't talk much to anyone, and only seemed to answer direct questions if he felt like doing so.

'I dunno, Jack,' he replied slowly. 'That's what gets my goat. They won't gimme no release date, will they.'

'Didn't the judge say how long when he sent you down?'

Mark shook his head. 'He said I had to be locked away for the safety of society.' Lynn looked at him and waited. ''S what he said, Jack, he did. If they'd only say when I could go out, I think I'd be all right. Know what I mean? It'd give me something to concentrate on.'

'Maybe we ought to try and do something about getting you a release date.'

'Could you? That'd be t'rific.' He saw Mark smack his hands together excitedly, as though Jack had already achieved that for him. Some chance, Brian Smith thought. He glanced at Steve Collins, who was with him. He smiled. He had heard the conversation too.

It was a quarter past eleven and the entire wing, apart from the nonces, was in the exercise yard. Forty-two men moved around in a circle in pairs, six paces apart. Talking was permitted between each pair but not with the pair in front or behind. Brian Smith wanted to walk with Lynn, and felt aggrieved that Mark took what he considered was his rightful place. Prisoners weren't allowed to walk in threes or he would have stepped right alongside. Instead he found himself in step with Steve Collins as he had done on several occasions recently. He recognized what Collins was doing. He was winding him up, never missing an opportunity to point out how close he thought Lynn and Mark were getting.

'It's nice the way Jack is taking an interest in him. Got the simple fucker eating out of the palm of his hand. You'd think he was his Dad, wouldn't you?'

Smith didn't comment. Knowing himself to be a lot brighter than the average con he could anticipate what this man was up to before Collins did himself, and although he suspected his motive was nothing other than a means of relieving his boredom it didn't stop his feelings of jealousy whenever he pointed out such things.

Collins sought him out during association that evening, finding him sitting on his own in the threes' TV room. The television was broken, which was why the place was deserted.

'Tucked up in Jack's cell like a couple irons, they are,' Collins said. 'You'd think he was giving him one.'

Finding himself reacting again, Brian Smith said, 'You should watch what you say, Steve. Either one of them could put you away.'

A smile crossed Collins's face, like he suddenly realized he had gone too far and was now trying to retrieve the situation. 'You got no sense of humour, Bri', 's your trouble.

You got to let go a bit, son, learn to recognize a joke. They'll end up carting you off in a straitjacket.' He sat and took out his tobacco and rolled a cigarette fatter than he normally did. 'Anyway, an educated lad like you ought to be writing his petition to the Home Secretary, not Jack.'

'What a waste of time,' Smith said. 'There's only one way that loon will get out. The way I plan to. I'm not waiting until they say when.'

Collins said, 'Yeah, that's right. You ain't got a release date either, have you, Bri'?'

'Sooner than anyone thinks,' Smith said. 'I'm not going to sit here and rot, waiting while they decide when it's safe to let me back into society. I'm going to do something about it. You see.' He was normally close-mouthed, and immediately regretted saying as much so.

'Put us in, 'you got one plotted up,' Collins said.

But Brian Smith was back in control now. How seriously Collins had taken his intention to escape, he couldn't tell. The real danger was that Collins was a man who didn't want to miss out on anything going off around the wing.

'The thing is, Brian, I got dough on the outside, a lot of it. And I've still got a lot of worthwhilc contacts. I'm no old mug. I'm not some silly fucking cowboy who could do no better than stick a shotgun over a building society counter with a video camera watching me the whole while. I could arrange to have a boat to take us off the island, across to France or Morocco. Anywhere we want.'

We? Brian Smith noticed how easily Collins included himself. Maybe the man was genuine, but still he hesitated.

'The thing is, if you're relying on Jack,' Collins said, 'you shouldn't. He's no value, no value at all. He'll get his appeal, get a result, he's a stoneginger. He won't want to make one, I guarantee it.' He paused. 'Think about it, Bri. Do yourself a favour, son. Put me in instead. You won't regret it.'

Brian Smith committed himself no further than to say he would think about it. Despite everything Collins said, logic told him that Jack Lynn was a better bet.

Unaware that he was the centre of anyone's attention, Jack Lynn carefully read through the petition he had written to the Home Secretary seeking some indication of a release date for Bobby Mark. The chances of getting it were slim, but it was worth a try, especially as it encouraged Bobby Mark and took his mind off his problems. There were a lot in this prison like him, and they probably had no more success with their petitions. He was doubtful if the Home Secretary ever saw them. What he needed was someone in Justice or the television programme *Rough Justice* to take up his case. But they only ever took on cases where there was a glaring injustice, not where prisoners like Bobby Mark had never denied their guilt.

'You gotta sign this now, Bobby.' He pushed the letter form towards Mark.

A worried expression came over Mark's face. 'Can you put down about them breaking m' specs? Makes m' headaches worse without 'em.'

'Well, I could put it down. But we'd be better off not putting that in now. I mean, you just give silly ballocks an opportunity to back it. Here, stick your signature on that. We'll tackle the MO about your glasses. All right?'

Mark accepted the advice and signed the petition.

Alan Parker appeared in the doorway, looking flushed.

'Jack, there's a couple of nonces on the twos, watching telly!' He sounded outraged.

'On their own?' Lynn was no less outraged.

'No, with two screws. 'S all part of silly ballocks' normalization plan – trying to integrate the nonces.'

'Fucking liberty! We can't have that.'

'Too fucking right. He'll have us twoed up with the dirty fuckers next.' Parker's indignation increased. 'I told some of the others to have a wander down there.'

'Tell some of them to get some boiling water from the urn, Al,' Lynn suggested. 'We'll scald the fuckers.' Just thinking about what some of the nonces on their wing had done enraged him so much he wanted them to die a painful, lingering death.

'Some are already getting it,' Parker told him.

'Let's see to the monsters, then.' He started out after Parker. Bobby Mark went with them.

In the TV room on the second landing Lynn found Menzies. The fine-boned child-murderer was sitting with another killer of children, the eggheaded Donald Ludlow, who was in his mid-thirties, but looked older. The fact that he seemed so unrepentant that he could have any expectation of getting out of his cell or leading any sort of existence there further enraged him. If the opportunity presented itself he, along with most other prisoners, would put the nonsense cases away. Most were unswervingly dedicated to that cause, even if it meant being charged again.

The two child-murderers were sitting between two warders watching *Coronation Street*, when Lynn arrived with Bobby Mark. None of the other Rule 43s on the wing had ventured out under the governor's new scheme to integrate them. One of the warders who looked after the second landing, Joe Marshall, glanced up, then turned back to the TV. With the arrival of other cons there were enough of them to overpower the two guards easily and murder the nonces. That prospect must have occurred to the two of them, they started to quake. Their eyes flitted nervously around at the arrival of more prisoners, none of whom was interested in the TV, but sat in chairs or leaned against the wall or sat on the edge of the table and stared at them.

Sweat broke out on the faces of Menzies and Ludlow as alarm visibly rose through them.

Collins came in, followed by Brian Smith. That made fifteen ordinary prisoners in the room and the atmosphere was so tense it crackled. Each of them ignored the TV, and watched for a signal that would spark things off. Steve Collins provided it as he stepped over to the TV.

'What's this rubbish you're watching?' he said. 'The other side's much better.' He switched channels, then again and again without bothering to identify the programmes. 'Ah, that's a load of ballocks.' He switched the set off.

There was no disguising that the nonces were the centre of attention then.

Like he was unaware of the tension, Marshall said, 'We were watching that, Steve.'

He was another Geordie, in his early thirties, and wore a clipped moustache. He also slashed the peak on his cap so that it hung almost vertically down his forehead and over his eyes, forcing him to carry his head erect in order for him to see. A number of the younger warders slashed the peaks in that way, like they belonged to some club. The older screws rarely did. Marshall's claim to fame along the walkways was that he had achieved the most overtime in a single week, doing ninety-eight hours actual. He was certainly as much a prisoner as any of them, Lynn thought, if serving his time less reluctantly.

'No one else was watching it, Joe,' Collins said civilly. 'Anyway, it'll corrupt these two, won't it?'

Marshall's glare circled the room, quickly assessing the gathering. 'All right, what the fuck's going on?'

'Going on?' Dunkerton said in apparent surprise. 'We just come for a bit of association. You know, the telly's broken on the threes. But what do we find? Fucking monsters forced on us.'

'You got kids, Micky, haven't you?' Lynn said.

'Yeah, I got five terrific boys. Think the world of me, they do. Come down and see me regular and everything.'

'I got kids too,' Collins commented. 'Nothing I wouldn't do for them. Breaks your fucking heart when you think what some wicked bastards here done to kids . . .'

'How'd you like these monsters getting hold of yourn?' Lynn asked. His voice trembled with emotion and he could barely get the words out. It was as much as he could do to stop from rushing them. 'Trying to make them go down on them like one of them done, listening to their cries, pleading with them not to, then strangling them when they wouldn't . . . 's what we gotta associate with . . .'

A prisoner working around the governor's office had got hold of some of the nonces' depositions which held all those details. Hearing them spoken caused all the fear and loathing that had been building to explode like the expulsion of a single breath from the prisoners. The two screws were suddenly on their feet, the two nonces coming up with them like their shadows.

'Back to your cells,' Marshall barked harshly at Menzies and Ludlow. 'Fuck off – quickly!'

They didn't need telling twice, but went like two hares suddenly breaking cover just as Alan Parker came along the landing towards the TV room with three other cons, each carrying a pint of boiling water they had collected from the tea urn on the ground floor. The two nonces ran straight into the shower of scalding water. In pain and confusion they hurled themselves along the landing.

Cons, forcing their way out of the TV room in pursuit, drove the two screws ahead of them. Lynn, like everyone else, was beyond the immediate control of these two warders. Ignoring their shouts to get back to their cells, they pressed on along the landing, joined by other prisoners. Which of the two screws was the first to reach the strategically placed alarm button didn't really matter. The effect of the bell starting up and drowning out all the other noise was immediate.

The news of the disturbance wasn't something Archibald Maudling enjoyed receiving at the start of his day. It made him angry. 'Why wasn't I telephoned at my home last night?' he demanded. He didn't listen when the deputy governor explained that he had decided there had been no need to disturb him. Maudling wasn't satisfied with that, even though the disturbance had supposedly been nipped in the bud. 'I know the signs,' he told his deputy, Chief Officer Carne and PO Allen as they followed him into his office. 'There's unrest, discontent – I can sense it fermenting. It was just such an incident that sparked last year's riots,' he reminded them. 'Am I the lone member of staff to recognize this?'

There was no reply from any of these senior officers.

He had little sympathy for the child-murderers, and wished he could get them transferred to Long Lartin.

'How are Menzies and Ludlow this morning?' he finally got around to asking.

'The MO treated them for superficial scalds,' the chief informed him. 'It shook them up more than anything. They'll be all right, a couple of days behind their doors. The way those lads on the twos went after them they might prefer to be left behind their doors for the rest of their lives, never being let out, having their food pushed through their door slots.'

Reading the files of those prisoners and seeing in print some of the things they had done to their victims had made Maudling feel sick. He had three children of his own and found it impossible to detach himself as he had gone through those details. He prided himself on being fair-minded and moderate in his reactions, but he wasn't convinced he would hurry to prevent any of those prisoners on Rule 43 from getting a beating. To see one of them suffering physically reduced his deep anxiety for his own children's safety. He didn't doubt how much they suffered mentally, but that knowledge didn't satisfy him, any more than it seemed to satisfy ordinary prisoners. These were thoughts he shared with no one.

He sat heavily behind his large, orderly desk. His office by contrast to the adjudication room was spacious and well-appointed; it had a carpet on the floor, and curtains; there were paintings and photos of his family and a cabinet containing cups and shields.

'Was it a premeditated attack?' he asked.

'There were no witnesses, sir,' PO Allen answered. 'The prisoners claim they were taking hot water to the TV room on the twos for their coffee when Menzies and Ludlow rushed out and crashed into them. Mr Marshall confirmed that, sir.'

'Animals,' he said unthinkingly, 'that's all they are. Not an ounce of decency or compassion in any of them. What hope is there of ever rehabilitating this particular collection of humanity even if there were the means?' He would have preferred to pass the more violent specimens on to Broadmoor, but unfortunately there was a limit to the numbers they could take. 'Keep them locked up after breakfast, Mr Allen. I'll see them in their cells, all of them.' He thought about that for a moment. 'I only wish I could keep them there the whole time.'

Along the landing there was a lot of noise from prisoners protesting about being kept banged up without being allowed to slop out after breakfast. Lynn knew that men regimented day after day as they were, forced to evacuate their bowels at set times, got into firm habits with such bodily functions. In the normal course of events they got to slop out half an hour after breakfast. Now, an hour past usual slopout time, they had a genuine need. Some prisoners were banging on their doors with tin ashtrays, others ringing their bells, others calling out. He heard the screws moving agitatedly along the landings, shouting through the doors for them to be quiet, telling them the governor was coming over.

'. . . I'm breaking my neck for a pony,' Micky Dunkerton shouted, hammering on his door.

'Then use your pot, if you can't hold it till the governor's been round,' Warder Westbury said as he went along the landing. He swung his keys against the door of the next cell. 'Stop ringing that fucking bell!'

'I wanna use the recess,' came the response.

'You can't!' He moved along to the cell where Bobby Mark was banging his door and wrenched the door open. 'What's this fucking noise? You want to be put back in hospital?'

Mark said, 'M' pot's full.'

'Why don't you try eating some of it?' came the reply.

The governor could hear the noise from across the prison and it irritated him. His one fear was that such a protest would start off something with the other prisoners, which was to be avoided at all costs. Demonstrations of this sort had the habit of spreading like a fire through a tenement.

The noise struck Maudling forcefully when the chief opened the main entrance to the wing. As he stood in the security vestibule and waited while PO Allen unlocked the inner gate, he bristled angrily. Someone would be on the punishment block for it, he decided.

'What's all this fucking noise, Mr Allen?' he demanded, as though incapable of identifying the protests for himself.

'They're complaining about not being allowed to the recesses, sir,' PO Allen snapped.

This only added to Maudling's displeasure. 'We'll see about about that,' he said. 'I'll show them they can't carry on like this. We'll start at the top, chief.'

The governor strode away towards the metal staircase, causing the two uniformed officers to put in a quick step to catch up.

'Open it up,' he ordered impatiently. The four of them were outside Collins's cell. No one had checked through the Judas hole, which ordinarily the landing officer would have done before unlocking the door.

There was no immediate sign of Collins as the door swung open. But when Maudling ventured into the cell with the chief and the PO he went rigid. Collins was in the corner with his trousers down, sitting astride his pot.

'Sorry, guv, I was took short,' he said with a smile.

Although a man sitting astride a pot, in this way, had a considerable physical disadvantage, the situation found Maudling psychologically disadvantaged. He wasn't about to accept that it was his fault that the prisoner was forced to this, but muttered a barely comprehensible apology and turned out. He would have to come back to question the man about his part in last night's disturbance, for he certainly wasn't going to do so while he sat in the corner defacating.

The next cell door was opened with the same lack of caution. There they found Dunkerton with his trousers down also sitting on his pot, which had been placed for convenience on his chair. His apology sounded no more sincere than Collins's had been. 'A bit of diarrhoea, sir.'

'See the MO,' Maudling barked and spun round out of the cell, more angry than embarrassed that his staff had allowed such a situation to develop.

His anger increased when in the next cell they found yet another prisoner on his pot. Maudling knew clearly what was going on. It was no coincidence that three men in succession were unable to control their bowel motions. Checking through the inspection hole in the door to the next cell they found Lynn in the same position; then Mark. They proceeded no further. Maudling turned back along the landing, trembling with anger.

'They won't get away with this, chief. Enforce every rule to a letter on this wing. I want the ringleaders of this little charade. We'll see who has the last laugh. They'll laugh on the other side of their faces.' He started down the stairs, not wishing to see any more prisoners.

Enforcing rules and regulations to the letter was perhaps the simplest way of punishing prisoners, doubly so for the satisfaction his officers had of knowing they were behaving perfectly legally. One of the most effective uses of the rules was to unlock men three at a time for their meals, and making sure they were locked back in their cells with their food before the next three were let out. It guaranteed that everyone but the first three got cold food; meals that weren't appetizing when hot were even less appetizing when cold. The whole process generally took over an hour, when normally it would have taken no more than fifteen minutes. The same painfully slow process was applied when slopping out. Privileges were severely curtailed; the no-talking rule on moving from one place to another was enforced. Offences against discipline were frequent, resulting in many prisoners appearing before him or his deputy. There was no doubt in Maudling's mind who would be the final winner.

To begin with, frequent references were made to the incident which had started the rule enforcement as the prison staff sought the ringleaders who had organized the scalding of the nonces. But when they got nowhere with that tack the whole matter was suddenly dropped, only the strict enforcement of the rules stayed. Eventually they would be relaxed again, but meanwhile some of the prisoners were getting angry with the regime. Knowing what could so easily happen in this situation. Lynn found himself persuading prisoners to refrain from taking action. Most of them knew instinctively that if any one of them protested, then he would be put down on the block as the ringleader.

More warders than usual watched them as they exercised around the yard in pairs, even though the enforcement of rules was being relaxed slightly.

As Lynn walked around with Bobby Mark, Steve Collins, who was six paces behind with Brian Smith, said, 'That was a result, Jack, doing them fucking nonces, whatever way you book it. No one was nicked, was they? Everyone stayed behind his door.'

'What did it achieve though?' Lynn wanted to know. 'Apart from all this aggravation.'

'What!' said Collins. He sounded surprised. 'We showed silly ballocks that he can't normalize the monsters. They didn't give us much for it. We ain't worse off, are we?'

'We're no better off either.'

'No talking, you two,' a warder yelled, running along the yard towards them. 'You're on report.'

They had finally found the ringleaders.

Time didn't exactly slip away for him, but it did pass, even though he counted the minutes and the hours as they grew into days, then weeks. Time passed more quickly when he wasn't behind his door, and was allowed to associate with other prisoners.

Lynn was counting the days and weeks to his appeal. He had yet to be given a date, and he didn't know how long it would be before it got on. That in-between time was his actual sentence, notwithstanding the result he might or might not get. That was time that couldn't be returned to him. The prospect of not having his conviction overturned and having to do the remainder of his sentence was something he couldn't bear to think about.

Time passing brought his first visit from his wife nearer, and the prospect excited him. He would have preferred Dolly to bring his daughters down to see him, and much as he wanted to see them he knew they had too much to talk about, too many adjustments and accommodations to try and make first. He got a visit for two hours every three weeks, and that wasn't nearly enough. Their letters didn't help either. Deeply disturbing problems that were thrown up by this forced separation couldn't be gone into in a letter, not when you knew the screws were likely to read it. That thought inhibited every word he ever set down on the page. He wanted to tell her of his sexual needs, how much he wanted to make love to her, and have her write of such things to him; however, he got angry thinking about such things being gloated over by others, or their intimacies being dipped into and shared among the prison staff like some confiscated contraband. They couldn't even write about money or how those problems might be resolved; he could only read between the lines about the aggravation Dolly was getting from the Social Security.

The letter he was writing in his cell during association was taking him a long time, the exercise causing him to think concentratedly about his wife and family, which in turn was causing him a dull feeling of frustration.

He looked up, welcoming the distraction as Brian Smith appeared in the doorway, bringing a paperback book.

'Oh sorry – are you busy, Jack?' he said uncertainly. 'I haven't seen much of you lately.'

'Writing to the Missus, 's all.' He turned the standard letter sheet face down – not that there was much in it. 'I'll see her before I finish it at this rate.'

'Due for a visit, are you?'

''S not before fucking time.' He watched the younger man, waiting to see what he had in mind.

''S that book on Buddhism I was telling you about.'

He slid the book into the narrow shelf over the bed and waited. Lynn watched him, knowing he was feeling uncomfortable and wondered why he couldn't come right out and say what he had to.

'You got a family who visit you, have you, Bri'?'

Smith said, 'I have a family, but they wouldn't even visit Cowes now. It was one of their properties I destroyed. They're very concerned about their property. Do you resent me for that?'

'What? Taking a chainsaw to your ancestral home?'

'No, not exactly – coming from that background.'

'I might if you had tried pulling any strokes on account of it. You're all right, I'd say.'

The cloud over Smith lifted and he smiled. 'Did you think any more about what I mentioned?'

'About the other thing?' Lynn said cautiously.

Smith turned and checked the landing outside the cell. 'It's all clear. The thing is, Steve Collins approached me. He wants to be put in.'

'He might be very useful to you,' Lynn said generously. He could see Brian Smith was trying to put pressure on him to get him to commit to his escape plan.

'Possibly he wouldn't prove terribly reliable.'

'I do fancy some of it, Bri'.' He was badly missing his wife and children. 'Let me think about it some more.'

Even that small commitment seemed to delight Brian Smith. He smiled and clapped his hands. 'Yes, of course. Of course. I'd wait for you.'

Ordinarily Lynn would have formed his own opinion about a con, and formed it quickly, knowing whether he was a wrong 'un or not, whether he could trust him or not. Brian Smith didn't fit into the pattern of most cons, most of whom would have gained acceptance there by virtue of the villainy they did or the sentence they drew. Their deps' were their calling card in there. On its own, Smith's unspecified sentence wouldn't have gained him acceptance any more than the nonces' long sentences would. But Collins had befriended him and he wasn't considered a mug by anyone. But still Lynn wasn't sure that Brian Smith wasn't simply doing Collins's bidding.

In the twenty-feet-square mailbag shop where security

prisoners worked, Lynn was at one of the three benches with Alan Parker and Bobby Mark. Conversation, though not officially permitted, was condoned by most of the screws, who tended to stay at the end of the shop with the discipline screw.

'What d'you think about Brian, Al?' Lynn was saying, glancing towards the warder, who wasn't looking in his direction but at Steve Collins, who was wandering around the shop. 'Is he a serious prospect to make one with?' Of necessity he talked quickly, his voice barely above a whisper.

'Serious as any, I s'pose,' he replied. 'He keeps well closed up.'

'That's what I thought.'

'He'd be safe enough, Jack. The thing is, he ain't got nothing to lose by having a go, has he?' It wasn't an argument against getting involved with him as far as Lynn was concerned.

'I ain't exactly got a lot, have I?' he said matter-of-factly.

Alan Parker arched his eyebrows and tightened his lips, acknowledging the point.

Their attention went to a uniformed warder who came into the shop and had a few words with a white-coated screw. Lynn knew it was about his visit, and was already on his feet when the white-coated warder approached.

The movements book that went everywhere with him was something he was growing to resent more than any other single object. For that more than anything made him feel like a numbered parcel rather than a person. It went across to the visiting block with him.

The visiting arrangements here were tolerable. The large

room in the visiting block had eighteen tables in a line. On one side of each table there was a single chair, on the other side, two or sometimes three, prisoners being allowed up to three visitors. But such visits weren't for Lynn. As a category 'A' prisoner he was taken past this room and across the corridor to one of the small, secure rooms that were a bricked-on addition to the prison. Lynn was escorted into one of these cubicle-like rooms and told to sit at the table which, apart from the two chairs, was the only furniture. One concession to progress was the absence of bars at the windows of these cubicles, but instead three glass bricks, the same as most modern police cells had, and which were even harder to break.

Lynn was kept waiting, and was convinced it was done to wind him up. His wife must have arrived or they wouldn't have called him down. He tried to stay calm, but found it increasingly difficult. When the door was unlocked from the outside he was startled. He stood as Dolly was brought in. He expected one of the screws in with them to tell him to sit, but neither did.

Dolly was wearing a summer frock and looked terrific. She looked as good as he could ever remember seeing her, despite the anxiety in her face, and the fatigue which he tried to deny to himself was there.

One of the screws spoke to his colleague. Lynn couldn't hear what was said, but the uniform who had shown Dolly in went out. The other one was locked in with them. Lynn was acutely conscious of that man, who inhibited him now. He and Dolly embraced and he kissed her self-consciously. He wanted to press himself against her, press himself into her, feel her body against his. The sexual images he had of her were still sharp in his mind and it was Dolly he thought about when he masturbated.

'How are you, love?' His voice was quaking with emotion.

She tried to speak, but couldn't get beyond her greeting, and that was barely audible. Her face crumpled as though no longer able to take the strain. She turned her head but couldn't hide her tears.

The warder directed Lynn into his chair. Physical contact wasn't permitted other than on greeting and departing.

'Ah, Doll,' Lynn said after a moment, uncertain how to react. 'Come on, love, sit down. Don't upset yourself.' He looked confused, instinctively knowing he had nothing to offer her. He bent over to physically comfort her.

'Sit back there,' the warder said to him.

Lynn looked at the uniform, having no understanding of the man or what made him do what he was doing. He considered protesting, but didn't.

'I'm sorry, Jack,' Dolly said through her tears. 'It's just, I dunno . . . I dunno, lovey.'

At one time she had been able to cope and had helped get him through his previous prison sentences. She hadn't enjoyed it for a moment, he had known that, but she had survived. Now he didn't know if she would. Twenty years was longer than anything before, too long for the mind to grasp or measure. The thought of her not being as much with him on the outside was tearing him apart.

''S murder,' Lynn said, feeling crushed by those thoughts. 'C'mon, Dolly, don't upset yourself, love. Don't give these slags the satisfaction. They nicked enough off us as it is – the no-good slags. C'mon.' He watched her as she tried to check her tears. He searched for something to say that might deflect her thoughts, but nothing came to mind. Everything he wanted to say was either directly related to their present position or would simply serve as a reminder of it. Finally he asked, 'How are the girls?' It was the wrong question, but then almost any question would be.

She caught her breath again. 'They're missing you, Jack . . .'

That suddenly being openly acknowledged caused him a lot of pain. He arched his eyebrows to try and ease the tension at the back of his eyes. 'Both all right, are they?' It took a lot of effort.

Dolly nodded. 'They wanted to come down with me . . .'

He knew all this, they had been into it in their letters, deciding it would be better to leave it for a couple of visits.

'They wanted me to give you their best love . . . Sandra won't settle to nothing, keeps asking about when you're coming home . . . Christ, when I think about what them rotten fucking policemen and that judge done to you . . .' Her anger came bubbling through. 'Them girls'll be grown up 'fore you're out . . .' She began to sob again.

'No, they won't, love . . . they won't,' he insisted. 'I promise it won't be like that.' He could see that she wasn't convinced and reached across to reassure her. Then, glancing at the uniform, he hesitated, withdrew his hand and looked helplessly at his wife.

'I'm sorry, Jack,' she said, taking a tissue from her dress pocket and pushing it against her nose and eyes. 'Coming here, upset like this . . . sorry, love. It's just . . . just . . .'

She seemed to search for the words to express what she felt, but finally words failed her. 'One visit every three weeks, it's hard to cope . . . I'm sorry, Jack.'

''S all right, love.' He nodded wearily. 'They wind you up so much you can't think of nothing to say, hardly, till the time's all gone. Does your brain in.'

'Tommy ran me down in his cab,' she said, wiping her eyes again and smudging her mascara slightly. 'He's been great, he has. There's nothing he wouldn't do for us, and my Mum. She sends her love.'

'How is she?'

'She's all right, Jack, you know how she copes. I want to reach over and touch you, Jack. I want to hold you and feel you against me . . .'

Lynn closed his eyes and a tear slid from under each of the lids. He turned away, hoping she wouldn't see them.

'Tom said if there's anything he can do for you, let him know.'

Offers like that one reassured him, made him think that all was not lost. Lynn nodded gratefully. 'He's a diamond, your Tommy, he really is . . .' He paused and considered her, wondering how he might reassure her. 'Dolly,' he said in a whisper. 'I won't do the twenty, that's a promise. We'll have some sort of life, the girls and us, we will.'

Bewilderment came into her eyes. ''S all I keep thinking about, Jack. That somehow they're gonna release you, only I don't know how . . .'

'I'll get a nice result,' he said firmly. 'The brief was well confident when I saw him. D'he say anything to you?'

'Just about selling the house. How much I expected to raise, what was owed on it. I had some estate agents round.

The market's still not very good. But they seem to think it would sell if the price was right.'

'It's got to be enough for Gladwell to do the biz,' he said. 'Did they say how much?'

'Both seemed to think about fifty-five was about right.'

'That don't seem like much.'

''S what the agents said, in this climate. It might improve if the interest rates go down a bit more.'

Lynn thought about the sale price, if they could get it; how much his brief would claim for doing what he planned to do, and what there might be left for Dolly and the kids to live on. Whatever was left over he knew it wasn't going to be enough, any more than it was to show for all the villainy he had done.

'Where you and the girls gonna go?' Lynn asked.

'We can move into m' Mum's, till we get another place,' she said, practically. 'I put m' name down for a council house, but they're not easy to get with so many being sold. I expect we'll get one of them high-rise flats. We'll be all right at Mum's. The girls want to go there. They don't mind. Their friends won't be too far . . . they make friends all right, kids always do . . .'

'Dolly,' Lynn said, interrupting her slightly manic conversation. 'I'll make it up to you, losing your home and everything, I promise.' He knew how much that had meant to her. 'After the appeal we'll get somewhere in the country, with a real country kitchen.' Their eyes met momentarily, then quickly glanced away, as if neither wanted the other to read the doubt there. 'What about the Social Security? What did they say finally?'

'I had a right ruck down there. They reckon m' money'd

been stopped because of the house, till it's sold. 'Cos we own it, that is. Stupid, innit?'

'They can't do that,' he retorted, having no control over his frustration. The warder stood off the wall. Lynn glanced at him and pulled himself back. 'It might be fucking months before you sell it. They must know what the market's like.'

''S what I told 'em. But they don't listen half the time. I expect they're just being difficult. They wouldn't give me m' fare down here neither . . .'

'The liberty-taking bastards!'

''S all right, Jack, we're managing,' she said. 'We are. You know me, I'll be down those offices first thing tomorrow. They got to give us something. The way they carry on you'd think it was their money they was giving you.'

'I'll see if I can get the welfare in here to do something. I don't s'pose they'll do fuckall. But I will make them have a go.'

'It wouldn't matter, Jack, we wouldn't starve. There's been a lot of offers from your friends and different people. A lot of neighbours have stopped and asked if they can help. They've given a few quid an' all, 's amazing. Remember that old Edna Roberts round the corner – she sends her best. She gave the girls a fiver each out of her pension the other day. She ain't got nothing herself.'

Such generosity touched him. But as he thought about the offers, he knew it was merely an avoidance, something to stop them saying the things to each other they ought to be saying. He glanced at the warder and, seeing his attention elsewhere, Lynn still resisted reaching over to touch his wife. 'If only you got a bit of privacy here. You can't say fuck all, not how you feel or nothing without those slags listening . . .' He closed his eyes and allowed his imagination to run for a moment. He started to get an erection and felt worse for it, not better. 'How's it been, Doll?' he whispered. 'You look terrific.'

'Don't, Jack.' She closed her eyes, as if trying to close off her needs. 'I can't tell you how much I miss you.'

'I'll make it up to you, Dolly, I promise, love. Somehow I'll make everything up to you and the girls. Tell them that. We'll have our own Christmases and the birthdays what got missed, and the holidays. We'll do 'em all when I get out, you see.' The words had a hollow ring. The disbelief he saw in her tear-clouded eyes forced him to look away finally.

A dull ache caused both by frustration and the confusion he felt sat at the back of his head and neck as he moved along the echoing thoroughfare, on escort back to the workshop. He was thinking about his wife and his daughters. The prospect of not seeing Dolly for another three weeks set his feelings in a turmoil; the thought of the Social Security making her struggle for what she was entitled to angered him.

'Oi! Where the fuck d'you think you're going? Home?' the warder said as Lynn went on past the mailbag shop.

He spun round, as if to challenge the warder, who simply pulled open the door and pointed into the shop.

Alan Parker said nothing to him when he resumed his seat, like he knew how upset he was, and was best left. But Steve Collins showed no such consideration. If there was one prisoner who would add to his distress it would be Steve Collins. Any vulnerability he noticed was like a scab that he had to pick at until fresh spots of blood appeared.

Stopping by his bench with a pile of canvas cut for mailbags, Collins said, 'Good visit, Jack?'

'Yeah, terrific,' Lynn responded as if in a coma.

'Always nice seeing the old lady. Let me know the next time she's coming down,' he offered. 'I can put you in touch with a screw over there, 's well bent,' – glancing round to check that the warders weren't too close. 'Could make life really nice for you down there. Know what I mean?' He winked.

Lynn looked up from his work. 'That's handy.'

'He'll even let you give her one if the price is right.'

'Leave it out, Steve, for fuck sake,' Parker said. 'What's wrong with you? What are you trying to do?'

'I'm trying to do him a favour,' Collins said, and moved away to his own place at the bench in front.

'He's a no-good slag at times,' Parker said quietly.

Lynn didn't respond.

Thoughts troubled him as his fingers worked, stitching the thick seams of the canvas sacks, but there was no solution that he could see. His troubles were all that occupied him, and he paid no attention to his work until a white-coated screw loomed before him.

'What the fuck's this?' The warder produced a metal tape from his pocket, ran a length out and put it against some of the stitches Lynn had sewn. 'Letters'll fall through those. The Post Office want eight stitches to the inch, no more or less. That's eight, for your information,' he said, holding up eight fingers. He then indicated an inch on the tape. 'There's an inch. Got it? Eight stitches to the inch. Get and unpick them.' He checked a finished sack. 'And that one.'

From the moment he became aware of what the screw

was actually saying his struggle to stay in control was lost. There in front of him was a uniform, who was rucking him, only right then he wasn't in a fit state to take it. The rejection of his work, which at best earned a pittance that went no way to helping his family, seemed to epitomize his problems and their battle for survival without him. Frustration first caused tears to cloud his eyes, then his mind to fog over. Anger exploded out of him like there was no end to the pressure behind it. He hurled the work on the floor. 'This is fucking silly,' he screamed, hardly able to get the words out. 'It's silly. I got a wife out there and two kids trying to fucking well live on Social Security while I'm sewing silly fucking mailbags for some rubbish amount and you slags tell me they're no fucking good. Why'nt you slags give us some proper work so's we can go and earn a living for our families, you slags!' He was screaming at them now, and trembling with rage, hurling materials, mailbags, anything to hand, about the room.

The two other warders in white coats ran forward to assist their colleague. As they tried to take hold of him, Lynn hit one of them – Warder Evans – splitting his nose, causing a fountain of blood. At the first sign of the disturbance getting out of hand the watchful discipline warder hit the alarm button. The clanging bell drowned out the noise, but didn't deter Lynn, or Bobby Mark, who jumped up to help him. It took no time at all for a dozen warders armed with heavy batons to answer the alarm call.

Sitting behind the bare desk in the adjudication room, Maudling looked a picture of self-righteousness and at that moment Lynn hated him more than anyone. He was standing toeing the line in his too-large carpet slippers, the two warders either side of him. He was aware that everyone in the room was watching him, waiting for an excuse.

Through the cuts and bruises on his face he was barely recognizable. The open flesh over his lips and around his eyes was puffy. This wasn't something the screws in the workshop had done to him, nor would have attempted in front of all those other prisoners, most of whom would certainly have stepped in if that had happened. Instead he had been carted off to cells down on the block, where eight screws had first set about him, and then Bobby Mark. All he had tried to do was defend himself, knowing that to have put himself about and done more damage would only have made things worse for him. He had lost consciousness twice during the beating, but was sure that hadn't stopped the screws. He knew how they reacted: one of their own kind had been hurt so they had gone on until all their anger and hostility towards him and Bobby Mark, and all prisoners in general, had been momentarily used up. He hadn't seen Bobby Mark since they had been removed from the workshop yesterday, but hoped he had fared better than himself.

Just what sort of a mess he looked, he could tell from the way he felt and the way people looked at him. However, the governor didn't bat an eyelid at his condition, but then he mostly avoided looking at him anyway.

'It's beyond my scope to hear this case,' the governor informed him, having listened to the three warders, each of whom corroborated the others' evidence. 'Regrettably I lack the authority to punish you sufficiently.' His guilt was clearly already decided upon. 'I am going to refer your case to the Visiting Committee to deal with, though I doubt even they have sufficient authority to punish you as you deserve. Personally I should like to see you flogged; it's the only punishment the likes of you seem to understand. However, the Home Office in its wisdom has ruled against such practice.' The governor sighed through his nose, making it sound more like an angry snort. 'You will be confined to a cell in the punishment block pending your hearing. Take him away.' He made a dismissive gesture with his hand, without looking at him.

'About turn,' the chief ordered. 'Outside!'

Lynn turned briskly, despite the pain such movements caused. There was no case to be made, not here. After all, he had put a screw in the hospital. As he was escorted out he heard the governor say, 'Keep him away from other prisoners, Mr McClean. I want him to have no contact at all until he goes before the Committee.'

Out of the adjudication room, Lynn was taken to the holding cell, where his shoes were returned to him but he didn't get to put them on. Instead he was ordered out in his socks.

The escort marched him along the block to the section gate. Beyond it Jordan stood in the familiar stance that some screws adopted, legs apart, arms folded across their chests. He made no attempt to unlock the gate, but simply grinned. This was the first he had seen of him, having been off duty when he had been brought down yesterday.

'The man who likes to beat up warders,' Jordan said. 'You didn't make much of a job of it, Jack.'

Lynn simply stared back through the bars, knowing he daren't say a word. This uniform would be looking for his excuse, too.

'We got your mate down here. He didn't do any better. Simple fucker.' He waited, but when Lynn didn't reply he unlocked the gate and curled his index finger at him, before heading off along the corridor.

At the open cell door Jordan stopped him and leant close to him until Lynn could feel this man's damp breath on his face.

'Try it on with me,' the blond screw warned, 'what you look like now is a beauty contestant compared to how you will look. Understand?' He didn't wait for a response. 'Inside.'

Without a sign of any kind Lynn stepped into the cell. He stopped with his back to the door and waited for it to slam, then the grille shutter to slap open, and close a short while afterwards. Finally, now he was alone, he let go, letting the pain wash over him. There was even more pain – if that was possible – when he lowered himself to the bed, and he bit down on his tender lip to stop himself crying out. He was determined not to give those bastards the satisfaction of seeing his suffering or to hear him cry. He wanted to report sick and seek solace and release in painkillers, but didn't for the same reason.

Lynn eased himself on the bed, trying to find a less painful position. He was bone-weary from both the punishment he had taken and the fact that he had been unable to sleep last night. He was still unable to lie in one position because of the pressure the weight of his body caused. His back and ribs had taken a lot of stick. Fleetingly he wondered about Bobby Mark, feeling a pull of affection towards him for steaming in to help as he had.

Two days and nights crawled away with him in this tender state, when he was not fully aware of anything other than his pain. Tiredness forced him to sleep, then he would wake suddenly in a paroxysm of pain and soaked with sweat, fearing another beating. He missed the meals that were pushed into his cell, for eating was painful too; nor did he exercise and slop out; then the pain began to ease and become more bearable. The more he moved the easier movement became.

The third night he was able to sleep, but was awoken by cries from Bobby Mark in the next cell but one. The brief freedom he had had from pain in sleep caused him to momentarily forget. He sat up too quickly for his own good, and winced. He expected to get more of what Mark was getting, and was disconcerted when nothing happened. He watched his door, but there was no one outside as far as he could tell. He waited and listened, growing more uneasy.

'Bob?' he called firmly through the silence of the block. 'Bobby? You all right?' There was no reply. He launched himself cautiously off the edge of the bed, and hesitated before pressing his finger against the bell. He wondered as he did if it was wise to remind the screws that he was still around. He didn't want any more stick. But he needed to find out about Bobby Mark, to know if he was getting another beating, even though there would be nothing he could do about it.

With no response to the bell, and no further sound from Bobby Mark, he thought about springing up to the window and calling along the block. But he knew that even if he had the energy to jump up and catch hold of the bars, he wouldn't have the strength to hang there for long. So reluctantly he pressed the bell again. Still there was no response. Eventually he went back to bed, back to sleep, hoping that it was nothing more than a nightmare Bobby had had.

While on the block prisoners were supposed to have an hour's exercise in the yard each day. If you got twenty minutes you were doing well. It wasn't convenient for staff to exercise prisoners as they should have been exercised: too many prisoners and too few staff was the usual excuse. There was the additional problem in that the governor wanted him completely isolated. But even so, when he was escorted through the block and into the yard he was surprised to find he was the only one there, apart from a warder with an Alsatian outside the wire. There was no immediate reason why others weren't out. It wasn't raining, and there certainly were others down on the block.

'Where're the others?' he asked through slightly puffy lips.

'No talking,' the warder said, 'or you're back inside. Just walk like you're s'posed to.'

That puzzled and disturbed Lynn. Something was up, he didn't know what, but wasn't about to answer back to try and find out.

In the early days of this current stretch in solitary, he didn't even see the trusty, so had no chance of finding out what was going on, or how Bobby Mark was. The food tray was handed to him by a screw. He hadn't long been eating his evening meal when there came the sound of crashing from another cell. A tray was flung against the wall. He knew it was Bobby before his muffled shout, 'I'm not eating that shit,' confirmed it. A scuffle ensued; a cell door slammed; then silence. Lynn waited for what seemed like hours before rising to the bell, but then he stopped. He thought about the possible consequence, and questioned whether he could do Mark any good by getting involved. Finally he decided that he couldn't. He turned away.

After eating his food, he sat at the end of the bed with his back against the wall and drew his legs to his chest, imagining the screws were going to rush in and tell him to stop thinking about Bobby Mark. He felt guilty about Bobby; he should have helped him. Bobby hadn't held back when he had been in trouble. He bloody well should have done! Lynn argued with himself, as you had no chance against all them warders. They always got back at you somehow, even if they had to wait months for their opportunity. But even so he concluded that he ought to try and find out how Bobby was at least.

He rose decisively and went to the bellpush and stabbed his finger against it. He'd have no problem if old Reg Allison answered it, but didn't think he'd get any response at all. He was startled when the shutter on the grille slapped open and the fleshy face of Oliver Dorman appeared on the other side.

'What are you ringing the bell for now?'

Lynn hesitated. This screw was one of those who had worked him over when he had first been brought down to the block. 'I want to go to the library,' Lynn said.

'That any way to ask?' fatty Dorman said in a reasonable tone. 'Say it properly. Then I'll consider it.'

'Yes – I'd like to go the library, please, Mr Dorman,' Lynn said, and then saw the mocking smile.

'The library's closed.' He slammed the shutter.

Anger burst out of Lynn. 'You no-good bastard!' he shouted, heedless of the consequences.

The shutter slapped open again immediately. 'What did you say?' the warder asked, his tone still reasonable.

It seduced Lynn a little. 'Bob Mark? How is he?'

'What, you mean the big fella? He's as good as gold. Released this morning, he was. I expect he's home by now. Wouldn't be surprised he's not giving his old lady one.'

With difficulty Lynn checked the rage that was rising through him.

'Anything else?' Dorman asked, smiling.

'Yeah,' he said calmly. 'Get cancer, you slag.'

It might have been a particularly sensitive point. If it was, then he knew he would be made to suffer for his remark. But for now the warder simply slammed the shutter.

As he hurt less and less, so he began exercising, then increased the duration. It helped to move the stiffness that lingered from his bruises. He could feel himself getting fit again, and found it a good fccling comparcd with how hc had been a week ago.

'Keeping in shape?' Reg Allison said as he opened the cell for Lynn to slop out after his last meal of the day. 'That's the idea. It doesn't do to mope around, getting depressed.' He waited as Lynn rose and wiped the sweat off his face with his towel. 'Put your slops out, son.'

'What's the chances of going to the library, Mr Allison?' Lynn asked. He had nothing to read apart from Gideon's Bible.

'You're s'posed to be denied all privileges,' Allison said,

slightly embarrassed. 'What sort of books d'you read? I'll see what I can do.'

'Anything'd be handy. That Bible's getting a bit thin.'

He went out to the recess with his pisspot.

Lynn was surprised when Reg Allison opened his cell later that evening and gave him a book to read. He decided this was the single screw with any feelings, until Jordan opened his cell door later that night. Oliver Dorman stood behind him, his arms folded across his chest.

'Where did you get that?' Jordan demanded. 'Give it here.'

'I brought it down with me,' Lynn lied, instinctively trying to protect the man who had given him the book. But then wondered if he hadn't been set up by Allison to give these two an opportunity to come into him.

'Stand up when you address an officer,' Dorman ordered.

Lynn complied. He didn't want to fight them.

'All right, where d'you get this book?' And when Lynn didn't answer, 'You're on report.' They took the book.

To his surprise they proceeded with the charge and pushed the report under his door. In the morning he was taken for adjudication. His form on which to answer the charge, had he a pencil in the cell to do so, was taken back. He was made to change into slippers and led in front of the deputy governor, who found him guilty and gave him three days' solitary as if that was something different from what he was already doing. The only true difference it made was the extra black mark on his prison record should the need arise for him to go before the Parole Board.

As his bruises and cuts diminished so the screws relaxed the instruction about keeping him isolated. Brian Lang, the block trusty, was the first to make contact when he brought food. But there was little opportunity to pass on information, as the warder stood at the door while the food was handed over.

'Forgotten the condiments, Bri,' Lynn said cheerfully one evening. The warder on duty took no exception to such exchanges. He moved back along the block.

'What d'you hear about Bob?' Lynn whispered, leaning close to the trusty.

'Give him a right good spanking last night, they did.'

Lynn had heard some of it, having hurled himself up to the window. He had called along to Bobby Mark, but hadn't got any reply. 'What was the upset over?'

'That no-good slag put dirt on his grub again –' Lang stopped abruptly.

'What's this, a love affair?' Dorman said, suddenly filling the doorway.

'Don't make yourself sick on that lovely grub, son,' Lang said, and laughed, as though taking the piss.

Later that night when most of the other prisoners were in bed asleep, their lights out, Lynn was sitting on the floor reading the few pages that were left in the Bible. He looked up suddenly, hearing two people out in the corridor. For a moment he thought perhaps one of the screws was checking through the Judas hole. Something was going on out there, but what it was he didn't know and couldn't speculate on. Cautiously he rose to the door and listened. There was a gap of a quarter of an inch where the grille in the door hadn't been closed completely. At the acute angle he saw the corridor in the direction of Bobby Mark's cell. They stopped. But then he saw and heard no more until Bobby Mark shouted, 'Fuck off, you bastards. Leave me alone.' His words were so clear that he might have been in the corridor. But there was no way he could be, Lynn reasoned. He waited, pressing his cheeks harder into the door to sharpen the angle of his view through the crack.

Suddenly the light went off in the corridor and he heard giggling as they scuffled past. Anxious, frustrated silence followed as he tried to work out what they were up to. Finally he had it when he saw Bobby Mark out of his cell and caught in the beam of a flashlight. The dirty bastards had opened his cell door!

'Bobby! Bobby!' he called, but the warning was too late. The screws were onto him.

'Where d'you think you're going?' Dorman demanded.

Lynn pressed himself harder to the door.

'You trying to escape, you fuckwit?'

There was a sound of running feet, followed by some swift blows. From the cries it was evident who was getting the worst of it. The scuffle went on for a few moments, then there was silence. Maybe they had knocked him unconscious, or perhaps he had managed to get back to his cell. Whatever the outcome, Lynn knew that somehow he had to do something for Bobby Mark, get him a result, or he'd wind up topping one of those screws, if not both of them.

He had spent fifteen days in solitary confinement before he got to go in front of the Visiting Committee. The procedure was the same as adjudication. First his shoes were removed and he was given slippers; then the the charge sheet was taken back from him. The charge of gross personal assault on a prison officer, namely Officer Evans, was boldly stated. But he chose to make no reply to it.

The Visiting Committee comprised two male JPs and a woman with CBE after her name. The three members present was the minimum for an adjudication. The chairman, Edward Wykes, a lean, bespectacled pillar of the establishment, wasn't someone Lynn felt he would want to talk to if they were on a desert island together. He sat behind the small desk, with the other two either side of him. Maudling was present also, sitting off to the side a little way, as if to suggest that he wasn't influencing any decision they might arrive at. Besides his escort there was Chief Officer Carne, PO McLean, the two assisting warders from the mailbag shop and Officer Evans, who had a huge plaster across his busted nose. Lynn was sure the dressing was larger than it ever needed to be, and doubted if it was necessary at all at this late date. But it was effective in signalling the shockingness of the assault.

This procedure was, as far as Lynn was concerned, no less a farce for the supposed independence of the

Committee. Everything about the hearing favoured the screws. While he had no representation, and no right to call witnesses. The Committee had the power to confine him for a couple of months or add extra time onto his sentence, or they could send him out for trial by a judge and jury, but rarely took that course. From the start of the hearing he knew he had no chance of winning. He stated what had happened, telling how he was upset after a visit from his wife and leaving it at that. There was no justification for having assaulted the screw. He hadn't been attacking him personally, rather the system of which he was part, but didn't expect sympathy from this little firm, who saw nothing wrong with the system.

Afterwards he was taken out while they decided what to do with him. He didn't for a moment think that they would consider any alternative to finding him guilty, but he was shocked that they needed less than five minutes to reach that conclusion.

On calling him back in, the chairman said formally, 'Having deliberated at length on the evidence against you, and taking into consideration your emotional state at the time, this committee finds the offence proven. No matter how distressing a visit from your wife might be, it does not mitigate assault, much less the type of gross personal assault to Officer Evans. Such behaviour is outrageous, it's barbaric. If you were beyond the confines of this prison, appearing before my bench, I wouldn't hesitate in seeking for you the maximum sentence.'

He caught a glimpse of PO McClean across the room. The prospect seemed to please him. For his own part Lynn was neither surprised nor disappointed. It was what he had come to expect.

'Prison officers have emotional problems also. At times these can be as acute as any prisoner's. They don't relieve their frustrations by assaulting prisoners,' he said.

Words of protest almost flew from Lynn. Only, saying some of the things he knew went on wasn't going to help either him or Bobby Mark, not here. Maybe if he got it out to a newspaper or television company.

'What a sorry state our prisons would be in if prison officers relieved their frustrations on the inmates,' Wykes continued, as though he seriously believed they didn't. 'Your sort of behaviour simply cannot be tolerated.' He paused like he was expecting Lynn to interrupt, and when he didn't, 'Anything further to say before we pass sentence?'

Now Lynn hesitated. There was so much he had to say. Too much. The words, struggling to get out, were smashing into each other and prevented him saying anything finally. 'No, sir,' he somehow managed through his confusion.

'Very well. The sentence is one hundred and eighty days' loss of remission; stoppage of earnings for a period of twenty-eight days; cellular confinement for a period of twenty-eight days.'

It was a result he could hardly believe. His glance flitted across to PO McClean, who looked disappointed. The expectation was that he'd cop at least an extra year, or be sent out to be dealt with by the Crown Court.

The magistrate paused to consider him as if reading something in his face. 'Do you wish to say something to this committee?'

His invitation surprised Lynn. Then with thoughts growing calmer, he hesitated and glanced at the governor.

'You need have no fear of being victimized, if that's what inhibits you,' Wykes said as though he personally was able to guarantee that. 'Mr Maudling?'

Maudling cleared his throat. 'If a prisoner has a complaint and makes it through the correct channels we will do all we can to remedy it, provided it's found to be valid.'

The chairman seemed satisfied. 'That's fair enough,' he said.

At that moment Lynn was conscious of everyone's eyes on him. Some of them were hating him, some fearing him, others probably merely being curious about him. He wondered where he should start. There was so much wrong with the system. 'Well, sir,' he began cautiously. 'I know I was out of order whacking Mr Evans like that –' Contrition was a good start, he thought, it would lull them. 'I'm sorry I done it. But the thing is, things build up for you when you're inside. You gotta have some of it yourself to know what it's like. There's no way you can tell just coming in for a visit. It ain't the same. You gotta taste it and smell it and feel it. You gotta be here and experience how unjust the system is even when it's not trying to be. It frustrates you the whole time, stops you thinking and acting like a man, makes you like a restrained child who ain't allowed to do nothing. That's a part of you. Then suddenly you get a short visit from your wife, and everything comes crashing in on you. All the time you're banged up you can't do nothing for your family, and all the while you can't help them you can't reassure them, you're wondering what's happening to them, if they're all right; if they're managing. Then your Missus comes to see you and tells you the problems, or you see it in her face if she don't crack, and there's fuck all you can do. You don't even have time to adjust to seeing her, to sit down with her and begin to sort things out. I mean, so much has built up you can't think of the things you need to say you're so anxious. The thing is, if they'd find us some proper work, so we could go and earn a wage to send home and support our families, then half them problems would vanish, so many of them are about money. It really ruins you, does you up in the head, knowing how they're struggling and you're just rotting in here, either sewing a few mailbags or making a few toys or sitting in your peter.

'I mean, prison's only s'posed to restrict your liberty, to stop wrong 'uns getting their living. But it does worse than that, it punishes your family, and does you up in the head 'cos you know it's happening. You can't wonder at villains getting released and going straight back to work, prison don't exactly rehabilitate them; you're fit for nothing when you get out. Unless you're allowed to make one or two decisions for yourself you forget how to; it's demoralizing, it strips away all you need to survive on the outside. 'S hard for ordinary people to see some of what's going on inside you. I mean, I know a lot of cons ain't exactly lovable, and down here you got the worst of 'em. But all this place is, is a dumping ground for the problems society can't cope with. 'S all. And everyone gets treated the same – diabolically.

'I dunno, the system's all wrong. It's unjust, it treats you like some low life form. Dogs in Battersea get better treatment, they do. I mean, this little lot takes all your self-respect, takes all your dignity. What are geezers in here, after all? I mean, they're only the villains what got caught. What are those people on the outside, most of them? Villains what didn't get caught. People in here are entitled to something, well, some of 'em. But this lot, it wants everything, dun it? We got nothing left.' The words finally stopped bubbling out of him and he felt exposed and vulnerable.

There was a pause. Wykes seemed embarrassed. He cleared his throat and said, 'You've obviously given matters a great deal of thought.'

'It's what builds up inside, sir,' Lynn said humbly.

The Committee didn't seem to know quite how to proceed. His emotional outpouring probably embarrassed them. He felt embarrassed himself now and wished he had kept his mouth shut.

'I'm sure where your points have any validity, the Home Office has them under review.' The chairman glanced towards the governor, who nodded. 'No one wants to see men stagnate when they could otherwise be useful, productive members of society.'

'Tell me, Mr Lynn,' the only woman member of the Committee said, 'what dignity or self-respect did you leave those guards when you smashed them to the ground with your shotguns?'

'I didn't, did I? I didn't smash no one with no shotgun. No way. I was fitted by the filth. They decided it was my turn, and that was it!' Anger flashed through him like petrol vapour igniting, and he felt two escort warders press tighter to him and grip his arm.

'A jury of twelve men and women thought differently.'

'Only with a bent judge. All the Bill what got up in court perjured themselves. It was a get-up from the go. I mean, what fucking chance you got . . .'

'Watch your language,' the chief warned.

Beyond caring, Lynn said, 'Well, go on, nick another hundred and eighty days off me. What's the fucking dif'?

Bang me behind m' door for as long as you like, don't alter the facts one fucking bit, does it?'

No one pursued the point. Wykes said, 'You're appealing against sentence?'

'Yes, sir. Just waiting for it to go on.'

'Well, good luck,' the chairman said. Lynn closed his eyes in face of the inadequate remark. 'Was there anything else, Lynn?'

He glanced over at PO McClean, hating the Ulsterman more than the two IRA men behind their doors on the wing probably hated him. But he wasn't afraid of him. He said, 'I'd like to make a complaint on behalf of another prisoner, Robert Mark. He's being held in solitary and getting a regular beating from the screws. The dirty slags steam into him for no reason at all.'

'That's a very serious allegation,' Wykes said formally. 'Have you followed the proper complaints procedure, taken it to the governor?'

'No, sir. Wouldn't do any good, would it?'

Maudling bristled at this, but didn't comment, as though to do so was beneath his dignity.

'Do you wish to name the officers you bclicvc are involved in this mistreatment of a prisoner?' Wykes asked.

Again Lynn hesitated, wondering if this was a smart move. They might try some kind of retaliation against him, or if they didn't they almost certainly would against Mark. 'No, sir.'

'Very well,' the chairman said. 'This committee takes note of your complaint, and will inquire fully into it. That's all.'

Lynn was escorted out to start his sentence in chokey.

During the relatively short time he had been at the prison he had made what he thought was an insightful observation about his fellow prison workers. Some might have thought it more a judgement, but if it was, then he included himself in it. The prison staff comprised more than a few of life's failures. A minority seemed to have taken up the job as a vocation, but more had tried somewhere else and failed. Failed to get into the police force – the examination being too stiff; failed the fire service; some had even failed to make it as traffic wardens! The prison service was the easiest of all civil service entrance exams; to enter you were required to pass the easiest of medicals, and you only needed to be five feet six inches in your socks. A number of people retiring from the armed forces, people who suddenly found themselves lost without that regimentation, came home to the prison service. Everything that attracted failure was to be found here in abundance; lack of change, secure employment, automatic power over a less fortunate section of society, strict regimentation. Few of his uniformed colleagues recognized or accepted the fact that they became prison officers because they were failures, and most deluded themselves about the worthiness of the job. Paul Hardiman harboured no such delusions, but felt no less at home.

An equal number of failures were to be found among

those like himself who formed the professional body of the prison service – the doctors, welfare officers, clerics – only most of those seemed to have less recognition of their failing. Perhaps being better educated they were better equipped to disguise the shortcoming in bullshit, or jargon. Some simply denied it by rigidly demarking the authority carried by their position, allowing no possible challenge to it.

Paul Hardiman, the prison chaplain, not only felt he was a failure, he was convinced he looked one also. He had a damp, crumpled appearance which seemed to inspire confidence in no one. The skin on his fingers was heavily bitten around the nails and often raw, so raw at times that he was afraid to touch any of the surfaces in the prison for fear of getting Aids. Pathological fear robbed him of sleep; it robbed him of his peace of mind. The possibility that he had already contracted Aids gnawed away at him but he was too frightened to go and have the test.

Feeling the need to remove himself from the pressures of parish work following the break-up of a relationship he had had with a young ministrant, the prison chaplaincy seemed ideal when it arose. His bishop had recommended him to the post, almost too fulsomely. It suited Hardiman perfectly for here there was never any need to measure oneself, while providing abundant opportunity to condemn others as worse failures if need be.

'Evening, Oliver,' Hardiman said cheerfully as he stepped up to the section gate in the punishment block. 'All seems very quiet,' he observed, and drew on his cigarette, which was now burning against the filter tip.

'All gone down the pub, Rev,' the fat uniformed man joked as he relocked the gate. 'Who d'you want to see, as if I can't guess? Wasting your time with that one, you are, Rev.'

As he followed the broad back he smiled and threw his cigarette stub onto the floor. He knew that annoyed them.

Lynn was face-down on the cold stone slabs doing press-ups, counting as he did so, going with ease. He seemed to ignore them, but Hardiman smiled at the prison officer. He was prepared to wait, watching the glistening muscles on Lynn's back. His friend had been very physical like this.

'You got a visitor!' Dorman informed him.

Hardiman waited, a little embarrassed that he was being forced upon Lynn in this way. He looked at the prisoner, then at Oliver Dorman, and finally inclined his head towards the door, indicating that it was all right for him to leave. From the look on Dorman's face he clearly had the inclination to lift his toe into Lynn's ribs, but he went out instead, slamming the door. Still he waited without speaking. He took out his cigarettes and lit one, not considering if this prisoner might object. Most didn't. Some cadged cigarettes. There was no ashtray, so finally he threw the spent match in the pot in the corner.

'Fifty,' Lynn said, mostly for his own benefit it seemed. He was sweating, but showed no other sign of strain. Had he tried doing press-ups like that Hardiman knew he'd be doing more than sweating.

'That's the idea. Keeping fit. Healthy body, healthy mind.' There was nothing coming back from the prisoner and Hardiman became more embarrassed. 'Would you care for a cigarette?'

'Don't smoke,' Lynn said.

With a nod he said, 'Very wise, especially here. I'm sure that's all the prisoners ask to see me for half the time. Yes. Keep trying to give it up. It's silly, really.' That was something else he had failed at, but he didn't want to tell Lynn, assuming he hadn't already guessed. There was another pause. He didn't know what more to say to this man. He felt awkward, and small talk didn't come to him easily. He felt Lynn's unease and wasn't sure how to dispel it. 'I came to see if I could assist you – with any of your problems.'

The statement seemed to take Lynn by surprise. 'You? What the fuck d'you think you can do?'

That wasn't the reaction he had hoped for. He watched Lynn rise off the floor and get his towel and mop the sweat off. The rough cotton being dragged across the stretched muscles was an exciting sight.

'Perhaps it'd help if you'd tell me the problem?'

Lynn said, 'I never had any religion. To be honest, I've only ever gone to church when friends got married, 's about all.'

'Your cell card says you're C of E.'

'I was going to stick down vegetarian – for the different food you can have. If you don't stick down C of E as well you're banged up while the others go to chapel.'

'Is that all the service means to you, a trip out of your cell?' He had the best attendance at his services ever here in prison, but still it hurt slightly when he thought about why it was that prisoners came.

'You ain't exactly Billy Graham, are you?'

Hardiman smiled, accepting the slight. He knew the power of his oratory fired no one's imagination. He sighed and said, 'Does God not address himself to you in any way?'

Ash tumbled down his coat. He brushed at it, then flicked his cigarette in the direction of the pisspot.

'While I'm stuck in here, down to fuck all? T'rific. He might if I was to get a nice result.'

'The apostle Paul was imprisoned, and endured great hardship.'

'Talk like a prick! What about that no-good slag who put me in here? Be fair! What about him? You lot make me fucking die, you really do. You're all in this together. Supporting each other, pretending what is going on is right.' He shook his head as if trying to clear it. 'Coming here and telling me Paul was imprisoned.'

Embarrassment prickled Hardiman's face and he tried to detach himself from it. 'You sound very bitter, James,' he said, sensing he had Lynn's first name wrong, but not seeking to correct himself.

'Wouldn't you be? Wouldn't anyone?' Lynn demanded.

'There are no easy answers as to why such things happen,' Hardiman said. The obvious answer was that men usually went to prison for committing crimes, but he was sure Lynn didn't want to hear that. He had no suspicion that the system often got it wrong, or that it ever did, and had no reason to suppose it had this time.

'That no-good fucking detective wanted me put away.'

'Cast your burden on the Lord. He will sustain you. He may not offer immediate solutions, but it does help to tell Him –'

'How the fuck's He helped you?' Lynn said uncharitably. 'I mean, you're doing time just like anyone else. You don't even have a key! You have to wait for the screws to unlock the doors just like me.'

'Maybe this is a penance.' Mostly he avoided thinking about it.

'I tell you what, pal, you couldn't get a living outside. I mean, look at what sort of people is working in here. Where else could fucking rubbish like that get a living? Look at some of them screws, they fucking well deserve to be this side of the door.'

This was another truth, one that made him realize how apt his job was. 'If you wish, James,' he said, focusing his attention away from his own problems, 'I will pray with you.'

'What for?' Lynn asked. 'Me getting a result on appeal?'

'That's a start. God will listen. I know He will.'

'If it's the same to you, I'll put my bit of faith in m' brief. I mean, I always believed in things I could see and touch. 'They open the gate and hand me a ticket back to London, that I'll believe in.'

'Let me help you some way. Trust me, James. Anything you tell me will remain in the strictest confidence.' He hoped he didn't sound as desperate as he felt. This might have been his last chance.

Lynn blew down his nostrils and turned away.

Hardiman watched his back as he flexed his powerful shoulders like he was getting rid of tension. He wanted to reach out and put his hands on this back and ease the suffering he knew was locked away there. His nerve failed him.

'Can I offer you no comfort?' Hardiman asked.

'Tell you what, you could do one thing for me.' Lynn gave rise to some expectancy in the chaplain. He waited. ''S a lad on the block here called Bobby Mark. You could try an' do something to stop these dirty fuckers picking on him, 'f you're man enough. 'They keep it up, I'll top one of those bastards. I swear it.'

'You're mistaken, Lynn,' he said firmly. He wasn't about to listen to accusations of that nature. 'These are decent chaps doing a difficult and unpleasant job. You're mistaken, I know you are.'

Lynn looked at him. ''Course I am,' he said quietly. 'Fuck off, wanker. Go back and let the governor brown you.'

Hardiman closed his eyes momentarily, then turned away. There was no point in staying when the prisoner started making remarks of that nature.

For the record he wrote a report on the meeting he had had with Lynn, setting down everything he could remember of their conversation, putting it down in a way similar to that the warders used to relate details of charges they brought against prisoners. He also ventured an opinion as to Lynn's mental state. It wasn't optimistic.

This opinion he expressed to the deputy governor the following morning as they walked to chapel. Hardiman was dressed in a surplice and carried a Bible. On Sunday he tried to avoid smoking until after chapel. He succeeded but rarely, other than to make himself irritable, or worse when he broke his pledge to himself.

'I don't pretend to be a qualified psychiatric worker,' he was saying, trying to avoid sounding obsequious, 'but I have certainly seen any number of psychopaths, and I recognize one in Lynn.'

'I'd have thought you fairly well qualified,' the deputy governor said, 'and Lynn is not very clever after all.'

'He's very insistent that he's innocent and the police are persecuting him.'

The deputy governor said, pushing his glasses up the bridge of his nose, 'His sort never know when to give up. If ever.'

'Well, I suppose there have been some spectacular miscarriages of justice come to light lately.'

'That's what the liberal press maintain. But clearly someone did the crime those so-called innocent people were convicted for.'

'Well, if persistence is ever to get him released, who knows, Lynn might get out earlier than we think,' Hardiman said. 'His "nothing to lose" attitude can only work against ordered society, especially in here.'

'You think he'll prove disruptive if put back on the wing, Paul?'

Encouraged by the deputy governor's regard for his opinion, Hardiman said, 'I certainly do.' He felt a sense of power that for the first time he was in control of. 'He'll always find morons in here whom he can impress with his anarchy. He's the type of prisoner who might be better off serving his entire sentence in isolation.' A wave of feeling that came over him then left him breathless. Yet he had no recognition of what it was about Lynn that reached so deep into him.

With a smile, the young deputy governor said, 'The Home Office hasn't come round to that one yet.'

Hardiman looked at him and shook his head, showing what he believed was his sense of regret. 'Something of the sort has to come on stream for the future.'

'Well, maybe some more morally acceptable version of the now disbanded sensory-deprivation special control units. I know this particular governor wouldn't demur at keeping the likes of Lynn locked in such a unit. I wonder how long he would continue to insist he was innocent in one of those?'

Paul Hardiman hoped Lynn would be around for a long while, but was immediately ashamed of the thought. He set aside both the thought and the shame by lighting a cigarette, and immediately felt worse.

'Leave it!' Lynn told a prisoner who came towards the dinner trolley on the ground floor where the trusty was waiting to serve out the food.

'We gotta do something about Bobby Mark. See about getting him some proper medical attention.'

'Leave off, Jack, I'm starving,' the prisoner protested. It was a feeble response, for he could see Lynn meant business.

'Bobby's up there dying, by the sound of it. Pass the word.'

Lynn stopped another prisoner as he came down the stairs. One or two were getting through despite his efforts. Some of them not only wanted to get their food but would eat it regardless of Bobby Mark. The big loon maybe didn't mean much to them, but what they wouldn't want to do, he knew, was go against him, or get out of step with everyone else on the wing.

Mark had got off the block a few days after he had, with all his cuts and bruises healed. He had settled back into the routine of the wing without any trouble, but had then started complaining about pains in his stomach. The pains got worse, and he had vomited a couple of times. The MO hadn't been any help when Mark had reported sick, and simply declared him fit for work. He did little more the following day when Mark was unable to get up. The doctor diagnosed indigestion, and continued to declare him fit for work. That was when Lynn decided they would have to have a protest.

Word quickly went round as the screws began unlocking. The threes were solid to a man. Alan Parker went along the second-floor landing telling cons about the hunger strike. Frank Timper stopped anyone on the first landing from going to collect their food. It all looked solid enough. Lynn went up the stairs and watched from outside his cell. He was as hungry as any, but more determined than most.

Apart from the warders creeping uneasily about, the wing was silent, and the slightest noise echoed up to the trussed roof. There was no activity at all around the food trolley on the ground floor. The trusty and the two warders, who were close at hand, watched nervously, as though uncertain about what was happening.

As Lynn watched from the balustrade outside his door he saw PO Allen emerge from his office on the ground floor. The noise at meal times was usually deafening. Now not even a television set could be heard.

'Are they all fed, Mr Rogers?' Allen asked.

'Just coming for you, sir,' Rogers explained. The voices sounded reedy and came up the building like ping-pong balls being batted around. 'They've all stayed in their cells, refusing their food.'

'Why? What's the problem?' The PO snatched the lid off one of the containers to inspect the food. The reason for their refusing might have lain there. Lynn smiled.

'They're protesting over Mark.'

'Right,' the PO said. 'Feed the nonces. There's no way they are going to refuse their food.' He marched off back to his office.

Clearly Chief Officer Carne was being summoned. The position hadn't changed by the time he was admitted to the wing. He was met by PO Allen and two warders.

'All still refusing, Mr Allen?' Carne asked.

'Yes, sir,' Allen snapped. 'All still refusing.'

'Who got it started, d'you know?'

Their glances came up the building through the safety wires, but Lynn made no attempt to move. Someone would have to state what the situation was about. It may as well be him.

Chief Officer Carne turned his look back to PO Allen. 'I might have guessed. Have any demands been made? Is everyone involved?' He walked along to the food trolley and lifted one of the lids. He sniffed, then nodded, as if satisfied that the food was wholesome. Lynn wanted to shout out to ask why he didn't eat it, but didn't.

'What does the MO say?'

'He's on his way over to see Mark now, sir.'

When the chief got to the cell with the MO, and the other uniforms close behind like No 23 buses, Lynn went along the landing and waited near the open door. He wanted to make sure they did nothing they shouldn't.

'What's the word?' Carne was asked after a few moments.

'Same as it was this morning, I'd say. A bit of indigestion. I'll give him something.' The doctor nodded.

Lynn's medical knowledge didn't even extend to first aid, but he was doubtful as he watched his friend writhing on the bed.

They suddenly all turned out of the cell, where they confronted Lynn. He straightened and became alert.

'You haven't collected your dinner,' Carne said. 'Do so.'

Shaking his head slowly, Lynn said, 'When something proper's done about Bobby Mark . . .'

'You saw the MO examine him.'

'He needs a proper doctor, not that toss-pot.'

To his surprise, no one there gave him an argument.

'Refusing to obey a lawful order. You're on governor's,' Carne informed him finally, and wheeled away followed by the others.

'Collect your dinner,' Carne ordered when they stopped at the door to Brian Smith's cell. Lynn followed them there.

'If someone medically qualified cares to look at Mark, Chief,' Brian Smith said courteously. 'Then I will.'

'Refusing to obey a lawful order? Come on, lad.' He waited, like he was expecting Brian Smith to respond to reason. 'Who put you up to it? This one?'

'Chief?' was all Brian Smith said and winked.

He went on report. The uniforms wheeled away.

'. . . As a man of some sensibility, one who has seen a lot of suffering in his time,' Collins announced, making a speech when confronted by the chief and his gang, 'I cannot stand idly by and allow a fellow prisoner to suffer in need of proper medical attention . . . 's that right, Jack?'

'Ballocks!' Carne interrupted. 'You kneecapped a business rival with six-inch nails. So don't give me this old rubbish.'

'A man can change, Mr Carne, mend his ways.'

'Get your food. I won't tell you again.'

'Do something about Bobby Mark, then I'll eat, pal.'

All Carne could do finally was put him on report. As he did every prisoner on the wing, apart from the nonces.

The prisoners felt a sense of victory for the solidarity

they had achieved, even if they hadn't advanced Bobby Mark's position.

Then, when word went round that the governor wasn't going to bother seeing any of them, Lynn wondered if it was a victory after all, and how long they would stay solid when they looked at the next meal being sent back to the kitchen.

That test never came. Bobby Mark had an ulcer that ruptured. His pain was then so intense, his sweating so profuse, that if the doctor hadn't called an ambulance and sent him to hospital one of the screws would have done so.

When the ambulance crew carried Bobby Mark out on a stretcher – escorted to the hospital by two screws – all the prisoners on the wing cheered. Like Lynn they felt a sense of elation, of triumph. It had cost them a meal, but that was little enough. They could feed off their victory for a while.

'What the fuck were they doing, Jack? Washing the fucking blood off?' the man said angrily, glancing round at the screw in the legal visiting room. 'Do you know how fucking long they kept me fucking well waiting? Just because they're doing time for the rest of their fucking lives they think everyone's got time to waste.'

Jack Lynn glanced round at the warder, almost feeling embarrassed for him. Alex Gladwell's managing clerk didn't look like he was going to stop rucking the screw. Lynn doubted if it was this one who had caused the delay anyway. Neither solicitors nor their clerks, in his experience, behaved like this man, and he wondered if it would reflect at all badly on him or his case.

'What a bunch of fucking wankers,' Trevor Reid continued. 'They all deserve to be in here for life.' He ground his cigarette into the floor. 'It's an out-and-out fucking liberty, you being in here, Jack. But you see if we don't get you a nice result. These fucking wankers will be sicker than fucking parrots when we do.'

Again Lynn glanced round at the screw. Then back at Alex Gladwell's managing clerk. He was in his early thirties, older than his boss, and looked more like a villain than someone who worked in a solicitor's office. He wore his hair long and tied at the back, and seemed to enjoy his openly contemptuous manner towards authority. Then he had nothing to lose, Lynn assumed. Reid glanced round at the warders, who were in the room with them, and shook his head. 'It's fucking outrageous that you can't talk to your lawyer in private. We'll whisper so the wankers get earache.'

Lynn wanted to smile, but didn't. Instead he said, 'How's it going, then?'

Reid glanced round at the two screws again. 'It's such a fucking liberty not being allowed to conduct this meeting in private.'

One of the warders said, 'You are in sight of but out of hearing of an officer, sir.' He was quoting the text.

'I s'pose you're both fucking deaf.' He turned and winked at Lynn, then leaned across the table to him. 'Alex asked me to pop down and see you,' he whispered. 'Got some right good news, we have. Your appeal's been set for two weeks tomorrow. But that's not all, Jack. Your chances look very good. We did a bit of work out at Abbey Wood nick. Managed to pull out some info'.' He smiled and waited a moment, glanced at the screws and leaned still closer. Lynn could scarcely stand the tension. 'The second half of the proceeds from that robbery you were supposed to have had, it turned up intact. What's more, it turned up well before you went to trial.'

'The dirty no-good fucking slags!' The words burst out of Lynn and he rose out of his seat, making the screws alert. 'That proves it then, don't it?'

Reid waved him back down and glanced at the prison officers, then leaned in again. 'It goes a long way. What it suggests is there was a conspiracy against you from the off. That the fifteen hundred pounds found in your possession couldn't have come from the robbery like the Bill claimed. That statement they had from the cashier at the Gas Board was a get-up.'

'What does it amount to, Trev?' Lynn asked, a vein of excitement running through him. 'Will it do it?'

'It gives a lot of weight to the grounds for your appeal.'

'But is it gonna come to a nice result? That's the thing.'

'I'd say it would. We'll slaughter that detective.'

'Fuck I,' Lynn said, greatly relieved. He closed his eyes to stop himself crying. 'Cor, you done brilliantly. That *is* good news.'

The feeling of excitement he carried back to his cell caused him to laugh to himself. Little shudders of pleasure rocked his body. He thought about gaining his freedom, about walking free on the outside, and he wanted to shout his news for everyone in the prison to know. But he was frightened to, in case someone came along and somehow stole it from him. He didn't want to think about that. He thought instead about his family, and Dolly, how, throughout the months he had been locked away, she had kept hoping and keeping faith with him. She was a diamond and he didn't know what he had done to deserve such a wife.

His excitement about his future prospects aroused him sexually as, back in the cell, he continued thinking about his wife. He found himself getting a hard-on, and closed his eyes and imagined he was alone with Dolly, in their bedroom. He saw just how it would be when he got out, like it had been in the past. It had been good then, almost perfect. The image stayed sharp and clear on the back of his eyelids as he imagined himself running his hand up her strong, well-shaped legs, under her skirt, feeling her moist crotch, and as he did so he reached into his own flies. She hadn't any pants on and he eased her legs apart. She let him enter her, first with his finger. He saw himself stroking her, keeping the rhythm he was making with himself now. She began making those low moaning sounds of pleasure. He could hear them as clearly as if she was on the bed with him. I love you, Dolly, he told her over and over in his thoughts, and his breath came faster as his excitement increased. He imagined her excitement increase, her wetness as her need became as great as his. He pulled her skirt up her thighs and slid on top of her. He didn't fumble, not then. Her hand found him and helped him guide him into her. His penis was hard and reaching. He could feel her arms clasped around his back, like they were never going to be apart again, and her lips were so soft on his. No matter how hard she pressed them against him . . . Suddenly he ejaculated, his body going rigid with the intensity of that surging pleasure. He rocked and he ached and he tensed every fibre of his body before release. When it was finally over, he kept his eyes closed, not wanting to return to the harsh reality of that cell.

Now, with the prospect of his appeal coming on soon and the near-certainty of getting a result, the time he had left became fairly easy for him. In a curious way he even began to enjoy it, especially the company of good villains. He enjoyed also suddenly being able to laugh at the screws, who would have to serve their time until they retired. One thing that seriously worried him, however, was the thought of Bobby Mark and Brian Smith remaining behind. He had come to feel responsible for them, and both seemed to rely on him and expected something from him. He would now walk, leaving them with theirs to do and little chance of getting early release. He didn't quite know what to do for them, if indeed he could do anything. He would have a go at the Home Office about Bobby Mark, but beyond that . . . Prolonging his own stay inside wasn't going to help either of them in any way.

From where he sat at the table in the threes' TV room Lynn's gaze fell on Bobby Mark, who, fully recovered from his stomach operation, was across the room, connected to the TV, like it was a life-support machine. Other prisoners were equally entranced by a stunt motorcyclist appearing on *Blue Peter*. Lynn brought his attention back to what was being said at the table. It had started off as an intelligent discussion about police corruption, but had eventually come round to story-telling. Each of the prisoners had a story to tell about how they were fitted by the police, or how the Bill had earned off them; probably every con in the prison, in every prison, had a similar story to tell.

'I did some business with the filth on the Squad,' Micky Dunkerton was saying. 'Me and a pal of mine plotted up some gear what some other villains had had off. It was about a hundred and eighty grand's worth of scotch. Well, we steamed in and nicked the whole lorryload off them, had a reliable placer lined up, everything. Then about ten CID jumped us, right boary geezers, all tooled up with pickaxe handles. "You fucking move, we'll split your heads right open." They meant it an' all – they had hold of us. Well, first we thought that they were other villains on the same firm, I mean, we didn't know. Then they told us, like. That was your pal, Steve,' he said, glancing over the table at Collins. 'Alan Greene, one of the DIs down there. He took about four grand off us, pumped us right up about some help.'

'Well, how bad's that?' Collins wanted to know.

'Terrific,' Dunkerton responded. 'He sent another squad out the next day and nicked us again along with the placer.'

'He always was a snaky bastard, that one,' Collins said, suddenly disassociating himself from the DI.

There was a silence at the table. Collins was the focus of attention, like he was responsible for Dunkerton's misfortune. It was illogical, but that was the way most villains reacted.

Turning to Brian Smith, Collins said, 'How come a bright boy like you ever got sent away, Brian? I'd've thought a psychiatrist could have got up in court and got you a nice result, especially with your background.' Then suddenly the negative attention was on Smith. He represented the monied classes, and everyone there knew they all got different treatment by the courts.

"'Talk fucking silly, Steve,' Brian Smith snapped. 'My old lady took me to all sorts of trickcyclists when I was a kid. We seemed to camp in Harley Street. What she was doing was looking for the right one – the one who would confirm just what she wanted to hear. Finally she found him. He was in a class of his own, this one. He said to her, "Mrs Smith, I can tell you exactly why your unfortunate son burns things." "Yes, yes," my old lady replied, hanging on his every word.' He told the story well; all the cons at the table were silent with expectation. '"He's a fucking arsonist, madam!"'

The laughter that exploded around the table, which seemed to be at Collins's expense, was finally interrupted by a shout from Bobby Mark across the room.

'Here, why'd he do that?' Mark said, shouting at the TV. 'That's fucking stupid, why'd he do it?'

'To think we starved ourselves for that,' Collins said.

'What's the problem, Bobby?' Lynn wanted to know.

'He jumped the river on his motorbike,' Mark explained. His confusion was bringing him close to tears. 'It's stupid, he could've gone on the bridge. I'll smash that fucking set, I'll smash it!'

'Leave off, for fuck sake,' said one of the prisoners around the TV warily.

'They'll bang him up again, 'he starts,' Collins cautioned.

'Bob! Bobby? Don't worry about it, son,' Lynn said firmly. His words seemed to have a calming effect on Mark. He turned towards Lynn, waiting for some direction. 'Come on, we'll do another petition to the Home Secretary about getting you a release date. They must've tore your other one up.'

Mark hesitated, slowly becoming aware that everyone was watching him. He glanced towards the TV. The motorcyclist had gone. 'Can I bring m' pudding?' he asked.

Lynn winked at him and rose as the danger passed.

As he emerged from the TV room with Mark another prisoner came hurrying along the landing.

'Jack,' he said breathlessly, 'we got that new molester trapped on the twos.' Judging from his excitement Lynn would have expected him to have been offering an escape route.

'Where're the screws?' he asked.

'They're all below. Al's getting Bayliss to brown him.'

'Get the others, Davy,' Lynn said, jerking his thumb towards the TV room. He inclined his head at Mark, indicating for him to follow, as he started down the stairs.

In his cell on the second floor, cons had trapped the newest nonce, whose door had been left unlocked during association, almost certainly on purpose. Mervyn Latimer was an articulate, owl-like man in his mid-twenties. He was very scared and was becoming more fearful as more cons crowded into his cell. Veins bulged on his wide forehead as his terrified eyes darted over the implacable faces before him, faces of men consumed with hatred and fear. Lynn wondered briefly, as he pushed into the cell, if it was right to involve Bobby Mark in this, if he knew what was going on.

'I know what you're thinking. But you're wrong. You are. I didn't molest young boys. I can explain, I can make you understand. Listen, that's not how it was, you must believe . . . I had a relationship with the son of a friend, who I loved. I loved him very much.' The words seemed to be slapping against a stone wall, but he persevered. 'It was no different from loving a woman, just as meaningful. No different. We loved each other.'

None of these men wanted to understand that kind of love. Buggering other prisoners out of physical necessity was something entirely different to them.

'How can you condemn me?' the nonce said. 'How can you attack me for what I did? It's no worse than some here have done. Some of you have attacked and robbed old women, have even murdered people . . .'

That wasn't the sort of argument they wanted to hear.

'Not children, you filthy fucker,' a con said angrily.

Suddenly, like he wanted to provoke them to do whatever they had planned, he said, 'Most of you have done worse – at least I loved him. You can't attack me for that, it's not fair. I'm no different from you. You've done far worse . . .'

'Don't say we're the same, you filthy bastard,' another prisoner said, lunging at the young man. 'I never done no boy in, you fucking bastard . . .'

'I loved him, you morons, why don't you understand . . .' The words were lost in the hostility he invited. Prisoners surged forwards, landed punches and kicks on him in a buzz of hatred.

Suddenly the attack ceased, and they folded back, leaving Latimer on his cell floor whimpering and bleeding. The reason wasn't that they thought he had had enough punishment, but that Alan Parker had arrived with Bayliss, a middle-aged homosexual who was HIV positive. His need for sex was as bad as the need for drugs any addict ever had.

'There you are, Bayliss,' Alan Parker said, indicating the young man on the floor. 'Didn't I promise you something a bit tasty?'

'What, are you lot gonna watch?' Bayliss said. His lips parted in a smile of anticipation.

Seeing the physical shape Bayliss was in, Lynn doubted if he had much to smile about these days.

On the faces of the cons who watched the performance as it started, there was both a revulsion and a fascination. Behind the shudder that went through Lynn there was also a sense of satisfaction in knowing that this nonce was not only being hurt but would be likely to carry that hurt with him for the rest of his life. There was no doubt that he was being hurt physically from his cry of pain as Bayliss anally raped him, while two of the other prisoners twisted his arms and held him.

When it was over, there remained with Lynn some of that deep sense of disgust, the loathing, even the shame, that had driven him to want such punishment meted out to people like this. He tried to tell himself that the nonce had got a little of what he deserved, but it didn't shake the feeling loose from him. Part of his revulsion was for that which he feared might be in himself. Finally he turned out of the cell with the other prisoners and almost ran back to his own cell to hide, not wanting to talk to anyone about what had happened.

They had had a nice result, having weighed off a nonce without anyone being nicked, without any of the screws even showing up to investigate the noise. But why did he not feel particularly good about it?

There were no reprisals over what had happened. No one went on governor's report, no one was charged or even questioned about the incident. The truth was that the warders were probably more pleased than anyone that a nonce had got a little of what he deserved. There was no way they could not have known about what happened, if not from the prisoner himself, then from one of the grasses on the wing. Instinctively Lynn came to realize that other prisoners probably felt the same way he did, for none of them discussed what had happened, which was unusual. He wondered if any of them regretted it as much as he did. But he didn't want to talk about that either. What worried him slightly was whether he would be involved in seeing something like that done again, given the opportunity. He didn't know the answer. Nevertheless, what they had done continued to disturb him for days after. Maybe he was changing, for more and more he was questioning himself. Was that sort of response the answer? Probably it wasn't any more than him or any of the other prisoners being banged up was the answer for what they had done. Slowly it began to dawn on him that imprisonment was a short-term answer that satisfied some need society had to punish, rather than something that addressed the problem. What he didn't know was where that left him.

'You know,' he began, uncertain about speaking his thoughts, 'that nonce we got hold of the other night. Would you say that was right, Al?' They were in the workshop, Lynn talking out of the side of his mouth and giving an eye to the discipline screw.

''Talk silly, Jack,' Alan Parker replied like he was never more sure of anything. 'Look what he done to that young boy he was s'posed to have thought so much of. You wouldn't think. He's got a lot more coming too.'

The reply made him uneasy. 'I dunno' He stopped

abrupty as the screw in the booth looked up from his newspaper. He was merely admitting another screw to the workshop. 'Look at the wicked strokes Steve's pulled. I mean, I done people with axe handles. He did an Old Bill,' – indicating Bob Mark. 'You done security guards . . .'

'But they're fair game,' Parker said. 'I mean, they expect that, don't they?'

'They're still people, Al.'

'What? Not once they put a uniform on! Anyway, they didn't do what that wicked fucker did. You think about your own kids, Jack, think about nonces getting hold of one of them. It don't bear thinking about, does it?'

Lynn knew he was right, but still his unease remained.

One of the white-coated warders approached the bench. 'There are some police officers to see you.'

'Oh yeah? What do they want?' Lynn replied. He panicked for a moment, thinking it might be DI Pyle calling about something else in the frame, now his appeal looked like going well. Alan Parker echoed his fears.

'S'pect there's another fitting, Jack, 'you get a result.'

'Fuck 'em. Tell them there's nothing I want to see them about.' It was his prerogative.

'Watch your language,' the screw admonished, 'or you'll be on governor's. You'd better see them. They're CIB.'

'Oh, why didn't you say so in the first place? Yeah, I'll see those filth all right.' There was only one thing the Complaints Investigation Bureau could be coming to interview him about: that was his complaint against the CID arising out of his fitting. 'They've certainly taken their fucking time.'

The two plain-clothes police officers were sitting at the table in the legal visiting room when Lynn was escorted in. They both had black briefcases before them on the table, along with a folder of papers. One of the detectives said he was a chief inspector. He was a thin-lipped, thin-faced man with a blond moustache, and thinning hair. The other, a sergeant, was thinner, and had round shoulders. Lynn cared for neither, anticipating that they weren't there to help him get any sort of result.

'Sit down, Lynn,' the sergeant said.

Lynn didn't move from where he stood just inside the door. 'You want my co-operation, pal, try being a bit civil.'

Taking immediate control of the situation, the chief inspector said, 'Don't let's be difficult, Mr Lynn.' His tone was civil. 'You made a complaint against the police. If you don't wish to proceed with it, we can as easily go back to London.'

Lynn stood looking at the two men, trying to get a better purchase on the situation but couldn't. Finally he sat opposite them.

'I'll be outside if you need me, sir,' said one of the warders who had escorted Lynn there.

The significance of his departure wasn't lost on Lynn. Anyone of his own visitors and the screws stayed in.

'Care for a cigarette?' The DCI offered a packet.

'What's that, an inducement to have me go easy?'

'If you like,' the chief inspector said. 'You know this is no easier for us . . .'

A note of laughter spun out of Lynn and skidded across the table at him. 'Don't talk like a prick, for fuck sake!' he said angrily, not pleasing either of these men. 'I'm doing twenty years. You're outside. You talk about it being no easier for you! What do you take me for, a mug? That slag Pyle, the dirty no-good slag – he fitted me. He ought to be in here.'

'The complaint against him has yet to be proven. That's what this interview is about, to try and establish the truth.'

'He fitted me all right. He told me himself, he did. Said I was well overdue. That's what he said. Without any conscience at all that wicked fucker nicked twenty years off me in cold blood – just to keep his numbers up. Fucking robbery, it is. He's robbing my children of their father, 's what he's done. Ruined my family. I've had to sell m' house and everything else. They're on Social Security, my family are. What a no-good fucker, that one. He manufactured all the evidence, he did, and what he didn't fit me up with, he went and left out in court so it wouldn't support my story.' He stopped abruptly, suddenly feeling that he was talking too much, and that what he was saying was making no impression on these two.

There was a pause. Then the DCI said, 'We would like a full statement, Mr Lynn. Whatever details you can give us, however apparently trivial they might seem.'

Lynn wondered if he should say anything. These men were after all policemen, colleagues of the man he was trying to have nicked. Why would they want to see one of their own nicked?

'Oh yeah, I got details, if your lot would take any notice.' He intended leaving it at that, but, having started, his grievances poured out. 'Where was I at the time that robbery took place? I'll tell you, I was in bed with my Missus, that's where. But she's the wife of a villain so why would anyone believe her? Pyle didn't arrange that, of course – for me to have that sort of alibi. But what he did arrange was for a villain called Cliff Harding to go and lolly me right up. He had previously nicked that slag with a shooter and held the charge over him. You see if he went and subsequently nicked Harding with that shooter. 'Course he didn't – the no-good slags had a deal. But the best is yet to come – my bit of dough, the money I was s'posed to have had out of that Gas Board – fifteen hundred quid, right? What Pyle put up in court. What he didn't tell the court was that the missing money from the robbery had already been recovered by the Bill out at Abbey Wood, the whole lot, intact, all in the money sacks. It's down in black and white, proving that my dough didn't come from the Gas Board, that I wasn't involved. See if you can wash over that little lot.'

Having made the statement, he panicked in case he had revealed his hand, and wondered now if they wouldn't simply slip out to Abbey Wood and remove the evidence.

The two policemen seemed unimpressed.

'We'll need a statement, Mr Lynn,' the DCI said, like he hadn't told them anything worthy of note. 'Perhaps you'd like to take it all down, Tom,' he said to his colleague, like this was routine for them, like they had heard it all before.

The date of his appeal approached like Christmas for a child, never seeming to arrive; then when at last it was on at the Appeal Court in the Strand it seemed like it would never be concluded, as if he would never hear the result. He was distracted while waiting for word, and convinced at times that he had got his result but it was being kept from him by the screws. A sense of impatience was building up in him, and he was beginning to feel frustrated again. Christmas had arrived but he hadn't got his presents.

Coming down for his midday meal after being unlocked, Lynn was a little late, others were ahead of him waiting to get their food. Automatically he went to the front of the queue. No one protested about the move which he accepted as his natural right.

'What's the word, Jack?' a prisoner who was waiting asked. 'D'you hear how it's s'posed to be going?'

'No, not a fucking word,' he replied despondently, taking the food away on his tray.

On the first-floor landing he met PO Allen. 'D'you hear anything, Mr Allen?' he said.

'The governor'll call you down when the result comes through. He'll put you out of your misery as soon as he can.'

Lynn paused and watched the warder go on down the stairs, doubting if this man cared one way or the other. He felt like throwing his food over him, suspecting as he did that PO Allen was part of the conspiracy. But he knew that if he did throw the tray they would make him serve his chokey before giving him his result. That would delay his reunion with Dolly and the girls.

The slop-out bell sounded. When Westbury unlocked the cell door Lynn was waiting with his pot. The gross, muttonchop-faced warder seemed to be grinning at him like he had a secret that he wasn't about to share.

'No word yet, Jack?' Brian Smith asked as he came along the landing with his pot.

'Those bastards're just keeping me on the hook.'

'I wouldn't be surprised,' the younger man replied. 'It's not an experience I've had myself. I never bothered with an appeal, but I can guess what it must be doing to you.'

Lynn smiled and put his free arm around Smith's shoulder, counting him a real friend. Smith was honest enough to say what his feelings were about the appeal – they were confused. As a friend he wanted him to get his result, but as a prisoner who had to endure an indeterminate sentence himself he said he saw him as a light at the end of a long and dark tunnel, a possible means of escape, and so didn't want to lose contact with him. Lynn had promised they wouldn't lose contact whatever happened.

Just before stopping work that afternoon the escort warders came and collected him to go before the governor. His movement book, correctly signed, went with him. This would be the last time, he decided, as he was taken into the governor's office, marched in there by his escort in the same manner as he was taken into the adjudication room. They stood close to him should he not get his result and try and take it out on the governor. Their presence didn't bode well, he thought fleetingly, and a feeling of panic struggled towards the surface. He forced it back down as he tried to shut out the negative thoughts. He would get a result, he had to. Apart from the governor, Carne was the only other officer present.

'You know why you're here,' the governor said, then avoiding his eyes he glanced down at his papers, as if to remind himself.

No. No! . . . Instinctively Lynn knew what the result was. He started to tense his muscles until they were rigid and causing him pain. Pressure was coming down on him like a heavy weight, bringing pain first behind his eyes, then in his shoulders and neck. His breathing became more shallow until he wasn't sure if he was breathing at all.

'We've had notice of your result on appeal,' Maudling stated. 'There's some good news for you, I'm pleased to say.'

Relief washed through Lynn, wave after wave, and he started to breathe again. The air tasted so good as it went down into his lungs, and as it came up he started to laugh.

He almost didn't hear the governor as he said, 'The appeal court judges have reduced your sentence by three years to seventeen years. It was thought the original sentence was too harsh –'

'Seventeen?' The laughter died in his throat, his muscles began to cramp again.

'However, they could find insufficient grounds to justify reversing the original decision of the lower court; therefore the conviction stands. Further, you have been denied leave to appeal to the House of Lords.'

'They can't, they can't!' Words burst out of him on

a wave of emotion. 'Those dirty cunts, they're in it together, beaks an' the filth! Those other dirty cunts fitted me up . . .'

'Watch your language!' the chief officer warned him. The escort tensed themselves in anticipation.

'Seventeen years. I can't believe it . . .' The magnitude of this stunned him. Where was his result? He had been promised the new evidence would do it. He wasn't dead, but they had just buried him.

'I realize this must be a disappointment,' the governor said, squaring the papers on his desk and avoiding looking at him. 'The Appeal Court's decision is final, so I want you to start to settle down now. You must accept it. A simple adjustment is all that's required and you can be out in twelve years' time, still a relatively young man.' Maudling squared the papers before him once more. 'Make life difficult for us,' he went on, 'and we will respond by making life very difficult for you. So keep your nose clean . . . try to earn maximum remission . . . be sensible, serve your sentence the easy way. Time will soon pass, you'll find, provided you settle down to it.'

This man was mocking him, Lynn decided. He clearly had no real idea what life behind bars did to you, both physically and mentally. Seventeen years – out in twelve – behave yourself – he was reeling and having difficulty staying in control. Thoughts of his wife and children swam through his head. This news would break their hearts. They were as wound up as he was about him getting out. He could barely grasp the significance of the length of the separation. The girls would be gone by then, they'd have forgotten him; likely Dolly would take up with someone else, while all he could do was wank his life away. The prospect of doing seventeen was sickening. He couldn't do it, couldn't sit here and do his time. Too many people would get hurt if he had to.

'That's all,' Maudling said. 'Dismissed.'

'About turn! Move out,' Chief Officer Carne ordered.

In a daze Lynn turned and walked out, hardly noticing the firm grip the two screws at his side had. They didn't realize it but their grip was holding him up. He was teetering on the edge of chaos, unable then to separate that on the outside from the inner chaos he felt.

Emotion churned through him as he was escorted across to the wing. In his anger and pain he was ready to strike out and hurt somebody, anybody, as if to spread pain around would relieve his own suffering. Seventeen years! His head pound as he again thought about his children, about his wife. Dolly would be fifty-five by the time he got out, if he got out. How could he expect her to wait that long for him? Carol, his eldest daughter, would be thirty, and Sandra would be twenty-seven – grown women who would have made lives of their own. The nausea he felt had no connection with the contents of his stomach, it was a feeling that no amount of vomiting would alleviate. He was sick at heart. The only way he would find relief was for someone to receive pain from him, someone who was responsible for his being here or was contributing to that. DI Pyle was the one he truly wanted to hurt, but that bastard had proved he couldn't be hurt, and he didn't imagine the complaint he had made against him, currently being investigated by CIB, would do it. Especially not in view of the Appeal Court's finding.

As the door was opened to his cell on the threes, he turned with a cry of anguish that reached out from the deep within and he launched himself at the two escort screws. The move was left too late for they anticipated him, quickly slamming the door. Lynn hit the solid riveted steel plate with the full force of his charge. With his fists he pounded the door as though it were a uniform and would yield to punishment. The flesh on his knuckles tore open and blood spurted from between his fingers, but at that moment he felt no pain; the suffering inside was too great. 'You dirty fuckers! You no-good dirty fucking cunts! I was fitted by that dirty fucker!' he screamed, over and over until he was hoarse from shouting and exhausted from pounding the door. Tears streamed down his face, but right then he wasn't aware of those either. Finally he had nothing left and became silent and still. Then he felt physical pain, and it began to dominate his emotions and he was grateful for it. He wrapped his towel around his knuckles, uncertain how he had come by the injury, and lay down on the bed and quietly cried. But when he began thinking about his predicament again he immediately dredged up fresh hostility, fresh hurt, anger, hatred. Someone was going to suffer for what they were doing to him. He prayed for it to be someone responsible for this, but finally anyone would do.

The warders didn't unlock him for supper or association that evening, nor to slop out. They were too wary for that, he assumed, and wisely left him behind his door to get used to the idea that he was in for seventeen. The first through that door was going to get it.

However, that wasn't how it came out. After wrestling with his feelings alone for two days he was no more ready to settle down to serve his time, but he was enough in control by then to know that if he was going to get out he had to be cunning.

Attacking screws and hurting them would in the long run, he knew, only hurt himself. Instead he thought about Brian Smith and the plan he had to get out. Later, when the landing screw opened the door for association, he stepped out quietly and went along to see Brian Smith.

The young blond lad was lying on his bed reading a newspaper when Lynn stepped into his cell. There was silence as they looked at each other, both knowing why he was there, but both a little embarrassed now.

'Sorry to hear about the appeal result, Jack,' Brian Smith said at last. 'It was really bad luck.'

Lynn laughed at that. 'One way to put it, Bri,' he said. 'What a turn-up. Knocked me sideways, it did.'

There was another pause. 'I see the Bill are not having it all their own way, Jack,' the younger man said, showing him a newspaper story about two villains at the Bailey getting a result because of allegations of police corruption involving detectives on the Squad.

'Some of those who are in trouble are quite senior officers,' Smith said.

'I expect they'll all end up with a commendation.' It was a fact of life. Putting his head out of the door he checked along the landing, making sure there was no one about. 'You sorted that one you was plotting, Bri, have you?'

'No. Not at all,' Brian Smith said, sitting forward on the bed. 'It's more or less been in limbo, to see what happened with your appeal.' He seemed awkward about that.

Lynn didn't hesitate. 'I'll have some of it with you.'

'That's fantastic,' Brian Smith said excitedly, like there

could now be no possibility of their not making it out. His enthusiasm made Lynn feel hopeful.

'What's the chances of putting one more in, Bri'?' he asked.

'Who? Not Steve Collins? That's trouble.'

He shook his head. 'Leave off. That ponce's about the last person I'd want to take those sort of chances with. I was thinking about Bobby. I mean, there's no other way he's gonna get out, is there?' He hadn't even hinted at the possibility to Mark yet, but felt sure he'd want some. 'There's no way I would leave him behind, unless he blanks the offer.'

Brian Smith hesitated. 'To be honest, Jack, I hadn't thought about three. Is he well enough to try one, do you think – after his operation?'

'I'd say he was,' Lynn said. 'He'll be all right.' He checked the landing again.

'Would you not go without him?' Brian Smith said. 'I mean, if there were some sort of problem with him?'

'I want to make one as bad as you, Bri'. I wouldn't put a gun to your head or anything like that.'

Smith nodded. 'Well, if you think he'll be all right.'

'Good as gold. You see. What d'you have in mind?'

'I have some keys which I made. They'll get us out of the wing. What we'll have to do is knock out the landing screws.'

He waited apprehensively, and Lynn could see he wanted his agreement.

'Knocking out screws won't be easy, but it'll have to do unless we find something better. What about outside?'

'I haven't worked it out. Any suggestions you have would be useful. We have the dog patrols to cope with and both the fence and the wall, and the security cameras.'

'Yeah, they want some thinking about.' He glanced at the younger man, seeing the anxiety in his face. 'But they're just details, Bri'. There ain't a problem what can't be overcome.'

'Look . . . is it all right there?' Smith nodded towards the landing.

'They'll all be watching telly.'

From inside his mattress Brian Smith produced two sets of keys and a large handmade knife.

'Fucking stroll on!' Lynn exclaimed. He had seen prison chivs before, but nothing like that. 'Where the fuck d'you get that?' he asked, taking the weapon and examining it.

'I made it. It'll do, Jack, won't it, if we take a hostage?'

'I'd say so. 'S hope you don't have to stab no one.' He handed the knife back.

'What about the keys? Any chance you can look after them? They're a bit of a problem. I don't like leaving them here during the day, and they run the metal detector over us as we leave the metal shop. I don't really know why I made two sets,' he said apologetically, as Lynn took the bulky keys.

'Yeah, I'll have one set, 'course I will. I'll give Bob the other set to mind . . . shush!' Lynn cautioned suddenly, hearing someone on the landing. Brian Smith thrust the knife back into his mattress.

Collins appeared in the doorway. 'What you up to?'

'Leave off, Steve,' Lynn said. 'I thought you was a screw. Bri' was just about to go down on me.' He winked at Smith, sharing the joke.

'You got one plotted up!' Collins said intuitively. 'You're trying not to put me in, you fuckers.'

'Shut up, Steve, for fuck sake. You'll get us all nicked.' Lynn checked the landing and found it clear.

The situation presented him with a problem, whether or not to bring Collins in on the breakout. Neither of them wanted him, but he wouldn't be easily put off with lies, and was jealous enough to ruin it for them if he wasn't included. An idea came to him to allay this man's suspicions.

'Steve, come here. I wanna talk to you.' He signalled to Brian Smith to be cool and led Collins out.

'What's the score, Jack?' Collins asked, having preceded him into his cell. 'Don't take me for an old mug.'

'I'm not. If I get something going, I'll put you in,' he promised. Lynn watched him closely to see whether or not he was convinced. 'I want a favour, Steve. That screw you got straightened over on the gate, the one who can do something about improving visits – any chance he could do one for me?'

'I would've thought so. You have to bung him. I mean, it comes to dough.' He hesitated. 'The thing is, he's got to have the money up front. What did you have in mind?'

'To be honest, Steve, I wouldn't mind giving my old lady a taste, if it can be done. I can't even remember what it's like when I have a wank.' He lowered his voice as if to emphasize his shame. 'To tell you the truth, Steve, I was thinking of browning Brian.'

There was no doubt that that convinced Collins for such information immediately put him in control of the situation.

With a sympathetic nod, Collins said, 'It does you up in the head, son, don't it, not having a dip.' He smiled. 'You know who it is over at the gate who arranges it? 'S the PO, Gordon Walters. But whatever you do, Jack, don't try to jib him for his money. It's gotta be there if he does the business.'

'It will be, won't it.'

'It's easily enough arranged. You just get your party to contact his party on the outside – I got an address back in m' cell. You tell him what you want and when. He'll tell you whether it can be done, and how much it will stand you in.'

'He's all right, Steve, is he?' Lynn asked. 'He's not likely to go the other way suddenly and nick me?'

'He's been as good as gold with me. Times I've given my old woman one on a visit. Don't worry, I'll put you in.'

Although the idea of making love to his wife wasn't the prime object of the exercise, suddenly it was growing in appeal, and he convinced himself that it might be essential cover to disguise what he was doing from both Collins and the principle officer in charge of the gate. He smiled and put his arm around Collins's shoulder. 'Good luck, Steve. You're a diamond.'

It took Lynn over a month to arrange the details. He had to wait for his next visit from his wife. This wasn't something he could write to her about. At first she was sceptical, saw all sorts of dangers and dire consequences, then finally warmed to the idea. The arrangements were fairly easy to make and cost three hundred pounds. It would have been cheap at treble the price, he decided, if everything went to plan. How Dolly got the money he was afraid to ask.

The plan, arranged through the gate PO, for him to make love with Dolly on her visit after next was essential to his escape plans. The details he had to give her was something for which he needed privacy.

The clock didn't move the afternoon of that visit as he awaited Dolly's arrival. When at last he was called out of the workshop and escorted across to the visiting block by two screws, he was afraid of planting one foot in front of the other in case he did something wrong and was sent back. His anxiety didn't pass unnoticed. 'What's wrong with you?' a screw asked.

'Nothing, sir,' Lynn said. 'Excitement, I suppose.'

Doors and gates were unlocked before him and locked after him in familiar, rigid routine. In the corridor where the category 'A' prisoners' visiting cubicles were situated, alarm spread through him. There were visits in progress in each of the four areas. He wondered what was going on, and assumed something had gone wrong with the plan, that the PO had taken his money with no intention of producing what he had promised. He immediately began thinking of ways he could get back at him, when Gordon Walters put in an appearance in person.

'Everything all right, Mr Berridge?' the PO asked, as if he had no notion of what was happening here.

'A bit full up,' the screw said.

'Yes, a mistake was made on the gate,' Walters replied. That was where all the visitors were controlled from. 'Stick him in here for now,' he said, going along the corridor and pulling open the door of a holding cell.

Dolly was already waiting there for him. Lynn almost fainted with excitement when he caught sight of her.

Motioning him inside, Walters said, 'You got twenty minutes.'

Lynn was about to protest that the deal was for an hour of privacy with his wife. But he knew any argument might have cost him this visit altogether.

Inside the cell Lynn clung to Dolly, enjoying feeling her soft warm body pressed to his, smelling the perfume she was wearing. He had all but forgotten what it was like to hold her in his arms.

She voiced most of his doubts. 'I can't believe this is happening. I can't believe it, Jack.' He could hear anxiety and caution in her voice and it worried him.

'I been walking round in a daze ever since the appeal. That knocked me giddy. Now this . . . I mean, I can't believe any of it. I can't believe any of it's happening . . .'

'I know. I know, Doll,' he replied quietly. 'I feel the same.' He just wanted to stand there holding her, reassuring himself that he was feeling what he was feeling. They were silent for a few moments, then he whispered, his lips close to her ear, 'We're gonna make one out, Doll, me and a couple of others . . .'

'Jack . . .?' The information startled her, but he kept a firm grip on her and stopped her signalling any surprise.

'It's all right. 'S gonna be all right. I promise you. I'll tell you in a little while. 'S one or two things you got to do,' – he assumed she would without question. 'Just relax, love, try and relax. Come on, we only got twenty minutes.' Her body was hard and tense in his arms. 'The way I feel I can't see me lasting two minutes.' He ground his hips into her, letting her feel how hard and reaching he was at that moment. He began to caress her but her tension made him more anxious. The circumstances weren't conducive to love-making and Dolly always had to feel at ease before she could get anything out of it. Even the thought of the girls coming into the room and interrupting them was enough to put her off. 'Take it easy, love. Come on, it's all right. It is,' he counselled, running his hands over her stiff body. Minutes seemed to tick away with the speed of seconds. He didn't like rushing into this but knew he had no choice here.

'No one won't come in, Jack, will they?' Anxiety gave her a pained expression.

'No, 'course they won't,' he said. 'It's all arranged.'

But she wasn't convinced.

He pressed on regardless, caressing her large breasts. He put his hands up her jumper and unfastened her bra. There was no feeling in his hands – he had forgotten what her breasts felt like. Pushing panic back he quickly ran his hands down her thighs, and lifted her skirt. Still he felt nothing as he brought his hand up over her tights and pushed roughly into the top of her pants. Delight rushed him as he remembered how thick and bushy her pubic hair was, but as he moved down to find the opening of her vagina he met with resistance from Dolly. He let out a tiny cry of protest. Finally she parted her legs, but that didn't seem to improve the situation. She was very dry. He persevered. Awkwardly he eased her back with him onto the narrow bed, but she was like a board. They didn't say anything to each other as he dragged her tights and pants down her legs and over her feet. He was trying to invent his excitement in his actions. A sigh escaped from him at the sight of her, and his breathing quickened, but then he saw her glance nervously towards the door. He pretended to himself something different as he knelt and put his tongue against her. The taste and the smell brought a rush of memories, but no feeling of pleasure, rather pain. Still Dolly was unable to relax for a moment, and time was running out. The seconds were resounding in his brain like hammer blows. He moistened her vagina with saliva, knowing he would have to forget her needs for the moment and simply answer his own before it was too late. Doubt crept into his brain, and he questioned his own ability to do anything in these circumstances. What if PO Walters was watching at the Judas hole? His erection, which had been so demanding, started to fade. Anxiety drenched him. He zipped open his fly, but recession was affecting everything! Not understanding what was happening, or why he was like this in the face of his urgent need, he started to get angry. The bromide that was put in the tea was the cause, he decided. He began to get more angry as he tried in vain to penetrate Dolly. She caressed him but to no avail.

Then when their time ran out, having failed to achieve

sexual intercourse or relief of any kind, he hurt with the kind of rage that people killed in. Dolly was in no better state, and blamed herself for the dismal result.

'I'm sorry, Jack . . . sorry, love,' she said over and over, crying the whole while. 'I'm not helping, am I . . .'

He was so wrapped up with his failure to get what he wanted that he was hardly aware of her or her problem.

'Jesus, that's never happened before . . .' he was saying.

'It's this situation. I mean, like this, 's not natural . . .'

'All that fucking gear they stick in your tea . . . what a time for it to happen.' He thought fleetingly of the men he had stiffed since being inside. Having had no problem on those occasions, he now wondered if he was going the other way. 'I was looking forward to this. Cor, you don't know how much, Doll. Too much, I s'pose.' He pulled her closer to himself.

''S my fault, Jack. I was so tense. I'm sorry.'

'I'll get back to my peter and get a raving popcorn, you see. Wish I could take you back there for a little while.'

'It is nice being with you like this, Jack, even if it's for such a short time.' She clung to him like a child.

'We'll make a proper job of it when I get out,' he whispered, his lips close to her ear. It was time to talk of the things she had to know about the proposed breakout. ''S one or two arrangements you gotta make for me.'

''S it gonna be all right, is it?' she asked. It was her only question about the entire plan. The rest she would do unquestioningly. ''S it gonna be all right?'

'To be honest, Doll, I don't know. But I gotta try. I mean, what have I got to lose?'

She pulled back from him slightly and looked at him.

'That's the truth,' he said. 'Prison is hurting, Doll, more than I know. It will go on hurting all the while I'm here.'

'What d'you want me to do?' she said.

'Get Tommy to get us some cars. We'll need at least two. One to get us away from here, the others for the change-over. We'll want clothes as well. Some for a big geezer, some for a much smaller one. And a bit of dough, 'f it can be got. Passports and stuff like that for getting out of the country I can arrange easily enough myself when I'm out.'

'Is that all you want me to do? It's not much.'

'No, but it's important. Can you do it all right, Doll?' If he thought for a moment that she couldn't he wouldn't have asked her.

She nodded.

He hardly had time to kiss her again before PO Walters returned to inform them this little session was over.

Both Brian Smith and Bobby Mark grew more and more excited as the plan firmed and the date to try for going out drew nearer. They had decided to go on the first night of the new shift. At times Lynn wondered if they'd ever reach that point without being tumbled. For his own part he was able to keep closed up but constantly had to warn the other two. The excited, whispered conferences they often dropped into signalled something was going off.

Then that which Lynn most feared happened. How, he didn't know, but assumed it was the work of a grass of some kind. There were so many who dearly loved to carry any piece of information to the screws. Maybe he had been careless with the keys he was minding. Or perhaps an attitude or a chance remark had alerted the screws, who were constantly listening out for such things.

Lying in bed after lights out, listening to the quiet on the wing, he found the quietness there like no other anywhere. A con coughing, or ringing his bell; getting up for a leak; striking a match, or muttering in his sleep, were all noises which echoed through the building. Then as he continued to listen he became aware of another noise, one infinitely more sinister: marching feet. Not the soft shuffle of the single warder moving along the landing with the almost indefinable squelch of rubber-soled boots. There was more than one of them out there, he realized, and he became more alert when the movements stopped outside his door. Despite his alertness the cell light suddenly coming on and the door being simultaneously thrown open, still managed to startle him. PO Allen stepped into the cell, flanked by two warders. They looked like they meant business, standing with their arms folded and their legs apart in a challenging stance.

'Up!' PO Allen barked. 'On your feet! Now.'

'What?' he said, recovering himself. 'What's it all about?'

'Outta that bed 'fore we drag you out.'

He didn't need another warning, but rose quickly and shivered even though the cell wasn't chilly.

'Take those off,' Allen ordered, indicating his baggy vest and pants. 'Let's see if you're concealing anything on your person.'

Straightaway Lynn knew what was going to happen. 'M' prick's about all,' he said.

'Watch your lip. Just do as you're told.'

The two warders flanking the PO eyed him menacingly, ready for any sort of resistance.

He didn't resist now, but struggled out of his vest and pants.

'Right, turn round, bend over, legs apart, let's see if you're hiding anything up your ass.'

'You go and fuck yourself,' he protested. 'If you want to look up my ass you get the MO in here.'

They glared at each other, Lynn feeling a trickle of sweat running down his back. After a few moments, the PO said, 'Right, get them back on, and get out on the landing. Don't you so much as scratch your nose unless I tell you you can.'

He obeyed quickly. Not in expectation of lessening his predicament, but not wanting to give them any excuse.

'Turn over every stitch in here,' the PO told his subordinates.

A desperate, sinking feeling came over Lynn as he stood against the balustrade and watched the search progress. It was as though nothing was worthwhile any more, everything was hopeless. He knew he might as well give up. If he had learned then who it was who had grassed him, he would have killed him. But immediately he realized even that was pointless.

Each piece of bedding, and furniture, and all his personal effects were scrupulously searched, and one by one were brought out of the cell and placed on the landing. Night-time searches were something screws sometimes did when they wanted to upset prisoners and put extra pressure on them. Instinctively Lynn knew that this wasn't what was going on. Here they had purpose and method.

Finally the cell was empty apart from the half-full pot that stood in the corner. One of the screws was pointlessly checking the walls for loose bricks. It was a waste of time.

The black and white stippling on the walls was designed to make the removal of bricks immediately apparent. PO Allen stopped his search and pointed to the pot on the floor. Lynn had purposely used it to dump in rather than go to the recess before he had been banged up, so the warder seemed somewhat reluctant to lift it. When he did there was nothing beneath it.

For a moment hope spluttered through him as the PO swivelled on his heels and came out of the cell. Maybe they didn't know and wouldn't find what he was hiding after all. He tried to keep the pleasure he felt off his face as Allen stood and looked at him. But then the principal officer reached past him and took the plastic spoon from the tray on the table and went back into the cell.

Hope suddenly died in him. He knew it was on top.

With the spoon PO Allen raised the two homemade keys from the pot. His face – which up until that point was wrinkled with disgust – now broke into a satisfied grin.

He spent eight days on the punishment block awaiting the arrival of the Visiting Committee. Attempting to make an escape was a sufficiently grave offence to be dealt with by the Committee. Meanwhile he had been questioned several times about the proposed escape. They wanted to know how he came by the keys, and who he had planned to escape with; who was going to help him on the outside. Lynn told them nothing. There was a chance Brian Smith and Bobby Mark would try it on their own, though how far those two would get on their own, even if they got outside thc prison, he didn't know. Probably both would prove equally lost and easily be recaptured, but that wasn't any reason they should be denied their go.

The evidence presented to the Committee was short and to the point. He was caught bang to rights, and he saw no point in denying his intention. On the back of the charge form he simply stated his original case that he was innocent, that he had been fitted up. He had nothing further to add. He didn't expect any result, and even before he was escorted out he heard the new chairman saying to his colleagues, 'The evidence against the man is overwhelming, I think you'll all agree . . .' What chance did you have when this man didn't even bother to give the appearance of going through the motions? Whatever his sentence was, he was resolved to try to escape wherever and however the opportunity presented itself.

In the adjudication room there was no murmer of disagreement from anyone on the Committee, the governor noted with surprise. He knew his chief officer and POs Allen and McClean would have been in agreement with the chairman also, but they weren't asked their opinion.

'The question is, then,' the chairman said, 'probably the single most important question when it comes to deterring miscreants within the prison system – how are we to punish the intractable prisoner such as this Lynn?'

Mrs Marlow, the only woman on the committee, caught the governor's eye and smiled. 'The only answer, I'm afraid . . . though not very progressive . . . is total incarceration, total isolation.'

'I don't know if we can be progressive with the likes of Lynn,' he said, smiling back at her, 'The best we can hope to do is defeat him.'

'Was there a psychiatric report?' the chairman asked, without bothering to check through the pages in the file before him. Had he done so he'd have found it.

'There is,' the governor said. 'But on the occasions when the psychiatrist saw him he was wilfully uncooperative. The summary of the report is that he is dangerously self-centred, and has strong psychopathic tendencies.' Before adjudication Maudling had glanced through both the reports by the psychiatrist and the one made by the prison chaplain. 'It seems he's compelled to work wilfully against any ordered society.'

'That's borne out by his record here over the past eight months,' the chairman observed.

Encouraged by the line the Committee chairman was taking, Maudling said, 'For the sake of my staff and the safety of my prison officers I'd like to see him placed under special control. Oh, I know those units were designed for terrorists primarily, but this man is virtually unmanageable. Sensory deprivation might be something he would respond to.'

Maurice Pollinger, a large, florid-faced magistrate who looked like a comic postcard impression of a publican, said, 'One can overcome one's moral objections to terrorists being held under such restraint – but this man still maintains he's innocent.'

Governor Maudling said evenly, 'He's likely still to do so when he's eventually released!'

'There have been some quite worrying miscarriages of justice in recent years.'

At that the chairman's face puffed up, reducing his eyes to slits, capped by spiky brows. 'The Appeal Court has given its ruling,' he said. 'Three eminently qualified judges have decided the safety of his conviction. I think we can reasonably abide by that decision in clear conscience. What do you feel, chief?'

The question threw Chief Officer Carne, and he hesitated. He seemed slightly confused and Maudling was able to guess why. 'Well, the units worked, sir, there was no doubt about that. They broke the hardest of prisoners – the few that got put in them. But they came in for a great deal of criticism from the Civil Liberties people.'

'Yes, that's why the Home Office closed them down,' Maudling said sharply. 'But of course it's *not* those vociferous, armchair liberals who have to confront these people.'

There was silence in the room for a moment or two after that. It was as though no one had anything to propose that was a practical alternative to units that were no longer available as a means of punishment.

Clearing his throat, the chairman said, 'I suggest we give this man the maximum sentence, see if that dulls his rebellious spirit. Fifty-six days cellular confinement; forfeiture of all privileges; one hundred and eighty days' loss of remission. All agreed?'

No one on the Committee demurred and the chairman accepted that as assent. Then Pollinger almost reluctantly raised the unthinkable: 'How might we deter him in future if the need arises?'

Therein lay the inherent weakness of giving anyone the maximum sentence in a system which paid lip service to liberalism. It was a question neither Maudling nor anyone else had an answer for, and it depressed him deeply.

No flicker of surprise passed Lynn as he heard his sentence. As far as he was concerned he might as well have done his time on the block as in his cell, and privileges weren't such that he missed them. As for the loss of six months' remission, it was meaningless in the context of the seventeen years which stretched before him interminably.

He settled easily into his solitary routine of exercising, eating, reading, masturbating and sleeping, with the light on the whole while. At night he had to put his clothes outside the cell. They were returned to him at morning slop-out. This was to prevent him escaping, but he knew the thinking behind it was nonsense, as his only way out would be via the door, and the clothes were left in a neat pile outside the same door.

He had been on the block for about a week after sentencing, and was in bed reading for a couple of hours after lights had gone out in the rest of the prison, when there was a sudden commotion, shouting and alarm bells, accompanied by dogs barking and running feet. Immediately he knew the break had gone off and he felt elated by the initiative they had taken. Disappointment followed soon after as the noise suggested that they hadn't got far.

He sprang out of bed, he jumped up to the window and caught hold of the bars. Then he pulled himself up with ease to look out. Every prisoner whose cell overlooked the yard must have done the same. He knew they were at their windows, even though he couldn't see most of them. Shouts of protest came hurtling down from the wings.

'Leave them alone, you dirty slags!'

'They was only exercising.'

'Leave 'em be, you dogs!'

'Go home and catch your old woman at it.'

'Get down from them windows!' a voice boomed from across the yard, 'or you'll all be on governor's.'

'Go and fuck yourself, you dog!' came the reply.

What followed then was a game the screws played trying to catch whoever had called out the insult. They'd accuse someone of it, expecting him to answer with a denial or the name of the real culprit. Sometimes it worked.

Lynn couldn't see either Brian Smith or Bobby Mark, but knew they must have been captured for things quietened outside. Then he knew for certain they were caught by the noise that swept through the block as they were brought in. He dropped down from the window and went to the door. There he could hear the warders coming along the central corridor of the block like an angry swarm of wasps, driving Brian Smith and Bobby Mark ahead of them. Both of the prisoners were shouting and sounded scared. He wondered if they had been beaten. Realistically he knew if they hadn't been then that wouldn't last. They must have hurt at least two guards in the escape bid, how badly he couldn't guess, but that wouldn't make any difference to the screws. They had an excuse to hurt them back.

The sound that came out of Brian Smith chilled him. It was the sort of terrified scream that Lynn hadn't experienced since he was a child, when he had learned to live with his fears and overcome his need to scream, knowing no one would ever answer them, certainly not his parents.

Angry, scrabbling noises passed his cell door, then a door along the corridor was thrown open and Bobby Mark screamed as he was hurtled in. It sounded to him like Bobby struck the wall and was then hit by a gang of warders as he rebounded. The noises increased his frustration.

'Thought you'd make one out, did you?' he heard Dorman shout. There was no reply. The silence that followed worried him more than the sounds of violence. He pressed his ear first to the door, then to the wall, then, he went back to the door. Finally, like a slap in the face, he heard a cry of pain from Bobby. He held his breath.

'You probably killed that officer you hit,' someone shouted.

Another voice screamed, 'You ought to be topped for that, killing a prison officer.'

'You fucking maniac, that would be too good for you . . .'

'You're a monster. A fucking monster . . .'

Fear spread through him as the words pierced his cell like metal-jacketed bullets. He was terrified for Bobby Mark and Brian Smith in case they had killed one of the warders. He heard more cries from Bobby Mark. It sounded like fists, feet, and sticks were used to thump him. He could almost feel the anger coming off the walls. Helpless, and frustrated, and angry by turn himself, Lynn found wave after wave of nausea washing over him. There was nothing at all that he could do.

A would-be escaper getting some stick, especially one who had hurt a screw, was almost an inevitable consequence, but he hadn't expected it to go on for so long. Hours passed and still there was toing and froing along the corridor and shouts of abuse. There was no response when he rang his bell. He didn't sleep at all, but kept a wakeful vigil, as if that could help either Bobby Mark or Brian Smith. With the arrival of the morning wake-up bell, he felt an illogical sense of relief, half-believing nothing more could happen to those two in the daylight. He could get no information from the warder who unlocked his cell for him to slop out. Nor from the trusty who brought his food.

The first sign of anything that gave him any true relief was during exercise with three other prisoners who were on the block. They had been in the yard for about five minutes when Brian Smith was brought out. He fell in line with them, shuffling along six paces behind Lynn.

The first opportunity he got, Lynn turned and said, 'Sorry you didn't make it, Bri'.' He didn't comment about his condition, there was no point. Brian Smith would have known how bad it was from the way he almost certainly felt.

'At least we had a go,' he mumbled through his swollen lips.

'Yeah, you done all right . . .'

'Eyes front!' a warder yelled. 'Keep moving.'

They walked on in silence for a while, but Lynn couldn't keep his peace, there was too much he wanted to know, not least why Bobby Mark hadn't been brought out. Exercise was their only point of contact.

'Where's the other fella, Bri'?' he asked, dropping back to shorten the gap between them. Then as though Brian Smith hadn't heard the question, 'What happened to Bobby?'

'I didn't see him after they separated us,' Smith said with difficulty. 'I think they gave him a lot of stick, Jack.'

Despite all that he suspected from what he'd heard, that information disturbed him more.

Throughout the whole of the day he was unable to get word on Bobby Mark. Even Brian Lang, the block trusty, wasn't able to tell him anything about his condition, having been kept out of his cell. That Lynn found particularly ominous. The following night there was a lot of noise along the block corridor. He imagined it to be the sound of people hurrying anxiously, but tried to allay his unease by telling himself this was only a reflection of his own anxiety. A door banged. Someone said something in a muted tone. What the fuck was going on? Another door banged. His unease increased, especially at the cry he was certain came from Bobby Mark. It was like that of an animal before it finally gave up its struggle. There was fear and desperation in the noise.

With no means of telling the time, other than by the

natural succession of day and night, or the bells which meant the commencement of something, everything was a between-times for him, but he learned to judge sections of time with a fair degree of accuracy. After the waking-up bell, he knew exactly how long it was before slop-out. This morning it was late, and he wondered why. There was a lot of activity that wasn't involving him. Sounds of the comings and goings of various parties. The uneasy feeling he had last night recurred. Jamming his finger against the bellpush produced nothing. Next he tried kicking the door, but in his bare feet he made little impression, and there was nothing in his cell with which he could effectively bang. He tried the bellpush again. His finger was aching by the time the shutter was eventually opened. It was Warder Allison there.

'Why you ringing this bell?' he demanded.

'My pot's full,' Lynn said. 'Why ain't we slopped out?'

'You think you're the only one on this block? Just be patient. There're more important things going on this morning.' He was about to close the shutter.

'Mr Allison?' he appealed. 'Is Bobby Mark all right? He was going on a bit last night.'

The warder hesitated, and glanced back along the corridor, before saying quietly, 'He topped himself last night, he did. Hung himself in his cell . . .'

The words turned his stomach and left him breathless when he tried to speak. Finally he managed, 'What the fuck you talking about?'

'Found him this morning, Jack,' the old screw said gently. 'Just be patient, son, don't add to our problems.' He closed the shutter.

'Wait!' Lynn shouted. 'Wait a minute,' he pleaded,

but got no response. He stood at the door, pain fighting disbelief, and making his world spin. He tried blocking the information, telling himself this wasn't true, that the screws were getting at him, to crack him. But each obstacle to belief was quickly ruptured and awareness seeped through. All that he heard last night, all that he had felt, confirmed that Bobby Mark was dead. What he knew with total conviction was that it hadn't happened like they said it had. 'They murdered him,' he concluded quietly. 'You fucking bastards!' The expression wasn't enough for him. 'You fucking bastards, you murdered him!' he said over and again. But the words rattled ineffectually around his cell, as anger surged through him, demanding greater release. Rage mushroomed and he turned it loose on his cell rather than himself, hurling his pot at the door. He watched the stains spread like blood before his eyes. Next he wrecked his bed, and using a broken spar, he smashed first the window, then the protected light fitting; he ended up by pounding the door with the same piece of wood.

By the time his cell was eventually unlocked, he was hoarse and exhausted and could offer no resistance to the screws who grabbed him and dragged him out and into another cell. This was a stripped cell with not a single item of furniture or furnishing apart from a plastic pot. This he was informed was how he would serve the rest of his chokey. He sat with his back against the wall, and his forearms resting on his knees, his head slumped forward. A screw chancing to look through the Judas hole might have believed he was asleep, but he wasn't, despite the closed eyes. He was crying, but trying to hide his tears. He had thought a lot of Bobby Mark, more than he wanted to acknowledge; how much he was missing him, wondering how he could pay back these bastards for what they had done. But then other thoughts started creeping in, more worrying thoughts, some that were suggesting to him that perhaps he couldn't pay them back; that he couldn't win; that this dangerously corrosive system was slowly breaking him down, despite his resolve that it never would.

For the whole of the two months he was on the block he nursed his hurt, and cried with regret over the death of Bobby Mark; nurtured his hatred for the system, and pumped up his anger at those responsible, but all the while he was trying to reconcile his feelings with some practical course of action. There was none he could take for as long as he remained in solitary. Protests would go no further than the governor, and if he made accusations against the warders on the block, accusations he couldn't substantiate, such action would merely result in more trouble for him. So too would any physical attacks on them. All he could do therefore was bide his time, await his opportunity.

When he got back on the wing he found the subject of Mark's death a past issue. It had left some surface anger, but nothing he could work up into a strident protest. He would like to see the entire wing barricaded on a landing, or out on the roof tearing up the slates and hurling them, refusing to budge until the newspapers and television had got hold of their grievance. But most of his fellow prisoners were apathetic, and he suspected that Steve Collins had some influence on the prevailing attitude. It was his form of paying back for not being included in the escape attempt. 'Who was Bobby Mark anyway?' he had heard Collins say. 'Just some simple lad who was category "F" and liable to turn it all in himself anyway.'

'That's not the Bobby Mark I knew,' Lynn told the gathering up in the threes' TV room. But it made little difference.

He tried again.

'What's wrong with you, Steve? You're doing the screws' job for them. They definitely topped him,' he said adamantly. 'They done it all right.'

'No way will you convince me different,' Collins said. 'But who's gonna believe it, Jack? I tell you, son, it's a nonstarter.'

'Someone's got to,' he argued, 'we kick up enough fuss. We should have a right ruck about it. We're worth fuck all 'we don't.'

'They had a coroner's inquest, Jack,' a con said, fiddling nervously with his tobacco tin. 'He took his life while the balance of his mind was disturbed, didn't he? That was the verdict.'

'They didn't fucking well call me as a witness, did they? They didn't call Brian Smith.'

'You reckon it would have made some difference, Jack?' Alan Parker said. If anyone was prepared to protest over the issue, it was him. So perhaps it was a nonstarter after all, Lynn thought, but remained undeterred.

'There was no way he could've tore those cotton duck sheets to make a rope. I mean, he was a strong lad, sure, but 'you tried them, have you? It's ballocks him hanging himself. They give him too much stick, that's what. Hanging him like that was the only way they could cover it up.'

There was an uncomfortable silence around the room.

'You'll get us all nicked, Jack, that's what you'll wind up doing,' Collins said.

'How fucking hard's that?' Lynn demanded. 'Bob's dead.'

'But you gotta be a bit practical, son.'

Lynn had to check an inclination he felt to leap across the table and hammer Collins. He finally convinced himself that the snaky slag wasn't worth getting nicked for.

Shortly after that the meeting broke up and cons slipped away quickly to their cells as if fearing he would corner them and press them into some kind of action.

Smuggling out a stiff to his brief to ask him to do something was the only alternative course of action left open to him, he decided, but that would be a slow process and would relieve little of his frustration. Despite learning to temper his anger with cunning, the pressure he felt to do something was acute.

Micky Dunkerton, immaculately dressed in his prison uniform, with a clean shirt and wearing a tie, was lying on top of his bed reading when Lynn pushed into his cell. There was an awkward pause as they looked at each other. This sort of encounter with him, one to one, was something most of them seemed to want to avoid, but they couldn't lock their doors against him.

'Ready for the off, Micky, are you?' Lynn said.

'I'd say I was, Jack.' There was another pause, and for a moment or two Dunkerton refused to look at him. 'Sorry I can't do nothing about a protest, Jack. But I only got one more day before they shift me to Ford, know what I mean?'

Lynn nodded. He understood Dunkerton's position: now the end of his sentence was in sight he was being moved to an open prison to acclimatize him to the outside world. With that much to lose it wasn't reasonable to expect him to put himself on offer.

'Silly ballocks'd block you out of spite.'

'I liked Bob Mark. Bit simple, but a nice lad. I'd like to have helped, but you know. I'm even calling the screws "sir" now.'

Lynn smiled. 'Got something in mind when you eventually get shown the door, Micky?'

'I daren't even think about it, Jack. I'll draw a bit of Social Security for a few weeks; give the old woman a taste – 'I can still get a hard-on. Then I s'pose I'll have to look for a bit of work. I mean, I'm still a blagger, Jack. If there's anything to blag any more. I hear there's no money about.'

'Someone's still got some, Micky.'

'Then someone'll put one up to me and I'll go for it. What else can you do? Can't live on Social Security all your life like some of them parasites.'

'You'll get on your feet. You soon adjust. They'll let you have a couple of home-leavers from the Ford.'

'That'll be handy. Know what I mean?'

There was a short pause. 'Any chance you'd take a letter out for me? 'S nothing in it for you, Micky – 's about Bob's death. I wanna see if my brief'll do something. I mean, if you don't fancy it, 's all right – I don't want to fuck your chances.'

'No, I'll take a chance, Jack. Least I can do. It'll go easy out of Ford.'

Lynn felt a surge of relief as the pressure eased off him. 'Good luck,' he said. 'He might do something – m' brief.'

'They took a fucking liberty with Bob Mark,' Dunkerton said. 'You gonna try and make another one out, Jack?'

'I've gotta try, Micky. You just go off your fucking head otherwise. Know what I mean?' He looked at him, suddenly realizing that his question had a purpose. 'You got something in mind?'

'Make sure no one's about,' Dunkerton said, climbing off the bed.

Lynn checked and found the landing was clear. From the door he glanced back at Dunkerton and watched him lift the top end of his bed. Then, removing the base cap from one of the tubular legs, he slid out one half of a pair of wire cutters and a hacksaw blade. The other leg held the second half of the cutters and the bolt that it fitted together with.

'I've had these about three years, can you believe. I was thinking about making one. But the time kept slipping away. Then I got m' parole. I didn't know who to give 'em to – I don't trust no one else, Jack, to be honest. If I left them here and they was found, I'm yanked back in. They're safe enough. What about him?' he said, indicating a budgerigar in a large home-made cage. 'You want to have him transferred to your peter?'

'Poor little fucker, he's doing life,' Lynn said. He waited to see what Dunkerton had in mind, knowing how he felt about that bird –

'There's a rope ladder in the bottom.'

'Oh, nice one, Micky,' Lynn said. It was like winning the football pools. 'Did you have something plotted up?'

'Of course – the time I been in here.' He gave him all the details of the escape plan he had worked out.

The following evening after lights out Lynn went to work on the bars of his cell with the hacksaw blade. Leaving one bar on the extreme left of the window, he fastened the sheet rope to it and climbed out. He had no anxiety about the rope made from strips of cotton duck sheets tearing as he lowered himself. Taking extra care not to make a sound as he went past the windows of the cells below him, he lost count of the estimated length and how much rope he'd have left. He felt anxious in case it was too short. It fact he had plenty. When he dropped to the ground he found himself in the exercise yard, which meant there was a fence between him and the wall. Although that meant extra work cutting his way through the wire, there was some advantage in that there would be no one in the yard at that time of night to look towards the building and see the rope hanging down. Cutting the wire was difficult with home-made cutters and he didn't think they were man enough. To his surprise, they were, but as he came out on the far side of the exercise yard he almost ran into a dog patrol. At that point he had no option but to go forward. He sprinted across the open compound to the lee of the wall, where he pressed himself into the shadow formed by the abutment. Alarm seized him as he looked towards the wing and saw the rope hanging down. The screw who was approaching only had to turn to see it too. Light seemed to be reflecting from it like a beacon. He heard the warder talking to his dog, and either the man or his dog or both would surely hear his thrashing heart. His mouth was dry and he tried to moisten it, but couldn't. At that moment he felt more helpless and vulnerable than he had ever felt before in his life. He watched as the warder and dog passed not more than twenty feet from him. If he turned his head a little to the right the screw would have seen him.

Tension and anxiety slipped from him as he watched the

warder depart. He could scarcely believe his luck had held, but he was drained and unable to move for a few seconds. When at last he did he carefully unwound Dunkerton's rope from his waist, made certain the hook was securely fastened – earlier doubts about whether the home-made hook was strong enough to hold his weight were partially dispelled by the worth of those home-made wire cutters. He hurled the hook up the wall. It found a hold first time, catching on the razor wire close to one of the Y-shaped brackets that held it. With relative ease he hauled himself up the rope, hand over hand, adjusting the blanket he had brought as he went. Getting that blanket out over the wire when he reached the top of the rope was the most difficult part of the whole operation. It meant hanging there by one hand, his feet dangling in mid-air. The thought of it sickened him, as he had no stomach for heights, but then he had less for another sixteen plus years inside. It took three attempts to spread the blanket on the razor wire before he could pull himself onto it without cutting himself to pieces. By this time the muscles in his left arm were saying they had had enough and were about to give up. He struggled awkwardly onto the blanket. Barbs came through the folded cloth and cut into him when he rested on the wire. There was no way he could avoid it, his weight caused the rolls of wire to shift like a spring the whole time.

So preoccupied was he with keeping his balance on the shifting wires as he hauled up the rope to lower over the other side that he didn't notice the closed-circuit security camera on the wall opposite as it swung round in his direction.

There were eight cameras that he was aware of covering all aspects of the perimeter wall. He only needed to avoid three at any one time. How long he had spent on the wire he didn't know precisely but knew it was too long when he saw the camera swing his way. He prayed the watcher in the gatehouse had other things on his mind.

The bells starting up startled him, shattering his prayer. He lost his balance and wobbled and reached out and grasped frantically at the wire. The razor barbs sank into his palms as his hands took his weight. He could feel them going deeper into the flesh. The pain shot back down his arms and he let go. He hit the ground hard, but managed to get up, intending to run, only couldn't; the pain in his feet caused him to collapse as he tried to move. Even if he had been able to run there was no longer anywhere to run to with about a dozen screws closing in on him. He simply lay on the ground, clasping his bleeding hands and grinning up at them defiantly.

What the Visiting Committee would adjudicate on his escape attempt was a foregone conclusion. The maximum fifty-six days cellular confinement; loss of all privileges; one hundred and eighty days' loss of remission. He expected nothing less. However, he was surprised when later the same day he was taken out of his cell and back along the block to the adjudication room. Having been weighed off with the maximum, Lynn puzzled as to what more they could give him. All too soon it became abundantly clear.

The governor was behind the desk on his own when he was wheeled in. The Committee had gone, but Chief Officer Carne was present, along with PO McClean.

'You are clearly a man who is determined to learn nothing from experience,' the governor said, straightening and bending a paperclip and refusing to look at him. 'Well, understand this, I am equally determined that you will learn, however painful that experience.'

'Like you done with Bobby Mark!' Lynn said, the words exploding out of him. 'You done a t'rific job there.'

'Quiet!' Carne ordered as if by reflex.

Maudling raised his hand, an amused smile dancing brightly across his face. 'Let him shoot off his stupid mouth, chief. He will learn finally that every offensive remark, every display of disrespect, will be to his cost.' He paused and nodded to the uniformed officers, then turned back to Lynn. 'The fifty-six days' cellular confinement you were sentenced to this morning will be unlike any you have previously experienced. Firstly you will have no privileges whatsoever, not even a letter from home; you will have positively no contact at any time other than with warders on the punishment block; you will be in a stripped cell throughout the day, your bed only being returned for you to sleep at night. Your clothes will be removed from your cell at night; the light will remain on the whole time. You will be observed by a patrol every ten minutes, day and night.' He paused and smiled again, then quickly glanced away.

'Terrific,' Lynn said. 'So what's any different?'

The governor slowly raised his hand, pointing the straightened paperclip at him. 'The difference is this: if any breach of discipline is reported to me, however minor, then your fifty-six days' sentence will begin from day one again, regardless of how much of it you have served. In other words, I want exemplary behaviour from you for fifty-six consecutive days before you will be released from solitary confinement.'

There was a brief silence.

Then Lynn said recklessly, 'You got some fucking chance.'

Another smile parted Maudling's thick lips, like someone with a secret that gave him the superior position. 'We'll see.'

By the time he had changed back into his shoes and had been escorted through the punishment block, PO McClean was waiting by the open door of his cell. The senior screw reached out and prevented him entering the cell. He was smiling too, like it was catching; lines were etched deeply into his masklike face. Lynn smiled as well, and widened it into a grin for the escort. They were unmoving.

'What I want from you,' McClean said quietly, 'is two months of impeccable behaviour. A single wrong word to any of my officers, or an offensive gesture, in fact if you so much as fart without permission, you'll be back to square one. Is that understood?'

'That's all ballocks,' Lynn said, believing he could take anything they put on him, and keep up the aggro for as long as they did.

'You'd better get anything you want to say off your chest while you've got nothing to lose,' the PO said reasonably. 'Tomorrow you'll only have fifty-five days left to do.'

Lynn stared at this man, trying to read his eyes, what he could see of them under the acute angle of the peak of his hat. They were cold and dead, even though the face mask was still smiling, and for a moment he felt scared. He tried to push this fear away.

'I'm going to enjoy watching you break, you fucker. I'm going to get such a hard-on from hearing you beg my staff not to put you on report when you slip.'

'I wouldn't count on it,' Lynn said.

'Inside. Now not another word out of you.'

Lynn ducked into the cell and the door was slammed after him. He stood waiting, half expecting the shutter to open and the PO to say something else. But nothing happened. As he waited he experienced a curious feeling of isolation, something that hadn't happened to him before in solitary. He wondered why he felt this way now. Possibly it was because he had been told he was being isolated. He tried to dismiss the feeling. But it wouldn't go away. There was nothing in the cell, not a stitch of anything with which he could distract himself, and out of nowhere a daunting feeling suddenly rose up in him at the prospect of serving this fifty-six days.

The shutter snapped open to reveal Warder Dorman's smiling face. The screw said nothing, but simply looked in, before closing the shutter. That happened every ten minutes, or thereabouts, and by the third day Lynn was beginning to admit to himself that this exercise was wearing on him. There was nothing he could do which wouldn't be seen during this personal inspection by the warders, and his options were pretty limited. He could do press-ups, use his pot, masturbate, walk up and down, or lie on his bed, when he had his bed in the cell. He began to tense instinctively as the shutter slid back. There was no contact when his food was served to him. No longer did the block trusty bring it into his cell, but instead the tray was handed to the screw, who opened the door and passed it in. Except, that was, when Dorman was on duty. Then he had the trusty put the tray on the floor, and would slide it inside with his foot, treating him as if he was contaminated.

'Why don't you just throw it on the floor, you slag!' he screamed when Dorman did this at suppertime. It was his first outburst for three days. Holding in all his anger had caused him too much pain.

Dorman's immediate response was to slam the door, as if ignoring the remark. Then the shutter snapped open when he was safely outside. 'That's going to cost you the three days you've already done.'

'You no-good slag!' Lynn shouted and hurled his tea at the warder. The shutter was quickly slammed, and Lynn had to live with his pint of tea on the cell floor until his bed was returned to him later that evening. Then he was given a bucket and mop and told to clean up the mess. He missed his tea that night.

In the exercise yard he was equally isolated, moving round in a circle within the wire sometimes for a lot less than the hour he was supposed to have for exercise. He rarely saw other prisoners, not even at a distance, and when two passed beyond the compound wire he felt elated. One of them called out, 'How's it going, Jack?'

'T'rific,' he responded instantly, but regretted doing so, knowing it was to his cost.

'Inside!' a warder ordered. 'You're on report.'

That meant going back to square one, losing the ten days he had so far done. Lynn looked at the uniform contemptuously. 'You silly bastard,' he said. 'I can keep this up as long as you.'

He was put on report for not getting out of bed quickly enough after the wake-up bell in the morning – the cell was cold, and being made to stand around in his pants and vest, waiting to get his clothes back, wasn't appealing. There was no sense of justice here, and the multiple injustices within the penal system were magnified on this type of chokey. He was put on report for not folding his bedclothes neatly when putting his bed out. He was put on report for damaging prison property when he was caught keeping a record of his days in there by scratching the wall with a stone he had smuggled in from the yard. Soon he noticed a pattern in the way they were putting him on report: each time letting him go a little longer, as if they were building up his hopes before charging him and taking him in front of the governor. There was no defence that Maudling would hear. The fact of being on report meant he was guilty.

Slowly Lynn learned to repress his feelings, but not

without pain; he began to watch and check the whole time how he behaved. It required a lot of concentration, and at first his concentration was not good. When he analysed what was happening to him, he told himself that the system wasn't in fact breaking him, or wearing him down, but rather that he was learning to be more cunning.

He managed to go for three weeks without being put on governor's report. The sense of achievement this gave him was shattered when, after breakfast and the second slop-out of the day, he was told by a screw that he was going up before the governor. He hadn't done anything, and he appealed to the warder's better nature.

'I don't know about that,' came the reply. 'I was just told to bring you up.'

This fitted the pattern of letting him get more and more well-behaved first, and gain a little confidence, and maybe believe he could make it off the block after all, when they knocked him back.

'Your behaviour record is abysmal,' He was told as he stood rigidly to attention, toeing the line in the adjudication room. 'Forty-seven days you have been on this type of punishment. Had you behaved yourself it would have been finished in another nine days. But clearly you're a man who prefers to do things the hard way. Out of forty-seven days your longest period without breach of discipline is currently twenty-two days . . .'

'Yes, sir,' Lynn readily agreed.

Maudling removed his glasses like they were too heavy for his face. 'No, sir,' he said. 'You've been making complaints against my staff. Allegations to the effect that members of my staff were directly responsible for Robert Mark's death.'

Lynn waited, fearing the worst. A knot of tension spread into his chest and across his shoulders into his neck, making breathing difficult and causing the back of his head to ache.

'Whilst you are perfectly entitled to make complaints against staff, even one that brings about their suspension pending an inquiry, we do have legitimate procedures for it. It is an offence to make complaints via smuggled letters, as you did in the case of Officers Dorman and Jordan. You will lose the twenty-two clear days.'

'That was before I started this lot, sir,' he protested.

Maudling wasn't interested. 'Your fifty-six days' cellular confinement begins again from day one. This of course has nothing to do with the fact that two officers *have* been suspended as a result of your illegal action . . .'

'You fucking liar!' The words burst out of him.

'Take him away,' Maudling said, returning his glasses to his nose and letting his glance rush across the Lynn.

Reg Allison was one of the warders who escorted him back along the block. 'You shouldn't have been that way with him,' he advised. 'He won't forget that.'

As they reached the cell, Lynn looked at the old man, accepting that he meant well. But he didn't reply.

'Why not toe the line?' Allison went on, as though that wasn't something he had been trying to do. 'Be easier in the long run.'

Lynn nodded wearily and went inside the cell. The door was slammed. He tensed, expecting the shutter to snap open. He began to wonder if he would ever get out of solitary. At that point he recognized in himself the same feeling of despair, of desperation, that Bobby Mark had experienced over his seemingly never-ending prison sentence.

* * *

Dolly Lynn felt helpless and frustrated over what was happening to her husband. She was trying to do something to stop the treatment Jack was receiving, but feared it wasn't enough, that she wasn't achieving anything worthwhile. Nothing seemed to be happening as a result of her visits to the prison and meetings with the deputy governor. Now she had a letter from Ronald Hazelwood, her local MP, asking her to call in and see him at his next surgery and she wondered what, if anything, he could do. He had seemed fairly sympathetic when she had gone to see him after Jack got nowhere with his appeal, but he hadn't managed to do much about that, despite writing to the Home Office minister. Following word from a recently released prisoner about the treatment Jack was getting, the MP had listened patiently when she had gone to see him, but had wanted to interview the prisoner. She didn't know where to contact him, and that had lessened Hazelwood's enthusiasm for the case.

The MP's surgery was in an empty shop with a curtained window in Kentish Town Road. The office in the back room was shabby, the furniture was old and worn and had the appearance of having been donated by the Social Services. Sitting behind the small trestle table with its scratched linoleum covering was the thin, round-shouldered MP. He had long, lank blond hair and round, modern glasses. He rose and shook her hand warmly.

'I'm glad you could come in, Dolly,' he said in a familiar way. 'Sit down.' He sat on the opposite side of the table and opened a correspondence file. 'Sorry if my letter alarmed you, but I think it's better to meet and talk, rather than me simply telling you the position of things by post. Has your husband's situation changed since we last had contact?'

'No, I still ain't received a visiting order. I been down there again without one. Said I weren't gonna go away until I saw him. But it didn't do no good. The deputy governor said I couldn't see him.' She paused, to stop herself crying. She didn't want to think about the situation with Jack, and at times even wondered if he was still alive. That was a silly notion, she told herself, but she knew what had happened to Bobby Mark. She massaged her dark-ringed eyes and looked away from the MP. 'They said he was in chokey still, and had all his privileges took away.'

'I'm afraid that was confirmed by my inquiries at the Home Office,' Hazelwood said. He seemed slightly embarrassed, and Dolly didn't know if that was a good or bad sign. 'I'm not sure they're allowed to stop his visits. I can't seem to get information about that. He's considered a persistent and disruptive troublemaker. As a result they seem to jump on him for every minor infringement of the rules.'

She had been told all this. What she wanted was new information about Jack. 'He made a complaint about the death of another prisoner what's got two screws suspended. That's all he's done. That's why he's getting all this stick, it is.' Anger surfaced through her sense of defeat.

'The Home Office showed me a catalogue of disciplinary charges against your husband, Dolly.' He paused. 'I wish there was something more I could tell you. I know there is a huge bias in favour of the prison service at these disciplinary hearings. We should try to get some reform, so that prisoners can be represented at their hearings by a solicitor. I think the European courts might be more helpful there.'

'He's been over four months down on that block, sir,' she said. 'I know what that's doing to him.'

'Let me get this right, Dolly,' Hazelwood said, sitting forward like he had suddenly woken up. 'Are you saying he's been in solitary confinement for over four months? Is that what you are telling me, seriously?'

'Yes, he has. And I ain't been allowed to visit him.'

'Gosh, I didn't fully appreciate that. I'm sufficiently familiar with the prison rules to know that fifty-six days is the maximum a prisoner could be confined to a cell for punishment. I'll go back to the Home Office, Dolly. I'll tackle the minister again about this. See what he has to say. Certainly I'll endeavour to get your visits reinstated. Leave it with me.'

'Something's got to happen,' she said ominously, 'or Jack'll wind up hurting someone. I know him well enough. He won't be able to take much more of it.'

'I'll get back to the Home Office first thing. I'll tackle the minister personally about your husband's case. She's not a bad sort at all. I'll see if I can get some action on this.'

She hoped he wasn't being over-optimistic, but she wondered at his smile. It was professional, easily found. Dolly wasn't reassured.

During his time spent in prison he had become used to sleeping with the light on the whole time, and during his months on the block he had become equally used to the door shutter opening every ten minutes or so, even though his instinctive reaction was to tense; what he hadn't grown used to was the warders who reached into his sleep in the night, wrenching him violently into wakefulness. Sometimes they were real, sometimes they weren't, and sometimes he was unable to distinguish between reality and unreality.

Hearing a long, sickening scream, Lynn pulled himself clear of the shallow sleep that held him and found himself wet with sweat. The scream had ended, but he didn't think he had imagined it. He sat up in the narrow bed and listened. The punishment block was silent, save for the metallic sucking noise that seemed to go on all the while; that wasn't something he imagined, but was the very atmosphere of the block. It was ever present at night, like all the pain and suffering was being expelled. It disturbed him.

A marked change had come over him, both psychologically and physiologically, one he noticed in himself and worried about. He was a different person from the man who had been put down here six months ago. He had shrunk in stature, and knew he had lost weight; his shoulders were constantly hunched and tensed; he blinked as though with an eye affliction, and he was jumpy, starting at the least sound. His resolve to beat the system was no longer with him; further, he knew it was a nonsense even to attempt it. Instead you had to be cunning, he told himself, play it their way.

He tensed now on hearing someone move along the corridor outside the cell. The centre of his interest was frequently the door, and he often found himself staring concentratedly at it.

The shutter slid open and a warder peered in without speaking. Lynn stared back until his eyes began to water, and he averted his gaze.

Sleep wouldn't return now. He had no idea what the time was, but he would lie in his bed until the wake-up bell sounded.

The bell startled him, even though he was listening for it. He rose at once, having too much to lose to be put on report for lying in bed after the bell. Straightaway he began folding his bedding into a neat pile, glancing anxiously towards the door, expecting somehow to be caught out, but not knowing how. These past few days had found him anxious indeed, for having almost reached his goal he was terrified of being kicked back to the start. Quite how he had all but managed fifty-six straight days without offending, he wasn't sure, but believed the screws were looking closely for something to pull him up on, some reason to back him, to make him start chokey all over again.

The cell door opened and a warder said, 'Bed out!'

With brisk movements he brought his bed out and placed it in an empty cell opposite his own, the blankets were folded into a neat square and placed on the end.

Automatically he reached for his pile of clothes as he came back across the thoroughfare.

'Leave those. Did I tell you to touch those?'

'No, Mr Wright, I thought . . .' he began feebly. The warder who had opened his cell each morning for the past week had always let him get dressed first. This was it, he thought, he would be put on report. He checked a tremble which started in his jaw.

'Don't think,' came the reply. 'Just obey orders.'

The warder's glance left him as he stepped into the cell. Lynn saw those beady eyes circling the empty space, searching for possible infringements of the rules. He waited anxiously, feeling hugely grateful when he was finally ordered to dress and slop out.

After breakfast he received a surprise visit from the governor. The governor, his deputy, or the chaplain looking in on prisoners was supposed to be a regular occurrence on solitary. In fact he rarely saw any of them.

'Stand up for the governor,' the warder ordered.

Lynn scrambled off the floor and stood to attention as Maudling and PO McClean stepped into the cell.

The governor looked him up and down, but no expression passed across his face as he said, 'You're to be congratulated, Lynn. You have now managed fifty-four consecutive days without offending against discipline. Quite an achievement. We're pleased with your progress.'

'Thank you, sir,' Lynn replied smartly.

'It's taken you six months. Most prisoners might have learned a great deal quicker. However, two more days and you'll be able to return to normal routine on the wing. Doubtless you won't wish to repeat this exercise.'

'No, sir.'

The governor nodded his approval. 'In a closed society such as ours, we cannot and will not tolerate disruptive elements. Good order depends on it. You've taken a long while to understand this.'

'Yes, sir.'

'Well done.' He removed his spectacles from his nose as he started away, but then turned back again. Lynn held his breath. 'Incidentally, as you were so concerned about Robert Mark's death, you might care to know the result of the Home Office inquiry which you were instrumental in bringing about. It upheld the coroner's verdict, that he took his own life while the balance of his mind was disturbed. It completely exonerated the two officers you named. I thought you might like to know. You might like to apologize to them. But that's up to you.'

This was his supreme test. After a moment, he said, 'Thank you, sir.' All traces of disappointment or anger, all his sense of frustration and injustice, were totally subjugated.

The governor's eyes darted over him, and away. 'Don't let yourself down during these next two days,' he told him, then wheeled out.

Possibly the governor, pleased with his progress, had told the screws not to wind him up too much over these last two days. He prayed that was the case. Everyone seemed pleased with him, that he was getting through; certainly he seemed to get less pressure. Gradually he was lulled into believing that he would finally make it out of chokey. He began to relax a little, and even started to allow himself to feel excited about getting back to the wing; that was until he heard from one of the warders that Jordan and Dorman were back on duty. The news was like a punch in the stomach that left him breathless and feeling sick. He knew for sure it would only be a matter of time before those two got round to him.

Each time the door opened fear seized hold of him and he quaked. Those last two days seemed longer than the entire time he had spent on the block.

Perhaps the governor had told them to keep away from him. He prayed and prayed that was the case. His prayers weren't answered. They got to him on his last night. He was in bed curled in the foetal position, too anxious to sleep, though he lay very still, hoping to give that impression, hoping he would be left alone. He heard the key as it turned. His eyes came open in alarm, but that was the only part of him that moved as the door swung open and they stepped inside. He could feel their menacing presence as they waited in silence. He was sure they could hear his teeth chattering.

'All right, get up!' Jordan suddenly barked.

'Move. Move!' Dorman ordered when Lynn didn't respond quickly enough. 'Or you'll be on report. Were you playing with yourself? You dirty little wanker, were you?' he demanded, like this was an offence against discipline.

'No, sir,' Lynn said quickly.

'I believe you, Jack, thousands wouldn't,' he said, like they were old friends.

The governor had told them to behave! Just as he started to convince himself, Jordan switched.

'Right, remove your clothes, bend over, legs apart,' he ordered.

He had on only his pants and vest, and wasn't in any frame of mind to argue.

Meanwhile Dorman had begun searching the bedding, pulling it apart and dropping it messily over the floor.

'We suspect you have escape tools hidden here.'

From his bent-over position, Lynn said, 'No, sir. Honest, sir.' All the while his feeling of desperation was increasing.

'Or smuggled correspondence,' Jordan put in. 'You know he's the one who caused our suspension, Oliver.' His colleague might not have known.

'Oh well, in that case tell him the result of our paid holiday.'

'Reinstated without a stain on our character. That's what the record reflects, Jack,' Jordan informed him. 'Doesn't that please you? Doesn't it warm your heart?'

'Yes, sir,' Lynn agreed, turning his head.

The two of them looked at each other and smiled.

'You lying fucker!' Jordan bellowed and thrust his baton hard up Lynn's anus and sent him crashing headlong into the wall as he tried to stop it. 'All right, get up. Anything here, Oliver?'

'Nothing. Or he's a better man at hiding it than I am at finding it. Unless he's hidden something in his pot again.'

Jordan smiled at that and turned to Lynn as he hauled himself off the floor, holding his ass. 'All right, pick it up.'

He hesitated and looked at the screw, hoping there was some shred of decency in him. 'There isn't anything in the pot, sir, apart from what I used it for a couple of times in the night.' The faces before him were implacable. Finally he picked up the pot and turned to them with it, hating them more than anything, knowing what they were doing to him, but hating himself more for going along with it.

'Right, fish in there among them turds,' Jordan ordered. 'With your hand. Let's see if there are any escape tools hidden there.'

Again he hesitated. He looked at the warder, then at the pot, and back at Jordan. He had a simple choice, obeying their order and praying he'd get out of chokey, or throwing the contents of the pot over these bastards and having his fifty-six days begin all over again. He saw alarm flash across Jordan's face, but knew really there wasn't any choice. By squeezing and squeezing his feelings, he made them all but disappear, he was finally able to plunge his hand into the pot and fish around to the satisfaction of these two warders.

They smiled.

He smiled as tears ran down his cheeks. He knew he had made it.

Progress for him was swift now that he had learned how to behave and was thinking the way the prison authorities wanted him to think. He soon got his clothes back in the cell with him at night, and got to sleep with the light out for the first time; in almost no time at all he even got onto the coveted working parties that moved around the prison, doing odd jobs and being supervised by only a single warder.

The current working party he was on was landscaping a small patch of ground outside the governor's office. Lynn and a prisoner from another wing were working together, digging holes to plant some trees.

'Dig fast enough, Jack,' his co-worker said, 'we could tunnel out before silly ballocks even notices.'

'Be handy,' Lynn said, not taking him seriously.

The other prisoner checked around, as if making sure the supervising warder wasn't within earshot, then said, 'You fancy making one, Jack? I mean, 'you seen that ladder in the maintenance shed? How hard would it be to do that padlock and have the ladder against the wall?'

Caution spread through Lynn now as he wondered what he was getting himself involved in here. He didn't know this lad who he was working with, certainly he didn't know enough about him to try to plot one out with him, even if he had had the inclination. But then suddenly he saw what this was, and became frightened. It was a get-up; someone had put the con up to this to test him. He thought back, trying to remember what he had said, whether he had said anything that could be construed as conspiring to make a break.

'Old Bill who nicked me once said to me, "You can't do your time, don't do the crime." I mean, that's fair enough. 'You're at it, you expect to be nicked sooner or later. It stands to reason. The only chance you really got is doing your bird, doing it their way, know what I mean?'

The younger prisoner shrugged. ''S up to you. I thought you was a million.'

'Me?' Lynn said. 'They're letting me do an Open University course. Education's the thing what makes the dif'.'

'Hold up.' He turned as the white-coated warder approached. ''S that deep enough, Mr Evans?'

'That'll do nicely,' the warder said, inspecting the hole. 'Just knock the stake in first, good and firm. Make sure you spread the roots out when you put the tree in.'

Lynn did as he was told, then held the sapling as his partner shovelled earth over the roots.

'Jiggle it up and down, Jack,' the warder said. 'Settle the roots in. It's going to be there for a long time.'

'What sort of tree is it, Mr Evans?' Lynn asked, with a compelling need to make conversation, as though that was the only way to eradicate the doubts he was afraid they might erroneously identify in him.

'Copper beech, can't you read the label? Ten or fifteen years you'll have a nice-sized tree there, Jack.'

The words didn't go lightly past Lynn. Instead they forcefully reminded him that he had all those years yet to do. This warder would have retired long before, but he would still be around to watch that sapling grow into a nice-sized tree.

EPILOGUE

The feeling of anger and hostility was palpable among detectives on the Squad. They were being singled out for the failings of the police, the failings of the whole institution of law and order, and the failings of the government to get on top of crime. It was ballocks, Pyle decided. It was grossly unfair, and what was happening to him personally was worse than grossly unfair. The result of the extensive and prolonged corruption investigation, which had been started by an outside force and was now being continued by CIB, was that seven villains, who had ended up in the dock at the Old Bailey and been found guilty, were now being released because detectives on the Squad had fabricated evidence against them. That wasn't the sole cause of the general ill feeling, which had started when policemen, some of them senior officers – some retired, others under suspension – had been arrested in highly publicized raids on their homes, and had been charged variously with conspiracy to pervert the course of justice, accepting bribes, conspiring to sell bail and weaken evidence. Included among those was Detective Inspector Maurice Head. Pyle had been interviewed five times under caution, but had so far managed to avoid suspension. He knew it was only a matter of time now before he was nicked. Two villains he had put away were going up to the Appeal Court for a second go, only this time round they had evidence from Esda tests that showed statements had been rewritten some time after their interrogation – Chief Superintendent Jeymer had authenticated the notes, deliberately confirming the wrong dates. Further they had evidence that detectives had lied in court by stating on oath that the notes of the interview were contemporaneous.

'Probably ninety-five per cent of the CID do it,' Pyle said angrily to his governor. 'I mean, most of us have bent one at some time or other. How else d'you put these fuckers away when courts bend over backwards to free them?'

'Oh, I don't know, Fred,' DCI Simmons said. He was less angry, Pyle knew, for although what was happening reflected badly on him, he wasn't facing a nicking.

They were at the bar of The Feathers. There weren't many other policemen drinking there at that time of night.

'I mean, why single out the Squad, Tony? What most of them were doing is what has to be done.'

As he watched the DCI concede the point in an undemonstrative fashion, Pyle wondered if he wasn't saying too much here. For all he knew this colleague could be talking to CIB.

'There's nothing fundamentally wrong with the men who do the job,' Pyle said. 'But I tell you if we aren't let do the job any way we can, and if the courts don't back us up by keeping those bastards behind bars, there's going to be a serious breakdown in law and order. Especially now with all these out of work people who can't meet their mortgage payments. Crime is the only growth industry.'

Most of the time he knew who it was who was doing the villainy, who it was he had to put away. That simple. The problem was that villains weren't governed by any code of conduct when they went out to make one, they weren't subject to rules like the police were, and Pyle saw no valid reason why he should be when he sought to put them away and make society a better, safer place. Most detectives had their own borders, their own guidelines, their own sense of what was right in such matters. And detectives were honourable men after all, especially those on the Squad.

'That's what's gonna happen, Tony,' he said. 'It's all gonna break down. We'll only take so much stick, then that'll be it. The men in the job won't have any incentive to go out and feel collars. Not if they're going to get nicked themselves for doing it.'

The chief inspector nodded. 'You'll get a result all right, Fred. Then I expect you might even be seconded to the Bureau.'

'The danger is, Tony,' Pyle said, ignoring his feeble joke, 'once they start looking at one or two you put away, where do they stop? The Appeal Court could end up turning over every result I ever had. Especially those that were a bit swift. Fucking depressing, isn't it?'

He finished the scotch in his glass and motioned to the barman. There was time for one more before he went off to his meet.